MY BFF

RUTH PHILLIPS OAKLAND

Meryton Press

My BFF © 2009 by Ruth Phillips Oakland

Layout by Ellen Pickels, cover design by Ellen Pickels and Lauren Oakland.
Cover photo from istockphoto.com, used with permission.

ISBN: 978-1-936009-01-5

Published by Meryton Press, Pembroke, Massachusetts USA

Dedication

to my family
Mike, Lauren & Jillian
for their love and never-ending support

Acknowledgements

Great thanks to Clare, tJean, Stacy, JaneV, Saulonchic, Tomaholic, Jillian, Ellen and Cjoki who all assisted in the editing of this story as it was written. Also my thanks to Moushele and the women of the Meryton Press who convinced me to publish and assisted in creating the final volume.

Finally, my thanks to all the wonderful members of The Meryton Assembly. You are the best cheerleaders an author could ask for.

PROLOGUE

Pemberley, the Darcy family estate
Derbyshire, England

"FITZWILLIAM GEORGE ALEXANDER DARCY!!"

His Aunt's voice could be heard coming down the long hall at Pemberley and through the heavy oak doors of his father's study. "Where is my nephew?!" The voice grew louder — if that was at all possible — as the lady came closer.

Darcy looked to his father with pleading eyes, but the elder man was focused on the doors, bracing for the hurricane that was his sister-in-law. They did not have long to wait. The doors burst open and the indomitable figure of Lady Catherine de Bourgh rushed through. Immediately, Darcy felt as if all the air had been sucked out of the room with the entrance of his aunt.

Her eyes passed briefly over the elder Darcy in their quest for the object of her considerable ire. "Fitzwilliam!" she spat as her eyes finally rested on the young man's face. "I have just heard the news and came here immediately to make my opinions known! What a fine mess! You should be ashamed! If the press finds out about this, you will make your family a laughingstock! And the foundation for which your family has labored tirelessly for over one hundred years will be ruined! What can you possibly have to say for yourself?"

Darcy felt every one of his Aunt's words like a bullet striking him in his gut. He had failed, and his family could suffer because of it.

"Now, Catherine," his father calmly interjected, "you are blowing this out of proportion. The sum is relatively small, can easily be repaid and the Darcy family, as well as the foundation, will survive virtually unscathed."

"You have always been too lenient with that boy, George." His aunt now turned her anger toward the elder man. "You gave him too much responsibility too soon. Why he's barely twenty-one years old, and an astronomically high IQ cannot make up for a ridiculous lack of common sense! If you had allowed me to oversee his project, *this* would never have happened! How could you have been so blind? The boy was too besotted to act with any kind of rational thought. Now this 'Rebecca' person will get away with ten thousand pounds. Of course, your son will learn nothing from this patched up business!"

Darcy was wallowing in self-disgust, and it didn't help that his Aunt and his father were having a conversation as if he weren't in the room. He felt the overwhelming need to defend himself, but no words came to him. His Aunt was correct. Because of his relationship with Rebecca, he had given her a position from which she stole funds from his project.

"Catherine," again the elder Darcy attempted to be the voice of reason, "Wills has offered to repay twice the amount of money from his yearly allowance. As for Rebecca, we may still press charges."

"Press charges?!" His Aunt's eyes appeared ready to explode from her face as her arms flailed about to punctuate her words. "Have you lost your senses? You know the press will never get enough of this type of scandal. It will never end! First the arrest — then the trial! Then that trollop will probably file some type of counterclaim alleging sexual harassment. This could go on for years! No, George, please tell me you are not possibly considering this! I insist I have my way in this matter! The family name is surely more important than ten thousand pounds!"

At that moment, Darcy wanted the earth to open up and swallow him whole, never to be seen again. How could he have been so stupid? Why couldn't he see that Rebecca was no different than all the other scheming girls he had known?

"Catherine, you forget yourself." The edge in his father's voice was unmistakable. "I am the head of the *Darcy* family and the *Darcy* Foundation. The decisions regarding the care of both are mine alone!"

Under other circumstances, the young man would have enjoyed watching his father remind his Aunt that, as much as she wanted to be, she was not a Darcy. At this moment, however, it was no comfort. Darcy felt he deserved every insult and condemnation his Aunt could hurl at him.

"Need I remind you, George, that you named him 'Fitzwilliam?' That is *my* family name! I am also related to you through marriage, so any scandal that touches your name touches us all!" Although his father was not moved in the slightest by this little speech, Darcy struggled to keep his stomach from upending his lunch onto the carpet. "The very least you can do is to remove him from the advisory board until he is mature enough to do the role some credit."

Darcy's eyes shot up to meet his father's, and the look on the younger man's face registered all his fear and anxiety.

"No." George Darcy's calm voice had the desired soothing effect upon his son. "I have no intention of doing any such thing. Someday, the leadership of the foundation will pass on to Wills. The best way for him to learn is to remain on the board. There is no shame in making mistakes as long as one is willing to accept the consequences of one's actions and to learn from them. I have every confidence that Wills has learned a great deal from this one."

"I have!" Both adults looked shocked to hear the young man speak. "I can promise you that I have learned a valuable lesson from this experience, and I will *never* permit *this* mistake to happen again." The elder Darcy bestowed a warm expression of pride on his son.

"You are the one making the mistake, George." His Aunt was still furious, her face purple with rage. "If you don't come to terms with the shortcomings of your children and make me the successor to the foundation, you will be sorry indeed. If you do not follow this recommendation, I will know how to act! Can you not see —"

"Catherine!" The elder Darcy's cold voice put a stop to her ranting. "The Darcy Foundation has always been run by a Darcy and always will be. There are decades ahead for Fitzwilliam to learn from me before he takes over. I have no doubt that he will do very well when the time comes. I will not discuss this further." George Darcy moved to open the doors to the study. "If you wish to see your sister, then now would be a good time. Anne is having one of her 'good days.' If not, I bid you good afternoon."

No one in the room would have suspected that the anticipated decades ahead would last no more than eleven months.

CHAPTER 1
LIFE IS BETTER WITH GOOGLE

Longbourn School for the Performing Arts
New York City, NY, USA
Seven years later

Fitzwilliam Darcy was annoyed. When he, his sister and cousin arrived, he was told that Dr. Bennet was in the building but not at her desk. Although he was assured that she was expected soon, they had now been waiting over half an hour.

Darcy was extremely impressed by Dr. Bennet's proposal for a joint project between the Longbourn Institute for the Performing Arts and his family's foundation. He had wanted to find a project to expand music education in underprivileged, intercity neighborhoods. If successful, this project could become a pilot program he could take back to London. More importantly, this could be his opportunity to move the foundation in a new and significant direction — something of which his parents would have been proud.

The added benefit was that his sister had been accepted to Longbourn as a freshman that autumn, and he had purchased a townhouse on Lansing Street in upper Manhattan within just a few blocks of Longbourn's campus. A project in New York would allow Darcy to reside with Georgiana in the city. As the closing with the attorneys was that afternoon, Darcy decided to stop by to meet with Dr. Bennet one day earlier than expected.

At that moment, however, his sister was not foremost in his mind. *She's looking for millions of pounds; the least she could do is be here!*

The small waiting area served four offices, the doors of which were spaced around the perimeter. The furniture was stiff and uncomfortable. The walls were decorated with opera posters, and the bulletin boards were covered with what Darcy was sure were items of useless drivel. His sister was amusing herself across the room looking at some photographs on the wall. Sitting next to him, his cousin was bouncing his right knee and humming softly to himself.

"Geoff," Darcy snapped at him, "why are you wearing that ugly tie, and could you stop humming? It's irritating!"

"I don't understand why you're so angry. You can't tell me you expected her to be here to meet us. I know you hate to wait, but if you're going to be consistently early, Darce, you must consistently wait." Geoffrey Fitzwilliam smiled tolerantly at his cousin. "And for your information, this is not an ugly tie; it is my *lucky tie.* I wore it because I am about to meet a very pretty woman."

"What?" Darcy became more annoyed. "Where are you going? I thought we were going to walk Georgie around campus."

"Dr. Elizabeth Bennet *is* the pretty lady!" Geoff adjusted the knot in his tie. "Don't you Google someone before you meet them?"

Darcy looked at his cousin with growing exasperation. "Her resume was part of her proposal. What more do I need to know? Verifying her credentials was your job. Regardless, she has enough degrees to be at least thirty-five years old."

"Regardless of what her impressive resume says, the picture of her on the Longbourn website tells me she is a fox, and I never pass up the opportunity to impress a fox! By the way...if she's thirty-five, I'm the King of Siam! My guess is that she's around twenty-four. She holds only two more degrees than you and you had those by the age of 25."

"That's one *less* degree, Your Majesty," Darcy interjected.

Geoff grinned wider. "Google says differently!"

Darcy heard a feminine voice down the hall call out, "Jack, I'm going for coffee. Want something?"

Darcy let out a huge sigh. "Well as long as we're waiting…" He walked to the hall and spotted the owner of the voice. A young woman wearing a red tank top and a pair of frayed, dusty jeans was heading towards them. Her long, brown ponytail swung from the back of a Boston Red Sox baseball cap.

"Miss!" Darcy called as he waved at her. When she approached him, he spoke

again. "Get me a small black and two with cream and sugar." He handed her
a twenty and walked back into the waiting area.

"I can't believe your gall!" Geoff laughed.

Darcy's haughty look matched his clipped reply. "She was going for coffee
anyway, so it's not an inconvenience. She's obviously a starving student as she
can't afford a decent pair of jeans, so I'll make it worth her while." He lowered
his voice. "And by the way my dear cousin, *that* was a fox!"

Geoff was stunned. "Is this my perpetually indifferent cousin commenting
on a pretty girl? I'll have to take a closer look at this *student*."

When the young woman returned, she walked into the waiting area where
Georgiana was reading the caption below a photograph on the bulletin board.
Georgiana looked up and smiled apologetically as she took her coffee. "Thank
you," she whispered. The young woman winked at her and put the remaining
cups and the change on the table next to Darcy.

"You may keep it," Darcy insisted, pushing the change toward her.

"Are you sure?" she asked gratefully.

"Of course," Darcy replied as his eyes discreetly scanned her from head to
toe. *She's gorgeous!* Her five-foot, six-inch-tall body was displayed to its best
advantage by the form-fitting top and jeans. Her hair looked like silk, and
Darcy imagined running his fingers through it and caressing…*No, wait! Slow
down, Darcy; she's a student. Think of something else!* "You wouldn't possibly
know where Dr. Bennet is? We've been waiting a long time."

"I most certainly do!" she replied earnestly. "Why don't you go in and have
a seat." The young woman smiled as she waved her hand toward Dr. Bennet's
office and then walked back down the hall to deliver a coffee to the aforementioned Jack.

Darcy sat back with a self-satisfied smirk on his face aimed directly at Geoff.
"I don't see what you're so proud of," Geoff teased, "bribing a poor student to
get what you want. However, I must agree with that bit about her being a fox.
Too bad we're so moral about hitting on the young and innocent."

"No doubt she's young, but with a body like that, I sincerely doubt the innocent part." Darcy's voice once again lowered. "*Those* are most definitely *real*."

"A man would willingly lose himself in that cleavage for days!" Geoff added,
looking forlornly towards the door.

"Stop it right now! You two make me sick!" Georgiana hissed, and the two
men knew to look appropriately apologetic. "Look, you don't need me here,

so if you don't mind, I'll just hang out in one of the practice rooms down the hall. Beep me when you're ready to go because I don't want anyone to know I'm related to either of you!" She then swept out of the door in a huff.

With Georgiana gone, Darcy looked around the office. The furniture was typical, low-budget, academic stuff. There was a high-back piano against one wall, and another was lined with diplomas. He stood up to read them and noted that Dr. Bennet was certainly well traveled in addition to being well educated.

"Darcy, this isn't like you. Typically, you're rolling your eyes when I comment about the women we meet." Geoff scanned his cousin's inscrutable expression when he noticed a small kink in the armor — a slight softening around the mouth. "You're smitten! Good Lord, you are! Why else would you be acting like this?"

Now Darcy *was* rolling his eyes, but his cousin continued. "Love at first sight. I can't believe it could happen to you — you, of all people!" Geoff knew he was laying it on thick, but opportunities to tease his cousin were rare and not to be squandered.

"Well now—" The young woman suddenly appeared in the doorway and spoke sweetly. "I'd like to thank you gentlemen for coming here. It would have been very difficult for me to come to London this week."

"Excuse me. We are waiting for Dr. Bennet," Darcy stated sternly.

"I am Dr. Elizabeth Bennet," she replied with a smile as she took her seat behind the desk. The silence within the room was deafening.

"Why didn't you tell us that earlier?" Darcy finally broke the silence, his cold tone effectively communicating that he was not amused at her little joke. "I would never have asked you to get us coffee if I had known. I thought you were a student."

The smile widened on Elizabeth's face as she spoke pleasantly. "First of all, Mr. Darcy, you didn't *ask* me to get coffee, you *told* me to get coffee. Secondly, having recently been a student myself, I would never abuse one by reducing him or her to the position of errand boy."

Darcy was confused. It was obvious she was pointing out his faults, but she was speaking in such a friendly manner that it was difficult to take offense.

"Finally, Mr. Darcy, don't you Google someone before you meet them? My picture is readily available on many websites including Longbourn's. How do you think I know that you are Fitzwilliam Darcy and that this *gentleman* next to you is Geoffrey Fitzwilliam?" Elizabeth's emphasis on the word "gentleman" had the desired effect. Geoff coughed with embarrassment.

Darcy was another matter entirely. He could not believe his ears. Here was this woman applying to his foundation for money, and she was treating him as the butt of some joke! At least he thought she was, but he still wasn't completely sure. Wasn't she the least bit concerned that he would simply walk out and take his millions with him?

At the same time in the back of his mind, he was wondering where he'd heard that Google phrase before.

Geoff interrupted his thoughts. "You weren't dressed as casually in any of the pictures I found on the Internet." Now Darcy remembered where he'd heard the phrase, and he wasn't pleased with Geoff's self-satisfied grin. His cousin was pouring on the charm, but by the look on Elizabeth's face, it was clear she wasn't buying any of it.

"I will not apologize for the condition of my clothing, Mr. Fitzwilliam. I was not expecting you until tomorrow; therefore, I did not hesitate to help a student dig a harp from a very dusty storeroom. My clothes notwithstanding, if you are willing to discuss business with someone so young and innocent — oh, yes," she said looking pointedly at Darcy, "doubtfully innocent — perhaps we can get started."

Darcy didn't know what to do first: flush with embarrassment or splutter in indignation. The decision was made for him when Elizabeth began discussing the Riverside Community Center Project. After about forty-five minutes, Darcy had to admit he was impressed, and he knew that if he were impressed, the Advisory Board members of the foundation would be impressed also.

Elizabeth handed each of them a disk. "I have prepared a PowerPoint presentation which I hope will help your Board visualize the implementation of the project; however, I was hoping to take you to see the Community Center while you are in town."

Geoff was thankfully now all business. "I think that's an excellent idea; however, we will need you to come to London to make a presentation to the Board. We must obtain their recommendations before final approval."

Elizabeth punched up a calendar on her laptop. "I can be in London any day the first two weeks of August. Are you anticipating resistance on their part?"

Darcy replied, "Their role is to advise the foundation. My cousin Geoff, his brother, Richard, and I are the officers of the foundation. The final decision will be ours; however, we will take seriously the opinions of the members of the board. There will be a few who will oppose the project, so it is important that we have all their questions dealt with immediately and in person."

Elizabeth saw the wisdom of this plan and agreed to come to London as soon as possible. Darcy and Geoff consulted their PDA's[1] and a date and time were set.

"Would you be available to tour the Community Center tomorrow morning?" Elizabeth inquired. "It appears that the appointment I *had* scheduled for 10:00 a.m. is now available."

"Where shall we meet?" Darcy asked, trying not to look uncomfortable. Somehow, this woman managed to get under his skin and make him squirm.

"We can meet here. The Community Center is just a few blocks away, and we can walk there if that's acceptable." Darcy and Geoff agreed that it was. "I'm hoping to speak to your sister while you're here, Mr. Darcy. It appears that I am to be her advisor for the next academic year."

"What happened to Professor Albright?"

"I'm afraid she had a heart attack a few days ago and will not be returning to Longbourn for some time. Last night the faculty met and divided up her students. If Georgiana is unhappy with the decision, I am sure another professor would be happy to take her on."

Darcy thought about this development. "Geoff, would you mind going down the hall to find Georgie?"

Geoff hesitated. He could just beep Georgiana on her phone, but finally he got the hint that Darcy wanted a moment to speak to Elizabeth alone and took off down the hall to the practice rooms.

"Miss Bennet," Darcy began.

"Dr. Bennet," Elizabeth corrected.

"Dr. Bennet," Darcy began again. He couldn't do anything right with this woman. "I must apologize for my earlier remarks, and I hope my behavior will not prevent us from working together or affect my sister's relationship with you here at Longbourn. I want to assure you that I am just as eager to see this project succeed as you are."

"I appreciate that, Mr. Darcy," Elizabeth said in her most professional tone. She then turned her attention down the hall to where Georgiana was approaching with Geoff. Her tone lightened considerably as she approached the young student. "Ms. Darcy, I'm Dr. Bennet. I was hoping to have a word with you in my office."

1 Personal Digital Assistant

"Dr. Bennet, I would have recognized you *anywhere*," Georgiana gushed, looking first at Darcy then Geoff. "Not only did I Google you, but I saw the picture of you on the bulletin board in the waiting area. You've got a lot of guts wearing that hat in this town!"

Elizabeth laughed. "I like to live dangerously." She then turned to Darcy and Geoff. "I'll only keep her for a few minutes." As if of their own volition, Darcy's eyes followed her into her office. *That is one beautiful arse.* He then began to berate himself mentally for the improper thoughts directed at his sister's advisor.

He walked over to the bulletin board where Georgiana had stood before his disastrous comments about Elizabeth. He saw a large photograph of a group of students. Elizabeth stood out wearing the Red Sox cap. The caption beneath it read: "Dr. Elizabeth Bennet (front and center) captained the winning softball team at the annual grad student picnic on June 16th."

"Brrr...is it me or did it suddenly get really cold in there?" Geoff mused as he looked over Darcy's shoulder at the picture and then laughed. "I don't know who set us up best — the lovely Dr. Bennet or your lovely sister."

"I'm going to have a talk with that girl when we get back to the hotel," Darcy muttered.

"I think I need to burn this tie."

Darcy did not get to talk with his sister when they got back to the hotel because she had a talk with him. Her tirade began the moment they were back in the limo. "I sincerely hope the two of you learned a lesson today about judging people based on appearances. Oh, the comments about her breasts! How can either of you face her again? And trust me you will have to face her again. There's no way I'm giving up the opportunity to work with one of the most brilliant musicians of this or any century because you two *gentlemen* have yet to learn how to behave in public!"

Believing he deserved this scolding, Darcy was allowing Georgiana to vent at him until this last bit of information came out of her mouth. "Come on, Georgie. 'The most brilliant musician?' Don't you think that's overdoing it a little?" Darcy finally got a word in but regretted it soon after.

"Oh, Wills, I know you would never bother to Google someone before you met them, but didn't you look at the pictures on the walls of the waiting area! She is Elizabeth Bennet — 'Bethy' Bennet!" Darcy looked at his sister questioningly. Georgiana, exasperated, took another breath and continued. "She's the child prodigy that Dad took us to see when I was nine. Don't tell me you don't remember. She couldn't have been more than fifteen, and she was playing concertos with the Royal Philharmonic Orchestra. I have all of her CDs. Surely you remember the poster of her that was on my bedroom wall for years!"

Realization began to dawn on Darcy. He did remember the concert and the poster — not to mention the T-shirt, lunch box and backpack. Darcy was nineteen years old at the time and resisted going to the concert, but his parents were insistent, and Georgiana was so excited to see her idol. He groaned inwardly as he realized he had been fantasizing about groping his sister's childhood idol.

He was grateful when the car pulled up in front of the hotel and the driver, Mr. Sparks, opened the door to let them out; however, Georgiana was not quite done. "Oh, and Wills, it was so kind of you to give the struggling college professor, classical recording artist and Grammy award winner the change from your twenty!"

Darcy entered his hotel suite and closed the door to his bedroom firmly behind him. He walked over to his desk, fired up his laptop and Googled *Elizabeth Bennet*. He found hundreds of results. First, he opened the Longbourn site. Her picture was featured as the newest member of the faculty. He had to admit that if he had seen this picture before, he would have recognized her immediately. *No one could forget those eyes.*

He found her academic accomplishments were far more extensive than what she had disclosed in her proposal. Apparently, she narrowed down her resume for him, only giving the accomplishments that related to her position in the music department, her business degree and her volunteer work with the Community Center. *So, she wasn't a braggart. Not what I would have expected from someone who had her face on a lunch box.*

What Darcy learned at the Longbourn site astounded him. Here he found out about her numerous advanced degrees in a wide variety of subjects from music to business and history. More websites highlighted her recording and performing career, and he clicked links that played her recordings while he continued his search.

He found many articles about "the shock heard around the music world" when she retired at the age of sixteen to pursue an academic career. There was apparently a great deal of speculation about her intense touring schedule as there were frequent hospitalizations for exhaustion. The most surprising fact was that she then disappeared into virtual obscurity. The dates of the articles confirmed her age as only twenty-four. She was more than brilliant; she was a genius. *She is definitely not my type.*

Darcy couldn't read enough. He ate his lunch in his study as he kept opening websites and reading more about this amazing woman. His search was interrupted by the arrival of the attorneys who conducted the closing for the house on Lansing Street. Once informed that the deed was filed with the Registry of Deeds, Darcy, Geoff and Georgiana moved their bags into the fully furnished house. The remainder of the afternoon was spent with the decorator who would see that the few changes Darcy and Georgiana wanted made to the décor were implemented as soon as possible.

Pleading jet lag, Georgiana requested an early dinner and retired early, leaving Geoff and Darcy in Darcy's new study, enjoying a glass of brandy.

"She's a bit of all right." Geoff's voice cut through the peaceful strains of Vivaldi playing in the background.

"Georgiana?" Darcy looked to his cousin with alarm.

"Well, yes, she's growing into a beautiful woman, but that's not whom I meant. I was talking about Dr. Bennet."

Darcy's body began to warm as he remembered Elizabeth's supple body, the swell of her breasts, the curve of her hips, the perfection of her bottom and... *No, no, no!* Quickly he attempted to recover himself. "She's tolerable, I suppose, but not my type."

"And we all know what your type is." Geoff paused to make sure he had Darcy's attention. "Expensive!"

In response, Darcy grabbed his laptop, wished Geoff a "good evening" and headed for his bedroom.

Once alone, Darcy was determined to put Elizabeth Bennet out of his mind and began opening and answering his e-mail; however, after only a few minutes, he found himself continuing his earlier perusal of her Google results.

Four hours and many pages of results into his search later, Darcy found a website established by the family and friends of a young man named Billy Ray Collins. Darcy's interest was piqued as he read the account of a young man who was wrongly accused and convicted of assault by a sixteen-year-old girl named Elizabeth Bennet. The website lamented Billy Ray's unsuccessful attempts to obtain parole, which were followed by a plea for contributions to a defense fund. Amazingly, a statement from a woman claiming to be Elizabeth Bennet's mother recounted her daughter's lies and deceptions that resulted in the wrongful confinement of poor Billy Ray.

Was this the same Elizabeth Bennet? Darcy certainly understood that there were people who would do anything to make money on the celebrity of another. He discounted the whole website as rubbish and moved on.

Later that night as he tried to sleep, Darcy told himself that he had indulged his fascination with Dr. Elizabeth Bennet long enough. *She is definitely not my type.* Elizabeth was Georgiana's advisor. Quite possibly, he would be working with her through the foundation. All that made dating her impossible. Not that he would consider dating her in the first place. *She just isn't my type.*

Darcy had made an art out of being emotionally indifferent to women. He had been doggedly pursued by every money-grubbing, insincere, manipulating woman on the planet. After that fateful day in his father's study, he resolved never to allow another woman to get close to him. As his family and friends provided all the companionship he could possibly want, Darcy only sought the company of women to satisfy his baser needs. When the deep urge for physical release could no longer be ignored, he set up a date with a woman who understood exactly what was expected. He took his date to dinner and then to a hotel. He never spent the night, never introduced a date to any member of his family and never took a date to any place he called home.

Darcy didn't worry about having to marry and produce an heir. He had inherited the lion's share of his family's assets simply because he was the only son. However, he would be happy to be the first in five hundred years of Darcy men to allow his sister to provide the next heir of Pemberley. Darcy wasn't fond of children anyway.

It was because of this long line and these assets that Darcy was a very popular man in Britain. Paparazzi had shadowed his movements for years. However, because he had lived his life so predictably, they became bored with their assignments, and only the occasional photograph of him was published.

His life was well ordered and predictable, just as he liked it. Someone like Dr. Elizabeth Bennet would only make things complicated. *She is most definitely not my type. Not my type at all. No, not in the least!*

CHAPTER 2
OPPOSITES ATTRACT

The next morning dawned clear and bright; however, Elizabeth was not her usually cheery self. She had slept little the previous night thanks to a very handsome, very irritating gentleman whose memory would not allow her to rest. *Why?* This wasn't the first time Elizabeth dealt with a huge ego in an attractive package. In the past she was able to put these men out of her mind as soon as they were out of her sight. She had no trouble whatsoever dismissing Geoffrey Fitzwilliam and his horrendous tie — why not his cousin?

She felt no embarrassment in admitting a physical attraction to Fitzwilliam Darcy. He was a good-looking man with an athletic, six-foot, four-inch body and beautiful, light blue eyes that could appear as hard as steel at one moment, and then turn liquid silver with the brief flash of a smile. The embarrassment came when she found herself wondering what he looked like *underneath* that beautifully tailored Italian suit. She could just imagine the broad chest, narrow waist, flat abs, tight butt and — *No, no, no!* This was the man she needed to fund her project, not a potential love interest. *Absolutely not!*

She recalled the moment he became more than another face on the front page of a supermarket tabloid. It had been the third day in a row that Longbourn's president, William Lucas, gave her a lecture about how it would be impossible to find funding, let alone implement a project to expand the music programs at the Riverside Community Center. Elizabeth had a long-standing relationship with the Community Center, which among other things, supplied instruments and musical instruction to the children of low-income families. Lucas insisted that she needed to develop something more viable to bring money into Longbourn.

Elizabeth was channel surfing at 2 a.m., drowning her sorrows in a pint of Ben & Jerry's ice cream when she stopped at the handsome face of Fitzwilliam Darcy giving an interview on the BBC. He was explaining his frustrations in attempting to expand the work of his family's foundation to bring music education to children in underprivileged areas in and around London. Then he spoke those magic words: "I want the Darcy Foundation for the Performing Arts to become more involved in the development and implementation of such projects. We want to do so much more than just write out checks."

New York was a long way from London, but Elizabeth spent the next two weeks working tirelessly on creating her proposal. Her plan first estimated the funding needed to restore the Community Center building and install the latest in computer technology. Secondly, she detailed a plan to fund fellowships for Longbourn students in exchange for which the recipients would teach music lessons at the Community Center. Finally, she outlined a public relations strategy that would attract donations significant enough to insure the program's eventual financial independence from the Darcy Foundation.

With a great deal of hope, Elizabeth express-mailed her proposal to the Darcy Foundation. Two weeks later, she received her first contact from Geoffrey Fitzwilliam.

Elizabeth Bennet Googled faithfully. Last week, when first learning whom she would be meeting, she wandered through the many websites containing information about Britain's wealthiest man, Mr. Fitzwilliam George Alexander Darcy.

In addition to the position of President of the Darcy Foundation for the Promotion of the Arts, he was recently named CEO of The Darcy Company, a world-renowned financial powerhouse founded by his grandfather, Alexander Darcy. Both of Darcy's parents had died six years earlier in a private plane crash outside of Paris, leaving Fitzwilliam Darcy as the guardian of his then twelve-year-old sister, Georgiana, and head of a vast financial empire.

On the second page of results, Elizabeth found the tabloid articles highlighting Darcy's dating habits. The articles had several pictures of him in various cities across the globe. In each picture he was meticulously dressed in

designer clothing and had a model draped over his arm like an expensive ac-
cessory — rarely the same woman twice. In another article he was nicknamed
"Britain's *Model Man*." She laughed at the pun but was repulsed by his obvious
womanizing. No, she would definitely not be looking at Fitzwilliam Darcy as
anything more than a colleague, even if he was absolutely gorgeous.

Upon reflection, Elizabeth realized they did have many similar interests;
both began college at age 16, had degrees in history as well as business, and
seemed to share political ideals. The greatest similarity was their shared interest in expanding access to music education. So, in spite of his reputation as a
playboy, Elizabeth was initially determined to like him.

The meeting yesterday now had her doubting if even working together would
be possible. In his defense, he had no idea that the water-damaged ceiling
tiles in her office were removed for replacement or that, because the tiles were
removed, all sound in and around her office was amplified and funneled to
the area around Jack's desk where additional damaged tiles were also removed.
What she hadn't overheard personally was filled in by a most enthusiastic Jack.

Did the fact that he wasn't aware that he was being overheard excuse his
behavior? One moment he was making inappropriate comments to his cousin
about her appearance; the next he was cold, indifferent and haughty. His arrogance and conceit made her certain that he was the last man on earth she
could ever be prevailed upon to date. *"Date?""When did the word "date" come
in? I mean "work with." Yes, that's it.*

For all her academic and professional prowess, Elizabeth was not the most
successful woman when it came to dating. When she first entered Longbourn
as a student, she realized that her thirst for knowledge was so great that her
course load could not quench it. So she began years of double and triple majors,
which eventually lead to her impressive list of accomplishments and a most
prominent lack of social life. On her twenty-third birthday, her grandmother,
Isabella Bennet, sat her down for a serious talk about where her life was going.
Elizabeth was made to realize that it was time to stop hiding from life and
start living it.

Darcy's comment about her appearance casting doubt upon her innocence
was too close for comfort. It was an opinion apparently shared by most of the
men she was introduced to. Her best defense was "the quick burn" such as she
delivered to Darcy and his cousin the day before. Any man still left standing
was eventually either intimidated by her intelligence or frustrated by her impos-

sible standards for a relationship. Therefore, Elizabeth only dated a man once or twice before the eventual confrontation arose and the acquaintance ended. That she had developed the reputation as an ice queen was inconsequential to Elizabeth. She was not unhappy. She had her work, she had her friends and she had her sister.

At that moment, Elizabeth's phone rang. "Hello, Lizzy, it's Jane. I was hoping we could have dinner tonight. It looks like my internship will finally wrap up within the next few weeks and I want to tell you all about it!"

Jane was a psychiatrist currently interning at New York City Hospital. It was impossible for Jane to think ill of anyone, except Adolph Hitler. Even then, she would sometimes express that perhaps if Hitler had been loved more as a child, he would have turned out to be a fine human being.

"Okay, but this time, you're cooking. See you at seven!" Elizabeth hung up musing that Jane would certainly find something in Darcy's behavior that would reveal the kind human being that Jane believed resided in us all.

On a more positive note was the behavior of Darcy's sister. Elizabeth liked Georgiana Darcy as soon as she gave Elizabeth that smile in the waiting area. It clearly said, "I know who you are, but I'll let them find out for themselves."

She was pleased that Georgiana wanted to keep Elizabeth as her advisor. They talked of the girl's passion for music and her goals for the future. Bright, talented and eager to get started, Georgiana's enthusiasm reminded Elizabeth of herself, eight years ago when she first stepped foot on the Longbourn campus.

Without any effort by Elizabeth, her thoughts turned back to Georgiana's brother. She had wasted an entire night thinking about a man who would surely not give her a second thought. Laughing at her own folly, Elizabeth forced herself out of bed to prepare for the day and her eventual reunion with the dreaded, but still very, very, hot Fitzwilliam Darcy.

DARCY ENTERED THE WAITING AREA outside of Elizabeth's office at 9:30 a.m. to find she was already there. "Good morning, Mr. Darcy," Elizabeth spoke as she walked from her office to the waiting area. "Will Mr. Fitzwilliam and your sister be joining us?"

She was dressed in a navy blue suit purchased on sale at Bloomingdale's and altered to fit perfectly by her friend, Charlotte Lucas. Her hair was swept back into a French twist, but Elizabeth had pulled a few wisps of hair free around her face and neck to avoid the severe librarian look. She was dressed for battle.

"They will be meeting us at the Community Center at ten o'clock," Darcy replied apologetically. His six foot four inch frame was immaculately attired in a custom made, gray Versace suit. "I'm afraid I was too impatient to wait for them this morning. When I am ready to leave for an appointment, I find it difficult to stand around doing nothing. I simply must go, hence my habit of arriving early."

"Unfortunately, Mr. Darcy," Elizabeth continued pleasantly, "the Community Center does not open until ten, so if we leave now, we will have to 'stand around doing nothing.' Would you like to stop first for coffee?"

She was sweetly pointing out his faults again. He suppressed the squirm fighting to come out.

"All right," he replied, and seeing an opportunity to make up for yesterday, he added, "but this time you pay, and I keep the change."

The corners of his mouth turned up into a barely perceptible smile. Elizabeth eyed him quizzically. She reached into her purse and pulled a twenty from her wallet. "Deal!" she agreed, handing Darcy the bill.

As he reached out toward the bill, he noticed that without the shade of the baseball cap, the full beauty of Elizabeth's face was revealed. Her eyes were deep blue — almost violet — and framed with long dark lashes. Her lips were full and shimmered with a lightly tinted gloss. Her teeth were white, but not artificially white like, he had to admit, the teeth of every woman he'd dated in the last several years. *I wonder if her lip gloss is flavored. Perhaps mint or fruit? Mint would be nice… Whoah! Where did that come from?* Darcy suddenly realized that he was staring, and in an attempt to cover his behavior, he quickly snatched the bill from her fingers and motioned with his arm for her to lead the way.

Elizabeth took him to the coffee shop in the main dining hall and then led him outside into the grassy quad where they sat down on a bench under an old oak tree. "This is a favorite spot of mine — out of the sun yet in view of everyone passing by. I think I'm not really awake in the morning until I'm sitting here with my coffee."

"You can't get much stimulation from that," he said pointing to her decaffeinated coffee.

"Placebo effect," Elizabeth spoke conspiratorially. "I've always had a problem with caffeine, but I love the taste of coffee."

"Then why bother?" His face was expressionless. "It appears to me that what you hold before you is a cup of useless chemicals. One would be better off drinking plain water."

"Caffeine and sugar affect us both physically and mentally," she countered. "If I cannot justify my beverage simply by the pleasure of taste, how can you possibly justify your own when one adds the negative affects of both?"

"Dr. Bennet!" a voice called from across the quad, stopping the debate. A young man came running toward them and stopped in front of the bench, panting. "I'm sorry to intrude, but I missed our meeting yesterday, and yes, I want you to be my advisor! I hope it's not too late!"

"Okay," laughed Elizabeth. "Wait until you catch your breath, *and then* speak."

After a few seconds of heavy panting, the boy continued. "I'm Jacob Carter. I was one of Professor Albright's students before the reshuffle a few days ago. My computer crashed. I didn't get your email about yesterday's meeting until ten minutes ago, and I ran to your office only to find that you weren't there. I just spotted you across the quad and...well, here I am." He continued panting and was now bent over, resting his hands on his knees. "I can't tell you how excited I am to have been assigned to you. It's such an honor! When I realized I missed the meeting, I panicked. I just..."

"Stop, Jacob!" Elizabeth interrupted him with a broad smile. "Missing the meeting was no big deal. Can you see me this afternoon, about 4 p.m?"

"Of course I can! Thank you so much," Jacob said breathlessly. "I'll see you then. Good morning, Doctor," he said as he nodded his head to Elizabeth, and then in turn nodded to Darcy. "Sir." He then began running back across the quad.

"Does that happen frequently?" Darcy asked coolly. "Students showering you with their adulation?"

Elizabeth hesitated to answer. Was he simply inquiring or was he somehow insulting her?

"Fortunately, it doesn't. However, I must assure you the feeling is mutual. These students are so talented!" She almost blurted out *like your sister*, but Elizabeth got the impression that Darcy might think she was just attempting to flatter him and that would not do. It was bad enough she was having trouble concentrating on anything other than his gorgeous body sitting so close to hers in that extremely well fitted suit. She had to keep her wits about her or risk coming off as some scheming moneygrubber or even worse: a star struck idiot.

In the meantime, Darcy was having troubles of his own. Somehow, his attention could not stray from the curls resting on the back of her long graceful neck as a light wind tossed them around. The breeze brought a faint whisper of her perfume, and Darcy was sure he knew the scent but could not place the name or how he knew it. He caught himself leaning towards her. *This is madness!* If he was to maintain any dignity, there had to be a change in the situation immediately!

"Can we walk? I haven't seen much of the campus." *Georgie just dragged me all over it yesterday.*

Elizabeth stood up. "We can take the long route to the Community Center. If we take our time, you can see the main buildings on campus and we should make it in time for our appointment with the director."

They walked in silence for several minutes, each enjoying the scenery and the fine weather. Darcy felt his control returning as long as he didn't look at her. Now if he could just come up with some intelligent questions about the project. "How do the students get to the Center from the inner city?"

"Directly across the river from here is Meryton, one of the poorest neighborhoods in the area. There is a subway line directly from there to here. Although the Center is located in Manhattan, most of the children that come here are from Meryton."

As they crossed the street marking the boundary of Longbourn, their conversation was interrupted by a high, shrill female voice.

"Fitzwilliam Darcy! You're Fitzwilliam Darcy! I can't believe it! Felicia will never believe me! Oh, my God! Oh. My. God! OH…MY…GOD!" The girl standing in front of them could be no older than 16, but she carried a Fendi bag and an iPhone. "Oh, I just love you!" She quickly snapped a picture of Darcy as Elizabeth watched with amusement. The girl then ran off as fast as her four-inch heels could carry her while tittering into her phone, "Felicia, oh my God! You'll never guess…" During the entire encounter, Darcy had done nothing but stand perfectly still, his face a mask of cold indifference.

"Does that happen often," Elizabeth teased, "run down by an adoring fan in Jimmy Choo's?"

"Unfortunately, yes. I must admit, I do not share the same admiration for my fans as you do for yours. I don't sing and I don't act. My celebrity is derived purely from my family and fortune." His serious face dissolved into a genuine smile. "I am the Paris Hilton of Great Britain."

He had made a joke, and once Elizabeth recovered from the initial shock, she burst out laughing. When she had sufficiently recovered, she could not resist teasing him a little more. "You should do that more often."

"Do, what?" Mr. Cold Indifference had returned.

"Smile… Laugh at yourself… Relax a little… Be human. You take your pick." She gifted him with her most dazzling smile, hoping for a return of his heart-melting dimples. She was not disappointed.

What more could he do? He was captivated. The smile, although brief, reached all the way to his eyes, lighting his entire face.

The ice was broken.

GEOFF AND GEORGIANA WERE SURPRISED to find Darcy and Elizabeth engrossed in conversation when they met up at the Community Center. Georgiana was pleased that somehow her brother had made up for his previous bad behavior while Geoff was a little jealous of the camaraderie that his cousin and the lovely Dr. Bennet had developed in just half an hour.

They met the director of the Center and toured the music rooms and small concert hall. The building was large but in need of repairs and general maintenance that the yearly donations currently received by the Center could not possibly cover. There was not nearly enough funding to take care of the building, let alone pay staff and provide instruments to the students who attended. The Center's financial situation had become critical. Without the implementation of Elizabeth's program, it would surely close within a year.

"Well, Dr. Bennet, I really enjoyed the tour. There is so much potential here," Geoff stated as they made their way to the door. "We may occasionally act like Neanderthals, but please believe me when I say that my cousins and I have dedicated our lives to funding projects just like this. I believe I speak for all three of us when I say we anxiously look forward to working with you on this one. We will forward your proposal to the advisory board immediately so we can get this ball rolling."

Elizabeth was overwhelmed by the generosity of the three people before her. All right, overwhelmed by one and genuinely pleased by the other two. "Thank you. I'll be sure to make every effort to impress the advisory board and make this easier for all of us," Elizabeth offered. "There just are not words to express how pleased I am to hear your enthusiasm."

"As soon as I receive confirmation from the board for the date of the presentation, I'll contact you," Geoff explained. "I should expect this to happen within the next 48 hours."

"Thank you, Mr. Fitzwilliam. I will look forward to hearing from you."

"Please, call me Geoff. With Fitzwilliam being my family name and Darcy's first name, we both tend to avoid using it unless it's necessary to be formal. At this point, I think it's no longer necessary."

"Then you must call me Elizabeth."

Georgiana looked to her cousin. "Elizabeth and I dispensed with the formalities yesterday. A professor cannot address her student as 'Ms. Darcy.'" I'm sure my brother would like you to address him as 'Darcy.' Most people do."

Elizabeth looked to Darcy for confirmation of his sister's suggestion. Darcy had to admit that what he really wanted was to hear her call him "Fitzwilliam," slowly and softly, preferably close to his ear. Something about the way the name rolled off her tongue when addressing his cousin sent shivers down his spine. Then he quickly reined in his fantasy. It was best to stay with "Darcy." "Please do," was his simple response.

"Well then…" Elizabeth was ready for the meeting to end, especially with the way Darcy was looking at her. His penetrating gaze made her feel as if he could see right through her every defense. "I will get back to my office; I look forward to your call."

"Good days" were said all round and hands were shaken, the last between Darcy and Elizabeth. When their hands met, their eyes connected and something extraordinary occurred. Darcy felt as if he was falling into the bottomless depths of her eyes and that something unexplainable seemed to be passing between their connected hands. It was terrifying and yet intensely pleasurable, which made it difficult for him to let go. Desperately his mind searched for something to grab onto, to bring him back to reality. *Rebecca!* His hand abruptly pulled back, releasing her as he cast his eyes away.

After taking a moment to recover, he glanced back at Elizabeth to see her face mirror the stricken look of his own. He realized then that whatever had happened to him, Elizabeth had felt it too and was equally un-nerved.

Fortunately the other two had not noticed the exchange as they were heading for the waiting Mr. Sparks and the Darcys' limo. "I'll walk with Elizabeth back to her office," Darcy called to Geoff and Georgiana, "I left my briefcase there."

"Shall we drive by and pick you up?" Georgiana asked.

"No, I'll walk back."

Elizabeth wished Darcy had left with the others. Her defenses were on high alert already, and she was afraid she would handle the situation badly when left alone with him.

Darcy's thoughts weren't much different, but he felt they needed to deal with whatever it was that transpired between them a moment before. Unfortunately, he had no idea how and hoped that the time it took them to get back to Elizabeth's office would allow him to put together a carefully thought out plan.

Neither looked at the other as they walked back toward campus. "You didn't bring a briefcase this morning," Elizabeth stated sedately.

"No, I did not." Darcy waited a moment and then continued. "I don't know what to say."

"Then please, say nothing. It will pass. It must be a fleeting…thing."

Darcy couldn't understand why, but he was hurt by her statement. "Is that what you have found in your past experience with…" Darcy searched his brain for a word to describe it, "…attraction." It was way beyond attraction, but it was the best he could come up with at the moment.

It was not in Elizabeth's nature to be dishonest. "I don't have any past experience with anything like…what just happened." There, she managed to be honest without revealing too much. It was quite an accomplishment considering the present fuzzy state of her mind.

"That makes two of us." Darcy was frustrated and more than a little uncomfortable. It had been years since he did not have complete control over his feelings for any woman. He recognized he was in serious danger and he needed to extract himself from this possible entanglement without jeopardizing their future working relationship.

When they at last stood in front of the building that housed Elizabeth's office, she tried to keep her eyes averted, but found she could not. For some inexplicable reason, she was terrified and yet compelled toward him.

When their eyes met again, all his intentions dissolved and Darcy felt the overwhelming desire to throw away all the carefully crafted rules of his carefully ordered existence. He couldn't stop himself from confessing his feelings any more than he could control the magnetic pull between his body and hers. Darcy whispered as his head bent towards her, "I want so much to touch you again, but I know it would lead to disaster."

She raised her head closer to his so he could hear her softly spoken words. "I don't know if I should be grateful or furious at your honesty, but either way, I must agree with you. Disaster!"

"We're going to be working together. We need to control this." He now understood the term, *drunk with her beauty*, for surely only those words could describe what he was experiencing at that moment.

"I agree, but I need time and…distance from you to think clearly." Elizabeth knew that she was in a precarious spot. They were too close, and yet she could not bring herself to walk away.

Elizabeth's statement made sense to Darcy's brain but her acknowledgment that his closeness left her unable to reason thrilled every nerve in his body. He did not think it was possible, but it made him only want to touch her more.

Unconsciously, his face moved closer to hers, their lips only inches apart. Elizabeth could feel the heat from his body and his warm breath on her face.

Darcy realized that not only was her perfume Chanel No. 5, but he could detect the faint scent of mint from her lip-gloss. He wanted nothing more than to taste it.

His right hand reached up to brush her cheek, but this slight movement broke the spell Elizabeth was under, and she immediately stepped back. Darcy's hand grasped only air.

"Will I see you in London?" Elizabeth asked a little too brightly.

"Yes, of course." He also took a step back and looked around while he cleared his throat. It took a moment before he could look at her again. "Until then, Elizabeth," and he walked away.

Darcy realized that had Elizabeth not stepped back, he would now be passionately kissing her in a public place — behavior he had previously found insupportable under any circumstances. He was grateful that she, at least, had kept her wits about her; however, he also felt severely disappointed. Darcy had desperately wanted to kiss her in that doorway, and he desperately wanted to kiss her still. The inability to carefully regulate his desires was new and unnerving. This would not do! He could not allow himself to get involved, let alone in a situation so close to the one that had turned out so horribly, so long ago.

ELIZABETH WAS SITTING IN HER office staring at her computer screen. Her mind was filled with thoughts of how it felt when Darcy took her hand, how his eyes seemed to devour her soul and how soft and desirable his lips looked when they stood together in the doorway. Why had she moved back? *Fear.* When he moved to touch her, fear gripped her chest and she could not help stepping back. She knew it was the right thing to do; she had to protect herself.

Fitzwilliam Darcy was dangerous.

Dinner with Jane that night went exactly as predicted. At first they toasted Jane's success and the news that she would remain at City Hospital for her residency. When Elizabeth told Jane about Darcy and his cousin's rude remarks the previous day, Jane replied that, although the gentlemen had expressed themselves poorly, they obviously had very good taste for admiring her. Elizabeth could not help but fall to the floor with laughter at her sister's observation. It wasn't long before Jane joined her, and it took them several minutes before they could contain themselves.

As the evening progressed, Elizabeth would occasionally catch her sister's eye and say the word "fox." Then the hysterical laughter would erupt again.

Eventually, Elizabeth told Jane about her conversation with Darcy on their way to the Community Center, which in Jane's opinion only confirmed her assessment that Darcy would improve upon further acquaintance. Elizabeth omitted what happened later. If she couldn't explain it to herself, how could she explain it to Jane?

Before Jane went home, she and Elizabeth reviewed Darcy's Google results. Jane interpreted his haughty manner as a defense mechanism due to intense media scrutiny. When questioned about the man changing women as often as he changed underwear, Jane believed that behavior was representative of serious intimacy issues, undoubtedly caused by some past emotional trauma. Her conclusion: Underneath the cold exterior, Fitzwilliam Darcy was a lonely man, desperately crying out for love. That was the same diagnosis Jane gave for Jack the Ripper, and when Elizabeth pointed that out to her sister, the laughter recommenced.

That night as Elizabeth passed another sleepless night, she wondered how Darcy was feeling. Was he equally as disturbed by what had occurred that day, or was it already forgotten as he slept like a baby? Was he sleeping alone?

What did it matter? There was no way a man who could have any number of women in the world (and obviously did) would be willing to settle for a monogamous relationship with her. He dated exciting women who had a certain something in their air, their manner of walking. Isn't that what was required on the runway?

As dawn approached and she finally felt sleep overtake her exhausted mind, Elizabeth imagined how his lips may have felt if she had only been brave enough not to step back.

CHAPTER 3

EN GARDE

July 9th, "The Daily Gossip" (U.K.)
Photo caption: Fitzwilliam Darcy gets a personal tour of the Longbourn
Institute for the Performing Arts.
Story: "Our boy Fitz is back in the States this week as he tours the famous
Longbourn Institute. Sources close to the Darcy family say that little sis,
Georgiana, will be attending Longbourn this autumn. It's no surprise that
Darcy has found a beautiful tour guide...."

Darcy gazed out the tinted windows of the limo at the lights of Times Square. He was on his way to pick up his date, Vanessa. She talked a little more than he preferred, however, she understood exactly what was offered and expected, and she was a dynamo in the bedroom. Tonight he wasn't interested in conversation.

He had momentarily hoped that they might skip dinner and go directly to the hotel. That he entertained the notion of doing something so drastically out of his normal routine, no matter how briefly, was a clear indication of just how out of sorts he was. But he knew the women he dated counted on their being seen together and, if possible, photographed. He didn't want to suggest anything that might make Vanessa less than enthusiastic when they were finally in private. After two days of fantasizing about Elizabeth Bennet, he needed to get laid. Badly!

"Excuse me, Mr. Darcy. May I have a word?" Sparks knew the answer before it was uttered. Mr. Darcy never refused to allow him to speak, but Sparks knew he should ask anyway.

"What's on your mind, Sparks?" was the reply.

"I would like to thank you again for inviting me to work at Pemberley last spring. My mother is under the impression that I haven't adequately done so already." Both men chuckled at the last statement. Knowing Mrs. Sparks, Darcy had no doubt his driver was under strict orders to thank him.

"Please tell Momma Hetta that it was my pleasure. Kindly also relate to her again how much Georgie and I enjoyed her visit. How did she find London?"

"You know Momma. London was too loud one minute, absolutely charming the next; but she always felt like a queen. I can't tell you how much we both appreciated everything your staff did for us there."

"I'm glad you both enjoyed yourselves. The last thing I want is to be on the receiving end of a lecture from your mother! If she refused to let you drive for me, then where would I be? Jerking and bouncing through Manhattan at this very moment, no doubt!" Darcy hated riding through the city. All the sudden accelerating, stopping, honking, yelling, and swerving made each foray into its streets un-nerving. That was why he appreciated Sparks. Sparks could maneuver his way through the streets without jerking Darcy around in the back seat. Darcy immediately recognized his driving talents and therefore specifically requested Sparks from the driving service every time he traveled to New York.

"Oh, I don't think you have to worry about that," Sparks laughed, "Momma still speaks of you and Miss Darcy as 'among the sweetest children God ever placed on this green earth.'" Both men laughed at the quote.

Sparks enjoyed working for Mr. Darcy as he always conducted himself like a gentleman. He was respectful: never making Sparks wait around unnecessarily, never keeping him up all night unless it was arranged with Sparks in advance and never making him do anything that could be considered the least bit degrading. Mr. Darcy had class, and Sparks was proud to work for him.

So when Mr. Darcy invited him to work for three months last spring at his estate in England, Sparks was happy to accept. Darcy's usual British driver was taking a well-deserved extended vacation, and there was no one else Darcy felt could take his driver's place than Sparks. Mr. Darcy's people arranged everything — from the work visa to chauffeur's certification and travel plans. Although totally unnecessary, Mr. Darcy sweetened the deal by inviting — at Darcy's expense — Sparks' mother, Hetta, to come and spend a two-week holiday in England while her son was there.

When she learned about the tragic deaths of their parents, Hetta Sparks adopted the position of surrogate mother and spoiled Darcy and Georgiana with special soul food dishes she personally prepared in the Pemberley kitchen. By the end of her week at Pemberley, Darcy and Georgiana had both taken to calling her "Momma Hetta," and the Darcy's territorial French chef was happily in possession of Hetta's prized family recipe for sweet potato pie.

The second week of Hetta's stay was spent at Oakland, the Darcy's townhouse in London. Even though Darcy and Georgiana remained at Pemberley, the London staff was given strict orders to make Hetta feel like a most honored guest. Darcy also gave Sparks the week off so he could spend the week in London with his mother.

Sparks was overwhelmed with the generosity and kindness of the Darcys. He learned while at Pemberley that the treatment afforded to him and his mother were the rule, not the exception, for the Darcy staff. Although the line between employer and employee was not crossed while he was working, during his mother's visit, Sparks was made to feel like one of the family. Sparks had no doubt as to why every member of their staff was so loyal.

Mr. Sparks pulled up in front of the bar where Mr. Darcy was meeting his date. Sparks waited by the limo until the couple appeared, and Sparks quickly opened the door. Without a word, Darcy and his date entered the vehicle, and Sparks drove them to a local eatery. The privacy glass remained down. This did not surprise Sparks. Mr. Darcy hated public displays of affection, even within the relative privacy of the limo.

MR. SPARKS COULD TELL THAT Mr. Darcy was not pleased. After dropping the couple off at a trendy Manhattan restaurant, Sparks was startled when his phone beeped after only 20 minutes. When the driver picked up Mr. Darcy, he was alone. "Take me back to Lansing, Mr. Sparks," was his terse order.

"Very good, sir," was Spark's reply, and the drive back to Lansing was silent. Sparks noted in his rear view mirror that Mr. Darcy was staring out the window with his hand propped against his cheek. He looked miserable. When they pulled up in front of Lansing, Darcy informed Sparks he was going out again in ten minutes. Sparks had a good idea where they would be headed.

ELIZABETH BENNET WAS SITTING IN her "at home office," otherwise known as her bed. The cool blue and white décor reminded her of her grandmother's house on the outer banks of North Carolina. The warm summer breezes and sounds of the sea always helped her unwind and relax. Her bedroom usually had the same effect. When relaxed, she could compose her best work.

Tonight she sat with her Spanish guitar in her lap and her laptop computer resting on a table specially made to roll over the top of the bed. Her fingers flew through the complex melody and she closed her eyes, trying to feel where the song would take her. Tonight it was taking her nowhere. She didn't feel the festive mood the music was supposed to invoke.

She had been out of sorts since Fitzwilliam Darcy left her standing in the doorway of her office building. She put down the guitar, stretched back onto the pin-striped duvet, and rested her head on several of the decorative pillows scattered about the top of the queen-sized bed. She slowly breathed in and out, trying to release the tension in her body.

There was no way to force the music. She would have to put it aside for tonight and work out her frustrations some other way. Jumping out of bed, Elizabeth quickly dressed and grabbed a duffle bag and an oddly shaped case. She fled outside into the night air. The evening was warm and sticky as Elizabeth donned the ear buds for her iPod and walked the riverfront path.

DARCY ENTERED THE MANHATTAN FENCING Club in a foul mood. He could not have predicted how awful his evening with Vanessa would be. When she turned around to face him at the bar, he was shocked. Her breasts seemed to reach him long before she did. "Hello, Darcy!"

"Van," he stammered, searching for something to say. His eyes were large with astonishment. "What have you done?"

"They're fabulous aren't they?" she gushed, turning her body from side to side to give him and everyone else in the bar a better view. "A friend of mine gave me the name of her plastic surgeon. Well, there just aren't words to describe how *perfect* they are." She took his silence as encouragement. "And see?" she smiled broadly to reveal teeth so white, he was certain astronauts could see them from space. "I got overlays for my teeth. They're now as *perfect* as my breasts. One completely fabulous package, wouldn't you agree?"

"There are no words," was all that Darcy could come up with. He flushed with anger at the spectacle she was causing.

"Well, let's go. I'm starved, and" she added, almost as an afterthought, "I've missed your handsome face." Having planted a photographer in the bar, Vanessa reached up to kiss him, but Darcy quickly moved back. Vanessa was quietly cursing his aversion to PDA.[2] A friend told her that a picture of him actually kissing a girl was worth up to $500,000 from the tabloids. That was more than she'd made modeling in the past five years.

Once outside, Vanessa looked around to see if the photographer followed them. She was disappointed when she didn't see him as Darcy quickly hustled her into the limo.

At the restaurant Darcy tried to get a word in edgewise, but for nearly fifteen minutes, Vanessa never seemed to take a breath. He couldn't recall her being this chatty on their previous dates, but finally she managed to ask him how he was. As he felt this might be his only opportunity to speak all night, he couldn't help but ask, "Van, why the implants? You'll never do runway work again with…*those*," Darcy was trying to be polite, but his disappointment came through in his voice.

At first, Vanessa looked miffed at his reaction, and then she suddenly brightened. "Of course, you haven't heard! I'm not going to model anymore. I have a new agent, and he assures me I am perfect for TV. I have an audition in L.A. on Friday for a part in a new series about a bunch of teenagers coming of age. You know the type: lots of sex and angst. Well, if I wanted a chance at the part, I needed bigger boobs to fill out the bikini. So, wah-lah!" she exclaimed, framing her new breasts with her hands. Darcy expected them to squeak like a dog's toy when she pressed them together.

"I also know how everyone in Hollywood has brilliant teeth. They can't just be straight; they have to be perfect up close. The veneers cost almost as much as the breasts, but they're just so *perfect*." Vanessa flashed him another blinding smile.

"Aren't you a little old to play a teenager?" was all Darcy could think to say. If she said the word "perfect" one more time, he was going to vomit.

"Darcy," Vanessa was getting angry now, "don't tell me you don't like my breasts. All men do. Just look. Every man we passed in this restaurant couldn't keep his eyes off me," she paused for a moment before lowering her voice to say, "Besides, you'll get to meet them up close and personal! I'm sure all these men are green with envy!"

Suddenly the thought of seeing Vanessa's new assets up close and personal

---

2 PDA in this instance means Public Displays of Affection.

was making him green, and *not* with envy! Darcy had to admit he was not only un-impressed, he was repulsed. He needed to extract himself politely from an evening in the company of a suddenly very talkative Vanessa and her fake breasts, fake teeth and what he was sure was a fake tan.

"I'm sorry, Van." He tried to look apologetic. "This isn't going to work for me." He reached into his pocket and slipped her a fifty. "Take this for the cab home. Stay and eat. I'll clear the bill with the manager before I leave. Perhaps one of your admirers would care to join you."

"What are you talking about?" Vanessa asked him incredulously.

"You've made some decisions to further your career and I respect that. I just can't see you again. It's one of my requirements, Van. No implants."

Vanessa was furious, but she needed to try to salvage the situation. They'd yet to have their picture taken together, and with her audition in a few days, a picture in the tabloids could only help her chances. She was still hoping to inspire him to kiss her. She needed the $500,000 to pay the doctors, the bills for her new wardrobe and to place a down payment on a small condo in LA.

"Oh, Darcy," Vanessa leaned over and whined softly in what she thought was a provocative manner, "I was looking forward to acquainting your very big dick with my very big tits. I've missed you soooo much! I've been wet all day just thinking about you!" She demonstrated her point by running her hand up the inside of Darcy's thigh.

Unknown to Vanessa, the gesture and her vulgar remarks only made Darcy more repulsed, and he quickly made his excuses and left, paging Sparks on his way to find the manager. For Darcy, the only positive outcome of the evening was that he was able to leave Vanessa without her making a scene.

Once he was in the safety of the back seat of the limo, Darcy wallowed in his disappointment. *Why? She was beautiful and now she's turned herself into some cheap Hollywood Barbie Doll.*

Darcy couldn't understand the need for implants. He would admit he was aroused by a beautifully full décolletage (a picture of just one such décolletage within a tight red tank top came to mind), but it was the whole, real woman that aroused him, not just her parts. In addition, Darcy felt implants were unattractive. They defied gravity, the cleavage they created was unnaturally spaced and they did not seem to fit the body they were attached to.

The fake breasts, the overly white teeth, and the unnaturally colored skin meant beautiful Vanessa was now repugnant to him. He mourned the loss of her natural beauty even if she did not.

Now that his planned physical exertion had disappeared, Darcy needed to exorcize his disappointment with Vanessa as well as his fascination with Elizabeth Bennet from his mind. The only place he knew he could work himself to exhaustion at this time of night was the Manhattan Fencing Club.

When he entered the club, Darcy was spied by Dalton Vivash. Dalton and his brother, Aubrey, owned not only the Manhattan Fencing Club, but also the Trafalgar Fencing Club in London. The clubs were unique, as they remained open twenty-four hours a day, seven days a week to cater to the needs of their members. Darcy held memberships in both establishments, so he was well known to Dalton.

"Hello Darcy," Dalton called across the entryway. "When did you get into town, and more importantly, how long are you sticking around?"

Darcy shook Dalton's hand, "I got in a few days ago, and although I'm leaving on Sunday to go back to London, I'm planning to live in New York off and on for the next few years. My sister is a student at Longbourn."

"Excellent. This will certainly make things interesting around here. There are far too many of the senior ranks sitting around on their laurels these days. You should shake them up." Dalton was genuinely glad to see Darcy. He was dangerous with a foil, and things around the club had become far too predictable, except of course, for that one exception.

"There's someone you need to see — a new student. She came in about three months ago and has already surpassed Beard, Dinsley and Youngsdale. I've taken her on myself. I haven't seen such promise since you showed up, what's it been, about eight years ago?"

"Twelve," Darcy said dryly, "Youngsdale too? She must be good. So tell me how old is she? How much better do you think she'll get?"

"I've got her warming up for a match with Yates. You remember Yates: great ball of arrogance but not a bad blade."

Darcy's memories of Yates were not pleasant. A self-professed Broadway producer, Yates always claimed to have a play in rehearsals but never seemed able to bring one to opening night. Arrogant did not begin to describe him. "Do you think she can make a good show of it?"

"I think that not only will she make a good show, I think she can take him!"

"I'll have to see that, if for nothing more than the entertainment value."

"Good, come down to number three when you're dressed. We'll be underway, but it shouldn't be over by then."

"If you've taken a personal interest, she must be lovely!" Darcy grinned at his friend.

"You know me too well. Come and judge for yourself!"

Darcy parted for the men's lockers and changed quickly. Seeing Dalton again had put him in a good mood. This was what he needed. He was in his element here: no distractions, no disappointments and no thoughts of Elizabeth Bennet.

When Darcy entered room three, the match was in full swing. He heard the buzzer sound and saw that Dalton's protégé was up three points to two. Yates' body movements betrayed his irritation. *Yates was always such a hothead!* His opponent looked cool and calm, waiting for the next *en guarde*. Darcy stood next to Dalton. Foils flashed as the next point began. Yates had calmed down but was clearly well matched by the young woman on the other side of the piste.[3] She was quick and smooth. Darcy had to admire her control.

"She came here three months ago?" Darcy clarified with Dalton who nodded his head yes, not taking his eyes off the action.

Darcy inquired further. "Where did she train before?"

"She didn't."

"I don't understand."

"When she joined here three months ago she had never held a foil before in her life. Incredible natural talent! She's amazing!" Dalton was obviously beaming with pride.

"You're kidding me; she's far too advanced!" Darcy could not believe what Dalton was telling him. The woman before him had too much control, her movements too precise to be such a novice.

"Ah, my friend," Dalton explained, "years of martial arts training prepared her well. It doesn't hurt that she's a certified genius. Look at the fluidity of her motion, look at the control though every maneuver."

"She's a little reckless. That should pass with time," Darcy observed.

"Oh, Darcy, you must find fault! Take a moment and imagine. Through all that control and execution you can still feel her fire, her passion." Dalton sighed. "I can only imagine what she must be like in bed."

Darcy laughed out loud. "Don't tell me, Dalton! This must be a first! You've been giving her private lessons for a month. You must be seeing her at least three

---

3 The floor area in which a fencing match occurs. It is an area 14 meters (40 feet) long and 1.5 to 2 meters (5 feet, 10 inches to 6 feet, 6½ inches) wide.

to four nights a week, and you can only *imagine*?" He looked at the woman more closely with a growing respect. She was too smart to fall for Dalton's seductions, at least so far, and her body was…perfection. Darcy smiled to himself. *At least there is more than one perfect pair of breasts left in this city!* He turned his attention back to his friend who finally responded to his jest.

"Sadly yes, she's a challenge in more ways than one. It's said she has ice water in her veins, but when I see her like she is now, I know she'll be the hottest lay I've ever had."

"That's what I admire about you, my friend, always the eternal optimist! I am intrigued. Would you introduce us?" The buzzer sounded as soon as Darcy spoke. The point belonged to the woman who squarely hit Yates in the left shoulder.

Dalton was obviously pleased with the direction the match was taking. "I don't think it would be a good idea to introduce her to someone even marginally better looking than myself, at least until after I have secured her…affections. However, she's an intellectual — not your type — so I guess there would be little harm."

Yates was now furious. He paced back and forth. There was no way this novice was going to take him down 5–2! He needed to rouse himself and he needed to throw off her concentration. He approached the centerline of the piste. His opponent moved in to hear him.

"Ah," said Dalton, "time for a little trash talk." To liven up the sport, Dalton allowed opponents to address each other once during the match to either attempt to rattle each other's confidence or to place or increase a wager. When both opponents reached the centerline, Yates removed his headgear and spoke between his teeth towards the woman. Darcy couldn't hear what was said. Wagers were typically spoken only for the assistant recording them to hear. Dalton's protégé then removed her headgear. A tangle of dark curls was swept aside and Darcy's breath caught in recognition.

Yates sneered at Elizabeth. "Well, Miss Bennet, would you like to make this a little interesting?"

"That's *Dr. Bennet*." Elizabeth spoke calmly and leveled her eyes at Yates. "I'm listening."

"Dr. Bennet!" Yates felt his attempt at intimidation failing. "If I take this match, you have to meet me for dinner Friday night, you have to wear something alluring and you have to be *nice*!" Yates hoped his smile was both seductive and disarming.

Elizabeth made no outward reaction to his remark. *You're down two points, loser. Do you think I'm so enamored that the idea of a date with you will throw me off my game? How pathetic!* "If I take this match, which seems very likely, you will immediately bow down before me and kiss my hand."

"I'm not done yet," Yates was rattled by her confidence, "and I've been around this block a lot more times than you have, darling!"

"That's *Dr. Darling* to you. Then you agree to the wager?" Elizabeth looked every inch the ice queen.

Kissing her hand did not seem like a big deal to Yates, ahhhhh, but the date… "Agreed," he hissed back at her.

"Agreed," Elizabeth calmly spoke to the assistant. The wager was noted and the opponents returned to their starting positions.

"Yates is scared!" Dalton smiled broadly.

"It's not over. He could be hustling her," Darcy suggested.

Dalton looked to his friend and chuckled. "You believe that if it gives you comfort."

He then turned toward the match as the referee announced, "En garde," followed by, "Fence!"

It was over very quickly. Two clashes of blades and the buzzer sounded. Yates was staring in disbelief at Elizabeth's foil which had clearly landed on his chest, directly over his heart.

"Match, Bennet!" was announced by the assistant. "Performance wager owed, Yates to Bennet, to be performed immediately!"

Yates and Elizabeth removed their headgear and fencing gloves. Elizabeth handed hers to an assistant and stood at her end of the piste, holding her foil in her left hand and staring coldly at Yates.

Yates at first was clearly pissed, but he had to perform the wager as a good sport or Dalton would have him thrown out of the club. He squared his shoulders and walked towards Elizabeth. He took her right hand, looked her in the eye and raised it to his lips.

Elizabeth cast her gaze from Yates' eyes directly to the floor in front of her and back to his face. Yates had no choice; he had to kneel. Elizabeth then lowered her hand as far as possible, forcing Yates to bow very low. He looked like he was pledging his allegiance to a queen. Elizabeth got what she wanted, his public recognition of her skills as a fencer. Yates realized too late what he had agreed to.

"Touché!" Darcy whispered.

Dalton beamed. "Precisely!"

"Wager, Yates to Bennet, paid!" Elizabeth called out clearly to the room, which erupted in applause. The only people who did not join in with the celebrants were the few men who had shared Yates' fate over the last few months. They were quiet as they recalled their own humiliation as well as their vow never to underestimate Dr. Elizabeth Bennet again.

Elizabeth looked up to Dalton and a brilliant smile graced her face. Her eyes were shining and her face was flushed. Darcy thought she was beautiful beyond imagination, and he could have sworn a collective sigh went up from every man in the room as they looked at her. Her gaze shifted to the tall man standing beside her instructor and the smile faded but her eyes held.

Dalton noticed Darcy's unguarded admiration. "I see you share my appreciation for Elizabeth's beauty. She's a goddess!"

"Indeed!" Darcy agreed, mesmerized.

Elizabeth felt his gaze boring into her as their eyes met. She roused herself to accept a few more congratulations before making her way over to Dalton.

"Well, Master Dalton," she began once she was standing in front of him, "it appears your friend Yates and I were not quite so evenly matched."

"You were brilliant, my dear!" Dalton moved forward to embrace her, but Elizabeth kept one arm in front of her, creating space between Dalton's body and her own. She liked her instructor, but she knew his intentions extended beyond teaching her how to fence. As Dalton released her, her eyes once again found Darcy's which had not failed to notice this subtle defensive maneuver.

"Elizabeth, let me introduce you to my friend —"

Elizabeth interrupted. "Darcy and I have already been introduced." She had no choice, she reached out her hand to him. "Good evening, Darcy. I hope you and your sister are well."

"Thank you, we are both well. Congratulations on your brilliant win." Darcy reached out and took her hand.

Dalton was too busy enjoying the win of his protégé to notice the obvious chemistry between the two people standing right in front of him. "Darcy, you dog! You didn't tell me you knew Elizabeth!"

"I didn't know it was Elizabeth until she removed her mask," Darcy explained, still looking into Elizabeth's eyes and still holding her hand.

Elizabeth broke away first. "Darcy's sister is attending Longbourn this fall; I will be her advisor. We met yesterday when they were touring the school."

"Oh yes, Longbourn. I should have recognized the name when you said it,

Darcy, but I was distracted." Dalton exclaimed, "Such a small world is it not? Come, Elizabeth, you need a breather, and I promised Darcy a go at me this evening. Would you like to observe?"

Elizabeth thought it would be interesting to see Darcy fence. He must be very good for Dalton to bother sparring with him. For a moment Elizabeth imagined watching his muscles move, his taunt body springing across the floor. "I am sorry to miss the opportunity, but I do have an early morning tomorrow. Dalton, a pleasure as always. Darcy, good evening."

Dalton turned away, his mind on the next match while Darcy took Elizabeth's hand once again, allowing himself a moment to revel in the softness of her skin. This time he raised her hand to his lips and lightly brushed them against her fingers. "Elizabeth, 'til we meet again."

Across the room, another young woman saw it all and fumed. Caroline Bingley hated Elizabeth Bennet. Up until a few short weeks ago, Caroline's frequent, tedious trips to New York were made tolerable by the attention she received at this club. That all changed with the arrival of this upstart college professor.

Caroline did not understand how it had happened. Elizabeth was plain, she dressed with no flair and her skills with a foil were mediocre at best! Caroline was the darling of both the New York and London social scenes and the star of the Manhattan Fencing Club. Now, Elizabeth Bennet was all anyone seemed to talk about. After Elizabeth's little scene with Yates tonight, it would be even worse!

However, all of that was nothing to what was happening at that very moment. Elizabeth Bennet was standing with Fitzwilliam Darcy. *Her* Fitzwilliam Darcy! Caroline saw the way Darcy looked at Elizabeth, and her blood boiled as he kissed her hand.

No, this was not to be borne! Elizabeth Bennet had taken Caroline's place as the belle of the club and her place as Dalton's star student. She was also sure that Elizabeth had taken her place in Dalton's bed. Caroline did not yet know how she was going to prevent it, but she would not allow Elizabeth Bennet to take her place in Darcy's bed too, especially considering Caroline had yet to be there herself!

CHAPTER 4
ACROSS THE POND

August 5th, The London Star Gazer(U.K.)
Photo caption: Fitzwilliam Darcy attends last night's performance of the
London Philharmonic to benefit Princess Diana Charities.
(No story)

I will remain in control of this situation! I will not allow my passions to lead me astray! I can handle anything and anyone that comes across my path, especially one Fitzwilliam Darcy! Elizabeth recited this mantra over and over. *I can't believe this has become so complicated!*

Elizabeth should have been comfortable in the first class seat the Darcy Foundation had provided for her transatlantic flight, but her mind was far too troubled to allow her to enjoy it. She should have been excited at the prospect of presenting before the advisory committee, but instead, she couldn't stop focusing on one man who would also be in London. Elizabeth had not seen Darcy since that night, three weeks ago, at the fencing club. The passage of time had not diminished the sensation his lips had left on her hand, or his touch that had stirred her...well, everywhere!

As the pilot announced their landing at Heathrow Airport, Elizabeth wondered if they would again be swept away by the overwhelming chemistry they felt for each other. Not since she was sixteen years old had Elizabeth Bennet felt fear. She had become strong, indifferent, detached. She feared no man, at least not since Billy Ray Collins. Today, however, she was terrified.

As Elizabeth left customs, she found a fit, elder man in a blue suit holding up a sign with her name on it. He introduced himself as Mr. Thayer, the Darcy's driver. After confirmation of where she was staying, he assisted her into the antique Bentley and smoothly merged into traffic.

The scene when she arrived at the home of her Aunt and Uncle Gardiner was chaos. Children seemed to pour from the front door, and hugs and kisses were rapidly exchanged in the rush to get Elizabeth inside and out of the record-breaking heat.

Once Thayer had successfully deposited Elizabeth's bags inside the front entrance (made more difficult by all the assistance he received from the two eldest Gardiner children), he produced an envelope from his pocket that he delivered to Elizabeth. The driver than wished them all a good afternoon and excused himself from the noisy homecoming.

After a peppering of questions about her flight and the fancy car that delivered her, Elizabeth managed to extract herself from her young cousins long enough to open the letter.

Dear Elizabeth,

I hope you had an enjoyable flight. Georgiana and I wanted to welcome you with a basket of flowers in your hotel room upon your arrival, but as you did not divulge the location of your lodgings while in London, I hope you will accept our heartfelt welcome through this simple note.

Georgiana and I would like to extend an invitation for you to dine with us this evening. Please call 020-XXXX XXXX if you cannot attend, otherwise, I will send Mr. Thayer to pick you up at 7 p.m.

Very truly yours,
Fitzwilliam Darcy

Elizabeth's original reaction was to decline the invitation, but after consulting with her Aunt to make sure they had no other plans for her, she dialed the number provided.

AT OAKLAND, THE DARCYS' LONDON Townhouse, Georgiana burst into her brother's study. "Has she called?"

Darcy looked at his sister and smiled. "She just arrived, Georgie. I don't know if she's even read the invitation yet."

"I wish you had told her to call even if she was coming. Then I wouldn't have all this suspense."

"I'll beep you as soon as I hear anything, but if we don't within the next hour, I would assume she'll be here."

"If she does come to dinner, do you think we can get her to play for us? That would be amazing! Don't forget to beep me. I hate these walky-talky phones, but today they are beginning to grow on me." Georgiana blew out the door as fast as she entered.

"Please shut the door!" Darcy called after her but she was gone too quickly.

Darcy's PDA vibrated and he quickly touched the earpiece to answer. "Darcy here."

"Mr. Darcy," was the response, "Thayer here. I've dropped off Dr. Bennet and delivered your letter as instructed. I should return to Oakland in approximately twenty minutes.

"Where is she staying?"

"It is a private residence, sir, on Gracechurch Street," Thayer explained.

"Please see me when you return. Thank you, Thayer." Darcy ended the call, pulled his earpiece out of his ear and threw it on his desk.

"Damn! She's staying with friends, which means it's unlikely she'll come to dinner tonight." Darcy was surprised with his reaction. He didn't realize until that moment how much he had wanted to see her. A disturbing thought crossed his mind. *Could she be staying with a boyfriend?* He realized his sudden anger at that thought was unwarranted, but he couldn't stop it.

His phone rang again.

"Darcy here."

"Formal, business or casual?"

"Excuse me?" It took him a moment to realize with whom he was speaking.

"Dinner tonight. Your note didn't say how to dress."

"Oh, I guess more business-casual. It's just Georgie, Geoff and I. We thought your first night in town should be low-key."

"Thank you. See you then." Elizabeth hung up and Darcy was left staring at his phone. After a moment, he beeped Georgiana. "She's coming to dinner."

"How do you know so soon?" Georgiana sounded suspicious. "You don't have Thayer spying on her, do you?"

"She just called to ask how to dress," he answered defensively.

"Were you nice to her?"

Darcy spluttered at his sister, "Of course I was! What do you think I am?"

"I just wanted to make sure you didn't make any more stupid comments about her breasts!" she warned teasingly. Fortunately for Darcy, his sister couldn't see how uncomfortable her statement had made him. "You and Geoff had better be on your best behavior tonight or I'm going to throttle the pair of you!"

Darcy ended the call. He leaned back in his chair, and putting his feet up on his desk, he pondered the confused state of his mind. Elizabeth Bennet cut up his peace, drove him to distraction and was a danger to his well-maintained existence; and yet, he was practically giddy with anticipation at seeing her. "Lovely Elizabeth," he spoke aloud to no one but himself, "What have you done to me?"

WHEN THAYER ARRIVED IN HIS study, Darcy immediately began the inquisition. He was puzzled as to why Elizabeth chose to stay somewhere other than Oakland. Any other woman of his acquaintance would be thrilled with such an invitation. He told himself this was proof of some great fault, and if he could discover it, her spell over him would be broken and he could dismiss her from his mind.

"What was the house like?"

"Typical, upper-middle-class neighborhood. Well maintained brick townhouse." Thayer was surprised at Mr. Darcy's inquiry, but then again, Dr. Bennet was a lovely woman. Was it possible his employer had developed a chink in his armor, or was he sizing up the competition for a business venture?

"Friend or family?"

"She referred to the lady in residence as 'Aunt Maddie.' Everyone within the house addressed Dr. Bennet as 'Lizzy.' She was affectionately welcomed, sir. I suspect, family." Thayer delivered this information in an even tone, eyes straight ahead. He would never openly question anything Mr. Darcy did, but his employer's obvious satisfaction at the last response seemed to confirm Thayer's suspicions that Mr. Darcy's curiosity concerning Dr. Bennet was not entirely business-related.

Darcy looked expectantly at his chauffeur as if he was anticipating more information. "There were four young children in the house, sir. Other than that, there is nothing to tell."

"Thank you, Thayer. You will not be needed until you pick up Dr. Bennet at 7 p.m."

"Very good, sir." Thayer walked out the door of the study and headed for the kitchen for a cup of tea and perhaps a hint to the cook about the possible significance of tonight's dinner guest.

THAYER DROVE ELIZABETH THROUGH THE large wrought iron gates of Oakland and into the covered courtyard in front of the house. Elizabeth could not imagine that such a large house could be within the city, but practically unseen from the street. It was both magnificent and intimidating. *He's just a man, like any other. Two arms, two legs, one very broad chest, one... Oh, God, it's going to be a long evening!*

Elizabeth was let in the front door by a servant and tried not to gape at the beautiful marble floor in the entryway. Different hues of amber and beige marble formed the pattern of an immense sunburst, which radiated from the center of the floor to every corner. A magnificent chandelier was hanging from the high ceiling and a large marble staircase rose before her. Beautiful antique tables held freshly cut flowers, and matching silk-covered benches sat against the warm wood-covered walls.

Elizabeth caught her reflection in a nearby mirror. The large grey and white block pattern on her full cotton skirt was set off by the wide black belt at the waist. The white cotton button down blouse had very short sleeves and perfectly fit her body perfectly. The collar of the blouse stood up against the back of her neck and the front was unbuttoned to reveal, what Elizabeth felt was, a tasteful, but attractive amount of cleavage in which rested a double loop of black onyx beads. She had again pulled her hair up into its trademark twist. She looked as cool and sophisticated as the interior of Oakland, even though her feelings remained more like the uncomfortable 90-degree heat oppressing London that evening. She silently thanked her friend, Charlotte Lucas, for giving Elizabeth this outfit from her friend's collection of summer designs.

The servant led her to a pair of intricately carved oak doors that he proceeded to open and motioned for her to enter. Nervous did not begin to describe how Elizabeth felt. When touring, she had been to homes that were considered quite grand, but the home in which she now stood went beyond her experience. It spoke of taste, class and very old money. As much as she hated to admit it, Elizabeth felt a little intimidated. She suppressed the uncomfortable feeling and moved forward.

"Elizabeth!" Georgiana called excitedly and quickly approached her when she entered the room. "I'm so glad you could join us this evening. You look lovely!" Georgiana warmly clasped her hand and smiled broadly. She wore a white cotton, peasant style dress that made her look younger than her eighteen years. Her dark blonde hair hung loosely down her back.

"Thank you for your kind invitation. You have a lovely home." She hoped she sounded calm but sincere as the gentlemen approached her. Geoff was the next to shake her hand. "Elizabeth, I can't tell you how pleased I was to hear you'd be joining us for dinner tonight. I hope your trip across the pond was pleasant." He was in a navy blue suit, light blue shirt and a tasteful tie.

"Yes, Geoff, it was. Thank you and," she winked for emphasis, "nice tie!" Suddenly Geoff had a new lucky tie.

Elizabeth then turned to Darcy. He looked very much at ease in a pair of Ralph Lauren khaki slacks and a crisp, blue and white striped button down shirt. He offered his hand to her, palm up.

Elizabeth gently placed her hand in his. Darcy wrapped his fingers around hers as she tried not to audibly sigh. "Elizabeth, welcome. Would you like a glass of wine before dinner?"

She found a comfortable leather chair as Darcy poured her a glass of perfectly chilled chardonnay. The cut crystal glass caught the light from the nearby window, sending multi colored rays across the beautiful antique Persian carpet, resting on the highly polished oak floors. All of the walls were lined with books, thousands of them.

"So, Elizabeth," Geoff began in a cheerful voice, "Darcy here tells me you refused his invitation to stay at Oakland. Did the Queen have a room for you?" Elizabeth smiled at Geoff's jest.

"I have relatives in the city. My Aunt and Uncle would never forgive me if I came to London and stayed anywhere else. Though I must admit, I'm very fond of them, so it's no bother."

"Oh, I understand perfectly!" Geoff replied. "We have an Aunt in Kent who would never allow us to stay in a hotel." He added conspiratorially, "Though I must admit, I'm not very fond of her, so it is a bother!" All three cousins laughed and Elizabeth couldn't help but join in. Soon the four were talking comfortably.

Elizabeth was aware of Darcy's keen gaze on her. She couldn't decide if he was mentally undressing her or finding fault with her appearance. Retaliation seemed her best defense. "So, Darcy…I was reading in the newspaper that your company is opposing one of the urban regeneration projects in Stratford."

Darcy was impressed with her choice of subject matter. "Yes. It is a district filled with a great deal of historic architecture. We'd like to see that preserved instead of replaced."

"But given the limited funding for the project and the large number of residents in that community in need of housing, wouldn't preservation require a substantial percentage of the available resources to eventually house only a limited number of individuals?"

Thus began a discussion on preservation vs. progress. Darcy was surprised at how well informed she was on the issues involved. He really had to think long and hard when responding to her points. Finally, Darcy said, "Given the dissertation you wrote on historic architecture, I'm surprised at your views on this matter."

"You have found me out. I occasionally profess opinions which are not my own, all for the sake of a good discussion!" Darcy appreciated the honesty of her admission, as well as her abilities to debate. Too many women he knew simply agreed with his point of view. Elizabeth taking the opposing opinion intentionally to encourage intelligent discussion was a refreshing change.

Finally Geoff broke in, grateful for the opportunity to be included in the conversation. "I believe, Elizabeth, you would have made an excellent attorney!" Geoff noted that this was the first time he had ever known Darcy to enter into any lengthy conversation with a single, unattached, female guest. Most women they entertained were either too intimidated or too enamored to disagree with his cousin, who was usually content to allow Geoff to do all the talking. This was a strange development, indeed!

Geoff decided it was time to learn more about Elizabeth. Did she already have a boyfriend? Was she gay? All of his questions, which usually revealed the presence of a significant other, had yielded nothing so far. Geoff decided to try once again. "So, Elizabeth, what do you do in your free time?"

"I don't have a lot of free time. What little I have is spent walking, reading or simply playing music."

Darcy knew what his cousin was fishing for and would have cleared his throat in an attempt to remind Geoff not to be intrusive, except for the fact that Darcy was also dying to know if Elizabeth was attached.

Geoff had finally decided that enough was enough and went for the direct approach. "No significant other in your life, then?"

Georgiana's eyes widened in surprise at her cousin's boldness and cast him a warning glare.

Elizabeth smiled at Georgie to assure her she was not affronted. "No, Geoff. I'm afraid I haven't had much time for a relationship."

"Well, we'll have to do something about that, won't we?" Geoff gave her what he felt was his most dazzling smile.

Elizabeth decided to turn the tables. "So, what about you Geoff? No Mrs. Fitzwilliam stuffed around here somewhere?" Elizabeth glanced behind her chair and under a table as if expecting a Mrs. Fitzwilliam to pop up at any moment. Darcy was captivated by the way she was handling his cousin. Georgiana giggled.

"The only Mrs. Fitzwilliam in my life is my mother," Geoff paused, looking Elizabeth straight in the eyes, "at least, so far!"

Elizabeth waited a moment before erupting into laughter. "That has got to be the worst line I have been handed in at least the last two years!"

"I'll second that opinion!" Georgie chimed in, her laughter matching Elizabeth's.

When their eyes met, Darcy raised his glass in salute. *Touché once again, Elizabeth.*

"Ah, Elizabeth, you wound me to the quick!" Geoff laughed along with the others.

Darcy, who *had* been mentally undressing Elizabeth for the past half hour, was now aware of how uncomfortable his trousers had become. He wanted her attention and desperately tried to think of a topic on which to engage her in conversation once again.

A knock on the door was followed by a servant who announced that dinner was served. Georgiana led Geoff out the door first as he told her, "Well, I guess I'll just have to save my best lines for you, Squirt."

"Don't do me any favors!" she replied. Their laughter followed them into the entryway.

Darcy saw his opportunity. He stopped Elizabeth from following them by gently taking her elbow. "One moment, Elizabeth." He reached a nearby table and picked up a card, which he handed to her. "I thought you might enjoy using this while you're in town."

Elizabeth took the card. It was a temporary membership to the Trafalgar

Fencing Club. "I suggest you start with a fellow named Wickham." Darcy lowered his voice as he stepped closer to add, "He could use an attitude adjustment."

Elizabeth stepped even closer to him and softly asked, "And what of you, Darcy? How's your attitude?" Elizabeth wasn't sure where he was going with this, but she wasn't about to let him think he had the upper hand.

Darcy raised his eyebrows. *Is she flirting with me?* "Let's just say I've been buying my own coffee these days." He lowered his voice to a whisper as if sharing a secret. "Can't be too careful."

They were now standing very close to one another. He smelled clean, and his shirt was freshly pressed. She wondered how nice it would be to nuzzle his collar, breathing in the scent of both soap and starch. *A heady aphrodisiac.* She suddenly felt the need for some space and stepped toward the door.

"Thank you," she said gesturing to the card, "but I didn't think security would allow me to bring my foil on the plane. They frown on that type of thing, you know."

His eyes were dark as he fixed them on hers. "I may have a blade that would suit you."

"We'll see." Elizabeth smiled slyly and returned his look as they walked out of the library.

She is definitely flirting with me! With that thought, a very pleased Darcy led Elizabeth into the dining room.

LATER THAT NIGHT AS ELIZABETH tried to sleep, she thought about Darcy. What was it about him that made him so irresistible? He was handsome, intelligent, well built, charming and not to mention, loaded. More than any of those attributes, he was dangerous. Perhaps it was the danger that attracted her.

Elizabeth knew she had to resist. She could easily fall in love with him, and that would not do. He was famous for his aversion to commitment, and Elizabeth could not bear the heartbreak that was sure to follow. She must protect her heart at all costs.

Darcy was having no luck finding sleep either. He kept reliving their conversation after dinner as she browsed through his collection of foils. She would select a foil, take it through a few maneuvers, and then replace it before reaching for the next. He was enjoying the show for she was grace in motion.

The companionable silence that fell between them when entering the room was relaxing. The quiet was only broken by the click of her small heels hitting the marble floor as she walked from one blade to the next.

Finally, she picked up one of his finest foils. As she moved with the foil, he could sense that this one fit her well. "Tell me the story of this foil," she broke the long silence.

"What makes you think there is a story?"

"I've learned there's always a story with a foil. How it was obtained? Why it was cast aside? I'd like to know."

"Will it make a difference as to whether or not you borrow it?"

"Yes, I think it will."

"My father had that foil custom made for my twentieth birthday. He heard that the maker was well known for the superior quality of his work. He didn't realize a foil is something you can't purchase for someone else; he just wanted to give me something to show his support and encouragement." Here Darcy paused, thinking of how happy his father was the day he presented him with the foil. "It never felt right in my hand, but I used it for an entire year just to show him I appreciated the gift. One day he pulled me aside and told me he could see that I did not perform as well with it. He understood and was touched as to why I kept trying to use it, but he insisted that it was time for me to select my own."

"A gift of love." Elizabeth smiled serenely as she offered the handle of the foil to Darcy. "I don't think it would be right for me to borrow it. It belongs here with you."

The foil was recognizably expensive and finely made. That she would refuse it for sentimental reasons moved him considerably. "Please take it. I know my father would have been pleased that someone had the opportunity to use it, especially so talented a fencer."

Now it was Elizabeth who was touched as she pulled back the foil. "In that case, I will borrow it to please your father. That will continue the tradition. Thank you."

Her words awoke tender feelings within Darcy he thought never to feel again. He wanted to hold her, to tell her how much she had touched his soul, but instead he fought the urge and stepped back. She appeared to step back at the same instant and spoke in a playful manner. "Now tell me about this Wickham fellow you want me to take care of. Shall I run him through?"

"A lovely thought, but you are far too beautiful to be locked away in prison because of him."

"Ahhhh, and what makes him so unworthy?"

"It is a long story, and tonight has been far too pleasant to cast a cloud like George Wickham on it."

"That bad! Well, I assure you, I'll do my best to dispatch him!"

"I have no doubt you could; but I must admit, I hope you never have the need."

Darcy again laid his head down on the pillow and tried to focus on relaxing his body. His own actions had him puzzled; when not in her presence, he was constantly reminding himself to pull away, and yet once she was within 50 meters of him, he found any excuse to be close to her. The push and pull in his head exhausted him. He needed sleep, and perhaps tonight would be the night he would stop dreaming of her. *Hah, not bloody likely!*

ACROSS THE HIGHLY POLISHED HALLWAY of Oakland's upper floors, Georgiana's thoughts were more pleasantly engaged. She had noticed her brother's attention never waived from Elizabeth throughout the evening, and she decided that Darcy must be smitten. She smiled to herself to think that her brother, who appeared to be immune to female charms, was clearly affected. The best part was that Elizabeth was making no effort to attract his romantic interest. *Yes, my careful, self-controlled brother. I think you have met your match — in more ways than one!*

CHAPTER 5
THINGS HEAT UP

Mr. Thayer dropped Elizabeth at the corporate headquarters of The Darcy Company at 10 a.m., a full hour before the presentation. The day was bright and exceedingly hot. The outside temperature was at least 35 degrees Celsius and the humidity was high.

Elizabeth dressed in her most comfortable suit. The charcoal grey cotton skirt was slim and formfitting. The matching short jacket had three-quarter length sleeves, which covered a white cotton blouse. Her hair was in its usual twist, allowing what little breeze there was to caress her neck.

It was upon entering the significantly cooler lobby, that a professionally dressed man conducted Elizabeth to an elevator. "My apologies, Dr. Bennet," Charles Hayter said as they stood outside the polished steel doors, "the air conditioning is malfunctioning in all the lifts as well as other sections of the building."

On arriving at the top floor, Mr. Hayter led Elizabeth down a hallway and through a pair of steel doors. She found herself in a sizeable office dominated by a large chrome and glass desk surrounded by several overstuffed, dark leather chairs. Against one wall was a marble fireplace, in front of which was a sitting area containing a leather couch, coffee table and two additional chairs. Geometrically patterned carpets covered the marble floor and deadened the sound of her footsteps. Two adjoining walls contained nothing but floor-to-ceiling windows, and before one stood Darcy, looking out over the city.

He turned to address her. "Elizabeth, how are you this morning?"

"I am very well, thank you,"

Darcy turned to his assistant. "Hayter, any news on the air conditioning?"

"I'm sorry, sir. Because of the heat wave, we can't get our contractor to come before tomorrow morning. I reminded him how much we are paying for the service contract; however, it had no effect."

"Have we tried someone else?"

"Yes, sir. They all say they're too backed up with their current clients to make a trip for us."

"That is unfortunate." Darcy turned to Elizabeth. "I'm afraid there is no air conditioning in the conference room used for the committee meetings. It's very uncomfortable in there."

"There isn't another room in which we could meet?"

"None with the needed media displays. I'm afraid we may have to postpone until next week."

This was unacceptable to Elizabeth. She needed to return to New York on Sunday. "I think I may be able to take care of this. May I use your phone?"

"Elizabeth, I do appreciate your gesture, but, believe me, if the Darcy name can't get someone here, I can't imagine you can."

"You're not the only one in this room with significant connections," she teased.

Darcy motioned her to his desk. Elizabeth sat on the corner of it, leaned back behind her to pick up the receiver, crossed her legs and punched a number into the phone. She then turned on the speakerphone so the sound of the line ringing could be heard in the room. Darcy quickly dismissed his assistant and allowed himself the pleasure of admiring Elizabeth's shapely legs as they swayed back and forth while she waited for the call to be answered.

"Gardiner Commercial Heating and Cooling," a pleasant male voice answered.

"Hello, Sean. It's Lizzy. May I speak to Uncle Ed?"

"One second, Lizzy. It's bedlam here today. Half the city must be without air conditioning."

"Please tell him it's important." Music sounded from the phone as they were placed on hold. Not five seconds later, another male voice was heard on the line.

"Hey there, Lizzybear! What's up?!"

"I'm at The Darcy Company; several parts of the building are without air conditioning. If we can't get someone to fix it within the next hour, my meeting will have to be postponed."

"What about their regular contractor? I can't imagine anyone fortunate enough to win a contract with The Darcy Company would make them wait for service."

At this, Elizabeth looked to Darcy and arched an eyebrow. "They can't come until tomorrow. Is there anything you can do? I don't want you to slight your regular customers, but —"

"Don't worry about it, Lizzy. I can have Sean and a crew there in ten minutes. Who should they ask for?"

Elizabeth again looked to Darcy. "Mr. Musgrove is in charge of maintenance," he replied.

"Uncle Ed, the name is Mr. Musgrove. Thank you so much; I owe you."

"That means you're babysitting the gang tonight so I can take Maddie to the cinema."

"You got it! I'll talk to you later." Elizabeth ended the call and jumped off the edge of the desk.

"Well, Darcy, with any luck, this problem will be solved very soon."

Darcy grinned broadly after successfully tearing his eyes from her legs to her face. "Thank you. It appears I once again underestimated you." His smile was warm, and his dimples were simply adorable.

Elizabeth was momentarily speechless. Her eyes shifted slightly from his dimples to his lips. *I could just take a few steps, push up on my toes and my lips would meet his.*

Darcy's thoughts had also strayed. Having her invade his private space was unsettling. Not because she was out of place, but because she looked to be exactly where she belonged. She was standing close, too close. He once again felt the overwhelming need to reach out and touch her. *It would be so easy, just reach out my hand and... why is she looking at my mouth? Is there something stuck in my teeth?*

"Elizabeth, is everything all right?"

"Yes, of course." Elizabeth had to pull herself out of her thoughts. Embarrassed, she turned away and walked toward the windows. Darcy immediately sucked at his front teeth in an attempt to remove anything unsightly.

"Would you like a cold drink?" Darcy suggested as he checked his teeth in the mirror over a small bar. Fortunately, he saw nothing amiss.

"Yes, thank you." *A cold shower is more like it. Focus, Elizabeth, focus!* "Will I be meeting your cousin Richard today?"

"No. Like the rest of us, Richard's position with the foundation is not his primary occupation. He is with the military and has been out of the country for several months. He has reviewed your proposal and presentation by e-mail and has already informed us of his decision to support it."

Elizabeth felt a pang of envy, "I've noticed you are a very close family."

"We are, but we have our struggles like most families do. I'm sure you will witness a fine example soon."

THEY ENTERED THE CONFERENCE ROOM to find it full of people seated around a large, highly polished table. Darcy announced that the air conditioning was repaired and the room should be more comfortable in a few minutes. He then introduced Elizabeth to the board and sat down at the head of the table opposite the podium. Georgiana sat to his right, Geoff to his left.

The chairman of the board was James Fitzwilliam, the Earl of Matlock and Geoff's father. Lord Matlock suggested that due to the heat of the room, formality could be foregone, and he encouraged everyone to remove their suit jackets. Elizabeth was reluctant to do so and felt the suffering heat of the large room as she introduced the project. She was relieved when the room darkened and the media presentation began so she could nonchalantly slip off her jacket.

Darcy's eyes were immediately glued to her. What appeared as a conservative white blouse from the front was from the back... something else entirely! Not only were her well-toned arms exposed, but her entire back as well. The effect was incredibly arousing, and Darcy's trousers tightened in appreciation of the beautiful view Elizabeth was affording him. What little light remained in the room made her skin seem luminous and he indulged himself with ideas of what he would do if they were alone.

He was kissing her beautiful shoulders while stroking the silky skin of her back. He whispered "Lizzy" against her neck as he hungrily devoured it. With a swift motion, he swept her into his arms, placing her hurriedly on the large oval table, pushing portfolios and water glasses to the floor as he lay atop her. He crushed his mouth to hers in a searing kiss.

Darcy didn't realize a soft groan had escaped his mouth as he daydreamed, but both Georgiana and Geoff turned to look at him with astonishment. They then noticed the direction of his gaze, and looked back to each other. Georgiana's face broke out in a huge grin, Geoff's with a look of utmost confusion.

Under the table, Geoff nudged Darcy out of his daydream. Darcy was embarrassed at having been caught and attempted to recover his senses and turn his attention back to the presentation. It was difficult. While his mind was back in reality, his groin was desperately trying to drag him kicking and screaming back into fantasy.

Elizabeth could feel Darcy's gaze on her back. She leaned back to cover it, but her bare skin was sticky against the leather chair. Was he disappointed with her less than professional attire? *Look buster, it is a damn hot day out there, and I had no idea your air conditioning wouldn't be working.*

After about fifteen minutes, Elizabeth realized that the media presentation was about to end. Fortunately, the room was finally beginning to cool, and she quickly slipped on her jacket and stood to address the board just as the lights came back up.

After she finished her presentation, members of the board began asking questions. The most pointed questions came from Lady Catherine de Bourgh. Georgiana had warned Elizabeth the previous evening that Lady Catherine was the Aunt in Kent that Geoff had joked about and that she desperately wanted to take control of the foundation away from Darcy. She therefore used every opportunity to attempt to make Darcy look incompetent in front of the board.

That was obviously the point of Lady Catherine's questions today. She framed her inquiries in a way that voiced her obvious displeasure with the project. She was clearly trying to cast aspersions on Elizabeth's integrity as well as Darcy's judgment.

Darcy was grateful that Elizabeth remained the picture of professionalism during this inquisition. By the end of the two-hour meeting, Elizabeth had impressed the majority of the board, just as Darcy had predicted she would. Elizabeth was then excused from the room while the board debated the issue of funding.

While she waited in Darcy's office, Elizabeth felt confident, so it was no surprise when a jubilant Darcy, Georgiana and Geoff burst through the doors to announce the recommendation of the board: full funding for the Riverside Community Center Project and joint administration with the Longbourn Institute.

Geoff was ecstatic. "Aunt Catherine was a bull, but my father refused to give her arguments any credit. She was so frustrated she stormed out before the final vote."

"Let's go out to lunch to celebrate!" Georgiana announced. "Elizabeth, do you like Indian food?"

"I love Indian food!"

Darcy interjected, "Okay, Geoff, I'll pay the check if you get the car."

"Right! You and Elizabeth meet us downstairs in fifteen minutes," Geoff answered. "Georgie, would you mind coming along? I've been having trouble with my card key." Geoff and Georgiana then left the room, leaving Darcy and Elizabeth alone.

"You did it, Elizabeth! You blew them away. I think my Uncle James and Aunt Elinor are ready to adopt you into the family. The way they defended you against Aunt Catherine was a sight to see."

"How many of the board members are family?"

"All of them are related to me in one form or another. They're very protective of the family name while at the same time protective of Geoff, Richard and me. That's why their opinion is so important. That's also why it would be difficult to dismiss my Aunt Catherine. I must apologize for her behavior today. What she said about you personally was totally out of line."

"I understand. I believe every family has its less than stellar members."

"And just who are the less than stellar members of the Bennet family?"

Elizabeth looked quickly away from him. "I'd rather not go into that, if that's okay?"

Darcy sensed he hit a nerve and changed the direction of the conversation. "Well, your uncle is certainly not one of them."

"My aunt and uncle are wonderful. That's why I love staying with them."

"Do they frequently require their sitters to have several Ph.D.s?"

"No!" Elizabeth laughed, "Usually one Ph.D. is sufficient."

Without a conscious thought to direct their feet, each sentence of this innocent exchange had brought them a step closer to each other. They were now inches apart.

"I'm sorry you had to sacrifice your evening for us." He then added softly with a sly smile, "Lizzybear!" As he said her nickname, he leaned in closer.

Elizabeth let a slight chuckle escape her throat. "That name is reserved only for use by my father and uncle." She had to tilt her head up to look him in the eyes.

"I like it. It suits you." He then tilted his head down to return her gaze. "Lizzy," he whispered. The urge to touch her again claimed him, but this time, he didn't fight it, he let it happen. Reaching up with his thumb, he stroked the edge of her jaw from her chin to her ear. He then wrapped his fingers around the back of her neck.

The contact hit Elizabeth like a taser.[4] All thought was clouded; nothing mattered except the man in front of her.

His lips dropped quickly to hers. When he made contact with her mouth, it was no feathery, light kiss. It was immediate, spontaneous combustion. Lips parted, tongues engaged and suction was liberally applied. Darcy slipped his hands under her jacket, up to her shoulders and slid the garment down her arms. His hands then moved across her bare back, pressing her body hard against his.

Elizabeth's hands were not idle as she glided them up his chest to his broad shoulders. She then raked her fingers through his hair, its thick mass giving her the anchor she needed to pull herself tighter against him.

Her kiss was claiming his soul, pulling him into a warm, silk trap. He wanted more; he wanted all of her, and he wanted it now. It no longer mattered where they were, that Georgiana and Geoff would be waiting for them and there wouldn't be a condom within a hundred meters of their present location. Everything was Elizabeth and his burning desire to possess her.

He moved his lips from her sweet mouth, along her fine jaw to her supple neck. Her sigh of pleasure drove him on so that when his lips finally tasted the salty skin of her shoulders, it brought back vividly the memory of his earlier fantasy. He glanced about the office. There was no table; his desk would suffice, but then again, the couch would be so much more comfortable. He reached down, scooped her up into his arms and carried her toward the couch as his mouth once again claimed hers.

A small alarm seemed to be going off in the back of Elizabeth's mind. *This is going too far. Am I willing to do this with a man for whom I'm just another fuck?*

Darcy laid Elizabeth on the couch. His kisses began to run down her throat, across her breastbone and down into her cleavage as his hands caressed her breasts through the crisp fabric of her blouse. *Yes, I believe I am!*

As he kneeled before her, he continued kissing between her breasts while one hand reached down to slide under the hem of her skirt, expertly caressing her thighs. The pleasure of his caresses was causing Elizabeth to send her cautions to the wind. She would worry about the consequences later.

Darcy came up for air and began pulling at his tie. The phone buzzed. He ignored it as he kept his eyes locked with Elizabeth's. He then began to unbut-

4 Stun gun

ton his shirt. Elizabeth sat up to take over the task and he reached behind her neck, searching for some means to release the front of her blouse. The phone buzzed again, three times.

"Shit!" Darcy exclaimed. Three consecutive buzzes was the signal for an emergency.

He stalked over to the desk and picked up the receiver, "WHAT!" He was breathing heavily as he listened to the other end. "Tell her I've left the building." He rolled his eyes in frustration as he listened. "Stall her for as long as you can." He slammed the hand set back on the base, took a deep breath and turned back toward Elizabeth.

"I'm sorry. My Aunt Catherine is on her way here. She won't be stopped." Darcy quickly began buttoning his shirt and grabbed his tie. "I hate to ask this of you, but would you mind waiting in here?" He pointed to a door. "I don't want her to see you here…like this. It would give her fuel to slander both of us to the other members of the board. I promise I'll get her out of here as soon as possible."

Elizabeth stood up, mortified at her own behavior. She retrieved her jacket and stumbled into her shoes that somehow had left her feet on the way to the couch. She passed through the door Darcy had indicated into a private washroom, and the door closed behind her. She turned on the light and was shocked at what she saw in the mirror. Her lips were bruised, her hair was a mess and red splotches were visible on her neck and chest.

She understood perfectly why his aunt could not see her. It was written all over her that they were about to have sex. She felt hot shame rise from her chest to her face. How could she have been so stupid?

Elizabeth could hear voices in the office. She quickly turned off the light in the washroom, put the lid down on the toilet and sat down to wait.

"Well, Fitzwilliam, that was a fine display you put on today!" Lady Catherine's voice boomed. Suddenly in a lighter tone she added, "By the way, you have yet to greet your cousin."

"Hello, Anne," Darcy said evenly. "How are you?"

"She's appalled, that's how she is!" Lady Catherine thundered her response. "Do you know why? Because she was forced to sit and watch that disgusting harlot charm her way into a ten million pound grant! Are we to have a repeat of your previous debacle?"

"Aunt Catherine, Dr. Bennet is a well respected woman who presented a very sound proposal."

"Oh, please! It is clear that she has used her arts and allurements to pull you in. Once she had your support, the board had no choice."

"You know that's not true. Her presentation today—"

"Her presentation! Is that what you call it? I saw how she exposed herself today. Every man in that room couldn't take their eyes off her shameless display of flesh. Has that woman no sense of propriety? The girl is a fraud! That ten million will disappear, and we will be a laughing stock. Think of your duty to your family, to the foundation!"

"I have, Aunt Catherine, which is why I decided to bring Dr. Bennet's proposal to the board. You've seen her credentials. Her character is above reproach. Every aspect of this project runs through the administration of this foundation as well as Longbourn's. Dr. Bennet couldn't steal this money if she wanted to."

"I demand to be part of the oversight of this project. There is no way I'm going to allow this to proceed in any way that may damage our reputation."

"I'm afraid I can't allow that. You would do everything in your power to prevent any funds from being issued. That would destroy the project and I will not permit that to happen."

Darcy's phone buzzed. "Darcy here. Yes, of course. Tell them I will be down directly." There was a short pause. "Aunt Catherine, this discussion is over. Georgiana and Geoff are waiting for me."

"This is not the end of this discussion, Fitzwilliam."

"Yes, it is! Goodbye, Aunt."

Elizabeth heard the door open and was about to step out of the washroom when she heard another feminine voice. "Wills, why do you have to fight her on everything?"

"Because she and I see things differently. The foundation is too important for me to hand over to her." He paused and then spoke softly. "How are you, really?"

"I'm feeling better as I haven't had an episode in awhile. The doctors say it will happen again eventually; they're just trying to prolong the frequency. I don't know how long I have, Wills. Please, do what mother wants and marry me. I can't bear her ranting about it any longer."

"You know that can't happen. I don't feel about you the way a husband should feel about his wife. Maybe you don't have as much time as most people, but then that's all the more reason to marry someone who loves you."

"But I love you. I'll try to make you happy."

"Anne, you don't love me. You just think you do because that's what Aunt

Catherine's been telling you since the day she married your father. You have to start living your own life, not allowing your stepmother to live vicariously through you. You must realize she only wants us married because she sees it as a way to gain more control over the foundation."

"I can't do it alone. I'm afraid, Wills. Eventually I will no longer be able to take care of myself, and mother will not live forever."

"You don't need to marry me to insure that we'll all be around to help you. Besides, I'm not good husband material."

"I wouldn't mind the other women. Just as long as you came home to me eventually. And I think the right woman could make you good husband material."

"That would take a very strong woman, and Anne, we both know you're not that strong. Now Georgie and Geoff really are waiting for me. I have to go."

"Just say you'll come to dinner on Saturday night. If I go back with nothing, she'll be furious."

"No, I will not give either of you false hope. Take care of yourself." Elizabeth heard their footsteps reach the door. "Anne, it is not unusual for people with MS[5] to live very long, productive and happy lives. That could be you."

"Oh, Wills! Why does this have to be so difficult?" Anne sounded defeated. "Give my best to Georgie and Geoff." The door opened; there was silence, but Elizabeth decided to wait.

When Darcy opened the door to the washroom, Elizabeth's hair was repaired, her clothing in order and the marks on her skin faded. Darcy realized he had one more complication to deal with. His behavior had been unacceptable. How was he to take it back, to remove any hope he may have given her about his intentions?

Elizabeth was the first to speak. "Darcy, I think that in light of recent events, I should forego lunch. Please give my regrets to Georgie and Geoff. I'm sure if you explain your aunt's visit, they will accept that as a justifiable reason for my absence. There is no need to delve into anything else."

Darcy was confused. "You're telling me that you're not having lunch with us because of Aunt Catherine?"

Elizabeth eyes flashed dangerously, "Do you think I care what that old battle axe has to say about me? I should thank her for the interruption. By now I'm sure we would both be regretting our actions."

Now Darcy was mildly insulted. *You don't know me, Elizabeth. We wouldn't*

---

5 Multiple Sclerosis

be anywhere near time for regrets. By now, you'd still be writhing with pleasure beneath me, begging for more! Darcy glanced toward the couch.

"It was a terrible mistake. I know you must think me a horrible tease, but it is not in my character to seduce a man in his office. Now, I think I must be going. Thank you for everything."

His thought processes were in a muddle. He should be grateful she wasn't expecting more from him; instead, he was disturbed that she could so easily walk away. It suddenly seemed imperative that he keep her there. "Elizabeth, let's discuss this. Now that your proposal has been approved, we have to work together. You can't run away."

"There is nothing to discuss. We are attracted to each other. In time we will learn to suppress it. At this moment, I can't be in the same room with you."

"You can't disappoint Georgie and Geoff. At least come to lunch."

"Do you really expect me to sit through lunch with your sister and Geoff and pretend that I'm not affected by what happened? Explain to me Darcy; how can you do it?"

Darcy refused to see the problem. What was it that had made what happened between them such a big deal, especially if she didn't want more from him? (He was still having trouble with the fact that she clearly did not want more!) In the end, it was nothing more than heavy petting. Darcy's head was convinced, but the gnawing feeling in the pit of his gut was not. He stubbornly ignored his gut.

The phone buzzed once more, and Darcy picked it up. Elizabeth realized an answer to her question was not forthcoming. His silence incensed her more than anything he could have said. Was he so callous, so unfeeling? As he was explaining his delay to Geoff, she turned and walked out of the office, softly closing the door behind her.

Darcy felt the loss of her presence as keenly as he had the previous evening when she returned to her uncle and aunt's home after dinner. It was as if all the life in the room had left with her. Now it was nothing more than dead space. He tried to shake it off as he took the lift down to meet Georgie and Geoff. They were disappointed that Elizabeth had left but accepted that Lady Catherine's overheard insults deflated her celebratory mood.

Geoff happily spent lunch reliving Lady Catherine's defeat during the meeting. Georgiana, who was more sensitive, realized that her brother was far more affected by Elizabeth's absence than he let on.

CHAPTER 6

THE STORM

Elizabeth was alone in the Gardiner's sitting room. The only light was the flickering from the television as she used the remote control to run through the channels one more time, hoping something of interest would be on. No luck! She left the television on CNN-international and made her way to the kitchen to make some iced tea.

The air conditioning was barely able to keep up with the blistering heat of the now six-day heat wave. Her Uncle had been working night and day sending out repair crews to businesses all over the city whose air conditioning had broken down from the unusually high demand. Elizabeth had agreed to watch her young cousins while he and her Aunt had a well-deserved night out.

The children had been asleep for at least an hour, far too long for Elizabeth to be alone with her thoughts of what had happened that afternoon in Darcy's office. She knew she should be happy with the results of the meeting with the advisory committee. Her project was funded, and she could return to New York in triumph.

However, she couldn't shake her feeling of guilt over what had happened after the meeting. Why had she allowed it to go so far? *What do you mean, "allowed," Elizabeth? You initiated, you encouraged. You can't place the blame on him.* Lady Catherine's interference was the only thing that prevented the inevitable result of their actions.

A fresh wave of shame began to creep over her body. There was no suppressing it. She wasn't sure if she was ashamed because of what had happened or, rather, because she had enjoyed it so much. Darcy had awakened desires within her she had never known existed. Her brain wanted to forget, but her body wanted to remember.

The phone rang. Glancing at the caller ID, Elizabeth didn't recognize the number, so she decided to let the answering machine get it. It was better than trying to take down a detailed message for her uncle. The long beep sounded as Elizabeth was turning on the kettle.

"Eddy, dear. I heard from Lydia that Bethy was in London this week, so I know she's been in touch with you." Elizabeth froze at the familiar British accent mixed with a slight southern drawl. "Look, I'm in London for a few days and . . . damn it, I'm her mother and I have a right to talk to her. Please call me at this number and tell me what hotel she's staying at. I just want to say hello. I promise I don't want to make trouble. Please, Eddy. It's been years since I've spoken to her. Have a heart!" A loud click marked the end of the call.

Elizabeth looked down and realized her hand was still poised over the switch to the kettle. She turned it on, sat in the closest chair and stared blankly at the wall. It had been six years since she had last heard Frannie Bennet's voice.

Suddenly her last conversation with her mother played through her mind. By that time, eighteen-year-old Elizabeth had not seen Frannie for well over two years. She arrived at her father's house one afternoon to find her mother sitting in the living room, waiting for her.

At first Frannie was pleasant enough. Elizabeth's mother insisted that she was being treated for bi-polar disorder and she wanted to be a mother again, especially to Elizabeth. It wasn't long before the conversation turned and Frannie revealed the real reason behind her visit.

"So who are you seeing in New York, Bethy? There must be scads of handsome young men in the city."

"I'm very busy, Momma. I just finished a double bachelor's degree, and I'm beginning two master's programs in a few weeks. I don't have time to see anyone."

"Bethy, dear," her mother reached over to pat her hand. "It's been long past the time you should have stopped being so perfect. Give into temptation and *enjoy yourself,* honey! Trust me, sweetie, no man will ever ask some prude for a second date. A man wants to have a good time!"

"Momma, why can't you respect my decisions? Most parents would be proud that their eighteen-year-old daughter wasn't promiscuous."

"Oh, Deary, you don't believe that, do you? You're going to end up all alone, and then what will your high and mighty ideals do for you? They can't pay the mortgage or keep you warm at night. Only a man can do that."

"I'll pay my own mortgage, Momma, as well as the heating bill."

Abruptly, the syrupy sweet voice took on a definitive edge. "Don't you speak to me in that tone of voice, young lady! Besides, you've lost most of your money. You had it all! Crowds of people at your feet, a five-album record deal. Do you know how many classical artists get a five-album deal? None! By now, we should all be living in Beverly Hills and shopping on Rodeo Drive! But no, all you ever thought about was yourself."

"You stole enough money from me to *own* Rodeo Drive!"

Frannie stood and slapped her soundly across the face. "You've developed quite the fresh mouth, Missy! I'll have to speak to your father about how he's raising you."

Frannie then sat down again, and the sweet voice returned. "Now, I want to speak to you seriously about college, dear. All this school will only deplete your little nest egg and make men run the other way. Men don't like a smart girl, Bethy. College professors are boring. I should know; I was married to one for nineteen years!"

"Momma, you know I hate it when you call me 'Bethy.' Why won't you please call me by my real name, 'Elizabeth?'"

"The name 'Bethy' made us all rich. It got you the attention of a lot of men, too. That's why Billy Ray wanted you, because you were famous and a little pretty. You've never been as pretty as Jane, or even Lydia; that's why it is important for you to go back on tour. When you're famous again, you'll have all the men you could possibly want. Such a waste, Bethy! You were lucky to have caught the attention of such a nice, rich boy like Billy Ray Collins in the first place."

"He was a horrible man!"

The edge had returned. "Don't talk to *me* about men! What do *you* know about them? I can't tell you how disappointed I am with you. If you had been nice to Billy Ray that night, you would have come home with a big smile on your face instead of all this trouble! You don't know how he suffers in prison. You should be ashamed of what you put that poor boy through over the past year and a half."

"What *I* put *him* through? Momma —"

"Now, enough of all this foolishness, Bethy! I want you to come with me right now. We're going to see the D.A.,[6] and you're going to take back everything you said about Billy Ray. With any luck, I'll have him home in a few weeks."

"No, Momma. That monster is going to stay where he is for as long as I can keep him there. Does Papa know you're here?"

Frannie stood menacingly over her daughter. "Bethy, I didn't want to say this, but you've given me no choice. Someday Billy Ray's going to get out of prison, and when he does, he's going to kill you! I know that sounds unpleasant, but there it is." Only Frannie Bennet would label a death threat as *unpleasant*. "You've got to help him now and hope he'll find it in his heart to forgive what you've done! If you don't, well, I just might kill you myself. Billy Ray is my one true love — my soul mate. You're such a selfish and ungrateful child to keep us apart!"

At that point, Thomas Bennet entered his house. "Shut up, Frannie! Not one more word." Frannie always became quiet when Thomas yelled at her. She just couldn't resist a forceful man! If he'd spoken to her like that from the beginning, they might still be married — at least until she met her greatest love, Billy Ray Collins.

Thomas immediately led Elizabeth outside. "I'm sorry, Lizzybear. I didn't know she was coming, but she's leaving, *now*." Thomas Bennet was gentle as he led his daughter to her car. "Drive around for about ten minutes. When you get back, she'll be gone!" Her father hugged her tightly, put her in the car and watched her drive away. Elizabeth glanced back to see her mother standing on the front porch.

Thomas Bennet had been true to his word. That was the last time Elizabeth had seen her mother.

Even though it had been more than six years ago, Frannie's words that day still disturbed Elizabeth to her core. During this conversation with her mother, Elizabeth finally accepted that Frannie would never come around and be the mother Elizabeth wanted her to be. Frannie would always be ready to sacrifice her own child if she thought it would get her a man who was young enough to be her own son.

Her mother's betrayal had wounded Elizabeth deeper and more painfully than all the injuries Billy Ray Collins had inflicted on her that fateful night. Just hearing Frannie's voice again tonight had caused those wounds to reopen.

6 District Attorney: The attorney who represents the government in the prosecution of criminal cases.

Elizabeth was pulled from her reverie by the bell at the front door. Her aunt and uncle must have forgotten their keys again. Elizabeth believed that they must have returned early because they felt they were imposing upon her. As much as Elizabeth wanted to talk to them, they really deserved this rare night out.

Elizabeth pulled open the door, but instead of her aunt and uncle, she was shocked to find Darcy standing there. He was red-faced and sweaty from walking in the intense heat. "Elizabeth, I realize I'm probably the last person you wanted to see this evening —"

"You are," she replied dryly. "Why are you here?"

"I need to talk to you. May I please come in?"

Elizabeth nearly laughed when she realized she was dressed only in a pair of men's cotton pajama bottoms and a white tank top. "As you can see, Darcy, I'm not dressed for business. I'm coming into the office on Friday to meet with Geoff. Can it wait?"

Darcy's look was serious. "I think you are well aware I did not come here to discuss business."

Elizabeth knew it was no use. If he had gone to the trouble of finding her uncle's house in this heat, he would not be turned away easily. She was not in the mood to argue any more than she was in the mood to play hostess. "Come in." She left the door open and walked back down the front hallway toward the kitchen.

Darcy was left at the doorstep. He felt a little awkward at her reception but eventually followed her into the house. He took note of the inside of her uncle's home. It was neat and comfortably decorated. The signs of a houseful of children were everywhere: safety plugs over electrical sockets, cords carefully wrapped out of reach, and children's books left here and there. It reminded him of their family apartments at Pemberley when Georgiana was small.

Elizabeth was pouring water into a teapot as Darcy entered the kitchen. It felt comfortable yet orderly. She gestured to the teapot. "Chamomile-Mint… interested?" Elizabeth was already unnerved; she was not prepared for a match of wits with Darcy, so she wasn't going to encourage him to stay by being overly hospitable.

"May I have it on ice?" Darcy was hot and thirsty, and he welcomed the chance to cool down before they talked. They were silent for several minutes. Elizabeth moved methodically around the kitchen, putting biscuits on a plate and pulling out serviettes. Eventually, Elizabeth poured hot tea into glasses over-filled with ice, handed one to Darcy with a serviette, grabbed her own drink with the plate of biscuits and walked out of the kitchen. Darcy silently followed her into the sitting room.

Elizabeth placed her tea and the biscuits on the table in front of a large, overstuffed sofa and took a seat at one end. She had not bothered to turn on a light, as it felt cooler to keep them off. CNN would do.

Darcy lifted a small stuffed animal from the other end of the couch. Elizabeth reached out her hand to take it from him as he sat down facing her. Elizabeth turned toward him, tucking her feet under her.

So they sat, just looking at one another, sipping their tea for several minutes. Finally, Darcy spoke. "I've been thinking of our 'problem' for some time. I think I may have come up with a solution."

Elizabeth said nothing. She simply arched her eyebrow to demonstrate her skepticism.

Darcy was hesitant to begin. What seemed like a perfectly solid idea only a few hours ago was now riddled with holes. The setting he found himself in with her was so intimate and comfortable; he regretted that he had to disturb it. "I won't attempt to deny the physical attraction we have for each other. It is so overpowering, sometimes I forget myself."

She remained silent as she studied him. He was dressed simply in a pair of linen trousers and a light green polo shirt. Darcy ran his hands through his hair, clearly uncomfortable with what he had to say. He suddenly looked so vulnerable that Elizabeth felt sympathy rising up within her. *Did he come to apologize? Sweet, but totally unnecessary.* Elizabeth waited for him to continue.

"You must understand; I won't allow myself to become emotionally involved with someone; however, I realize that it is pointless to fight this…" here he searched for the right word, but the best he could do was, "…thing. Therefore…"

He paused again, got up and began to pace back and forth in front of the table, again running his hand through his hair. Elizabeth realized this must be a rare sight indeed. *The calm and carefully controlled Fitzwilliam Darcy is struggling!* She nearly smiled.

He stopped in front of the television, suddenly annoyed with the background noise. "Do you mind if I turn this off?"

Elizabeth reached out with the remote and pushed the power button. The room was plunged into darkness; the only light was from the streetlight coming through the windows. It was enough for Darcy to find his way back to the couch where he resumed his seat, focusing his eyes on his glass of tea.

"I think we should go away this weekend. We could leave early Saturday morning. I have a cottage in Brighton, on the water. It's small, very private. I'd have you back in time to catch your flight on Sunday night."

Elizabeth was confused. "How is going away for the weekend going to solve our problem? It seems to me that it will only exacerbate it."

"I think if we spent enough time alone...*together*...we would be able to ...satisfy...our...physical desire for each other...at least to the point where it would not be so...debilitating." There, he had said it. It was more difficult than he had imagined, but now it was out in the open and could be discussed in a rational manner.

Elizabeth was grateful they were sitting in the dark, for the blush that covered her face would have betrayed the calm voice in which she spoke. "Let me make sure I understand you. You are proposing that we spend two days screwing each other's brains out, which you hypothesize will get us over whatever this *thing* is that we have for each other."

Darcy finally looked at her. He couldn't tell if she was angry or not. He could barely speak the word, "Yes." Elizabeth wasn't the only one grateful for the dark. His stomach was tied in knots, and he thought he might be sick. "I don't mean any disrespect. We just can't go on like this. I'm finding it difficult to focus on anything, except...how much...I want you. I'm not sleeping; I'm barely eating. Something must be done!"

Elizabeth was desperately trying to come up with the words to respond to what he had said. The difficulty was she had not yet figured out how to react. On the one hand, she understood his struggle, for she felt the same way; but on the other, she knew she should be offended at the suggested remedy. She had to admit it all sounded perfectly logical, and yet she could not possibly consider it. Elizabeth was unaccountably amused by her confusion and could not help but smile at herself. Unfortunately for Elizabeth, Darcy took her smile as acceptance.

"I think this will be good for both of us." Darcy was suddenly feeling better; in fact, he was ecstatic! He expected her to accept eventually, but he thought she would at least resist at first. But, no, Elizabeth was too intelligent to play that sort of game. Didn't he admire her for her mind? Well, in addition to her…eyes. *Yes, eyes. They are hauntingly beautiful in the dark.*

He was feeling positive enough to lighten the mood and perhaps begin the weekend a little early. He didn't think he could expect to make love to her in her uncle's sitting room, but they were alone, and a few kisses would be very nice. He moved forward on the couch until he couldn't sit any closer without climbing into her lap. He took her hand. "I believe," he leaned forward to whisper in her ear, "you will find this to be an *extremely pleasurable* holiday." He moved to brush his lips against her cheek. She smelled heavenly and her skin was so very soft.

Elizabeth was lost in the sensations his attentions were producing. Then his last statement registered and her brain snapped to attention. Her voice was low but tense. "A little over-confident, aren't you? Do you consider yourself *that* great a lover, or is it merely the *thought* of being shagged by 'The Great Fitzwilliam Darcy' that will send me into fits of ecstasy?"

Lightning flashed outside the window followed by a soft roll of thunder. Although her voice was calm, Darcy heard the danger and immediately backed away. She stood and left the room. Darcy took off after her immediately. He reached out and stopped her in the hallway. "Elizabeth, what is the problem?"

"Shhhhhh." Elizabeth pointed upstairs and headed for the front door.

He caught up to her and repeated his question in a lowered voice. "What *is* the problem?"

"What happens if your little plan is only a temporary fix? To what level are you willing to go? Will we excuse ourselves to the broom closet each time we shake hands in public? Should we pencil in an extra fifteen minutes before each meeting for a quickie? Will I need to install a condom machine in my office at Longbourn?"

"Elizabeth, you are not being reasonable!" He would not admit it to her, but she had a point.

"Mr. Darcy, I am not *any man's* casual fuck! I apparently have a higher sense of self worth than the women with whom you typically condescend to *associate*!"

"Then what do you suggest? Shall I walk around drooling behind you, half-dazed with a perpetual erection? Would that satisfy your sense of superiority, Dr. Bennet?"

"*My* sense of superiority? Is your ego so large there is no room left in your head for rational thought? What I suggest, Mr. Darcy, is that I return to New York and we conduct all our interaction by e-mail and telephone. Right now

I have no desire to lay eyes on you again!" She emphasized her point by opening the front door. "Get out!" They were standing close together, their intense argument still being conducted in hushed voices.

"Do you think I haven't considered that option? My aunt will be watching my every move. We can't avoid each other without raising suspicions that could not only endanger your project but my credibility with the board. There is too much at stake here; this project is too important. We will have to work together — and in person."

In the past, Elizabeth had discovered silence was frequently more effective than words. It was a defense mechanism that had served her well, and she chose to use it now. She crossed her arms in front of her, looked him straight in the eye and glared. A flash of lightning illuminated the inside of the foyer, and the thunder that followed was getting louder.

Darcy couldn't understand what was happening. He was furious with her! How could she just stand there and say nothing! Never in his life had a woman made him lose his temper. What was even more maddening was the realization that he wanted her all the more because of it. *This is hopeless! Control ourselves, indeed! Impossible!* He stepped closer.

"We can't keep our hands off each other, Elizabeth; you must realize we're going to end up in bed eventually. I don't understand why we can't just do it and enjoy ourselves. Do you have something against a good time?"

His words — so much like Frannie's — hit her like a slap to the face.

"So you're a man who wants to have a 'good time?' That's too bad, Mr. Darcy, because I refuse to have a 'good time' with someone I don't care about. I deserve better than that."

They stood facing each other in front of the open door, oblivious to the increasing flashes of lightning and the wind blowing across their faces.

Darcy seethed. "Are you telling me you're the high and mighty protector of some distorted sense of morality? I can't believe it!"

"Why? Because, although I may be young, with this body I could not possibly be innocent?"

He was furious that she used his own words to insult him yet again! He had apologized. How long was she going to hold it against him? He stepped even closer to her. Speaking through clenched teeth, he hissed, "With all the men dying to get between your thighs, you expect me to believe you have remained so pure as to have never given into temptation." *This is unbelievable;*

MY BFF

she can't possibly think she's too good for me. "Don't stand in judgment of me, Dr. Bennet. You can't possibly have been madly in love with every man you have ever shagged!"

Her eyes widened in fury and Darcy saw the fire within their depths. He grabbed her shoulders, pulling her hard against his chest and without giving her time to react, planted his lips hard upon hers. Not a second later his breath was knocked from his chest as he found his entire body pushed forcefully against a wall with his right arm twisted and held firmly behind his back.

Maybe it was the aftereffects of Frannie's call; maybe it was the heat; maybe it was Darcy's forceful kiss; but somehow, Elizabeth was driven over the edge of reason. She released his arm, and as he turned back to face her, she shouted, "I have never shagged anyone…ever!" Her last word was accented by a loud *slam* as the wind sucked the front door closed.

The words were spoken in anger and without thought; however, the effect of them was immediate. All color drained from her face, which displayed a look of shock over what she had inadvertently revealed.

Darcy could not have been more stunned if she had run him through. As the meaning of what she said sank in, he began to shake his head back and forth. His eyes were wide with shock and disbelief. "No," his voice was barely audible, "You can't be." But it was true, it was written all over her face.

As silent tears coursed down her burning cheeks, Elizabeth grasped the handle of the front door and pulled it open again, desperately needing him to go without another word.

Darcy had no memory of moving from the spot where he stood in the front hall, but he suddenly became aware of the rain that was falling on his face and the flash of lightning that forked across the sky. He glanced back at the closed front door of the Gardiner home. *Touché, Elizabeth.* He didn't call for Thayer. Darcy's mind was so dazed, he didn't think about the possible danger as he walked back to Oakland in the pounding wind and pouring rain.

Inside the house, Elizabeth leaned back against the front door and collapsed to the floor. *Touché, Darcy.* She buried her face in her hands, and for the first time in six years, she cried.

London's record heat wave had finally broken in the most violent thunderstorm of recent memory.

CHAPTER 7
CAUSE AND EFFECT

"Darcy, Aubrey has just told me the most fantastic story!" Geoff burst into Darcy's office immediately after lunch.

Aubrey Vivash was not only a mutual friend; he was the fencing master of the Trafalgar Fencing Club and Dalton's brother. However, Darcy was not in the mood for club gossip this morning. "Geoff, don't you knock? Surely you must see I'm busy."

"I've never knocked before. Why should I start now?" Geoff flopped down in a large leather chair in front of Darcy's desk. "Now, my friend, I am going to tell you Aubrey's tale, for I know it will lift you from the foul mood you've been in all day."

Darcy was aware that he was in a foul mood. He'd barely slept again last night, and he was having difficulty focusing on the contracts he needed to approve by the end of the day. However, he knew it was pointless to argue with Geoff. "So, what is it? Has Caroline Bingley cancelled her membership at the club?" If that was the case, Darcy might feel just a little better. The woman may at one time have been his friend, but for the last few years she had become a royal pain in his arse.

"Everyone needs a dream," Geoff teased. "However, I promise this is almost as good. Shall I proceed?"

Darcy knew he didn't really have a choice. He sat back in his chair.

"Aubrey said that about 3 a.m. this morning, our least favorite person came into the club."

"George Wickham!" Geoff had Darcy's full attention. Wickham had been avoiding the club since his run in with Darcy last year. "So the bastard's turned up!"

"Oh, it's much more than that! Apparently, when he checked in, he perused the guest book and saw that our own Elizabeth was there and as *your* guest. You didn't tell me she fenced. You've been holding out on me!"

The mention of Elizabeth's name caused Darcy's stomach to churn. "I saw her fence in New York. She's very good."

Geoff noticed the flash of discomfort in Darcy's eyes. *Georgie might have something there.* "Well, Wickham proceeded to ply Aubrey for information about her. Of course, Aubrey knew she was from New York, and although she had only been fencing for a few months, she was already considered on par with a junior level. When Aubrey volunteered that he thought she was beautiful, George was off to find her."

"Oh, no!" Darcy groaned. Although he had teased Elizabeth about Wickham, he never believed they'd actually meet. He didn't think George would have the guts to return to the club, not even at 3 a.m. He also feared that with the state of mind he left her in last evening, Elizabeth may have been willing to believe one of Wickham's many tales of woe about the mistreatment he had received at Darcy's hand.

"Did he challenge her?"

"Don't jump the gun! I'm getting there!" Geoff was clearly enjoying his story, so Darcy hoped that meant an unhappy ending for Wickham. "Aubrey said he was informed by another member that George caught up with her immediately after she finished warm-ups. Wickham was his usual suave self and asked her a lot of questions about how well she knew you and how close you were. She was polite but less than forthcoming."

Darcy could picture the encounter in his mind. Wickham could not resist attempting to bed any woman Darcy knew, just in case she might be a prospective Mrs. Darcy. "So he didn't challenge her? Did he ask her out?"

"Darcy if you continue to interrupt, I'm going to stop!" Geoff found Darcy's impatience amusing. *Oh Darce, you've got it bad!* "Now, where was I? Oh, yes. Well, apparently Elizabeth said she was not in the proper frame of mind for a match and pointed out that George did outrank her. Well, our George was not to be deterred, so he promised to take it easy on her and assured Elizabeth she would benefit from his *years of experience*. Finally, she relented."

Darcy was feeling really ill now. He knew exactly the frame of mind Elizabeth was in last night. There was no doubt in his mind that she was at the club at 3 a.m. because she was too distraught to sleep. He felt responsible that she was exhausted and, on top of that, had Wickham thrust upon her.

"Aubrey was in the locker room when George came in to change. The pig was taking bets that he would be enjoying his breakfast in Elizabeth's bed! What is extraordinary is that he reserved the dueling room immediately. Perhaps George calculated that either his skills were so great or Elizabeth's so paltry, he didn't need to warm up!"

Now Geoff sat back and waited for Darcy's reaction.

Geoff was not disappointed as a smile spread across Darcy's face. "He underestimated her!"

"And no two people know more about the dangers of underestimating Elizabeth Bennet than you and me!" *Me even more so, Geoff.* Darcy's mood again darkened as he was reminded of how he had treated Elizabeth, not only at the beginning of their acquaintance but last night as well.

Wanting to put the smile back on his cousin's face, Geoff continued, "Well, after his bragging in the locker room, the match attracted quite a crowd, even for 3 a.m. George easily took the first three points. Elizabeth appeared to be tired and frustrated, so that's when George made his move."

"A wager!" Darcy could only imagine the type of wager Wickham would propose.

"You know Wickham's tactics well. The rest of the match took almost no time at all." Geoff knew the keys to telling a good story were talent and timing. He was expert at both.

"He gained the final points so easily?" Darcy's evident disappointment was the signal for Geoff to deliver the *coup de gras*.

"No, *she* took five points from *him*! Aubrey said once the wager was set, a dramatic change came over Elizabeth. She was the epitome of calm. Oh, you should have heard Aubrey going on about how fluidly she moved and how expertly she executed her attack!" The smile had returned to Darcy's face. "Aubrey said Wickham seemed too shocked by what had happed to react at first, but then he pasted one of those slick smirks on his face and tried to look pleased with the result. He didn't fool anyone; he was pissed!"

"I'm sorry I missed it."

"Oh it gets better, because George had agreed to a wager he had to perform immediately."

Darcy knew what was coming, but he let Geoff have the honor of repeating it. His cousin was obviously having a good time retelling the story, and Darcy could not blame him. It was priceless!

"So George was required to kneel before Elizabeth and kiss her hand. A rather classy and ladylike wager, I might add. Now, Aubrey said George turned to the crowd, gave them a wink and said it was his pleasure. He approached Elizabeth, kneeled and took her hand." Geoff paused here for dramatic effect. He had to admit to himself, he told the story so much better than Aubrey did.

"Before the bastard made contact with his slimy lips, Elizabeth abruptly jerked her hand away and called out 'Wager, Wickham to Bennet, paid.' Without a look in George's direction, she walked away to the cheers of the room!" Geoff didn't think it was possible, but for the first time in his life, he saw his cousin sitting there with that stupid, love struck look on his face that Darcy had criticized in his friends. *Oh, I've got to tell Georgie about this!*

Darcy was oblivious to his cousin's observation of him. His mind was full of Elizabeth. She was incredible! The twist on her usual form of punishment was brilliant! He never should have doubted her; Elizabeth would never put herself in a situation over her head!

Darcy finally stirred. "Did Aubrey say anything else?"

"Wickham could no longer hide his fury. Apparently he took his anger out on a marble pillar and managed to break his foil blade in half."

"Did Aubrey find out what Elizabeth had wagered if she had lost?"

"They were to have breakfast together, but there were no specifics. Needless to say, he lost quite a bit of money in addition to his pride!"

"You were right, Geoff. Your story did put me in a better mood."

"Elizabeth never ceases to amaze. I believe I could fall in love with that woman." The glare that passed over Darcy's eyes was so fleeting, most people would not have noticed it. However, Geoff was not most people. He knew Darcy better than anyone; perhaps even better than Darcy himself. Geoff knew that Elizabeth Bennet was the perfect woman for his cousin. He also knew it was unlikely that Darcy was ready to admit it.

Darcy tried to cover his momentary loss of control with humor at Geoff's expense. "Based on your comments at dinner the other night, I believe you already have. Somehow, I just never pictured you on the losing end of unrequited love." Good-natured laughter had again erupted between the two.

"I have not yet admitted defeat. I'll spend the morning with her tomorrow… in my office… alone! With no other distractions, she may begin to appreciate my considerable charm." *Well Darcy, perhaps the threat of a little competition will force you to react.* "Do you think I can borrow your couch?"

At first, Geoff had no idea the riot of emotions his comment had caused. Suddenly, the knot in Darcy's stomach returned, and he again felt ill. As he tried to hide his reaction from Geoff, his cousin was trying to figure out what he had said to effect such a change. Geoff stared in wonder at his cousin, who was obviously trying to avoid looking at either Geoff or the couch.

Geoff suddenly remembered Elizabeth's hasty departure the day before. She had agreed to go to lunch but then cancelled after overhearing some disturbing comments by Aunt Catherine. A woman who could handle George Wickham would not let Lady Catherine bother her. Something else was the cause of her cancellation, and Geoff now had his suspicions.

"Darcy, what happened on that couch?" Geoff asked the question with a grin he did not feel.

Darcy squared his shoulders, glared at Geoff and spoke defensively, "Exactly what are you accusing me of?"

"You're telling me nothing happened on that couch that I should be concerned about."

"I can't imagine what you're talking about." Darcy was a terrible liar, which was why he avoided the practice at all costs. The couch, however, was not something he was willing to discuss.

"Okay. Nothing happened. So you'll agree we should take Elizabeth out tonight to celebrate her triumph!" Geoff waited in anticipation for Darcy's response. Would Darcy fall into his trap?

"I have plans."

"Really?"

"A date." Geoff was even more suspicious. Was Darcy lying to get out of facing Elizabeth?

"With whom?"

Darcy turned to the computer on the credenza behind his desk and pulled up his calendar where Geoff could clearly see the name "Elise" and an address. "Still using The Service? After your experience with Vanessa, I thought you might give it up."

"A man has needs, Geoff. This is how I choose to handle them."

"It is my experience that cheap sex is cheap sex, no matter how much you pay for it." Geoff got up and walked toward Darcy's door. He then issued a parting shot: "We'll just have to celebrate with Elizabeth at the Garden Ball tomorrow."

Darcy's head turned abruptly to his cousin. "I didn't know she was invited."

"Dad asked her, and she couldn't possibly refuse him."

"Well, yes…all right," Darcy responded dryly, his eyes determinedly focused upon the contract in front of him.

So you are going to be stubborn. Geoff was looking forward to the battle to come. Who would win: Darcy and his pride, or the lovely Elizabeth and her multitude of attractions? Personally, he didn't think Darcy had a chance!

ELIZABETH ROLLED OUT OF BED at 2 p.m. Her head ached and her vision was foggy. *Six hours of sleep; it will have to do.* The cool shower didn't help. She felt as if she had run a marathon. Not even her match with Wickham had helped. She was worn out. She wanted to go home, and she never wanted to face Fitzwilliam Darcy again.

She had never felt ashamed about being a virgin. It was common knowledge among her friends who had a good time at her expense, scouting the clubs for "Mr. Right the First". Their teasing was good-natured, and she knew they cared about her.

Darcy knowing was another story. He didn't know her well enough to understand the circumstances. Part of her wanted to know what he thought of her now, part of her was terrified to find out. She wished the earth would just open up beneath her and swallow her whole.

"We will have to work together—and in person." His words echoed in her mind. How would he react when he next saw her? Would he ridicule her, pity her, or avoid her? Should she act as if the conversation had never happened?

Elizabeth dressed slowly and made her way down to the kitchen. She was surprised to find Aunt Maddie sitting at the table. "Lizzy, I'm so glad you're up. Are you ill?"

"Frankly, I don't know what I am."

"Would you like something to eat?"

"No, I'm not hungry."

Aunt Maddie poured a cup of herbal tea, added a generous teaspoon of honey and a slice of lemon. She placed it on the table in front of Elizabeth and sat back down.

"Do you want to talk?" Madeline Gardiner was more than Elizabeth's aunt. She was a child psychologist who had helped her deal with the aftermath of the Billy Ray Collins incident. The older woman was also the inspiration behind Jane's career choice.

"I know it would help if I did, but I don't know how to put my feelings into words right now."

Maddie spoke soothingly, "You seemed okay when you went to your meeting yesterday. I noticed you weren't as happy as I expected you would be with the result. Did something happen there?"

"It began there."

"Your uncle said you went out very late last night. Can you tell me where you went?"

"To the fencing club. I couldn't sleep and thought the physical exertion would help."

"When do you think you finally fell asleep?"

"The last time I remember looking at the clock, it was about 8 a.m."

"So, I take it this has something to do with the Darcy people?"

"One of them."

"Fitzwilliam Darcy?"

"How did you know?"

"There are only three 'Darcy people.'" Maddie smiled. "He's the most prominent, so he's the one I guessed first." Elizabeth smiled back. "Did you argue?"

Elizabeth's smile faded as she stared at her teacup. "Yes."

"Was it about the funding, or was it personal?"

Suddenly, Elizabeth poured out everything that had happened with Darcy. Their unusual attraction, their aborted tryst in his office and the entirety of their conversation last night.

Aunt Maddie was silent until she was sure Elizabeth was finished. She got up and poured Elizabeth another cup of tea and then looked her directly in the eyes as she spoke. "I know it is not the current fashion to be a virgin at your age, but if Fitzwilliam Darcy is a good person, he'll respect you for it. If he doesn't, he's certainly not worth the worry!"

Seeing that her words were having little effect, Maddie tried a different tact. "You have every right to be cautious, but you can't judge every man by the standard of Billy Ray Collins. Do you honestly believe Mr. Darcy is like Billy Ray?"

"No. There are times when he's coldly arrogant, but then I have seen him be warm and generous towards his family and even to me; but his reaction last night... He was so angry and then so...shocked."

"There is a reason he reacted the way he did, just as there is a reason he won't allow himself to become emotionally involved with women. You don't know specifically what that is, but there are some generalizations that we can assume would have an effect." Maddie paused a moment for this to sink in before she continued.

"We can assume that a man in his position in society has hundreds of women ready to throw themselves at him every day. They don't care *who* he is, just *what* he is. A man in that situation is sure to have experienced a disappointment or two. That alone could make anyone overly cautious." Elizabeth nodded in agreement.

"I think it's also safe to assume that few of these women have your standards for intimacy. That does not give him the right to misjudge you, but it may help you understand why he reacted the way he did." Elizabeth remained silent, absorbing her Aunt's rational words.

"Lizzy, I do believe that if the two of you are willing to accept each other for who you are, you can find a way to work together. Who knows? Perhaps you can be friends."

Elizabeth raised her brow skeptically.

Her aunt continued, "If either one of you is unwilling to do that, you may have to find someone else to administer your project. Is that what you're afraid of?"

Elizabeth thought for a minute. "No, it's not."

"Let's play the 'worst case' game. What is the worst thing you think could happen with Mr. Darcy?"

"He could break my heart."

Maddie reached out to take Elizabeth's hand. "Why would you give him that power over you?"

"I don't know!"

"That, my dear, is what you need to figure out."

MR. THAYER PULLED UP OUT front of Elise's flat. Darcy waited a moment before signaling to Thayer to open the door. He needed a moment to think.

Elizabeth's tear-streaked face kept appearing in his mind. It was as if he was somehow betraying her by going out tonight with Elise. He couldn't understand this reaction. She had asked for nothing and he owed her nothing, but somehow her revelation had changed him.

The movement of a passing walker brought Darcy back to the present. He needed this date tonight. He needed some sense of normalcy. Darcy reached up and tapped lightly on the window next to where Thayer was waiting. The door immediately swung open, and Darcy stepped out into the cool evening air.

Darcy had been very specific when he contacted The Service and requested a date with Elise. If she had undergone any plastic surgery, he wanted to know about it in advance, and he wanted an alternative *companion* for the evening. He was not about to have a repeat of the Vanessa disaster. The nameless voice explained to Darcy that Vanessa had not informed the service about her surgeries and apologized for the inconvenience. They assured him Elise had not had any procedures done.

Darcy breathed a sigh of relief as he e-mailed the results from his latest blood work to the service. An hour later, Elise's results were forwarded back to him along with her current phone number. It was all efficient and confidential. No names were exchanged with the service, only numbers. Privacy and anonymity were paramount for all concerned. Darcy had an unregistered Swiss Bank account specifically for this purpose. Six thousand Euros were deducted within twenty-four hours. This was his confirmation that Elise had agreed to meet him.

He called Elise to arrange the date and time. It was her choice where they would meet. As he and Elise had an established business relationship, she felt safe having him pick her up at her apartment. It would be no secret that Fitzwilliam Darcy was going on a date with model Elise Johansson; the paparazzi would see to that. The only secret was that he had paid for the privilege.

Elise looked lovely as she let him inside her apartment and quickly shut the door. "It's nice to see you again, Darcy." Her voice was low and sweet. She reached up and kissed him lightly.

"Are you ready?" he asked. She handed him her overnight bag, picked up her purse and reopened the door. They stepped into the street and walked toward the limo. Darcy let out the breath he didn't know he was holding. Everything was as it should be.

Dinner was at a restaurant that had just opened a few days before. It had received a lot of press and reservations were impossible to get, unless of course you were Fitzwilliam Darcy. The paparazzi was there in force, and Darcy knew Georgie would laugh to see the picture of him and Miss Johansson in tomorrow's paper.

The meal was excellent and the conversation pleasant. They discussed the weather, as the breaking of the heat wave seemed to be a relief for everyone. They also discussed the latest albums by several of Darcy's favorite classical and rock artists, as well as the newest exhibitions at the museum.

Darcy appreciated how Elise always prepared for their dates by studying up on the subjects he liked to discuss. She always dressed impeccably, behaved with grace and never smiled for the paparazzi. While she was with him, he had her undivided attention. She was expensive but worth every cent. Elise was a pro.

Keeping his libido under strict regulation was always paramount to Darcy. During a date, he never allowed his desires to come to the surface. He sat back and enjoyed the evening as it was happening, not heatedly jumping ahead. There was a time and a place for everything.

As dinner ended and they entered the limo, Darcy was feeling great. His world and his emotions were back in their correct order. Elizabeth was not completely gone from his thoughts, but he was confident that she would not interfere with his enjoyment of this night.

The hotel was one of the best in the city. Elise waited until they were in their suite and Darcy had dismissed the bellman before she excused herself to freshen up. While he waited, Darcy removed his coat and tie, unbuttoned his collar and placed a box of condoms on the table next to the bed. He sat in a chair and removed his shoes, carefully folded his socks, placed them methodically inside the shoes and then placed his shoes next to the chair on which hung his suit coat and tie. He was ready.

When Elise returned she was wearing only a bra and panties. There were no words spoken as Darcy met her in front of the bed. This was the moment he finally allowed his body to respond to his needs. He kissed her, letting his tongue pass through her lips. Elise responded immediately, running her fingers up his chest and moaning against his mouth.

Darcy knew immediately something was off. Her mouth tasted...wrong. It wasn't unpleasant, it just wasn't right. He pulled her tighter against his chest and kissed her neck. Her skin smelled...off. It smelled lightly of roses. He liked the smell of roses, and she had not put on too much perfume, but she smelled...off.

She moaned again. Her moans were beginning to irritate him. He knew he was not his usual amorous self. She had little reason to moan but did so just as often as when he felt he was in top form.

Darcy was not a man who normally gave into frustration, so he pressed on. He slid his hand up her back and unclasped her bra, caressing her shoulders as he gently pulled the straps down her arms. He had to admit that he wasn't thinking about it; he just did it. It was all habit and no passion. Elise pulled her head back and looked at him.

"You seem a little tense tonight. Here, let me." She pushed him back onto the bed and dispatched the remaining buttons on his shirt. He never allowed a woman to take the dominant role before, but nothing else was working, so Darcy was willing to give it a try. Elise kissed his chest as she reached down and stroked his penis through his trousers. She moaned again. Darcy wasn't aroused, he just felt…stupid. It was an unfamiliar and unsettling sensation.

Darcy sat up. Elise sat up beside him, resting her hand on his thigh but looking at the floor. He knew she would allow him all the time he needed, but Darcy also acknowledged there would never be enough time.

Elise had done everything right, just as she always did, just as she was paid to do. Yes, Elise was a pro. Her appearance, her conversation, her attention, her moans and caresses were not specifically for him, but for the man who paid for them. Tonight they just happened to be one and the same. They were nothing special, nothing unique, and they no longer turned him on.

Cheap sex is cheap sex, no matter how much you pay for it.

He was a little surprised that he didn't feel angry. What he felt was acceptance. He had settled for this for six years and now it was no longer enough. *Yes, Elizabeth. I know exactly what you have done to me.*

CHAPTER 8
THIS COULD BE THE BEGINNING OF...

August 8th, Celebrity Tattler (U.K.)
Photo caption: Fitzwilliam Darcy and model Elise Johansson enter Almo's
Restaurant last night.
(No story)

The garden at Hayes Hall was aglow with a million fairy lights as the band played soft jazz in the background. Lord and Lady Matlock held this event every August to thank those who assisted them in their various charity endeavors throughout the year. This year's Garden Ball was bigger than ever. A large tent contained beautifully decorated tables and a large dance floor. Several small bars were located around the periphery of the tent, and waiters serving a variety of canapés circulated among the guests.

Elizabeth stepped through the French doors from the salon onto the large, stone terrace. She walked forward to the railing that overlooked the garden and breathed in the fragrant air. It was hard to fathom one was only twenty minutes outside the city. The garden was filled with numerous varieties of blooming roses. The effect was beautiful and elegant.

"Dr. Bennet!" Elizabeth's attention was caught by James Fitzwilliam, the Earl of Matlock. He was standing to the side of the terrace with his wife. "We are so pleased you could join us this evening!" Elizabeth had liked the Fitzwilliams immediately when she had met them at the advisory board meeting. They were warm, intelligent and generous. Like their son, Geoff, they also shared a wonderful sense of humor that put everyone around them at ease.

"Lord and Lady Matlock, thank you for extending me your kind invitation. The gardens are beautiful!"

"Now they are even more beautiful with the addition of such a lovely lady!" the Earl responded as he warmly pressed Elizabeth's hand. Elizabeth could see where Geoff got his charm.

"James! Allow Dr. Bennet to settle in before you scare her off with effusive flattery." Lady Matlock's smile belied the severity of her words as she turned toward Elizabeth and took her hand. "Now dear, you must address me as Elinor and the Earl here, is James."

"Well then, I insist you call me Elizabeth!" She felt the presence of more guests behind her. "I hope we'll have a chance to speak later."

"Save me a dance, Elizabeth!" the Earl called after her as she walked away. He then made a low whistle as his eyes followed Elizabeth's figure down the elegant, stone stairway. "I can understand why Darcy was so distracted at the meeting. You know, my dear, you would look breathtaking in a dress like that!"

Lady Matlock gazed up at her husband adoringly. "You are the only man I know who can turn ogling another woman into a compliment to your wife."

The Earl quickly dropped a kiss onto his wife's cheek. "Ah, Ellie, you know you are the only woman for me!" They turned to welcome their next guest.

Under the tent, Darcy, Georgiana and Caroline Bingley were gathered near one of the tables. Caroline had arrived at the party early, knowing the family would already be assembled, and had attached herself to Darcy's arm like a leech ever since. Caroline was always clingy, but tonight she appeared desperate to keep hold of him. Darcy could not figure out how she had been invited. Caroline never spent a moment assisting any charity and she was not on the invitation list. *Was this one of Geoff's little jokes?*

Caroline had heard enough conversation to realize Darcy and Elizabeth Bennet were more than just casual acquaintances. Not only were they going to be working together, but Elizabeth would be attending the Garden Ball tonight.

Caroline immediately launched into a tirade of vaguely concealed insults. "Oh, I do hope she's trustworthy. What can you possibly know about her? None of us had ever heard of her before a few months ago, and now she's managed to get her hands on your millions! I hope she won't embarrass your aunt and uncle tonight. It's quite possible she will show up in something abominable!"

Georgiana was shocked at Caroline's outburst. "Caroline, Elizabeth would never embarrass anyone and —"

"Oh, my dear Georgiana," Caroline interrupted her patronizingly, "you are still too young to understand that those who do not have the advantage of society such as ours, cannot possibly grasp the importance of taste and elegance at an event such as this."

Darcy and Georgiana looked at Caroline's dress, looked back at each other and raised their eyebrows at her comment. Caroline was far too engrossed in scanning the crowd for anyone who might notice her on Darcy's arm to detect their expressions concerning her appearance.

Caroline was wearing a gold lamé sheath that hung loosely on her frame. Georgiana felt the dress fit so loosely that a thin strap might slip down over Caroline's shoulder and cause a major wardrobe malfunction at any moment. Caroline accessorized with a gold wire necklace on which hung a very large medallion. The necklace looked so heavy, Darcy thought the weight of it would pull her to the ground if she leaned over too far. Each of her wrists bore several inches of gold bangles with which she constantly managed to toy without loosening her grip on Darcy's arm. On top of her head, her unnaturally white-blonde hair was elaborately arranged in a concoction of twists and curls. She looked like an elaborate, gilded, Corinthian pillar.

By contrast, Georgiana wore a simple one-shouldered gown of pink silk that accented her slight figure and complemented her delicate features. The single diamond pendant she wore was a gift from Darcy on her sixteenth birthday. The matching earrings he gave her when she turned eighteen. Darcy believed that his sister's simplicity far outshone Caroline's gaudiness, and Georgiana was without a doubt the most beautiful woman at the ball — that is, until he saw Elizabeth Bennet.

Darcy's eyes locked on Elizabeth as soon as she stepped into the lights beneath the tent. She wore a strapless gown of sky blue silk that hugged her body from her breasts to her hips, where it flared slightly to the soft grass below. Her hair was swept back off her face and secured in a low, elegant chignon at the nape of her neck. The only jewelry she wore was a pair of diamond chandelier earrings and a diamond tennis bracelet. She took his breath away!

Caroline Bingley noticed the direction of his gaze and clutched the arm of his tuxedo so tightly that Darcy thought she would impale him with her gold, dagger-like nails if he attempted to move. "Oh look, Darcy, our little college professor has finally joined the party!"

Several people near Elizabeth had stopped to stare at the lovely vision she presented though it was clear Elizabeth was unaware of the stir her entrance had caused. "See what I mean," hissed Caroline, implying that something was significantly wrong with Elizabeth's appearance. "Oh, I do hope the Earl and Lady Matlock will not be embarrassed!"

A familiar-sounding, low whistle came from behind the group and they turned to see Geoff gazing intently in Elizabeth's direction. "I wouldn't worry about my parents, Caroline. They can handle the embarrassment!" His voice dripped with sarcasm as he moved past them toward Elizabeth.

Caroline cast Geoff an unseen frown. She despised Darcy's cousin; he always spoke to her in that same sarcastic tone. The only person she despised more was his twin brother, Richard.

Richard didn't bother with sarcasm. He told her straight to her face that she was petty, cruel and far too good a person to have to resort to such tactics. How dare he say such things to her? Who did he think he was? Thank goodness Richard was out of the country again so Caroline wouldn't have to spend the evening avoiding him. No, tonight there was no one to come between her and the object of her desire.

Caroline eyed Darcy as he was eyeing Elizabeth. He looked as splendid as ever in an Armani tuxedo. Tall, masculine, well groomed and exuding every pound he was worth. He looked the part of the young billionaire, and she looked the part of the wife of a young billionaire. She was certain that Darcy would realize her potential if she could just get his attention away from that hick bookworm! Caroline squeezed his arm tighter.

Darcy winced visibly. "Excuse me, Caroline." Darcy felt as if his arm was going numb from Caroline's death grip, and he wanted to extricate it from her long, gold hooks and escape! He decided he would excuse himself to get a drink and began to move away.

Before Darcy could make his excuses, she interrupted, "Oh, I'd love a drink." Caroline, suspecting his motives, intentionally cut off that line of escape. "I'll just tag along!"

Darcy would have to be more direct.

"I was not going for a drink." He gave her his most stern glare. Caroline knew where he was going, and she was determined he wasn't going without her, but she had no choice. She would have to relinquish her hold on him ... for the moment.

Darcy walked in the opposite direction to what she had expected. *Perhaps he just needs to use the toilet.* Caroline turned back to speak to Georgiana, but the girl quickly excused herself and went to join Geoff.

Caroline could not believe they had all left her standing alone. She did not think it was possible, but Elizabeth Bennet was surpassing even Richard in Caroline's ire!

Walking around the back of the tent, Darcy was trying to get his thoughts in order. He wanted to speak to Elizabeth but couldn't find the right words to say.

"Hello, Elizabeth," Darcy spoke into the dark. "Yes, I'm aware I was a complete arse on Wednesday night, but you never told me that you were a virgin." *Yes, like that bit of information would have previously come up in polite conversation.* "Good evening, Elizabeth, let's just pretend Wednesday night never happened. What do you say?" *Do you even have the right to address her by her first name? The last few minutes of your argument were conducted in rather formal address!* "Elizabeth, I know I behaved like a raving maniac, but of course that should not prevent you from speaking to me in private."

The previous night had been spent deep in thought. He knew he had to change his approach with her. He needed to display all the respect she deserved while keeping his galloping libido in check. It was going to be difficult, but for the sake of the project, it was necessary.

Darcy recognized that in addition to the intense physical attraction, he genuinely liked Elizabeth. She was intelligent, witty and a stimulating conversationalist, and that was the basis on which he would build his business relationship with her; but first, he had to find some way to convince her to speak to him. "Elizabeth, I must beg you to forgive me —"

"Wills, dear, who are you talking to?" Darcy turned around to see Lady Matlock approaching.

"No one, I was just thinking out loud."

"Unusual behavior for you. What's on your mind?" Lady Matlock had her suspicions but hoped Darcy would be uncharacteristically willing to elaborate.

His aunt was too perceptive, and he had no desire to discuss this particular topic with anyone. Darcy glanced about for a means of retreat. Seeing none, he decided a tactical diversion was necessary. "How is it that Caroline Bingley is here tonight? I wasn't aware she had a sudden change of heart toward the less fortunate."

Lady Matlock recognized a dodge when she saw one, but she knew it was useless to press her nephew. "She rang me this morning, said she just got into town and would love to come. I know she's become rather…unpleasant in recent years, but you were all such good friends after your parents died; I didn't think anyone would mind."

Darcy huffed. "I just stood through a tirade on the unsuitability of Dr. Bennet not only as a business associate, but as a guest at your party. This was followed by my having to painfully pry her fingers from my arm." Darcy rubbed the wounded appendage. "I would not be surprised if I need stitches!"

"Poor boy!" Lady Matlock gingerly touched his arm. "This is not like you to allow Caroline to rattle you. Shall I ask her to leave?" Lady Matlock knew Darcy too well to suspect he would say yes, but she was hoping to lead the conversation away from Caroline to the other lady previously mentioned. Darcy shook his head. "Perhaps Caroline would be discouraged if someone else was on your arm. Dr. Bennet perhaps? She looks quite lovely this evening."

The flash of alarm on Darcy's face told Lady Matlock all she desired to know. She pretended to ignore it, and Darcy quickly recovered his indifferent façade. "I wouldn't want to impose upon Dr. Bennet."

"If Elizabeth can handle your Aunt Catherine, then Caroline should not faze her in the least. Come, Wills, let's go say hello to her."

Lady Matlock led Darcy back into the tent towards a small bar where Elizabeth stood with Geoff, waiting for a drink. As they slowly approached, Lady Matlock stopped occasionally for a quick greeting to people they passed, and Darcy could only smile and nod when one of them would address him. The closer they got, the more anxious he felt. Unfortunately, Lady Matlock was keenly aware of his distress and enjoyed every moment of it. When they were within five meters, she whispered to him, "Relax, Wills! After the first 'hello,' you'll be just fine."

Darcy wanted to pretend not to understand his aunt, but it was too late to react. They were now standing behind Elizabeth and Geoff who were receiving their drinks from the bartender.

Elizabeth knew from Geoff that Darcy was at the party, and she felt jumpy from not knowing when she might see him. When she turned and unexpectedly faced him, her eyes grew wide with surprise, and she took a quick step back.

"Forgive me, Dr. Bennet, it was not my intention to startle you." Darcy's use of the more formal address was defensive. He didn't want to give her any reason to be angrier with him than she already was.

Elizabeth recovered quickly. She remembered her aunt's advice to try to get to know Darcy better. There was no reason to remain hostile when his manner was so civil. "Darcy, you're too kind. I should have been more careful of where I was walking."

For Lady Matlock and her son, this exchange was quite interesting. Geoff noticed Darcy's sudden use of "Dr. Bennet" and the apology in his voice that had nothing to do with startling her. Lady Matlock noticed Elizabeth's shocked reaction when she saw her nephew. When mother and son's eyes locked, a plan was wordlessly formed between them.

"Mother, you look divine this evening. Would you be so kind as to grace the dance floor with me?" The smile shared by mother and son demonstrated from which side of the family Geoff had received his good looks.

"It would be my pleasure. Wills," Lady Matlock turned to Darcy, "do dance with Elizabeth. It would be unpardonable for such a lovely young lady not to dance!"

Darcy did not want Elizabeth to feel any pressure. "Elizabeth, I understand if you would rather not dance with me."

Elizabeth widened her eyes in mock horror. "One can hardly defy one's hostess! I could never be so rude!" Until a few seconds ago, Darcy thought he would never again be the object of her playfulness. This response helped him to relax a little as he realized she was not angry with him. He smiled broadly as she tucked her hand into his extended arm.

"Shall we?" he asked as he led her to the floor.

As they stepped onto the parquet floor, Darcy took her right hand in his left and placed his right hand on her waist before spinning her around the floor. They were a physically stunning couple and moved gracefully together, claiming the attention of many of the other guests. Their conversation was tentative, but it was a step in the right direction. Each hoped it wouldn't be long before they re-established the easy banter they developed at Oakland her first night in London.

"You dance very well," Elizabeth complimented as they smoothly executed another turn in the foxtrot.

Darcy responded first by spinning her around. "My mother was determined that her children should know how to negotiate a dance floor with ease. I fear I did not appreciate ballroom dancing lessons at the time. I don't imagine most sixteen-year-old boys would."

Elizabeth laughed lightly. "No, I think not. Your mother must have been very proud of your achievement."

"Given my rather vocal opposition to the lessons, she was tactful enough not to mention it," he said with a smile. At a flourish in the music, Darcy gracefully dipped Elizabeth. She followed his lead effortlessly. "You also dance very well. Surely you must have taken dance lessons."

"I've been dancing since I was three, and except for a few teenage years when my touring schedule prevented it, I continued through my first two years at Longbourn."

"I imagine you excelled in dance as easily as everything else."

"I didn't attempt to excel in dance," she admitted. "That way I could stay in a class with other girls my age." He gave her a questioning look so she continued. "In dance class I didn't have to be the genius who needed special tutors or the freak who appeared on television every week. I felt…normal." She suddenly flushed at her confession. "I don't know why I'm telling you all of this."

"Perhaps because I'm one of the few people who understand exactly what you mean," Darcy suggested. "I was on my second advanced degree before I found myself in class with people my own age."

Elizabeth smiled appreciatively. "Precisely!"

Georgiana Darcy was extremely pleased to see her brother and her advisor getting on so well, and she was determined to keep Caroline Bingley too occupied to interfere. She was presently speaking to Caroline and kept their positions steady, with Caroline's back to the dance floor. Georgiana allowed her to drone on with advice on everything from where to shop in New York, where in that city are the best places to meet men of their particular social standing, and where Darcy could have disappeared to for so long.

Georgiana shifted her gaze when someone familiar caught her eye. She searched the crowd to see if she could recognize the figure. When she caught sight of him again, she froze in fear. *What could he be doing here? How dare he come?* Her loss of attention was noted by Caroline who turned to see what she was looking at. "Oh, George is here! When I told him about the ball this morning he didn't seem all that interested, but here he is! Oh, let's do say 'hello.'" Caroline turned to find that Georgiana had walked in the opposite direction.

George Wickham's attention was glued to the dance floor. He seethed inwardly as he watched Darcy and Elizabeth move gracefully to the music, laughing and smiling into each other's eyes. When he met Caroline outside the spa that morning, he could not have cared less about the Garden Ball as he was still trying to avoid Darcy. However, upon reflection, he thought *she* might be there.

He was still smarting from the humiliation Elizabeth Bennet had served him, and this might be his chance to get even. His initial plan was to avoid Darcy and get Elizabeth alone. Now, seeing the obvious attraction between her and his arch nemesis, he decided that more careful planning was in order. If he was clever (and George Wickham prided himself on being very clever), he could bring down Elizabeth and get some small revenge on Darcy in one brilliant maneuver.

"George, dear!" Caroline's sickly sweet voice called out across several tables.

"Damn!" George hissed to himself. If he were going to avoid Darcy's attention, he would need to stop Caroline from announcing his presence to everyone within a fifty-meter radius. He quickly walked over to meet her. "Caroline!" They hugged loosely and kissed the air near each other's cheek.

The plan struck him like lightning. Elizabeth may know her way around a fencing room, but a society function was his home field, and he would have the advantage. A compromising situation seen by the right people, and Elizabeth would be the laughing stock of the tabloids for weeks to come. Darcy would be furious, but Wickham would be long gone by the time the papers hit the stands.

"I see our friend Darcy is enjoying himself this evening." George motioned with his hand toward the dance floor. Caroline's reaction was predictable as she turned vividly red.

"Excuse me, George. I must save Darcy from that predator!" In a flash, Caroline was off toward the couple, and George slinked into the background to plot his next move. He saw his old friend, Denny. Denny loved a good scheme!

Darcy and Elizabeth were just leaving the dance floor when Caroline intercepted them. "There you are, Darcy. Eliza, we're so happy you could join our little group this evening. You look so sweet. I *sooooo* loved that look *last* year! It's Versace, is it not?"

"Good evening Caroline. I'm afraid my dress is not Versace. It was designed by a friend of mine and, therefore, one of a kind."

Caroline rolled her eyes at Darcy as if he was in on her private joke concerning the dubious origin of Elizabeth's dress. When Darcy did not respond, Caroline decided it was time to separate him from Elizabeth. "Darcy, I must speak with you, immediately." Caroline noticed his look of exasperation, and she became desperate to think of something that would drag him away from this little nobody. "Georgiana asked me to find you. The poor girl needs you right away!"

At this information, Darcy's look of annoyance rapidly changed into one of great concern. "Please excuse me, Elizabeth." Darcy turned to Caroline. "Take me to her immediately!"

As Darcy walked out of the tent, Elizabeth heard a familiar voice behind her. "Miss Bennet, I believe this is our dance."

Elizabeth turned around to face George Wickham who immediately snatched up her hand and pulled her to the floor. "We wouldn't want to make an ugly scene, would we?" Elizabeth had no choice but to acquiesce. She shivered with revulsion when he touched her waist and began to move her around the floor.

"What do you want?" Elizabeth's voice was as cold and steady as her gaze.

"Why, only the pleasure of your company. You look ravishing tonight, Miss Bennet. I hope my friend Darcy took the trouble to tell you."

"*Dr.* Bennet." Her icy gaze made him shiver for a moment, but he quickly recovered.

"*Dr.* Bennet? I had no idea. Are you treating the Darcy family for any specific malady? Perpetual haughtiness? Or are you here to remove the pole that is stuck up Darcy's arse?"

Elizabeth refused to react as she wished. "I'm not *that* kind of doctor."

"Ahhhh, an intellectual. Let me guess: English Literature, Music or, given the talent you are now so artfully demonstrating, Dance?"

"All of the above and so much more."

George was pleased. He was under the impression that she was falling for his charm and was now joking with him. This was going to be easier than expected.

"Impressive, but surely a girl as intelligent as you are must know that Darcy will have no interest in anything…permanent. You must have seen the morning papers. He leaves a trail of devastated hearts wherever he goes." George pulled her close to deliver in her ear what he thought was the crucial blow. "He eats little girls like you for breakfast!"

Elizabeth drew her head back from him. "Mr. Wickham—"

"Please, call me 'George.'" He gave her what he thought was his most passionate gaze and whispered huskily, "Elizabeth."

"George." She smiled her most dazzling smile. "Please address me as '*Dr. Bennet.*' I'm not interested in your views on Darcy's dating habits. Frankly, they're none of my business. However, I do enjoy the study of human character. I am fascinated to know how a man with such ridiculously obvious motives expects anyone to believe the poisonous morsels of knowledge he chooses to bestow."

George was taken aback by her statement. She was still smiling but she was definitely not joking. The song ended and she stepped back away from him and clapped for the band with the rest of the dancers. George was still stupefied when she bowed her head to him and walked away. It took him a few seconds to realize he was conspicuously standing alone in the middle of the dance floor. *This is incredible! This cannot be happening! This is not over yet!* He looked at Denny, nodded, and then followed Elizabeth out of the tent.

Darcy was practically running ahead of Caroline to locate Georgiana. Once he was outside of the tent, he stopped and, not finding his sister, impatiently waited for Caroline to catch up. "Where is she? Is she hurt?"

Caroline was out of breath from trying to keep up with him. "Relax, Darcy. Georgiana is fine!"

Suddenly Darcy realized that Caroline had lied to get him alone. "Caroline! I've had it with you and your silly games. Don't ever do that to me again! You scared me to death."

"You'll thank me later when you come to realize that Eliza Bennet is a gold-digger! You've seen her at the club. She eats nice men like you for breakfast!"

Darcy spoke with controlled rage. "When I want advice from you, I'll ask for it. In the meantime, stay away from me. I am so angry with you at the moment...I could do something...rash!"

"Oh, Darcy, *please* do something rash!" With that, she threw her arms around his neck and planted her lips on his. Darcy was startled and disgusted. He forced her fingers apart from behind his neck. The force required to pull her arms from his body threw her sprawling to the ground.

"Get away from me!" Darcy growled. "How many times do I have to tell you I am not interested?"

"I refuse to listen to you right now." Caroline held out her hand for Darcy to help her up. He didn't move. "You're obviously still under the spell of that little trollop! Someday you'll realize I'm the only woman fit to be mistress of Pemberley. When that happens, I'll be waiting."

"Don't hold your breath!"

She huffed as she brushed the grass from the back of her dress and, gathering what little dignity she had left, stomped off toward the house. Darcy took a few minutes to gather his wits and then headed back to the party. He entered the tent just in time to see George Wickham follow Elizabeth into the darkness.

Trying not to panic, Darcy decided it was faster to skirt the outside of the tent rather then try to cross through all the guests. When he arrived at about the place he last saw them, he desperately looked around for Elizabeth. Not seeing her, he followed a flagstone path though the gardens to a nook surrounded by tall hedges. There she was — standing alone — gazing up at the stars.

"Elizabeth," he called frantically. When he finally stood next to her, he could see she was fine. She looked calmly serene; her appearance was perfection. "Excuse me; I thought I saw someone following you. I was concerned."

"Do you mean *him*?" Elizabeth cast her gaze to the ground about three meters to the left of where they stood. There lay George Wickham, flat on his back as a loud groan escaped his throat. Darcy's fear dissolved into relief. "Yes, that's him." Darcy could hear George's labored breathing but couldn't resist a joke at his expense. "Is he dead?" he asked dryly.

"No." Elizabeth breathed an exaggerated sigh of disappointment. "You gave me strict orders not to kill him." The expression on George's face clearly showed his sudden suspicion that he had been set up again. Although the suspicion was false, neither Darcy nor Elizabeth had any inclination to enlighten him.

"You would be a vision in those orange jumpsuits they force prisoners to wear, but I believe that look is *sooooo* last season!" Darcy's imitation of Caroline inspired a large smile from his companion.

George groaned with the effort to sit up and then gave up and collapsed back to the ground. "George," Darcy said as he and Elizabeth turned to walk away. "I warned you that if you approached my family again you would find it very painful. Although I regret it was not done by my own hand, you can see — and feel — I was right."

Once they were out of hearing, Elizabeth turned a concerned face to Darcy. "Is Georgiana all right?"

"There was nothing wrong with her to begin with. Caroline decided it was time to separate me from a certain gold-digging man-eater and throw herself at me at the same time."

"Gold-digging man-eater? Ah, yes! That would be *me*. How did she get on with that?"

"Let's just say George wasn't the only guest to land on their back for inappropriate advances." As they walked along the path, they were approached from the opposite direction by Denny and three rather nosy matrons. Denny stopped when he recognized Darcy and Elizabeth, realized the game was foiled and moved his unwitting accomplices back toward the tent. Denny quickly slipped Wickham's camera phone back into his pocket.

Elizabeth looked at Darcy with an amused expression, "Poor Caroline! I met her at the fencing club and she's made it quite clear that she doesn't approve of me. How do you know her? She gave the impression that she's part of the family."

"She is. At least, she was. I've known her most of my life. Our parents were close friends. Caroline and her brother Charles practically grew up at Pemberley. My parents died with theirs when Mr. Bingley's plane crashed. Mourning together, we became inseparable, and Caroline was a great help with Georgiana. Then Caroline went off to Switzerland for two years after university. When she returned she was suddenly so obsessed with what I *have*, she no longer cared about who I *was*. I've tried to ignore it as Charles and I are still close and she *is* his sister. Tonight, when she lied about Georgiana, she crossed the line."

"I am sorry. I understand how it feels when someone you love disappoints you." Elizabeth looked off into the sky thoughtfully.

"That sounds like a story. Care to elaborate?"

Elizabeth smiled at him teasingly. "We haven't been friends long enough for that one."

"We're friends?" Darcy asked in astonishment. That she would even entertain the notion was more than he could possibly have hoped for.

She hesitated for a moment and then smiled playfully. "Yes. I would like that."

Darcy smiled back. "I have to warn you — I don't have much experience being friends with women. My last female friend was Caroline, and you see how that worked out."

Elizabeth couldn't help but tease him. "Does that mean you don't want to be my friend?"

"I'm willing to give it a try, but I imagine it will take a great deal of patience on your part. So what kind of things do male/female friends do?"

"I must admit that I don't have much experience with male friends, so we'll just have to make up the rules as we go along. I imagine you and I can do pretty much the same as you would do with your male friends. You say Caroline's brother is a close friend. What do you and Charles do when you get together?"

"Well, we eat chips — I mean, fries — and watch football — I mean, soccer."

"Please, Darcy, I speak several languages, including 'snotty Brit,'" she teased.

"I can eat chips and watch football. What else?"

"We play rugby. It's absolutely brutal!"

She gently lifted her hem to show him her heels. "That sounds like a spectator sport for me."

"Charles likes to drag me to clubs to meet angels!" Darcy added cheekily.

"I love to go to clubs, but I think the 'angel meeting' should be left to you and Charles."

"Agreed. Mostly we talk. Charles and I have a great deal in common." Darcy led her to a small bench between two large rose bushes.

Elizabeth took a seat. "I'm a pro at talking, and few people have more in common than you and I."

"That's true." Darcy sat next to her on the bench. "So, what about you? What do you do with your friends?"

"We don't watch football, but we do watch DVDs."

"I can do DVDs." Darcy pretended disgust. "No romantic comedies though."

"We don't go out to meet angels, but we do 'cruise hunks.'"

"I see." Darcy was enjoying this conversation immensely. "I'll pass on that one."

"We like to meet for drinks, and on Fridays we sing karaoke."

"Karaoke sounds more like a spectator sport for me. I had no idea you were such a showoff." They were both laughing.

"It is amazing what one will do after consuming enough liquid courage."

"Did I tell you how beautiful you look tonight? I must admit, it's flattering to think my new friend will make me the envy of every man I know."

"Well, I'm looking forward to the challenge of becoming 'buddies' with Europe's Most Eligible Bachelor."

Darcy rose and again offered his arm. "I believe, Dr. Bennet, that this may be the beginning of a beautiful friendship!"[7] She linked her hand back into the crook of his arm as they made their way to the tent. "See, we can do this!" Darcy said encouragingly as he covered her hand with his free one.

"Now, I do have to find Georgiana. If she knows George is here, she could be upset."

They were still linked at the arm when they found Georgiana. She was standing next to her uncle who had his arm around her protectively.

"Georgie," Darcy began sympathetically, "I have something distressing to

---

7 *Casablanca*, starring Humphrey Bogart and Ingrid Bergman, directed by Michael Curtiz, Warner Bros. Release 1942

tell you —"

"I'm all right, Wills," she interrupted. "As soon as I saw George, I found Uncle James."

"I've got security looking all over for that poor excuse for a man." The Earl's eyes scanned the crowd. "I won't rest until I find out how he got in here."

At that moment, Geoff joined them. "No one's seen him. Georgie, are you sure it was him?"

Darcy interjected, "Elizabeth and I saw him too. We left him down the path at the nook. He was flat on his back and in pretty bad shape. I imagine he's still there."

"Wills," Georgiana gasped. "You didn't fight? You promised me you wouldn't fight him. Did he hurt you?"

"Unfortunately, I didn't get the chance to touch him. It was Elizabeth!" Darcy smiled at her with pride, and Elizabeth colored as everyone looked at her in wonder.

"Well," Elizabeth looked to her audience and batted her lashes innocently, "What else is a girl with a black belt supposed to do?" Everyone burst out in laughter as the Earl pulled out his PDA and notified security of George's whereabouts.

"Excuse me, James," Elizabeth teased the Earl later when they were dancing, "Are all your parties this eventful?"

"I must admit, they are usually rather boring. It's going to be hard to top this next year! I may have to hire a few strippers." They both laughed.

Elizabeth whispered conspiratorially, "As long as you include a few male ones, I'll fly back to attend."

"Elizabeth, you are charming beyond description! I can understand why my nephew is so taken with you."

"I'm afraid you've misinterpreted the situation. We're just friends."

The Earl raised his eyebrows in astonishment. "Ah, my error. Do forgive me."

At the same time, Darcy was cornered by Georgiana. "So, my dear brother, what's the story with you and Elizabeth?"

"You'll be happy to know that we are now friends."

"Friends?" Her disappointment was clear.

Darcy laughed at his sister. "Sorry, Squirt. Elizabeth and I are going to be working together a great deal. It's important that we get along. I'm just surprised at how well we do."

"Friends?" Georgiana asked again as if she couldn't have heard right.

"I like her and I respect her. She and I have a lot in common. Why shouldn't we be friends?"

After the ball, the family gathered in the Fitzwilliams' library for a congratulatory brandy. The ball was a great success. After the glasses were empty, Darcy was the first to announce he was going to bed. Once he was out of the room, the remaining family looked to Georgiana who announced unhappily, "They're... friends!"

"Friends?" Lady Matlock repeated incredulously.

"Friends!" Geoff said firmly with a knowing look to his mother.

"Friends," the Earl of Matlock said with resignation. "That's what Elizabeth said too."

"Well," Lady Matlock sighed in disappointment, "so that's how they're going to handle this. Now there's only one thing to do. I bet twenty pounds they'll be lovers in eight weeks."

"Ellie!" the Earl looked at his wife in shock. He smiled broadly. "I don't give the boy eight days once he gets back to New York! Well, just to be fair, I'll take two weeks."

"I'll take sixteen weeks," Georgiana piped up. "Wills can be so stubborn."

Geoff stood up and regarded them all with a look of disgust. "You should be ashamed of yourselves! Darcy would be appalled!" Then Geoff grabbed a tablet to write down all the wagers. "I'll take twelve weeks. I agree that Darcy's stubborn, but let's not forget the 'Elizabeth factor.' She'll be tough to resist."

"Too bad Richard's out of the country," Lady Matlock lamented. "He would have loved a piece of the action." The whole group joined in her melancholy.

Georgiana brightened. "I'll e-mail him tonight. He shouldn't miss out."

CHAPTER 9

FINDING SYMMETRY

August 15th, London Society Weekly (U.K.)
Photo caption: Lord and Lady Matlock toast the beginning of their annual
Garden Ball on 7 August. This year's ball raised over £1,000,000 for Fitzwilliam
Charities.
Story: "Hayes Hall was the setting for Lord and Lady Matlock's Annual
Charity Garden Ball. The weather was heavenly and the scene delightful as
guests paid up to 5,000 pounds each to attend...."

August 25th, Celebrity Tattler (U.K.)
Photo caption: Fitzwilliam Darcy and his sister Georgiana dash through
Heathrow Airport.
(No story)

Georgiana Darcy was tentative. "Really, Elizabeth, I'd rather not. I like to sing at home and in the car but nowhere else."

"I heard you singing in the practice room. Your voice is lovely!" Elizabeth encouraged. "You need this class to fill out your schedule."

"What about the accordion? I'd rather play polkas than sing in front of people!"

Elizabeth looked at her seriously. "I don't believe there is an instrument on this planet you couldn't pick up and play expertly in less than three weeks.

School isn't about doing what you already know; it's about exploring what you don't." Elizabeth stood firm. "Just sign up for this voice class. I promise it will be filled with other people as reluctant to sing as you are."

"I'll think about it." As Georgiana turned to leave, she walked head on into a tall young man of about twenty. They both offered profuse apologies and flushed with embarrassment.

"Jacob Carter, this is Georgiana Darcy." As Elizabeth made the introduction, both students reached out to shake hands. "Jake will also be a reluctant vocalist this fall."

Jacob thought Georgiana had the bluest eyes he'd ever seen. Georgiana thought Jacob's smile could melt the coldest heart (and hers wasn't even chilly). Upon noting the reaction of the two, Elizabeth rolled her eyes skyward. Darcy was going to kill her.

AT 5 P.M., DARCY WALKED into the waiting area outside Elizabeth's office. His plan was to approach Elizabeth looking for Georgiana and then casually ask if she had dinner plans. He was new at this "friends with women" thing and didn't want to muck it up. Unexpectedly he found her speaking with his sister, throwing his carefully laid plans into turmoil.

He didn't want to eavesdrop so he kept his distance, just watching his sister with Elizabeth as he regrouped his thoughts. Ever since the Wickham incident, Georgiana was reluctant to open up to anyone new, and seeing her so relaxed with the woman who was her childhood idol was comforting. A "Plan B" was formed, and he moved into action.

He knocked on the open door and was greeted with two beautiful smiles. "Hello, how are you lovely ladies this afternoon?"

"Beware, Elizabeth!" Georgiana teased. "Every time he calls me 'lovely,' he wants something."

Elizabeth laughed as he dramatically clutched his heart. "Dearest sister, how can you of all people suspect *me* of ulterior motives."

"Because *you*, dearest brother, never do anything that is not well thought out in advance. So spill it! What are you doing here, and what do you want?"

"I was hoping to take you out for an early dinner. Elizabeth, would you care to join us." *Smooth, Darcy*, he congratulated himself. *Very smooth.*

"Sorry, but you'll have to go without me," Georgiana piped up and, turning to Elizabeth, added, "Jake and I are going to get a coffee and then grab the

subway to Times Square. He knows a great place to buy the sheet music we'll
need for voice class. I'm sure we'll find something to eat there." She glanced at
her watch. "I'm late! I'll see you two later." Georgiana kissed Darcy's cheek as
she swept out of the office.

"Who's Jake?" Darcy frowned.

Elizabeth grimaced. "Jacob Carter. You met him in the quad the day we
walked to the community center."

"Tall, good-looking guy who thought it was an honor to be your student?"

"That's him," Elizabeth responded reluctantly.

"And is there a reason you couldn't introduce my sister to some short, greasy
geek who spends his evenings playing video games?"

"Sorry. All the greasy geeks are going to MIT this year."

"I see." Resignation crossed his face as he sighed dejectedly. "Well, what about
you Elizabeth, can I interest you in dinner?"

"I'm afraid I also must decline. Tonight is 'girls' night' — no men allowed.
However, I'm not meeting my friends until later. Can I buy you a drink at the
Alumnae Club?"

His carefully laid plans a failure, Darcy decided that a drink was better than
nothing and agreed. Once they reached the club, they were shown to a table
by the windows, which gave them an excellent view of the river.

The room was full, but the tables were spaced far apart, and the voices were
kept low. It was the perfect place to meet and talk. A waiter approached the
table, but he was intercepted by an older man who was clearly in charge. "Dr.
Bennet, I am so pleased to see you this afternoon. Shall I bring you a glass of
the Symmetry?"

"That would be lovely, Mr. Hurst, and please bring a glass for my friend here."

Darcy was taken aback that she should presume to order for him. "Don't
look so severe," Elizabeth teased. "Trust me; this is something special."

In less than a minute, Mr. Hurst appeared with two glasses of red wine and
quickly excused himself as Elizabeth picked up her glass and held it forward,
waiting for Darcy. She watched as he took his first sip. He took his time, but she
was eventually rewarded with an appreciative smile. "This is excellent. What is it?"

"First you must promise to keep the secret."

Darcy gave her a suspicious look. "Agreed."

Elizabeth lowered her voice. "It's called 'Symmetry,' a blend of 1999 California Merlot and Cabernet from the Rodney Strong California Winery. It's

no longer available through regular channels. Mr. Hurst and I have an understanding. He uses his connections to find it, and I pay for it. The advantage is that I'm the only person here who can order it."

"Interesting, but isn't that rather illegal?"

Elizabeth raised her eyebrow in a playful manner, quickly glancing left and then right. "It is, hence the need for secrecy!"

"Who would have thought that such an upstanding young woman would be capable of such devious plotting? I know so little about you."

"That is a two-way street." Elizabeth eyed him carefully.

"So what do you say to an exchange of information? You ask me a question, and I get to ask one in return."

Elizabeth hesitated before responding. "We have to establish some rules. First, we must be completely honest with our answers."

"Agreed." He took another sip of his wine. "It goes without saying that all disclosures must be kept in the highest confidence."

"Of course. If a question is asked that one feels unable or unwilling to answer, we just say so. The other must respect that."

"Very wise. Any more or may we proceed?"

"I believe that will do for the present." She sat back in her chair. "So...do you wish to go first since this was your suggestion to begin with?"

Darcy thought for a moment. There was a question he was dying to ask. "Can I ask you anything?"

"Why not!" she said. "According to the rules, I can decline to answer."

He decided to go for it, leaned in and quietly asked, "How is it that a beautiful woman with...well let's face the truth, an incredibly fabulous body...is still a virgin at the age of twenty-four?"

"You don't start off easy, do you?" Elizabeth sat down her glass before continuing. "Believe me, it wasn't a conscious decision. I had a rather bad experience when I was sixteen. My reputation came into question and I had to defend it aggressively. Afterwards I decided that my behavior would always be above reproach. I buried myself in my studies to the point where I didn't have time to think about dating, let alone sex. When I reached an age where I no longer cared about my reputation in the small town in which I no longer lived, I was already past the age when most women had...lost it."

Darcy couldn't help himself from asking, "Did you ever consider just... losing it?"

"There were times when I considered it, but then I would remember that I deserved so much more than to just toss it away in the back seat of some car. I want to at least feel that I mean something to the man I have sex with, and I've yet to meet that man." She flushed with embarrassment. "I suppose that seems very silly to you."

"Don't underestimate me, Elizabeth. You have no need to defend yourself to anyone for having standards." He thought for a moment, but came up with one last question on the subject. He leaned in even closer and asked in a hushed voice, "Don't you have…urges…needs?"

Elizabeth smiled and whispered, "I believe I have perfected masturbation into its own art form." Darcy allowed his mind to wallow for a second or two in the delightful picture that popped into his head at that confession.

"Now it's your turn to ask me something," Darcy suggested as he leaned back into his chair. He was ready for a change of topic as he was already feeling a little hot under the collar.

"Yes, it is!" She smiled slyly. "What's your fascination with models?"

Darcy was hesitant to answer but felt that, after her honesty, he owed it to her. "It wasn't that I went looking for models specifically, and I don't just date any model — only a specific kind." Elizabeth raised her eyebrows, letting him know she was expecting more. He should have known it wouldn't be that easy. "I wanted to date women I found attractive and who understood that I wasn't interested in a relationship."

"In other words, you just wanted sex with no strings attached."

He looked at her expression carefully. It didn't betray her feelings. "Yes. Does that make you hate me?"

"Why should I be angry that you engage in consensual sex? It's not like you're lying to these women to get them into bed. I appreciate your honesty."

"You make me sound like a saint. Trust me; it's all far less aboveboard than you think."

"Enlighten me?" she asked, her eyes wide with curiosity.

Darcy wasn't sure if he should proceed. He was surprised at her tolerant reaction so far, but she was somewhat innocent. "You may be shocked."

"I'm not interviewing you as a potential husband! I'm your friend, and I promise to be as objective as possible."

"It's difficult to find women who don't eventually want to turn even a casual relationship into something more permanent. Someone I trusted gave me a contact to a service. Most of the women connected to the service are aspiring actresses or models." He waited here to see if she understood.

Elizabeth understood perfectly as her eyes grew even larger. "Aren't you worried about being caught? Surely you've heard of the Eliot Spitzer scandal?"[8]

"The practice is not illegal in the country where the actual transfer of funds takes place. There is a risk of public disclosure, but everything is conducted without names or permanent records so there is no documented evidence to implicate me." To Darcy's amazement, Elizabeth was not offended, in fact, she was intensely curious about the whole operation. After she peppered him with questions in which he revealed most of the process, she sat back with an astonished expression on her face.

"Six thousand a night! How much of that is paid to your date?"

"I pay a yearly fee to The Service. The entire six thousand goes to my date."

"Wow! I'm in the wrong business!" He couldn't help but laugh at her expression. Then she looked back at him with curiosity. "What about STDs?"

"Nothing's fool proof of course, but there are strict guidelines for blood tests and screenings that everyone on both sides of the transaction must adhere to. I've also done my part to support the condom industry. I'm a fanatic about it — always was."

"How long have you been using this service?"

"About six years."

"Every date you've had in the last six years has been through this service? All those women you were photographed with were part of it?"

"Every one," he confirmed.

Elizabeth looked puzzled. "You told me Caroline didn't care about you as a person; surely these women don't feel any differently?"

"I don't expect more from them. I loved Caroline like a sister. That's the difference."

"I'm afraid I'm not being clear." She hesitated to put her thoughts in better order. "You don't have relationships; you have transactions."

"That's the material point," he admitted.

"It all sounds so clinical! So artificial! Doesn't it seem like…rather less than sex should be? I admit I don't have any experience in the matter, but shouldn't

---

8 Eliot Spitzer is the former governor of the State of New York. In March 2008 he became part of a prostitution scandal, which eventually resulted in his resignation from office. http://www.nytimes.com/2008/03/10/nyregion…nd-spitzer.html

sex be something more?"

"I must admit that recently I've come to the very same conclusion."

Elizabeth regarded him thoughtfully before she continued. "So who was she?"

"I don't understand your question."

Elizabeth looked him straight in the eye. "The woman who made you settle for less."

Her perception unnerved him. "I'm sorry. We haven't been friends long enough for that story."

She smiled at his use of her own statement. "It's your turn, or have you had enough for today?"

"No, I have no desire to pass up this golden opportunity." Darcy thought for a few moments. "Whatever happened to Bethy Bennet?"

Elizabeth took a large gulp of wine and motioned to Mr. Hurst to bring another. "Bethy Bennet died a long and painful death eight years ago. Her demise began with a very public hospitalization for exhaustion, and she was buried forever as part of my parents' divorce. I was happy to watch her die!"

Darcy was shocked by the vehemence in her voice. "But you had so much. You had your own frickin' lunch box!"

Elizabeth's smile did not reach her eyes. "Ah, the merchandising! My mother's idea. Who ever heard of a classical recording artist on a lunch box? When I found out I nearly died of embarrassment, but apparently they sold very well in Europe and Japan."

"It must have been difficult to lose it all."

"I didn't lose it; I gave it up! I was touring for most of my childhood. I never knew what it was like to have a friend, have a home or go to school. I had four sisters and didn't know them. Music grew into a prison I couldn't escape."

Elizabeth's voice had become dead near the end of her story as she stared into the bottom of her wineglass. "When it was finally over, I got to do what I wanted to for the first time in my life. Most of the money I made was eaten up by lawsuits and taxes. I established trusts for each of my sisters and myself, and the rest I donated to charities. I got to know and love my sisters, and I got to go to Longbourn."

"Surely your parents knew you were unhappy? Why didn't they intervene?"

Elizabeth let out a disgusted laugh, "My mother was my manager. Frannie Bennet was in love with the fame I had and the money that came with it. Eventually she was skimming off the top, and I was being worked to death. I was hospitalized for exhaustion frequently. Momma didn't seem to have any trouble covering it up."

"What about your father?"

"My father was desperately in love with my mother. He didn't want to believe she was capable of abusing her position. When it got so bad he could no longer ignore it, he called my Uncle Ed to bring me home, and I was allowed to stop being Bethy Bennet. Momma never forgave him or me. It wasn't long after that they divorced."

Darcy's mind was reeling. It was hard to grasp what she had been through at the hands of her own mother. Darcy's mother had been kind, gentle and giving. It was difficult to picture Elizabeth's mother as cold, opportunistic and scheming. "Is that what you meant the night of the ball about people you love disappointing you?"

"Something like that, yes. Do you mind if we change the subject now? I feel like I'm depressing both of us."

"Of course. I believe it's my turn to answer a question."

Elizabeth didn't hesitate. "What about George Wickham? He told me he grew up with you."

"What else did he tell you? No, let me guess! Was it the story where I heartlessly take away the inheritance that my father left him, the one where I see to it he was thrown out of Cambridge to cover up my rampant womanizing, or the one where I undermined his position at The Darcy Company because I perceived him as a threat to my attaining CEO?"

Elizabeth couldn't help it; she laughed. "No, it was the one where you broke up his relationship with Georgiana because you didn't want to lose control of her inheritance." Elizabeth continued with mock concern, "He's madly in love with her you know!"

"Now that's a new one! He must be getting more action with the lost love angle." Darcy let out a laugh he didn't feel.

"I don't know about that, I didn't buy it, and I was pretty upset with you at the time! Of course, I also knew how old Georgiana really was."

"You'd be surprised how many people do buy it," Darcy said sadly. "The truth is that George's father was the groundskeeper at Pemberley and one of the few employees whose family lived on the property. Mr. and Mrs. Wickham honored my father by naming George after him. Being close in age, we grew up together, and I'd have to say he was my first best friend. Sadly, his parents had both passed away by the time George was sixteen, and my father was appointed his guardian. George tried to convince my father to adopt him. Of course, it never happened."

"George was accepted into a business management program at Cambridge, and he was tossed out after the first semester. Then it was pre-law at Oxford with the same result. My father gave him a job at The Darcy Company as a file clerk as he wasn't qualified to do anything else; however, he pronounced the job as beneath him and left both the company and Pemberley with the half a million pounds left in the trust fund my father established for him. At the time of my father's death, none of us had seen or heard from George in three years, but there he was — front and center — for the reading of the will."

"My father left him another million pounds, but George was outraged, expecting the estate would be divided into equal thirds. He hired an attorney in an attempt to contest the will, but his petition was dismissed immediately. Since then, he's been traveling around the world, telling anyone who will listen about his mistreatment at my hands."

"Was that why Georgie was so upset at the party?"

"No, it gets worse — much worse." Darcy leaned his elbows on the table and rubbed his temples. "I never told Georgie about the less savory parts of his history. It seemed harmless to allow her to keep her fond memories of George from her childhood. Last year, Georgie was on holiday with some friends at Ramsgate, a seaside resort in England, when she ran into George. About two weeks after her return, I received an envelope in the mail containing nude photographs of Georgie with a threat. I was to deposit two million pounds into a bank account on one of the Caribbean Islands, or else the photos would be sold to the tabloids."

"I noticed the body in the photos was not Georgie's. She has a rather distinctive birthmark that was conspicuously missing. The supposition of Georgie's head on the body was so perfect; she would have had to be carefully posed when photographed for it to fit. I had to ask her if she had posed for any photos lately, and I had to tell her why. She insisted I show the photos to her. What could I do? She was no longer a child. She revealed George had asked her to pose in some photos he would sell to travel magazines. That was why the pictures had to be posed so carefully."

"The betrayal devastated her. Even after I retrieved all the photos and insured no one would ever see them, she didn't leave her room for a week or our house at Pemberley for a month. I felt lucky to get her back to school last year. She's better now, except she would only come to Longbourn if I moved to New York while she was here. Your project was like a gift from heaven as it gave me a reason to relocate to New York without having to reveal Georgie's fears to anyone else."

"And you wouldn't let me run him through?" Elizabeth asked incredulously. "You are a saint! How did you stop him?"

"Money can buy a lot of things, even revenge. I'm not proud of what I did… I hired people to find George and ransack his flat. I had experts check the memory of his computer to see where he stored the pictures and then destroy them. We also destroyed the computer, but that wasn't enough. George was always very clever." Here Darcy dropped his gaze as if he was too ashamed to look at Elizabeth. "I had him…interrogated…until he revealed the location of every jump drive and hard copy of those photos. Then I had the shit beat out of him, just because I could."

Elizabeth reached over and took his hand. "George was lucky. If he had done that to Jane and I had your resources, he would probably be dead now."

He looked up into her eyes and felt as if Elizabeth's acceptance had lifted a huge burden from his shoulders.

Elizabeth looked over at Mr. Hurst and signaled for another glass to be brought for Darcy. "You were protecting your sister; there's nothing to feel ashamed of."

"I must offer you an apology, Elizabeth. I accused you of being the protector of some distorted sense of morality. I was so very wrong."

She understood the significance of those words and squeezed his hand in response. "I may not agree with every choice you have made in your life, but I can see the logic behind those choices, and I respect that."

He looked down at her hand on his. The familiar chemistry was there, but now it meant something so much more. He spoke very seriously. "If only there had been someone to protect you." He took his free hand and covered the one she had placed over his. "Now there is." He meant it. He would protect her from anyone that might hurt her — even himself.

"In case you hadn't noticed," she spoke playfully again, lightening the mood, "I'm a big girl now."

"Oh, I've noticed," he said cheekily. "But if you need me, just whistle. You know how to whistle don't you, just put your lips together and blow."[9]

She laughed, "That's the second Humphrey Bogart movie you've quoted to me. Do you do that often?"

"Sometimes the best words of wisdom are contained in the classics, whether Homer, Plato, Confucius or Humphrey Bogart!"

Elizabeth paid the check against his insistence, and they made their way back to her office. "Do you have plans for Sunday?"

Darcy smiled. "I think I would like to hear what you have planned before I commit myself. Given your history of illegal activity, you could be taking me on a wine-smuggling expedition."

She laughed. "Nothing so exciting. I need to get out of the city. I've decided to go hiking, and I thought it would be more fun to take a friend along."

As they reached the door to her building, he bent down and kissed her cheek. "I'll see you on Sunday."

That Sunday, Darcy and Elizabeth enjoyed a beautiful picnic along a mountain trail in eastern Pennsylvania. The following Wednesday, Elizabeth was invited to Lansing for lunch. The Saturday after that, they enjoyed dinner and a movie. Two days later, they met up after fencing for a late supper. And not long after, they were together nearly every day. It was, as Darcy and Bogart predicted, the beginning of a beautiful friendship.

---

9 *To Have and Have Not*, starring Humphrey Bogart and Lauren Bacall, directed by Howard Hawks, Warner Bros. Release, 1945

CHAPTER 10

THE PAPARAZZI POUNCE

September 6th, *The Daily Insight(U.S.)*
Photo caption: Fitzwilliam Darcy and his mystery lady enjoy the Yankees vs. Red Sox.
Story: "Last night, Fitzwilliam Darcy was again out with his mystery lady. A spokesman for the Darcy family did not identify the woman...."

September 21st, *Celebrity Watchers(U.S.)*
Headline: Darcy's Mystery Lady Identified!
Photo caption: Fitzwilliam Darcy's Mystery Lady is Dr. Elizabeth Bennet. Last night, they attended the opening of the independent film, "The Piracy Option," in New York.
Story: "Celebrity Tattler has learned the identity of the mystery woman Fitzwilliam Darcy has been seen with repeatedly in the past month. She is Dr. Elizabeth Bennet, Associate Professor of Music at The Longbourn Institute for the Performing Arts. Could love finally have hooked the elusive fish? Darcy publicist Frank Churchill says the couple are 'friends.' Like we haven't heard that one before!..."

Darcy awoke on a Friday morning with a throbbing, rock-hard erection. *Damn!* He'd been dreaming about her again. When the dreams first started occurring, Darcy despaired that his body refused to accept that Elizabeth was his respected friend, not some dream lover. He tried everything that came to mind to suppress his rampant fantasies but to no avail. Eventually, he gave up trying to control his subconscious.

Without opening his eyes, he reached into the drawer of his nightstand and pulled out a small bottle of lubricant. The loud "squish" announced that he had just emptied the bottle and caused him to open his eyes in disbelief. *Three ounces! At this rate, I'll need a gallon!* He moved his right hand under the blankets, below his stomach to the base of his penis. Relaxing back into his pillows and allowing his mind to drift back to the dream, he began the rhythmic stroking that would soon bring relief.

It had begun innocently enough. They were walking through the trees, and it had begun to rain, just as it had the day of their last hike. They headed for a small shelter. It was not a building per se — just a slanted roof on four posts. Why it was there or who built it didn't enter his mind. It was a dream and, therefore, didn't need to make sense.

While they waited for the rain to stop, they talked of inconsequential things: what his favorite food was, what time of the day she awoke on weekends, and how long they could each hold their breath. The last subject evolved into a dare followed by a competition. Elizabeth went first. She took several deep breaths in preparation for the final breath she would hold. Darcy watched with admiration the dramatic rise and fall of her breasts under her wet blouse. She caught his gaze, and he prepared himself for a well-deserved berating; however, she just laughed lightly and slowly began to unbutton the garment. As he stood in stunned silence, she eased the fabric over her shoulders, revealing a lacy bra, and then hung the blouse upon a nail on the post.

"Does that improve the view?" she asked huskily, causing his eyes to leave the swell of her breasts to meet her own. Elizabeth's fine eyes were filled with amusement and something else — desire! Her long, slender fingers moved to the clasp behind her back. With one swift movement, the bra was removed, revealing her exquisite breasts.

"What's the matter, Fitzwilliam?" she asked seductively as she hung the bra next to the blouse. "Cat got your tongue?" Somehow, the remainder of her clothing dissolved away and she stood before him, completely naked.

In the dream, he couldn't move; he couldn't speak. The frustration he felt only increased as she approached him and reached out her fingers to caress the bare skin of his chest. (Yes, he was naked too!) He desperately wanted to reach out to touch her. She was so beautiful, so perfect, so . . . eager. He didn't know where Elizabeth 'I'm not any man's casual fuck!' Bennet had gone, but at the moment, he didn't care!

Freed from the restrictions of his dream, Darcy pushed away the progression of the actual dream (in which he woke up in frustration) to allow his conscious thoughts to release both his tongue and body in the daydream. He gathered her into his arms and pressed her naked flesh hard against his own. His mouth covered hers in a deep and passionate kiss. "I believe you have found my tongue," he whispered against her lips when he came up for air before once again descending into the sweet, hot depths of her mouth. She moaned as he caressed the satin skin of her back, slowly, expertly guiding his hands to her fabulous arse. He grabbed her tightly there, and pulled her hard against his throbbing erection. His mouth moved to devour her neck as she reached to stroke his straining penis. The feeling was excruciatingly pleasurable. That was all it took. That was all it ever took, throwing him over the edge.

Darcy cast back the bedding as his body arched in the throes of an orgasm that seemed to go on forever. Over his lifetime, he'd shagged more women than he could count, but masturbating to fantasies about Elizabeth was the best sex he'd ever had. He couldn't explain it; it just was.

His PDA rang. Darcy tried to clear his still misfiring brain and reached out to grab it. He stopped suddenly when he realized his right hand was covered in semen and so reached out with his left and flipped open the phone. "Darcy here." He was still panting.

A bright cheery voice responded, "Hey, it's Elizabeth!" Darcy reacted instinctively. He grabbed the blankets and jerked them to his chest as if she had walked in and caught him.

"Can I call you back?" He wanted to put himself back together mentally and physically before speaking to her.

"I'm sorry. You're not alone?"

"No, no, that's not it at all, I'm just... about to take a shower; the water's running." He was a terrible liar, but there was no way he was telling the truth this time.

"Okay. I'll be waiting." She hung up.

Damn! Now I'll have to strip the bed before the maid comes in. He ran off to the shower and let the water course over his head as he pulled himself together. Darcy still marveled at the effect she had on him. He was acting like a teenager caught wanking off in the boy's lavatory at school. His thoughts went back to his fantasy. He realized that once again he couldn't allow himself to imagine them having intercourse.

She was a virgin. He'd never had sex with a virgin, so he had no point of reference. He could imagine, but it seemed disrespectful to do so, for as much as he desired Elizabeth, he knew they would never, ever be lovers. He turned up the cold water.

Over the past four weeks, Elizabeth had become his friend and confidante. He had never been so open with anyone in his life. He told her of the overwhelming responsibility he felt towards Georgiana. She told him about how she had skillfully avoided her mother for the last six years. She wanted to produce alternative rock albums and write her own opera. He wanted to expand the foundation and increase his involvement in human rights issues.

They debated any topic of interest, even those on which they agreed; one would simply take the opposing side for the fun of it. Elizabeth stimulated his brain in a way no one else could. The same was true for his body — hence the new morning ritual.

Once he finished shaving, he wrapped a towel around his waist and called her.

She answered quickly. "Hey, sorry I bothered you earlier. Is she gone?"

"There was no 'she.' I did not have a date, and I do not bring women home," he reminded her.

"You brought me home." *She's teasing me.* He wasn't sure he liked it when she teased him.

"That's different. I bring friends home."

"So, if I would have succumbed to your charms in London, I would have never seen the inside of Lansing?" *Still teasing.*

"That would have made things very messy." He glanced over at the tangle of sheets on his bed. *Not that they aren't messy now.* "I should thank you for coming to your senses."

"We have Lady Catherine to thank!" *Still teasing.* He was glad they had come to a place in their relationship where they could joke about what had happened in his office that day. What happened at her aunt's house was still a touchy subject. "Perhaps some sense of self-preservation would have eventually kicked in, but I must admit you're quite irresistible!"

"Not to mention handsome, hot and a fabulous hunk of prime beefcake. At least, that's what the tabloids tell me!" He could hear her laughter. *I'm teasing back! That's new.*

"Speaking of tabloids, that's why I called. If you're just up, I suppose you haven't seen the papers this morning?" Darcy groaned. This couldn't be good news. "They've identified your 'mystery lady.' Not just the British tabloids; the local papers have joined in. Apparently it's on the AP."

"I'm sorry, Elizabeth." He had hoped that they would have a little more time before the paparazzi began to hound her.

"You warned me, and I can handle it. I just wanted to ask if I could refer all reporters to your publicist. Since all the questions are about you and me, I thought it would keep our stories straight." Darcy thought for a moment. She was so damned practical. Caroline Bingley would have hired five publicists, all telling a different story to stir things up.

"I don't mind. However, if we use the same publicist, they'll assume we're secretly married." *I'm still teasing her.* He heard her laugh again on the other end of the line. "All right. I'm sure Frank will be thrilled with all the extra attention." Another thought crossed his mind. "Have the photographers turned up on your doorstep yet?"

"I've been very careful about keeping my address under wraps because of Frannie. I've already called Bill Lucas. He was unhappy at first but decided that any publicity could not help but be positive for the school. He's releasing a press statement that all photographers are barred from campus until further notice. I should be all right until one of them follows me home." It was clear she understood what she was dealing with. "The security in my building is pretty tight."

"If they start harassing you on the street, call me. I can get you a bodyguard."

"I just want to use your publicist! Let's not jump the gun. I'm a big girl, Darcy."

"As I've said before, I've noticed." *God, how I've noticed.* "The paparazzi can get pretty aggressive, and I don't want you to get hurt."

She was laughing again. "You really are a sweet man!"

"Don't tell anyone. I have a reputation to keep." *I'm teasing again. I'm getting quite good at this.*

"Wouldn't dream of it! See you at lunch!"

"Be careful." He heard the click too soon. She didn't listen to his last words, and he began to worry.

Darcy dressed quickly and walked downstairs to breakfast. Georgiana was already sitting at the table, laptop open beside a plate of toast and cream cheese. "Good morning, sunshine!" She called out at his less than happy face. "Have you seen the papers already?"

"No, but apparently you have. Is that why we spent thousands of dollars on a computer, so you could read *Celebrity Tattler* before the *Times*?" He gathered a plate of eggs and toast from the sideboard.

She eyed him with a mischievous smile. "There are times when reading the tabloids is profitable. Geoff and I had a bet to see how long it would take the press to identify your 'mystery woman' and pounce. Looks like I won!"

"How much?" She had a mouth full of toast so she held up five fingers. "Well, at least I can take comfort in knowing that you won. You can use that to offset the cost of your laptop. How long did Geoff guess?"

"Seven days. Aunt Ellie took two weeks; Uncle James took three weeks. Somehow, I knew Elizabeth wouldn't make it easy for those bloodsuckers. She's got too much class. Speaking of Elizabeth, how is your 'friend' this morning?"

Darcy winced. "She *is* my friend, Georgie. I don't appreciate the way you imply that it's more than that."

"My dear brother, I have many, many friends, some of them of the opposite sex, and I don't look at any of them the way you look at Elizabeth. Sometimes your gaze is so intense I expect her to spontaneously combust right before my eyes!"

"Like the way you look at Jacob Carter?" Georgie's smug face turned sheepish. *Ah ha! That got her. I am really good at this.* "Are things with you and Jake becoming serious?"

"We are '*friends*,'" and with a wicked grin, she was out the door.

Later, in his study, he checked his e-mail. Geoff caught him with an instant message.

    GFitz: C papers 2 day? E's a star.

  FDarcy: Call Frank Churchill. E 2 use our publicist, e-mail details.

    GFitz: U & E pretty cozy at game.

  FDarcy: FRIENDS! What's up with project?

    GFitz: Did u review contracts?

  FDarcy: Signed last night. Bets on G and J?

    GFitz: M says kiss already.

            D says kiss next week.

            I say G's 18, sex last week.

            R says he may b out of UK, but he's 2 scared of u 2 bet on G.

  FDarcy: R's a wise man! I'll take 20 on kiss in 1 month & U R DEAD!

    GFitz: Wishful thinking on both. G'afternoon.

  FDarcy: G'morning

DARCY ARRIVED AT ELIZABETH'S OFFICE at 12:30 for lunch to find her on the phone, talking excitedly. Her face was animated, and her free hand was gracefully waving about. He leaned against the door frame and smiled, struck again by her beauty. She noticed him and hung up quickly. "That was Longbourn's attorney. We can start set up for the project on Monday!" She was so excited she leaped across the room to hug him fiercely.

"That's great!" He hugged her back, unnerved at the familiar sensation that was a little too close to his fantasy to ignore. He pulled back quickly. "Does Mr. Hurst have enough Symmetry for us to celebrate at lunch?"

"He just got in another case. Let's go!"

Darcy and Elizabeth walked to the Alumnae Club. With the press banned from Longbourn's campus, it was the perfect place to go undisturbed and not be photographed. This was where they had their most intimate conversations and bared their souls to one another. After four weeks of lunches and after-work drinks, they knew each other better than most people did after years of friendship.

"Frank called this morning. There are a number of requests for the name of the person who designed the dress you wore to the opening last night. Would you mind if Miss Lucas' name was given."

"You're being sweet again," Elizabeth whispered a mock warning.

"I'll risk it if it will make you happy," he whispered back.

"I don't want anyone to think that I'm using our friendship for personal gain. Not even to promote Charlotte." She frowned and he was touched at her sincerity.

"If we don't give a name, the press will take a guess at who the designer is, and someone else will receive the credit. Your friend deserves to be recognized, and the publicity can only help her."

Elizabeth realized he was correct and conceded. He reached over and covered her hand with his own. "You are a rare woman, Elizabeth Bennet. The women I've known would jump at the chance to use me to advance their personal interests."

"I don't know where the women you know come from, but I feel the need to redeem the entire sex." She looked distressed. "You need to meet my friends."

"And just how are your friends different?" Darcy felt uncomfortable. It was one thing to meet Jane and perhaps Charlotte, but he was apprehensive about a whole group.

"They are driven. Each one of them has a dream to pursue that doesn't center on finding a rich husband. They are intelligent and interesting — not the least bit calculating and conniving. As a member of the sex you have maligned so frequently, you owe me this much!"

Darcy had to agree. "How much time do I have to prepare for this enlightenment?"

Elizabeth thought for a moment and then brightened. "Tonight is karaoke night. We all meet around seven at *tJean's*. It's a small club near campus. Fortunately it's not *girls only* night, so you can sit with us, and I'll concede to your bringing your friend Charles along so you won't feel so vulnerable."

"I do not feel vulnerable!" Darcy felt the need to defend his masculinity and vulnerability was an emotion he could not admit to. "I'll have to check with Charles since he's been complaining that I'm never available anymore, but I'm sure he'll agree. He's presently unattached and will jump at any opportunity to meet single women. There's not a woman alive Charles wouldn't love." Darcy frowned. "He's so trusting, so naïve sometimes."

Elizabeth eyed him seriously. He was brooding again. "Are you ready to tell me about *her* yet?"

He knew exactly what she meant and the sudden tension between them was uncomfortable. This was the first time she had brought up this particular subject since that first drink at the Alumnae Club four weeks ago. Memories of Rebecca were tucked safely away in a part of his mind he never wanted to revisit. He couldn't even bring himself to say her name.

"No, I will not discuss her." Darcy knew his answer was also an admission that there was a *her* to discuss. She seemed satisfied to let the matter drop, but Darcy was feeling exposed and defensive, so he turned the tables. "And what about you, Elizabeth? The defenses you've built are more than a response to an overzealous stage mother. Who's the ghost in your closet?"

Elizabeth felt the intense anxiety rise in her chest and all she could do was stare into her glass. Her distressed expression cut Darcy to the core, and his protective nature took over. His voice was cold as ice when he asked, "Who is it?"

Elizabeth didn't look up. How could she expect him to trust her if she wasn't willing to trust him in return? "If I tell you names, will it be enough for now?"

He nodded his head in response as she tried to gather her courage. *Why is it so difficult? Just say it!* "Frannie was far more destructive than an overzealous stage mother, and there's a man in prison, Billy Ray Collins." Her head abruptly rose to meet his gaze, but she quickly diverted her eyes. She felt naked and vulnerable.

Darcy's mind snapped with recognition at the name. His thoughts raced to the website for the man in prison. He re-read the site in his photographic memory and focused on the section with the statement from Elizabeth Bennet's mother. *Frannie.* When he hadn't known Elizabeth, he dismissed it all as rubbish. Now that he knew something about her relationship with her mother, the website gave enough clues to deduce the truth. The horror of it struck him like a sledgehammer. The attempted rape and her mother's betrayal were beyond his comprehension.

He needed to give her something to make her feel she had not made a mistake in trusting him with her confession. They needed common ground and Darcy knew what he had to do. He felt the wounds reopening deep within as he quietly spoke, "Her name was Rebecca, Rebecca Wickham. George's cousin."

Her eyes slowly rose with her understanding of what he had done. They sat for a long time, his hand still clasped over hers on top of the table. Darcy and Elizabeth looked into each other's eyes, each deeply appreciating the sacrifice of the other. With their shared revelations, the bond between them had strengthened beyond mere friendship.

When it was time to leave, Darcy maintained his hold on her hand as they walked back to her office. The comfort they drew from the shared contact soothed the raw emotions each had lain bare. The silent walk ended at her office where they were reluctant to part. Finally, he enveloped her in his arms, embracing her tightly. She gratefully returned his embrace and kissed his cheek.

Darcy released her, already missing the warmth of her body. "Shall Charles and I pick you up tonight?"

"I'm having an early dinner with Charlotte. We'll meet you there." He gently kissed her forehead and walked toward the exit.

CHAPTER 11
TIME TO LOOSEN UP

Charles Bingley bounded into the back of the Darcy limo like a hurricane. "Mr. Sparks, good evening! How is your lovely mother?"

"She's just fine, Mr. Bingley, thank you for asking." Sparks offered a smile — rare while on duty — but it would have been impossible to remain stoic. Bingley's high spirits and ready smile just had that effect on people — not at all like his sister, but Sparks chose not to dwell on that subject.

Bingley turned his attention to his host. "Darcy, this has been a splendid evening so far! I'm glad you could pull yourself away from your new friend long enough to spend a night out with me. I may not be as attractive as Dr. Bennet, but I hope you don't find me too boring," he teased.

"No, your company is excellent as always," Darcy replied dryly.

"I can't begin to guess where we're off to next; however, I do hope that wherever it is, there will be music and a dance floor. I'm in the mood to dance."

"When are you *not* in the mood to dance?" Darcy asked with mock annoyance, which did not fool his friend in the least. "Do you honestly think I'm going to take you to some seedy dive where you will dump me at the first opportunity to dance with the *angel du jour*!"

"Just because you hate to dance is no reason for me to dampen my own enthusiasm. Besides, nothing is more desirable to a woman than a man who can dance."

"Except perhaps a rich man who can dance," Darcy suggested helpfully.

Charles laughed. "Fortunately, you and I fall under both categories. A man must call on all his advantages when looking for his ultimate angel."

Darcy rolled his eyes. "Speak for yourself! I honestly don't know why I put up with you."

"Because I'm one of the few people in this world who can make you laugh. You, my friend, need to loosen up!"

Darcy creased his brow. "I do not need to 'loosen up.' I'm perfectly relaxed."

"Ha! You haven't been perfectly relaxed since our parents died. Come on, man! You've filled your life with so much responsibility, I don't know how you find time to breathe, let alone relax."

"And you call what you do relaxing? Freezing your arse off on Mount Everest or hiking to the North Pole…and that stunt last month in the Great Barrier Reef? How big was that shark you photographed? At least seven meters!"

"Oh, twenty at least!" Bingley teased. "So, are we going to a club?"

"Yes," Darcy said in exasperation. "We will be meeting up with Elizabeth. I hope you don't mind."

"Excellent!" Charles expounded, "Then I won't have to feel guilty about leaving you alone if I find an angel to dance with. But why couldn't you have told me earlier where we were going? Why all the cloak and dagger stuff?"

Darcy issued the one word answer: "Caroline."

"I see." The smile faded from Charles' face.

Darcy regretted the pain he was causing his friend, "I'm sorry, but I didn't want to ask you to lie to her about where we were going, and I was hoping to have a night out with you where your sister did not 'accidentally' run into us."

"I'm sorry, Darce. She's been even more tenacious since the press reports about you and Elizabeth appeared in *The Times*; but she is my sister, and I appreciate your not taking out that restraining order. Though God knows, you had more than enough reason to. I will try to talk to her again," Charles offered, "but I doubt it will do any good."

"I'd appreciate it. Now, let's not let this ruin our evening." Darcy knew how to return his friend to his previous good mood. "Elizabeth will be with a number of her friends…all female and single."

The bright smile returned immediately to Charles' face. "Really? How soon until we arrive?"

The inside of *tJean's* was a sea of bodies. and Darcy stretched his neck to see if he could find Elizabeth in the crowd. The lights were low, and the hum of a hundred conversations was nearly drowned out by the volume of the music. "This place is fantastic," Charles yelled so that Darcy could hear him over the noise.

A man was on the small stage singing a rendition of *New York, New York*.[10] "God, I hate this song!" Darcy complained to Charles. "Why is it that no matter where in the world I travel, if there's a karaoke machine, there's some fool who thinks he's Frank Sinatra?"

Charles laughed at his friend. "Loosen up and buy us a drink."

Charles snagged a passing waitress and ordered a Bass Ale. Darcy ordered a Bombay Sapphire Martini, dry, shaken hard until the ice splintered with only one olive. The waitress rolled her eyes in response, and by the time she returned, there was a tall, red-headed woman on stage belting out *My Heart Will Go On* from the movie *Titanic*.[11] There was only one song Darcy hated more than *New York, New York* and that song was it. Frustrated that he couldn't find Elizabeth, Darcy pulled out his PDA to text her.

The lights flashed as the woman finished her song and suddenly the room burst into loud applause and catcalls as the next performer took the stage. Charles noticed a group of women rush to the front of the stage. "Darcy, over there. A whole flock of angels!"

Darcy waved Charles away, focusing on the message he was entering with his stylist when a familiar voice caught his attention. He forgot his text message to give his full attention to the performer.

I love myself, I want you to love me.
When I feel down, I want you above me.
I search myself, I want you to find me.
I forget myself, I want you to remind me.

Her voice was playful and seductive; her movements as she danced across the stage were mesmerizing. Her violet dress was too short to be considered remotely proper and the song she sang was even less so.

The 'angels' standing before her joined in the chorus:

10 *New York, New York*, music by John Kander Lyrics by Fred Ebb
11 *My Heart Will Go On*, music by James Horner and lyrics by Will Jennings

I don't want anybody else.
When I think about you,
I touch myself.[12]

"She's a fox!" Charles claimed excitedly.

Darcy laughed. "That's what I said the first time I met her." At Charles' look of confusion, Darcy explained, motioning toward the stage. "That's Elizabeth!"

Darcy led Charles to a better vantage point to watch Elizabeth's performance. When she came to the spoken bridge of the song, she ran her hands along her body, giving anyone in doubt the exact meaning of the lyrics:

I want you...
I don't want anybody else...

Her hands slowly caressed her thighs and then moved up her hips to her ribs.

And when I think about you....
Ooooo, I touch myself.

The audience grew silent as her hands inched toward her breasts, holding its collective breath, anticipating when Elizabeth's hands would reach their ultimate goal. Then, just as the music reached its crescendo, she threw her arms out to her sides in the ultimate tease.

Darcy smiled broadly in response. Thunderous applause filled the room at the end of Elizabeth's performance, and Darcy tapped Charles to get his attention. "Come on. We're sitting with the 'angels.'"

Upon seeing Darcy, Elizabeth walked over to envelop him in a welcoming hug. "Hey, Darcy."

"Hey, Elizabeth." He spoke into her ear as he returned her embrace, "You are a very naughty girl!"

"I sing what I know!" she teased as she pushed up to kiss his cheek.

"You are amazing." He tightened his embrace as he offered his praises.

"That's what the tabloids tell me," she said saucily as she broke away.

Charles watched this exchange with barely concealed amazement. *Just friends,*

---

12 *I Touch Myself,* music and lyrics by The Divinyls. This song has a rather interesting part in the first *Austin Powers* movie.

my arse. No wonder Caroline has her knickers in a twist. Charles approached the pair to introduce himself. "You must be the incomparable Dr. Elizabeth Bennet."

Elizabeth turned away from Darcy to greet his friend. "And you must be the amiable Mr. Charles Bingley. I'm delighted to make your acquaintance."

"The pleasure is all mine," Charles replied, keeping up their mock formality.

"Shall I introduce you to my esteemed associates?" Elizabeth teased as she led the gentlemen to the table where the 'angels' were seated. With a wave of her hand, Elizabeth caught the attention of the group. "Ladies, this is my good friend, Fitzwilliam Darcy, and his friend, Charles Bingley. Gentlemen, pay attention as there will be a quiz later." This announcement brought a round of laughter from the table. "To my left here are Alexandra Chin, Cassandra Little and Sandra Gordon. These three are inseparable so they are collectively referred to as the 'Zandras.' To my right is Maria Lucas and last but not least, her sister Charlotte."

When the handshaking ended, Darcy sat securely next to Elizabeth, while Charles seated himself squarely in the middle of the 'Zandras.' A few minutes later, a waitress arrived with a tray of glasses filled with a pink concoction. "What are they?" Darcy asked, and then noticing the glow in Elizabeth's cheeks, he added, "and how many have you had?"

"Cosmopolitans. Two parts citrus vodka, one part orange liquor, one-half part cranberry juice and a dash of sweetened lime juice. Otherwise known as liquid courage!" At the end of her description, a cheer erupted from the 'angels' as they simultaneously raised their glasses and drank deeply. "This is round three, and you two need to catch up!"

With a graceful wave at the waitress and a rapid movement between Darcy and Charles with her fingers, another beer and martini quickly appeared before them. After about fifteen minutes and three more performers, Elizabeth leaned forward to speak so only Darcy could hear. "You, my friend, need to loosen up."

"What is this? First Charles and now you," he said flatly. "I am perfectly relaxed."

"Really?" She arched her eyebrow and smiled sweetly. "No one at this table wants anything from you but your pleasant company, and that you apparently left in the car with Mr. Sparks."

"I've been very pleasant." He sounded like a petulant child.

"You've said nothing to anyone but me since you arrived at this table. If that is what you consider pleasant, I'd hate to be around when you are actually rude," she teased while patting his knee maternally.

He lowered his eyes to his glass and then looked toward the stage where another performer had just finished singing *Hit me Baby One More Time*.[13] "I must admit I'm not very comfortable around people I don't know."

"Bullshit!" She was still smiling sweetly. "You've got ten minutes to gather your courage, then I'm throwing you to the wolves!" He didn't quite know what she meant, but the determined expression beneath her smile convinced him to down the remainder of his first martini and take a large swallow from the second.

The club's owner took to the stage and requested the attention of the crowd. "I'm sure it is a surprise to no one that, for the fourth month in a row, the winner of our karaoke contest is Lizzy Bennet!"

Elizabeth stood, leaving Darcy alone with her friends as she took to the stage to accept the adulation of the crowd and an envelope from the club owner, which he immediately snatched back from her. "And," the owner continued, "for the fourth month in a row, the bar tab for Lizzy and her friends has more than exceeded the amount of the prize money!"

The club again erupted in applause as the 'angels' also stood to take a bow. As she came down from the stage, a man asked Elizabeth to dance, and looking to see Darcy still sitting silently at the table, she accepted.

It didn't take a genius to figure out what Elizabeth was up to, and as Darcy was a genius, he immediately understood that she was trying to force him to talk to her friends. He took another large swallow of his drink and turned to Charlotte. "Let me congratulate you on the dress you designed for Elizabeth. My publicist tells me it's creating quite a stir in the press."

Charlotte turned her attention away from the tall man eyeing her from three tables away. "Thank you, but Lizzy could make a brown paper bag look like haute couture."

Darcy's mind momentarily pictured Elizabeth wearing nothing but a fragile, brown paper bag. He would have been happy to continue those musings for quite some time, but he knew what Elizabeth expected from him. "I must agree with you; however, you are very talented." Charlotte thanked him again, and turned her attention back to the tall hunk.

Darcy realized that Charlotte was content to allow the conversation to stop there. In the past, all he had to do was to get a woman to start talking

---

about herself and if given the opportunity, she would go on and on for hours. Suddenly, he understood this was not going to be easy. He looked across to see Elizabeth catch his eye from the dance floor. Another song began and she stayed with her partner. He was going to have to try again. "I'm surprised a design house hasn't made you an offer."

"Oh, I've received offers, but none that will allow me to retain control over my work and who I design for. Hopefully, a suitable offer will come soon. I'm getting a little tired of living with my parents." Charlotte turned to give him her full attention. "You may have met my father. He's president of Longbourn. He's a sweet man, but he tends to treat me like a five-year-old."

Darcy agreed that he had met William Lucas. This was followed by another awkward pause. "Are you designing anything else for Elizabeth?"

"Yes, a gown for both the Longbourn Fundraiser and the Human Rights Recognition Awards in January. Congratulations, I understand you are to receive an award for your work with the Ethiopians. Tell me, how you were able to convince them to release that woman and her daughter. I was glued to CNN for days, worried that they would be executed."

Darcy explained about the work he had done with Amnesty International and how, using the economic influence of The Darcy Company, they were able to convince the Ethiopians that it was in their best interest to release their prisoners. A half hour later, Darcy was surprised to find that he was still talking to Charlotte as well as Alexandra and Maria who were equally well informed on international events. Elizabeth had returned to the seat next to his, and he thought to impress her by asking Charlotte to dance. He didn't know if it was the three martinis he had consumed or the excellent company of Elizabeth's friends, but he was sure he was enjoying himself nearly as much as Charles was.

In the meantime, Charles was making good on his promise to dance with every woman at the table. Darcy ignored the look of shock on his friend's face as he began to dance with Charlotte, choosing instead to look to Elizabeth. A broad grin crossed his face at the look of approval he found in her eyes.

So the evening progressed. Darcy made a point to speak to each of Elizabeth's friends, and he had to admit to being impressed. All three Zandras played with the New York Symphony, and Maria was beginning her first year of medical school at Columbia. None made him feel that his assets, both financial and physical, were being inventoried, and he found himself relaxing more through the evening. Next, he asked Elizabeth to dance and could not help but admire her legs beneath the sexy short dress as he walked behind her to the dance floor.

Elizabeth was pleased with the efforts Darcy had made to break out of his comfort zone. She understood that it was not easy for him to go against his reticent nature, and to see him doing so for her benefit only endeared him even more to her.

She took a moment to admire Darcy's fluid movement on the dance floor. It contained none of the mindless jerking and bouncing of most of the men she danced with. She smiled at him and he took her hand and pulled her to dance closer, moving his hand to her waist. He seemed to be able to communicate wordlessly to her how he wanted her body to move so it looked as if they had been dancing together for years.

The admiring glances of the women around them did not escape Elizabeth's notice. Darcy was wearing grey trousers and a dark blue shirt that were expertly tailored to his body. Even if he wasn't famous, he would have attracted the attention of every red-blooded woman in the room.

She noticed one woman intentionally bump into Darcy from behind, and in a sudden act of possession, Elizabeth slid her hand up his arm to rest on his shoulder. He responded by pulling her closer. The heat of his body permeated her own as they moved with the pounding beat of the music.

Two songs later, they reluctantly moved apart, and Elizabeth was suddenly accosted by a white blur with blonde hair. Darcy's initial alarm was dispelled by Elizabeth's laughter, and after an enthusiastic embrace, the women broke apart. "Darcy," Elizabeth began, "this is my beautiful sister, Jane. She just got off her shift at the hospital and decided to join us."

"Darcy," Jane responded as she shook his hand, "I've heard so much about you, I feel we are friends already." Darcy had to admit that Jane was very pretty, but certainly not as beautiful as Elizabeth; however, there was something most unusual in Jane's appearance. While Elizabeth radiated sensuality and vivacity, Jane was ethereal, almost otherworldly. *An 'angel.' Where is Charles?*

Darcy didn't have far to look, for not four feet away was Charles, standing still as a stone in the middle of the dance floor, completely oblivious to his dance partner and staring dumbfounded at Jane.

"Don't worry," Elizabeth quipped to Darcy, "Jane seems to have this effect on most men. They usually snap out of it after a moment or two."

Darcy tried to get his friend's attention. "Charles, come meet Elizabeth's sister." Darcy had to repeat himself before Charles was able to come out of his trance. After a quick apology to the woman he was dancing with, Charles by-passed both Darcy and Elizabeth, walked straight to Jane, introduced himself and offered his hand. When Jane placed her hand in his, instead of shaking it, Charles raised it to his lips for a kiss.

Jane blushed prettily, looked down at her feet and then back at Charles. There they stood, just gazing at one another, the rest of the world lost to them. Elizabeth's quick glance to Darcy communicated the need to get the two love-birds off the dance floor. After seating Charles and Jane at their table, Darcy and Elizabeth stepped back to watch them: heads close together, hands still clasped, continuing to stare into each other's eyes.

"Is your sister seeing anyone?" Darcy asked as he put his arm around Elizabeth's shoulder.

"Not at the moment. Why?"

Darcy smiled as Charles kissed Jane's hand for the second time. "She is now! Let's dance."

Soon Darcy and Elizabeth were back on the dance floor, their movements being appraised by Charlotte, Sandra and Cassandra.

"You're sure they're still just friends?" asked Sandra of Charlotte. "That's dance-floor foreplay if ever I saw it."

"Lizzy was telling me just before he arrived that they were just friends. He certainly didn't dance with me like that!" remarked Charlotte. "Thank God they're not grinding."

"Do you think he'll be the one... you know... to finally 'do her?'" asked Cassandra with concern.

"If not," Sandra replied dreamily, "he can do me! Get a look at that ass!" At this all three women simultaneously turned their heads slightly to the right to get a better look at Darcy's assets.

"Brains, socially conscious, filthy rich and a great ass. Lizzy had better grab that man now; she can work out all her baggage with him after they're married."

"Charlotte," Cassandra cried, "the man changes girlfriends so frequently he must have a revolving door to his bedroom."

"He seems perfectly nice to me, and you can't deny the chemistry between him and Elizabeth. Statistics say 50% of marriages end in divorce. Darcy and Elizabeth would have just as great a chance at a happy marriage as anyone else."

"You can't believe all that crap you spout off about marriage!" Alexandra said as she joined her friends.

"I most certainly do! Before we know it we'll be too old to hang out in bars, and our biological clocks will be on their last battery. We need to strike while we can, and Lizzy's Mr. Darcy is better breeding material than most men she'll ever meet."

"He can dance too!" commented Sandra with an exaggerated sigh. "Not many men can dance like that, at least the ones who aren't gay."

"His friend dances well. Where is Charles, by the way?" asked Cassandra.

"Over there," Charlotte motioned with her head to the table where Charles and Jane were seated. "Another soul lost to the mind-boggling beauty of Jane Bennet."

"That's unusual," Cassandra looked at the couple that appeared to be in deep conversation. "Jane usually doesn't notice the afflicted."

Charlotte pulled in a deep breath, expelled it loudly and put her hands on her hips in determination. "Well, ladies, with the Brits taken out of commission by the Bennet girls, we'll have to fend for ourselves, and I've had my eyes on Mr. New York, New York all night!" Charlotte walked towards the gentleman, and soon after, all of the 'angels' were dancing.

Darcy and Elizabeth spent the rest of the night on the dance floor, dancing only with each other. With their pictures posted on the front of practically every tabloid in the city, it wasn't surprising that several club-goers used their cell phones to snap pictures of the couple.

As they left the club, Darcy offered to have Mr. Sparks drive the entire group home. Jane was dropped off first with a promise from Charles to call her the next day. The last to arrive home was Elizabeth, as she only lived four blocks from Lansing.

After thanking Sparks and wishing him a good night, Elizabeth was surprised to find Darcy standing behind her as she pulled out her card key. "What are you doing?"

"I'm seeing you to your door."

"It's only twenty feet from your car to my door," she laughed.

"I just wanted to make sure you arrived inside your building safely."

"You didn't walk Charles to his door," she teased.

"Charles isn't as cute as you are." He was smiling rather goofily.

"I think your friend is very charming."

"So do I, but what does that have to do with Charles?"

They looked at each other a moment before both burst out laughing. "That was not funny!" she said between spurts of giggles.

"It's amazing how witty one feels after four martinis!"

She managed to suppress her laughter and brushed an errant lock from his forehead. "I realize how uncomfortable this was for you tonight, and yet you managed to force yourself to speak to everyone."

"Your friends were certainly different. Perhaps they did manage to redeem the female sex."

"Don't nominate them for sainthood yet; I did catch Charlotte eyeing your butt a few times."

"I did too," he smiled, "but for some reason I didn't care."

"Perhaps it was that fourth martini," Elizabeth teased. "Well, we are only human, and you have a very admirable ass."

"Dr. Bennet," he waggled his eyebrows playfully, "I believe you're flirting with me."

"Is that not allowed, Fitzwilliam? I don't remember our establishing any rules regarding flirting."

The name Fitzwilliam rolled off her tongue, the "z" hanging in his ear before running down his spine to settle somewhere decidedly south of his belt. "Perhaps we should. The first is that you should not call me Fitzwilliam. It does *things* to me."

"*Things?*" she asked innocently.

"Yes, *things*." The look in his eyes told her exactly what *things* meant.

"All right. Then you have to stop looking as if you're mentally undressing me," she countered. "That does *things* to me."

A look of mock pain crossed his face. "That is too much to ask. Mentally undressing you has become my favorite pastime."

She raised an eyebrow in warning. "Now who's flirting?"

"All right! All right. I promise to try, but it won't be easy. Now I think we should continue to dance together as we look *fabulous* when we dance." Elizabeth had to laugh at his comical pronunciation of the word "fabulous."

"Agreed. I hope you will not object to occasional handholding." She brought attention to the fact that he was, at that moment, holding her hand.

"My, my," he said confusedly as he held up their clasped hands, "when did that happen?" He quickly kissed her hand. "As I have to give up mentally undressing you, I refuse to part with the right to hold your hand."

He became serious as he rubbed his thumb along her knuckles. "Elizabeth, we can't fall in love. It would ruin everything." She knew the warning was for her, and she took it seriously. "It should be our most important rule," he continued, "never to be broken."

"Yes. The most important," she agreed. "Now purely to satisfy my curiosity, just exactly what is your problem with falling in love?"

"Love makes people do foolish things. For example, one moment a man is a pillar of respectability, and then he falls in love. The next thing he knows, he is reduced to a sop called 'Muffin,' 'Sweetie Pie' or 'Pumpkin.'"

Elizabeth couldn't suppress her laughter any longer. "I can't imagine anyone calling you 'Pumpkin.'"

"Thank you," he said appreciatively.

"No, I think 'Baby' is much better suited to you," she teased.

"Baby!" he exclaimed, "Let me assure you there is positively nothing infantile about me."

"It has nothing to do with infants. I can only imagine that if a woman fell in love with you, she would want to sing to you all the time. The endearment used most in music is 'Baby.' For example," here Elizabeth softly sang, *Be my be my baby, My one and only Baby,…*[14]

Darcy was enchanted. Never before had the name 'Baby' sounded so perfect, and he fleetingly considered the legal requirements to have his name permanently changed.

"Of course," Elizabeth added, "I won't be singing that song to you since we are not allowed to fall in love."

"No, of course not," Darcy reached through the haze of alcohol to change the subject. "Now the ban on sex is obvious, but what do you say to a little harmless kissing?"

She gave him a most seductive smile before leaning in slowly. He lowered his face in anticipation as she drew close. Suddenly she diverted her aim and placed a quick kiss on the tip of his nose. "Good night, my most excellent friend." And with that, she disappeared inside the building.

Darcy turned around to find Sparks still standing beside the open door of the limo, eyes discreetly diverted and no expression on his face. "Yes, Mr. Sparks! To Lansing, please." He hesitated on his way into the seat and then lowered his voice, "Perhaps you can find an all night chemist we could stop at first."

Darcy was quickly in and out of the *Duane Rheade's Pharmacy* and sat

---

14 "Be My Baby", by Jeff Barry, Ellie Greenwich and Phil Spector, 1963

agitated in the back of the limo. "Is everything all right, sir?" Sparks asked.

With the last martini firmly in the driver's seat of his brain, Darcy blurted out, "Three ounces, Mr. Sparks! Have you ever heard of anything more ridiculous in your life?"

"Three ounces of what, sir?"

"Here in the States you sell everything in obscenely large quantities, and yet I cannot find personal lubricant in an amount greater than three ounces! Why?"

Sparks was completely at a loss, and yet it was clear Mr. Darcy was expecting some kind of response. "Sir?" was the only thing he could think of to say.

"Men masturbate!" Darcy exclaimed as if it was the most obvious answer. "From the morning after their first wet dream until the day the nurse takes their Viagra away, men masturbate!"

Sparks offered up his stoic expression and standard answer, "Yes, sir."

As Mr. Darcy began humming a song Sparks vaguely remembered from the first *Austin Powers*[15] movie, the driver began to catalogue all the firsts he had experienced with this particular employer that evening. Mr. Darcy was clearly drunk, he had filled the limo with people he had met in a bar, and he had left Sparks waiting outside while he talked to Dr. Bennet (not that Mr. Sparks minded; the conversation was quite entertaining). Finally, there was the rather one-sided discussion on the way back to Lansing. (Sparks felt it best not to dwell on that one for too long, for one cannot drive while engaged in hysterical laughter.)

His opinions on the availability of gallon-sized bottles of personal lubricant aside, (Did Mr. Darcy not Google? Sparks was sure there was nothing one could not find on the Internet.) Sparks' conclusion was that it appeared Mr. Darcy had finally learned to loosen up.

---

15 *Austin Powers: International Man of Mystery*: directed by Jay Roach, written by Mike Myers, released 1997

CHAPTER 12
A QUIET AFTERNOON

September 22nd, Celebrity Watcher (U.S.)
Photo caption: Fitzwilliam Darcy and Elizabeth Bennet dancing at the
nightclub tJean's in New York City.
Story: Last night Fitz Darcy hit the town with his ladylove, Elizabeth Bennet.
The evening began when Elizabeth performed a racy rendition of "I Touch
Myself" for her man. Witnesses reported that later the two were spied kissing
passionately in a secluded corner. Oh behave!!!

At about eight the next morning, Elizabeth was happily perfecting her favorite art form while fantasizing about her very best friend when the phone rang. She checked the caller ID, blushed profusely and then answered, "Daddy?"

"Good morning, Lizzybear! How is my favorite girl this morning?"

Their standing arrangement was that she would call him every Sunday morning. That Tom Bennet had called her and on a different day of the week was beginning to break through her thoughts. "Daddy, is everything all right?"

"Of course it is. Can't your old man call you?"

"I guess so." His response had not alleviated her suspicions. "So how are things in Hunsford?"

"Mary e-mailed a sermon to me this week about the danger of red meat to my eternal soul. Kit appears to be majoring in frat drinking instead of history, and as for Lydia…I found a young man trying to crawl out of her bedroom window last night. So in other words, there's nothing new in Hunsford. You still have three of the silliest sisters in the country."

"And how are you?"

"Missing you very much…and Jane, too, of course. There hasn't been a word of sense spoken in this house since the two of you moved out eight years ago."

Elizabeth could hear the loneliness in his voice. "You can always come to New York. I've got plenty of room and we can spend a few days playing chess and arguing over Nietzsche. You have colleagues you can visit over at NYU, and perhaps we can get Jane to stop wrestling with straitjackets long enough to come over for a dinner or two. I promise that, whatever we cook, it will involve a great deal of red meat."

She heard her father sigh heavily. "You know how difficult it is for me to leave the library. We have a new shipment of colonial manuscripts coming in soon, and there's no one else I can trust them to." After an uncomfortable lull in the conversation, Tom said, "While I've got you on the line, I wanted to ask about that young man I've seen you with in the papers."

"Ask what, Dad?"

The lightness disappeared from Tom Bennet's voice. "Do you know about that man, Lizzy? Are you aware of his reputation?"

Elizabeth always felt a little irritated whenever her father tried to be protective. Something like "too little, too late" always came to mind, and she didn't want him, or anyone for that matter, to worry about her anymore. "I know that he's a man who has done many great things. Did you read about the work of his family's foundation, about his attaining CEO of a financial empire or about his work with Amnesty International?"

"Lizzy, you know very well I'm asking if you are aware of his reputation with women."

"I am aware," Elizabeth said soothingly. "You don't know him, Dad. He's a good man and a good friend."

"Well, just be careful. I don't want you to get hurt."

"I know, Daddy. I'll be careful."

As rest of the conversation proceeded as usual, Elizabeth knew her father felt satisfied. He had done his fatherly duty in issuing his warning about Darcy, and now he could go back to his books without feeling any guilt.

DARCY AND ELIZABETH MET UP at the fencing club after she had finished her classes at the Community Center. Elizabeth was surprised that he practiced with her so often as he was clearly a far better fencer; however, she was learning a great deal from their sessions, and he seemed to enjoy himself, too. After a quick shower, they walked back to her co-op for lunch.[16]

When Elizabeth told Darcy that the security in her building was tight, she was not exaggerating. Upon entering the reception area, Elizabeth introduced Darcy to Mr. Anthony, known as "Tony." Tony was the head of security for the building, and he immediately required Darcy to show identification and sign in as Elizabeth's guest. As Darcy was expected to be a repeat visitor, an electronic file was established with his picture so that he would not need to go through the entire process each time he came to visit. Instead of being annoyed at the process, Darcy commented that he felt more at ease about Elizabeth's safety, knowing it would be very difficult for the paparazzi to gain entrance to her co-op.

Elizabeth's co-op was purchased with the majority of her trust fund, and she was very proud of it, even though it was far less elegant than any of Darcy's homes. She gave him a tour beginning with the long hall that began at her front door and ran the length of the unit. The first doorway opened to a large living room, where at one end was a red sectional sofa facing a cabinet that held her television and entertainment center. On the other side of the room was a parlor grand piano along with a number of guitars and violins all resting on display stands. The second door led to an eat-in kitchen, the third to a small bathroom and the fourth to a spare bedroom. The last door led to Elizabeth's bedroom.

"I'm a little nervous to show you this room," she admitted.

"Why?" he teased, "Is this where you keep all your black market wine?"

"No," she laughed, opening the door to admit them. "You're just overly fastidious and I've yet to tidy up in here today."

"I am not overly fastidious." He sat on her unmade bed to prove his point.

"Darcy," she said pointedly, "you neatly fold your napkin when you've finished eating and you keep a coaster on your desk for your coffee mug!"

He groaned in defeat as he lay back on her bed. He noted the soft yellow

---

16 An apartment building or a group of dwellings owned by a corporation, the stockholders of which are the residents of the dwellings. It is operated for their benefit by their elected board of directors. In a cooperative, the corporation or association owns title to the real estate. http://www.azpropertypro.com/glossary.html

walls, white wainscoting and blue and white striped bedding. The bedding smelled of Elizabeth and he resisted the urge to bury his face into it and inhale deeply. Instead he spread out his arms and looked up at the ceiling, "So, this is where all the magic *doesn't* happen."

Elizabeth could not help but laugh; however, a smart remark like that could not go unpunished. He received a red decorative pillow to the face. "Ouch," he exclaimed and then realized from how far away the pillow was thrown. "Good shot!"

"Oh, I'm a very accomplished woman. I throw pillows, tease masterfully and even manage to cook a passable pasta primavera."

He looked entirely too comfortable in her bed, and Elizabeth had to admit, the idea of joining him was very appealing. Like everything else he wore, his jeans and sweater fit him perfectly, and his amazing body lying among her blankets reminded her too much of her fantasies for comfort. She needed to retreat to more neutral territory. "Let's go; you can help me with lunch."

"Are you kidding? I'm still a little hung-over from last night, and your bed feels too good to get out of." He kicked off his shoes and swung his feet up onto the mattress. "Wake me when lunch is ready."

Oh God! He looks so … delicious! Elizabeth felt her breath begin to quicken. "Fitzwilliam Darcy, get out of my bedroom!"

"With an attitude like that, young lady, it is no wonder you're a virgin." He was rewarded for that remark with another pillow to the face.

She retorted, "I prefer the term 'sexually challenged,'" as another pillow landed in his face.

"You have deadly aim," he complained.

"Yes, and at least three more pillows," she pointed out.

Reluctantly he rose and followed her into the hall. Elizabeth prepared lunch while Darcy sat at the counter and entertained her with stories of his childhood at Pemberley. After the third story, she started to recognize a pattern.

"So from your point of view, Geoff, Richard and George were the instigators of all your misadventures, while you, Charles and Caroline were dragged along against your wills?"

"Precisely!" He smiled like an innocent cherub.

"Like that little discussion you and Geoff had outside my office on the day we met? That was entirely Geoff's fault."

"The perfect example!" he agreed.

"So your comment about my breasts being real was scripted by Geoff, who then held a gun to your head and forced you to say it?" She knew she had him when he shut his eyes and gritted his teeth.

"I concede." He held his hands up in defeat. "You are the master!"

She handed him the plates and flatware[17] to place on the table. "And don't you forget it."

After lunch, she surprised him with a rugby game she'd TiVoed the night before.

"That," she announced as she entered the living room with his Guinness, "is my seat!" In her absence, he had taken the corner seat of the sectional sofa, his long legs resting on the cushions in front of him.

Ignoring her statement, he stretched out his arms and settled back, "This is the most comfortable sofa I've ever sat on." He took his Guinness, and just before placing it on a coaster, he abruptly moved it slightly to the left, sitting it directly on the polished wood of the coffee table.

"All right," she conceded. "You are not fastidious! Now please put your drink back on the coaster."

He smiled and did as he was asked. "Guinness and rugby! Charles and Geoff will be green with envy!"

Elizabeth said nothing but looked again at his location on her sofa with a frown. He continued to tease her. "I believe it is considered proper etiquette to give your guest the most comfortable seat available." When she grimaced in response, he relented. "All right, I'll share, but you're a lousy hostess."

"Sue me," she suggested as she happily snuggled in next to him.

As he explained the rules of the game, Elizabeth sipped her merlot and tried to follow the action. After awhile the game became rather one-sided and Darcy became more interested in his friend than the match. He began stroking her arm where his hand rested, marveling at how smooth the silk of her blouse felt beneath his fingers.

Elizabeth sighed contentedly as she allowed her head to relax into his shoulder. "You are not only an excellent friend, but also an excellent pillow. I haven't been this comfortable in ages." Elizabeth stifled a yawn. "As I didn't get much sleep last night, I hope you'll forgive me if I drift off."

"Go ahead," he offered. "I'm not going anywhere."

Elizabeth turned her body toward him and draped her arm across his chest.

---

17 knives, forks and spoons

"Please wake me when the game is over. I never thought watching a bunch of buff men in little shorts, rolling around in the mud and sticking their heads in each other's crotches could be so boring."

"This was a very nice surprise, Elizabeth. You are a great friend, even if you can't appreciate a fine game like rugby."

"Remind me to think of some cheeky comeback when I'm not so sleepy." The last thoughts that crossed her mind before she drifted off were that Darcy was warm, wore the softest cashmere sweater she'd every felt and smelled really, really good.

Darcy pulled a blanket off the back of the sofa and covered them both. Sitting with her tucked against him as if she had been custom-made to fit there, he noticed how clean her hair smelled and how beautiful she looked without makeup. He was struck by her thoughtfulness in recording the rugby match and picking up the Guinness. They were small gestures of friendship, but for so long Darcy felt as if he had to take care of everyone around him. He had forgotten how good it felt to have someone take care of him instead.

He also had to admit that cuddling on a sofa was not something he normally did with his other friends. All right, it was something he *never* did with his other friends. He quickly rationalized that he and Elizabeth were determined to create their own boundaries in their friendship and to hell with anyone who disapproved. He kissed her forehead and hugged her closer before joining her in a much-needed nap.

OUT OF ALL THE DREAMS she had had about Darcy — and she'd had plenty — this had to be the very best! He was lying beneath her as she began to kiss his neck lightly. He reacted slowly at first, as if emerging from sleep, and then she heard his low growl of pleasure. Elizabeth moved to kiss his perfectly chiseled chin, his beautiful dimples and the corners of his soft lips until he turned his face to kiss her slowly, tenderly. She stroked his lips with her tongue and he opened beneath her gentle assault. He tasted so very sweet, and as their tongues brushed against each other in thorough exploration, she could not prevent the sigh of contentment that escaped from her lungs. She never wanted to wake up as she felt his hands caressing her back, then reaching down to pull on her buttocks, bringing her entire body closer...

Abruptly his lips left hers. "Elizabeth, I don't think we're dreaming."

Her eyes flew open to find his but millimeters from her own. "Darcy!" she looked at the position of their bodies and pushed away. "I'm so sorry!" Flustered beyond words, she could not bear to look at him. "Excuse me; I need a moment!" was all she could squeak out before fleeing down the hall to her bedroom.

"Damn!" Darcy swore. Immediately missing the warmth of her body, he closed his eyes, trying to decide how he was going to fix this latest debacle while allowing time for his erection to subside. He walked down the hall to stand outside her bedroom door and was reminded of all the times he stood outside Georgiana's room when she was upset. He decided to try the same tactic he used with his sister: humor.

Inside her room, Elizabeth was mortified. How could she not have known she was actually kissing him! Horrified about what he might be thinking of her, she paced back and forth, knowing she could not remain in her room much longer and yet not knowing how to face him.

"Elizabeth, please open the door." Her head shot up in response to his voice. "Look, when I accidentally snogged Geoff, I did not go running off to my room and shut the door." His plan worked like a charm; she could not stifle her laughter.

A few seconds later, her door opened a few inches and he could see her smiling eyes. "Was Geoff a good kisser?"

"Gentlemen never kiss and tell."

"So, what did you do?"

Darcy gently pushed the door open. "We talked about it." He reached in, took her hand and led her back to the sofa. "Look, we know we're more than a little attracted to each other. We just need to be more careful."

"What you must think of me!" She turned her head away in embarrassment.

"I don't believe I was screaming 'rape,'" he reassured her, "I thought I was dreaming, too." He gently turned her face back to look at him. "I'm curious though. Where do virgins learn to kiss like that?"

"I've kissed men before. I've kissed you before," she reminded him, "and I'm a quick study."

"I've noticed that about you." He looked deep into her violet eyes and a sense of loss washed over him. "Someday the right man will walk into your life and become the luckiest bastard on the planet."

"Thanks," she replied. "You'll be sure to point this lucky bastard out to me when he finally makes an appearance." He was grateful to see her smile return as she stood to look out the window. "It's still light out. How about a walk?"

They walked in companionable silence, enjoying the tree-lined walkway and the bright clouds reflected in the river. The day was unseasonably cold with a brisk wind, so they had the park to themselves.

Back at her co-op, Darcy goaded her into playing for him. They sat together on the bench while she flawlessly played Mozart's Piano Concerto No. 13 from memory.

After accepting his praises, she turned the tables. "Now you play something for me."

"What makes you think I play?" Sometimes he suspected she could see inside his brain.

"The entire time I was playing, you were moving your foot along with mine on the pedals. Not only do you play, but you have played this particular piece... frequently!"

"I confess, I used to play a great deal before my parents died, but then I gave it up. There were just too many other obligations that had to take precedence."

Elizabeth refused to back down, demanding that he also play something from memory. When he finally relented, he played Andrew Lloyd Webber's *Pie Jesu-Requiem*. Like everything else he did, his execution of the song was perfect. When he finished, they both were very quiet, moved by the reverence of the music. He was still staring off into space when he began to speak softly. "I played this at my parents' memorial service. Of course, there I played it on the organ at Pemberley Church. My mother thought it was the most beautiful piece of music she'd ever heard."

"It is lovely," Elizabeth agreed. "You must have loved them very much."

"My mother had been battling breast cancer for several years before the doctors finally agreed that it was beyond hope. She didn't have much time left, so my father asked the Bingleys to join them at our family's villa on the Mediterranean for a last holiday. Of course, they never made it. There wasn't much left of their bodies in the wreckage — only enough for DNA identification. The day of the memorial service was the worst of my life, but I tried to take comfort from the fact that they died together and my mother was no longer suffering."

Elizabeth took his hand in a gesture of comfort. "I'm sorry I forced you to play the Requiem."

He turned to face her. "I wanted to play it, and I wanted to talk to you about my parents. It's amazing really. I never talked to anyone about it before." A small smile tugged at the corners of his mouth. "What is it about you, Elizabeth, that makes me want to open my soul to you?"

"Don't ask me; Jane's the shrink," she teased gently as she brushed the lone tear from his cheek.

"Now, it's your turn. We should lighten the mood by playing something happy." He began rummaging through her sheet music. "Hey, what's this?" Darcy brought Elizabeth's attention to the top of a piece he selected where it was clearly printed, *In Everyway Horrible, words and Music by E. Bennet and J. Austen.*

Elizabeth scowled, "That is hardly a 'happy' song. I'm told it's very 'emo.'"

Darcy was too impressed to care. "I have this on my iPod! Why didn't you tell me you wrote for Excessively Diverted. I've been a huge fan of theirs for at least ten years. And this song... Wow! It's got to be one of my all-time favorites."

"I wrote this song a long time ago," Here she paused before continuing, "the year before my last tour."

"This song is so depressing," he said, pointing to the music to emphasize his point. "You must have been miserable when you wrote it."

"Oh it was much worse before Jay Austen got a hold of it! I included this song in a portfolio of Alternative Rock songs I wrote for a British record company. Apparently, Jay Austen was so impressed he wanted his band to record it. His only stipulations were to change some of the lyrics and add an instrumental bridge. Jay said without those changes the song was too depressing, even for him!"

Elizabeth rarely spoke of her time as 'Bethy' Bennet so Darcy gave her his full attention, hoping she would continue. This day his patience was rewarded. "I poured all my hostility, anger and disappointment into this song. One day Frannie heard it and forbade me to play it ever again. Of course, that only made me play it constantly. Later, when I started questioning her management of my concert schedule, Frannie went to extremes to try to control me, but I knew that as long as I could play this song, I was still fighting."

Darcy's curiosity about Frannie was getting the better of him, "define extremes."

"She practically worked me to death. Late night concerts were followed by early morning radio or television appearances. I'd go for weeks without a day off and that was used to travel. It's not surprising my health deteriorated rapidly. I was hospitalized four times that last year. The lawsuits due to cancelled dates began to pile up, and Frannie's response was to try to fit in even more performances."

"Once, when I was performing in Sao Paulo, she tried to force me to give a private concert to some wealthy South American businessman during which more than music would be on the program." The look of shock on Darcy's face let her know he understood exactly what she meant. "So you see, 'Bethy' Bennet was beginning to implode long before that final dramatic collapse in Vienna."

Darcy's reaction was to try to comfort Elizabeth, but she pushed his arms away. "No, I don't want or need anyone's pity. I fought back the best way I could, and in the end, I persevered. Now I am in complete control of my life, and I refuse to be anyone's victim!"

Not knowing what to say or do, Darcy remained silent. Finally, Elizabeth let a small smile play at the corners of her mouth. "Whenever I feel angry about Frannie, I try to imagine her face every time she hears that song played on the radio."

"She really hates it?" Darcy asked conspiratorially, a devious smile on his lips.

"With a passion!" The sparkle had returned to Elizabeth's eyes.

Darcy added, "It really was rather overplayed when it first came out. I heard it everywhere I went, restaurants, shops…"

"Oh, yes," Elizabeth agreed, "I believe there's a Muzak[18] version playing in elevators all over the country by now!"

Darcy smiled broadly. "One can only hope!"

"Now," she closed the cover over the piano keys to signal the end of the discussion, "I've been reviewing our last chess game in my mind and I think I've figured out where I went wrong. Care to let me try again?"

"On one condition."

"And that is?"

"You get me Jay Austen's autograph."

After a very close chess match where Darcy again emerged the victor, Elizabeth sent him home so that she could grade a stack of compositions she had promised to return to her students that Monday. Darcy made his way back to Lansing where he planned to read through the mountain of e-mails he received each day as CEO of The Darcy Company and catch up on some much needed sleep.

---

18 Muzak is a satellite radio system that until recently was known primarily for providing "elevator music" (those annoying, soft rock, instrumental versions of popular songs) you could hear not only in elevators but in doctors offices and department stores. Today Muzak offers a wide range of music to its commercial customers, but is still trying to shake off that stodgy image.

He ate a late dinner in his study, and as he finished responding to his e-mails, he received an instant message.

RFitz: It's Sat night. Why r u @ home?

FDarcy: Late night last night. U should have seen. I danced & drank way 2 much.

RFitz: A man leaves civilization for a few months, and everything goes to hell!

FDarcy: Very funny! Where r u?

RFitz: If I told you, I'd have 2 kill you. You know the drill.

FDarcy: I know, but I had 2 ask.

RFitz: Saw pics of U&E. Hot!

FDarcy: FRIENDS!

RFitz: Looks like my kind of girl. Introduce us when I get back.

This made Darcy think for a moment. Elizabeth was exactly Richard's kind of girl: smart, funny and determined. Of all the men Darcy knew, Richard would be the one to respect her most and would have the patience to break through her defenses, and perhaps she could get Richard to give up his lifelong crush. Darcy knew he really should try to get them together.

FDarcy: Not your type. Met any women where u r?

RFitz: The only women I meet are dangerous. Definitely not my type.

FDarcy: Any idea when u r coming back?

RFitz: After the New Year, then I M home 4 good.

FDarcy: U r going to resign?

RFitz: Yes. Liz II can find someone else 2 save her arse 4 awhile.

FDarcy: R u all right? This doesn't sound like u.

RFitz: I M tired, hot & haven't slept in 3 days. I M getting way 2 old 4 this job.

FDarcy: U R only 30 for God's sake!

RFitz: That's ancient N this business.

FDarcy: What r ur plans?

RFitz: Hoping my filthy rich cousin will open a branch office 4 me N the Caribbean. Nothing 2 elaborate, just a chair on the sand with an endless supply of margaritas nearby.

FDarcy: I'll see what I can do.

RFitz: If u & E decide 2 do the deed, keep N mind that I've got 20 on the last week in December. I'd appreciate u holding out as I could use the cash when I get back.

FDarcy: Friends, Friends, FRIENDS!!!

RFitz: Me thinks the lad doth protest too much!

RFitz: g2g

FDarcy : Don't get shot.

RFitz: That's the idea.

Darcy crawled into bed that night reliving the amazing kisses Elizabeth had given him on her sofa. Whoever the lucky bastard was, Darcy hated him already...with a passion.

CHAPTER 13
A BLAST FROM THE PAST

October 15th, Celebrity Watcher (U.S.)
Photo caption: Elizabeth Bennet's co-op, located in this building in Manhattan, will soon be tagged "for sale."
Story: Sources have disclosed that Elizabeth Bennet is planning to place her spacious Manhattan co-op on the market as she prepares to move in with boyfriend Fitzwilliam Darcy...

October 21st, Celebrity Tattler (U.K.)
Photo caption: Fitzwilliam Darcy and Elizabeth Bennet enjoy the fall foliage during a stroll through Riverside Park, New York City.
Story: Hearts are breaking worldwide with the news that Fitzwilliam Darcy has proposed to Elizabeth Bennet. Friends of the couple say that an early June wedding is planned in the bride's hometown of Hunsford, North Carolina and that Vera Wang has offered to design a lavish wedding gown reminiscent of Princess Diana.....

November 2nd, New York Society Weekly
Picture: Elizabeth Bennet in Charlotte Lucas at the Longbourn Annual Benefit Gala. Jewels by Harry Winston.
Story:.... Among the many prominent contributors present was Mr. Fitzwilliam Darcy escorting Longbourn's own Dr. Elizabeth Bennet. Dr. Bennet was resplendent in an ivory lace gown.... With her easy grace and shining wit, Dr. Bennet was warmly welcomed into the higher echelons of society....

"W hat's this?" Darcy asked, pulling a bundle of newspapers and magazines from his briefcase. "I most certainly did not put these in here."

Elizabeth glanced over the top of her computer screen. "I suspect your sister has again decided that we need to see the latest tabloids."

Darcy dug farther into his briefcase and finally extracted a flash drive, "This was what I was looking for. I was up working on these specifications until about 1 a.m., so I'm not sure what kind of shape the format is in, but the figures should be accurate."

To amuse himself while Elizabeth checked his spreadsheet, Darcy opened *New York Society Weekly* and propped his feet up on the desk. He was tired, but it was a good sort of tired, the kind that came from working hard and seeing progress.

Between his usual workload as CEO of The Darcy Company and working with Elizabeth on the set up of their project, he had been putting in a string of sixteen-hour days. However, he was not complaining. Elizabeth worked as hard as he did and the project set-up was coming along nicely. He turned to a page in the magazine that Georgiana had strategically marked with a yellow post-it to find a splendid photograph of Elizabeth in her evening gown and read the story beneath.

"Congratulations!" Darcy removed his feet from the top of Elizabeth's desk so that he could lean forward to show her the article. "You are now a member of the higher echelons of society. Before you know it you'll be taking tea with the Vanderbilts, attending charity luncheons with the Gettys…"

Elizabeth again briefly glanced over the top of her laptop before she resumed typing. "What? No Trumps or Hiltons?"

"The Trumps and Hiltons are new money. Certainly not worth your notice, *dahling*!"

Elizabeth laughed. "I was only welcomed because no one wanted to offend you and your billions. As soon as they realize we're not engaged, all those in-vitations will evaporate. Not that I mind. I'm not sure I really fit in."

"You underestimate yourself, Elizabeth. You were charming, intelligent and," he turned a page to point out a photograph of the two of them together, "you make me look damn good standing next to you!"

Elizabeth promptly grabbed the magazine and bopped Darcy on the back of the head with it. "You're enjoying this way too much! Did you at least try to tell anyone we're not engaged?"

"Do you think I should have spent my evening walking up to anyone who would listen and say, 'Look here old boy; that Bennet woman and I are not engaged?'" He harrumphed with indignation before continuing. "The few people who were rude enough to ask about the lack of a 'rock' on your left hand were told the truth. Is it my fault no one believed me?" He turned back to the magazine. "I must admit it was very pleasant not having every eligible debutante in the city thrust at me."

Elizabeth smiled at him indulgently, knowing how much he despised all the attention they had received that night. "I think my naked hand attracted more attention then the jewels around my neck. The necklace was exquisite. I hope you returned it to Harry Winston's unscathed."

"Have no fear; it has been taken care of." He reached out to take her hand. "You were by far the loveliest woman at the gala, Elizabeth. And for the first time I actually enjoyed myself at one of those parties. Thank you again for agreeing to go."

"As William Lucas' new 'money magnet,' I would have had to go anyway. Speaking of Lucas, we're meeting with him on Friday, and I'm sure he'll be far more interested in our report than our social lives."

"Of course I will!" William Lucas chose that moment to walk into Elizabeth's office. "How goes it?"

Elizabeth watched Darcy's transformation with amusement. Gone was the warm and funny friend of a few seconds ago, replaced by the cold and haughty man she had met three months before. "Dr. Bennet and I have made a great deal of progress, and we shall comfortably meet your deadline."

"Capitol!" Lucas expounded. Glancing at the magazine on Elizabeth's desk he added, "The Gala was a resounding success. Thanks to you two, we have had more than the usual amount of press coverage, which cannot help but increase short-term donations. When a certain *desirable event* takes place, the school will benefit even more so." William Lucas gave them both a knowing look.

"Bill," Elizabeth said with exasperation, "Darcy and I are not engaged."

"No, of course not," Lucas said with a wink. "I'll see both of you on Friday."

As soon as they were alone again, Darcy's severe expression melted away into a devastating smile. "See what I mean?"

Elizabeth could not help but chuckle. "How about a break? We've been at this since seven this morning, and it's now nearly eleven."

Darcy closed the lid on his laptop. "I'm starving. Let's take an early lunch."

They were talking as they approached the doors, and therefore were taken completely by surprise when, upon reaching the outside, they were assaulted by a sea of reporters and cameramen all shouting and pushing each other in an attempt to get closer to the couple. A few overwhelmed security guards were trying to keep the paparazzi in order, but were having little effect. One guard grabbed Elizabeth by the arm and forced them both back inside the building.

"What's happened?" Darcy impatiently asked the frazzled guard.

"We don't know," he replied shaking his head. "They just started showing up about ten minutes ago. Whatever it is, they are willing to risk being arrested to get to the two of you."

"What about the police?"

"They'll come as soon as they can. Apparently, there's a large fire in the Village at the moment, so they're tied up. You should be all right inside this building until they can get here." The guard returned to his post outside the door as Elizabeth and Darcy walked back to her office.

"What could it be?" Elizabeth asked with a twinkle of amusement in her eyes. "Has anything like this happened to you before?"

"No." Darcy's steely expression communicated his frustration. "Whatever has happened, it can't be good. Let's see if Frank knows anything."

Once inside, Darcy called Frank Churchill, placing the call on speakerphone so Elizabeth could hear.

Frank sounded more than a little exasperated when he took the call. "My phone has been ringing off the hook for the last forty minutes. Are you familiar with a New York 'shock jock' named Walter Elliot?"

Darcy had no clue but Elizabeth had heard of him from talk around the city. Elliot had joined the list of radio disc jockeys who used inflammatory material to attract their audience.

"Apparently less than an hour ago, Dr. Bennet's mother was a guest on his radio show, and the things that she said were rather…disturbing. The station has already set up a link on their website on which you can listen to the broadcast in its entirety. I think it would be best for you to check it out there than for me to try to describe what was said. Quite frankly, not even I have the stomach to repeat some of the things Mrs. Bennet said."

"All right, Frank. Once I've had a chance to check it out, I'll contact you, and we'll map out a PR strategy for damage control." Darcy looked at Elizabeth.

All the color had drained from her face, and she was staring blankly ahead, her breathing rapidly increasing. Alarmed, he ended the call.

"Elizabeth." When at first she didn't respond, he knelt before her, took her arms and gently shook her. "Elizabeth!"

Finally, she seemed to become aware of her surroundings. "Take me home, please! Can you take me home?" She sounded frightened, which only increased Darcy's alarm. He had never known a woman as strong as Elizabeth, and to see her so devastated was nearly more than he could bear.

He called Fred Wentworth, head of security for The Darcy Company, who arranged for a small army of bodyguards to aid in getting them out of Longbourn, into the Darcy limo and then into Elizabeth's building. It was a harrowing experience. The press of bodies as they made their way out of the building was awful. The limo pulled away to the incessant clicking of cameras and shouts of questions from reporters. A similar crowd waited outside Elizabeth's co-op building. Once inside the building, Darcy remained in the lobby to receive an update from both the bodyguards and Mr. Anthony.

Soon the police arrived and set up barriers to keep the front of the building clear, but the reporters simply set up camp in the park across the street. Darcy and Elizabeth were essentially trapped in her home.

When Darcy finally entered the co-op, he found Elizabeth sitting on one end of her sofa while Jane, who had arrived before them, sat at the other. He was puzzled at the physical distance between the two women. As close as they were, he expected to find Elizabeth wrapped in Jane's arms. Both had untouched cups of tea sitting in front of them and stared at Elizabeth's laptop, which was open on the coffee table.

Elizabeth looked to Darcy anxiously. "Georgiana?"

Darcy immediately sat beside Elizabeth and took her hands. "She's fine at Longbourn. I have a bodyguard escorting her around campus. Are you all right?"

It took a moment for her to respond, and then she took a deep breath and pointed to the laptop. On the screen was the radio station's website, complete with a large picture of Walter Elliot, a gaudy advertisement for Gowland's Lotion and the link to the interview with Frannie Bennet. "I was waiting for you," she said softly.

"You don't have to do this, Elizabeth. I can listen to it and then speak to Frank." Darcy looked to Jane for support but found her eyes averted to the other side of the room. Again, Darcy was puzzled.

Elizabeth shook her head. "I need to know what she said. I just wanted to be someplace I felt comfortable first." Darcy knew the look of determination on Elizabeth's face. There was no way he could convince her to wait until the shock wore off.

He squeezed Elizabeth's fingers gently and then reached over to the laptop and clicked on the link, bracing himself for the worst.

Elliot: Anybody who has at least one eye in their head and the ability to peruse a supermarket tabloid knows that British Billionaire Brat, Fitzwilliam Darcy, has a new plaything, Elizabeth Bennet, formerly known as Bethy Bennet. Rumors are flying concerning this newest attention-seeking, celebrity couple who, as usual, will not speak directly to the press but instead leak every detail of their private life to keep public interest. They claim to be 'only friends.' Well, we all know that really means they are trying to keep the wedding a secret, and Bennet is probably already knocked up.

Today, I have here in my studio the mother of Elizabeth Bennet, Mrs. Frances Bennet. Good morning, Mrs. Bennet.

Frannie: Oh, dear. Please call me Frannie. Mrs. Bennet is my ex-mother-in-law! Believe me, you've never met a bigger pain in the (beep). Oh, dear! Can I say (beep) on the radio?

Elliot: Sure, why not... So tell us, what's the 411[19] on your daughter and Fitz Darcy?

Frannie: You've got to be kidding! I doubt very much that Bethy is intimate with that young man. It's a pity; he is delicious! No, my Bethy is quite frigid, of that I'm sure. Why even when she was a teenager, she didn't believe in having sex. She toyed with the feelings of a number of young men in Hunsford.

Elliot: You're telling us that Fitzwilliam Darcy, Britain's 'Model Man,' is dating a woman who won't have sex with him? Now Frannie, that's a bit too much to believe!

Frannie: I know my own daughter, Walter. I can call you 'Walter,' can't I? You are just such a handsome man, such lovely skin. How do you keep your face so smooth?

Elliot: Well, I do take very good care of myself... but getting back to Bethy. Are you telling us they are not really engaged?

Frannie: Oh heavens no! Trust me, this Darcy must be gay and using Bethy to cover it up. The really handsome men always are, except you of course, Walter.

---

19 The numbers dialed on a telephone to get an operator to find out a telephone listing, also known as "Information." It has become a slang term for the word "information."

Elliot: Is that what your daughter told you? That Fitz Darcy is gay?

Frannie: No, silly. Bethy hasn't spoken to me in over six years. Can you imagine? Such a selfish, heartless girl to abandon her mother after everything I did for her. I was her manager, you know, when she was famous.

Elliot: So if you haven't talked to her in over six years. How can you claim to know the details of her relationship with Fitzwilliam Darcy?

Frannie: Walter, dear, an elephant never changes his stripes and Bethy will die a cold, self-righteous virgin.

Elliot: Frannie, I don't believe elephants have stripes.

Frannie: Spots, I meant spots.

Elliot: Spots? Now Frannie, you really should keep your hands to yourself....

Elizabeth stood up. "I've heard enough. Excuse me."

"Of course," Darcy replied, again baffled that Jane did not follow Elizabeth back to her bedroom but remained on the sofa. The remainder of the interview was simply more of Frannie's outrageous flirting with Walter Elliot, who despite his protests, sounded like he was enjoying it immensely.

Darcy turned off the computer and looked to Jane who now sat with her head in her hands. He asked in exasperation, "How could your mother do such a thing?"

Jane sighed heavily and sat back, looking up to the ceiling. "My mother was not always like this. When I was very little, she was a wonderful mother. Then when I was six and Lizzy was four, she was in a very bad car accident. She suffered from severe head injuries, spent months in a coma, and when she came home, she was different. We didn't begin to suspect the danger of those changes until Lizzy's collapse. Momma has apparently lost the ability to tell right from wrong, and that makes her behave in ways we don't understand."

"Can't she be locked away or something? The woman is a menace!"

Darcy was surprised at the anger in Jane's voice, "My mother is sick and needs help. With proper treatment, she can get better. Simply locking her up will solve nothing!" Jane stood up. "I'm going to check on Lizzy."

To say Darcy was taken aback would be an understatement. He could not believe that Jane was defending her mother after what she had said about her sister on the radio before millions of people. Darcy began to regret calling Jane and asking her to meet them at the co-op. He had expected Jane would help Elizabeth deal with this crisis; instead, they couldn't even look at one another. Apparently, the only thing that could come between the inseparable Bennet sisters was their mother.

Darcy made a call to Frank Churchill and then called Sparks to bring him an overnight bag. He didn't know how long Elizabeth was going to need him, but he would be prepared. Then he called Bingley who by then had heard about the interview and was frantic because he couldn't get through to Jane.

Jane emerged alone from Elizabeth's room and approached him apprehensively. "I'm sorry, Darcy. I should not have snapped at you. I appreciate that you're here for Lizzy."

During the past five weeks, Darcy had come to like Jane. She was warm and friendly and loved her sister unconditionally. It appeared that that was how Jane loved everyone, including her mother. Seeing the vulnerability in her eyes, Darcy reached out to comfort Jane. She responded by breaking down in tears. "I can't do this," Jane sobbed. "Lizzy's trying not to hurt my feelings, and I'm trying to support her without betraying my mother. I'm not helping either of us."

Darcy allowed her to cry until she composed herself.

"I have patients to see," Jane announced as she broke away and picked up her coat. "If I stay here, I'll just make things worse. Will you stay with Lizzy tonight? She'll try to send you away, but please promise me you'll stay anyway."

Darcy promised and then added, "You should call Charles. He's worried sick about you."

Jane smiled through her tears. "I thought you would be angry with me."

"I can't say I understand, but I know Elizabeth wouldn't want me to be judgmental. In fact, she'd be furious if I was."

Jane attempted a small smile in response and then left with a promise to call that evening. Darcy made a few more calls before walking back down the hall to knock gently on the door to Elizabeth's bedroom. When she didn't respond, he entered to find her on her bed, curled up in a fetal position, staring blankly at the wall.

Every protective instinct within Darcy rose to the surface. He gently lay down on the bed behind her and touched her shoulder. She stiffened in response, and he could feel her body's war to control her emotions. "I'm all right," she insisted. "You can go home now."

Darcy knew it was pointless to argue with her. She was the only person he knew who could match him when it came to being stubborn. Therefore, he tried a different tact. "Just humor me and let me stay? Besides, while it appears that there is no way for either you or I to avoid those vultures, if we stay here together, the press will be diverted away from Lansing and Georgie." She sighed and let him put his arm around her waist.

After a few minutes, he felt it was safe to say what he thought. "You don't have to be so brave all the time, Elizabeth. There's no shame in crying."

She took a huge gulp of air before responding, "I don't cry! Not ever!"

"Of course not," he replied indulgently, remembering the tears she'd shed in Gracechurch Street.

Darcy held her tightly, trying to give her all the comfort he felt she needed. He was eventually rewarded when he felt her body relax against his. They lay there for sometime before Elizabeth spoke. Her words were so quiet he could barely hear her.

"I went to live with the Gardiners after Vienna. A few months later, I went back to Hunsford to visit my family before I was to go to my grandmother's home for the summer. Frannie was surprisingly nice to me. She took me to lunch and shopping. I was so happy that I didn't want to question her motives, I just wanted to enjoy having a mother who cared for me."

"Billy Ray Collins was very popular with the teenage girls in Hunsford, so I was shocked when he asked me out on a date. At first, I said no as every instinct I had told me he was trouble. Even Jane agreed with me until Momma suggested it be a double date with Jane and her boyfriend. Trying not to disrupt the pleasant relationship I seemed to have developed with Momma, I finally relented.

"Billy Ray picked me up. We were supposed to pick up Jane at the mall where she worked and then pick up her date before heading out to a movie. It didn't take long for me to realize we weren't headed towards the mall. I demanded Billy Ray tell me where he was taking me, but he simply laughed and sped up the car. He made so many turns I had no idea where we were until finally he stopped at the end of a long dirt road. Then Billy Ray turned to me and said, 'You either part those lovely thighs for me or I'll leave you here and you'll have to find your own way home.'"

Darcy's grip tightened further around her waist as she continued, "I had no idea which way to go, but I bravely announced I'd find my own way home. Billy Ray was less than pleased with my answer and expressed his disappointment with his fist, repeatedly. Somehow, I got out of the car and tried to get away but he caught up with me. Eventually I was lying on the ground with Billy Ray standing over me, unbuttoning his jeans. I'll never forget the words he said, 'Frannie told me I should be prepared for you to put up a fight, but, I was determined to have you for my birthday. Now it's time to unwrap my present.'"

Darcy could not hold back his astonishment. "Your mother gave you to him ... for his birthday?"

"Yes," Elizabeth paused for a few moments before continuing, "but Frannie also gave me a present. The day before, she had bought me a pair of four-inch heels that she insisted I wear to impress Billy Ray. I impressed him, by God. I was dazed from the beating, but I could still pull back my foot and slam a heel with all my might into Billy Ray's testicles. As he lay writhing in pain on the ground, I got up and stumbled into the woods as far as I could until I collapsed against a tree. Eventually I could hear Billy Ray trying to find me, but the woods were too thick and it was getting dark so he gave up and drove off.

"I stumbled around all night. At daylight, I finally found a paved road and followed it until I saw a police car that had pulled someone over for speeding. I was taken to the hospital, and Billy Ray was arrested. Billy Ray had no scruples in implicating Frannie. That was when he revealed that they had been lovers since Frannie returned from Vienna. He was seventeen years old.

"Billy Ray's family was very powerful in Kent County. It was circulated that I tried to seduce Billy Ray, and when he didn't cooperate, I goaded him into hitting me so that I could extort money from his family. Even when several other girls in town came forward with claims similar to mine, the Collins family insisted on my guilt and his innocence. Therefore, it came as a shock when he suddenly pleaded guilty. Billy Ray received ten years in prison, and Frannie was sent off to a mental hospital where she stayed for nearly two years.

"My father could no longer deny my mother's failings both as a mother and as a wife. He filed for divorce and received full custody of my younger sisters. Jane, of course, was already eighteen. I petitioned the court and was awarded the status of an emancipated minor. I went back to London and the Gardiners until I started at Longbourn that fall. End of story."

Darcy was too stunned for words. The entire tale was so incredible; if he hadn't known Elizabeth so well, he would have been tempted to think she was exaggerating. However, Elizabeth was the most honest person he knew. No, it had to all be true. "I'm so sorry."

"No," she whispered vehemently, "I don't want anyone's pity. Please, anything but that. Billy Ray was the catalyst that forced me into karate classes. I refused to allow any man to ever have the ability to take physical advantage of me again." She let out a small chuckle. "Not even you, Fitzwilliam Darcy."

He smiled as he recalled his rather abrupt acquaintance with the wall in the foyer of the Gardiner's house. "I suppose I should be grateful you left my bollocks intact."

"I knew you didn't want to hurt me." This time her chuckle was a little lighter. "You just wanted to fuck me."

"Still do," his voice teased playfully while his body reminded him there was far more honesty in that response than he would care to admit.

"Well at least Frannie's little stunt today accomplished one thing: I'm in bed with a gorgeous man. She would be so proud." She laughed mirthlessly at that. The room was once again still as both were lost in their thoughts.

Once again Elizabeth broke the silence. "I had to tell you everything after what happened today. I'm sorry I waited so long to tell you that my mother was capable of such things or that there was a man in prison who wants very much to kill me when he gets out in a few years. I've been preparing for when some part of my past would come back to haunt me. Only now, it's haunting you too, and you have every right to be furious. You should go. Run as far away from me as you can possibly get."

"I'll do no such thing," Darcy whispered into her ear. "You don't think I'm going to allow a few photographers to bother me? I'm used to it."

"Frannie? You're used to things like Frannie? What she said about you…"

"Shhhh." Darcy gently stroked her ribs through her T-shirt. "This is not the first time someone has accused me of being gay, and personally, I respect gays far too much to be insulted. I spoke to Frank again, and he said that according to the blogs he's checked, everyone thinks Frannie is simply grabbing attention, and no one is taking her seriously."

"But that won't stop Frannie from appearing on every news rag or celebrity gossip show she can get to. This will go on forever, and you and I will be hounded everywhere we go."

"It will be over sooner than you expect," Darcy offered. "Brad and Angelina will adopt another baby, or Paris and Britney will be arrested again, and the paparazzi will move on. They're like sharks. They cannot resist the smell of fresh blood." After a few more moments of silence, Darcy said, "I'm not being fair. No one would care about what Frannie had to say if it was not for me in your life. It's your decision. If you want me to go away, I will."

Elizabeth reached back behind her head to brush his cheek, "No. I don't want you to go."

"So, we'll ride out this storm together?"

Darcy could hear the smile in her voice. "Yes. Together."

He inhaled the scent of her perfume. Today it was a barely discernible mixture of orange blossom and ginger. Spicy, exotic and yet light and playful — it was a perfect description of the woman lying beside him. She wore this scent most days, he noticed, saving the Chanel for more formal occasions like the Longbourn Gala.

He thought she could not possibly be lovelier, but that night, as she descended the steps after checking her cloak, he felt completely overwhelmed by her. Reminiscent of Rhett Butler in *Gone with the Wind*, he stood in his tuxedo at the foot of the steps, drinking in the sight of Elizabeth as the lace train of the ivory strapless gown trailed behind her like a waterfall on the stairs. The necklace he had borrowed from Harry Winston's graced her throat; however, the pearls seemed to pale in luster to her skin, as the sapphires, which matched the broad navy sash at her waist, could not compare to the deep violet-blue of her eyes.

In that moment, Darcy felt he was in great danger of falling in love. He had been a fool to think that familiarity would lessen his attraction to Elizabeth. Each day he spent with her only served to increase the supreme torture of desiring what he could not take, but Darcy was not afraid. He found the danger intoxicating.

Now, as he lay beside her, a new understanding took hold. She had somehow permeated his every thought, his every dream and his every desire. Elizabeth was a part of him, as much as his hand, his head or his heart. *Damn!* It turned out he was an even larger fool than he had supposed. He was way beyond danger.

He loved her.

The realization washed over him in wave after wave of emotional pain. He wanted her, the complete surrender of her body and soul, and yet he knew he could not act upon that desire. Just as Elizabeth would never allow herself to be vulnerable by becoming a victim, he refused to allow himself to be vulnerable by being in love. As he now admitted he was hopelessly in love, his only defense was never to admit it to anyone else, especially Elizabeth.

It would be best for both of them if he went back to England. Georgiana was doing well; he was certain his help in that quarter was no longer necessary. If he created distance, both physical and mental, then when the *lucky bastard* finally arrived, it would be easier for Darcy to let go. Perhaps? Maybe?

No, he would not leave Elizabeth. He would continue to endure this torture indefinitely, for he could not bear the thought of living without the light and life she had brought to him. She was his air and water, sun and moon, earth and sky. Besides, had he not just promised her that he would stay? Darcy sighed in painful acceptance of his fate.

Elizabeth rolled toward him as her eyes fluttered open. When they focused on his face, she smiled and his heart lurched. "Hey," she said, reaching out to stoke his cheek with her fingertips.

"Hey," he said in return.

"You must be starving. I'm sorry I'm such a lousy hostess." He was grateful for her teasing. It wasn't in Elizabeth's nature to remain unhappy for long.

"I was just thinking that very thing. Here I am, the kind supportive friend, and this is how you reward me?"

"I adore you, you know," she said, having no idea the effect her words were having upon his equilibrium. "Thank you for everything you've done today. This would be so much more difficult without you."

"I adore you too," he admitted grudgingly, causing her to laugh. "Can I get you anything? A bottle of water, a glass of wine?"

"Both," she decided.

They ordered Chinese delivered, and Elizabeth insisted they pull out their laptops and get some work done. She maintained her sunny disposition, but Darcy was not fooled. There were long moments when she would be still and look off into nothing, and as much as it broke his heart to see these small signs of her distress, Darcy knew better than to bring attention to them. He waited until she was smiling again to find some small excuse to squeeze her hand or give her a hug. It was only late in the evening when they were again snuggled into the corner of her couch that she sought the comfort he so desperately wanted to give her. She still would not cry but held onto him tightly as if clinging for her very life.

Except for bodyguard-escorted trips to Longbourn, Elizabeth and Darcy stayed inside her co-op for over a week before Britney was indeed arrested again, and the whole flock of reporters seemed to move en masse to Los Angeles, leaving just a few diehard souls behind to track Darcy and Elizabeth.

CHAPTER 14

ABANDONED INTERVENTIONS

November 15th, Celebrity Watcher (U.S.)
Photo caption: Fitzwilliam Darcy and Elizabeth Bennet at the Breast Cancer Research Fundraiser last night in New York. Dress designed by Charlotte Lucas.
Story: Designers Declare War! Sources say a war is brewing between Vera Wang and newcomer Charlotte Lucas over the rights to design Elizabeth Bennet's wedding gown. Wang, designer to the stars, was rumored to be creating the gown, but Elizabeth's close friend, Lucas, has designed every dress she has worn publicly since first...

November 20th, The London Star Gazette (U.K.)
Photo caption: Fitzwilliam Darcy and Caroline Bingley dining in London's West End.
Story: Darcy Cheats! Sources close to Fitzwilliam Darcy have reported that he and Elizabeth Bennet have had a major blowup over his alleged infidelities with London Socialite, Caroline Bingley. The two are now residing on separate shores of the Atlantic and Darcy is no longer hiding his new infatuation with Caroline. An intimate friend of the family confided, "It's over with Eliza. A sophisticated man like Darcy could never be happy with a little college professor..."

Jane Bennet turned from her sister's laptop to tease dramatically, "I'm so sorry to hear about your breakup with Darcy. It must have been devastating!"

Elizabeth removed another Fellowship application from the scanner near her desk and muttered in annoyance, "Yes, now there's no reason for Charlotte to hate Vera Wang. I was *soooo* looking forward to a good catfight!"

Charlotte put down her coffee. "I may just take Vera down anyway. She's just too damn cute for her own good." It took Jane and Charlotte several seconds to realize Elizabeth had not joined in their laughter. The sudden silence that enveloped Elizabeth's office was deafening.

"Lizzy," Jane finally asked with concern, "you don't believe Darcy is actually dating Caroline?"

"Of course not," Elizabeth huffed as she slammed down the lid of her scanner. "I just can't believe the lengths to which that woman is willing to go. Darcy suspects she's hired someone to follow him. Given the frequency with which she has 'accidentally' run into him since he arrived in London, it's the only plausible explanation."

Elizabeth glanced over Jane's shoulder at the picture in the article. "Darcy said he was dining out with Geoff when a waiter 'accidentally' spilled a glass of red wine down Geoff's shirt. Not a moment after Geoff left for the men's room to clean up, Caroline 'coincidentally' appeared out of nowhere and a photographer 'conveniently' happened to be there to snap that picture."

"And let us not forget who it is that calls you 'Eliza' and refers to you as 'the Little College Professor,'" Charlotte added. "Wow! This woman is obsessed!"

"Charles has told me Caroline has been somewhat jealous of you," Jane said, reluctant to speak ill of her boyfriend's sister. "She's rather cold to me as well."

"God, I want to ring her scrawny neck," Elizabeth hissed, "for being rude to you and treating Darcy like some prey to be shot, bagged and gutted!" Both Charlotte and Jane were surprised by the degree of vehemence in Elizabeth's voice.

Elizabeth was tired. Darcy was in London on business, and although he had been gone less than a week, she missed him far more than she had anticipated. Each night she found herself lying awake, wishing she could curl up next to him again. The news report that morning only served to push her over the edge from irritable to thoroughly pissed off.

"Ah-ha! You're jealous!" Charlotte cried as if she had just discovered the meaning of life. "I told Jane you were crazy about Darcy! Just friends, my ass!"

Jane smiled sweetly. "I knew you were in love with him too, Lizzy. How long have you known?"

Not wanting to admit her feelings, let alone bring up the subject of Frannie's radio interview and the subsequent publicity whirlwind that followed, Elizabeth shooed her sister from in front of her laptop. "I promised to e-mail Darcy these applications. Why don't you two go ahead to lunch? I'll catch up with you shortly."

"Lizzy," Jane said indulgently, not about to let this opportunity pass by, "it's good to recognize your feelings; then, you can deal with them."

"I don't want to deal with them!" Elizabeth insisted. "I will never be more to Darcy than a very good friend. I have accepted that, Jane, and you have to accept it too."

"But he loves you, too! I see it; Charles sees it; *hell*, everyone sees it!"

"Hell?" Charlotte interrupted in surprise. Jane had never before cursed with any word more shocking than 'sugar.'

Elizabeth responded firmly, "You can see all you want, but I know what Darcy's said. He does not want a romantic relationship, and he most definitely does not want to fall in love. It is for the best that our friendship remains as it is."

Charlotte countered, "He hasn't so much as looked at another woman since at least August; if he had, it would have been all over the tabloids. He may not want to fall in love, but that doesn't mean he hasn't."

"And what about you, Lizzy?" Jane asked. "I know you haven't dated much in the past, but you haven't so much as looked at another man since you met Darcy."

"Jane! Charlotte!" Elizabeth had lost her patience, then immediately regretted her outburst. With a voice far gentler she said, "I am so happy when Darcy and I are together. He understands me on levels no one else can. I won't risk what I have for something that can never be. I know this is difficult for both of you, but you have to stay out of it. You have to trust me to make my own choices."

"But when it ends, what will you do?" The thought of Elizabeth with a broken heart was just too much for Jane to bear.

"I'm sure my friend will design me a lovely straight jacket and my sister will use her connections to find me a nice padded cell in which to wallow in my misery." Elizabeth tried to tease, but seeing Jane did not appreciate the joke, she added, "I am going to enjoy this while it lasts. I refuse to waste time thinking about how miserable I'll be when it's over. You must promise that neither of you will be angry with Darcy. I went into this with my eyes open, and he has done nothing wrong." After looking at the long faces of her friends, Elizabeth set down the applications and announced, "Okay, let's go to lunch," effectively ending the discussion.

At that moment in London, Darcy and Geoff were sitting in front of the fireplace in Darcy's office, enjoying a glass of brandy. The evening was cold and rainy, and thick clouds obscured the view from the windows. They sat in companionable silence, listening to Darcy's iPod and relaxing after a long day of meetings. Geoff broke the silence when he noticed the smile on his cousin's face. "How is Elizabeth?"

"She's very well." The smile grew broader, confirming Geoff's suspicions of where Darcy's thoughts had been.

"I was thinking of returning to New York with you tomorrow. I've never experienced a U.S. Thanksgiving, and I can work from there just as easily as you can."

"No," Darcy said unapologetically. "The plane's overcrowded as it is."

Geoff's eyes flashed angrily, "It's a private plane for God's sake, and you're the only passenger…" In mid-rant he noticed the smile still playing on Darcy's lips. "You're teasing me? You? And I fell for it? This is incredible!"

Geoff looked at his cousin carefully. Darcy was slouched sideways in the leather armchair, one leg perched upon an armrest and the other sprawled out before him, his brandy held precariously in his fingertips that hung out over the opposite armrest. "Who are you?" Geoff asked with narrowed eyes. "And what have you done with my stubbornly serious cousin?"

Darcy's warm laughter reverberated from deep within his chest. "Oh, he's in here somewhere, but now he comes out mainly for public display, business meetings and 'accidental' run-ins with Caroline Bingley."

Geoff narrowed his eyes and looked harder at Darcy's relaxed features. "You're getting laid."

Darcy immediately sat up straight and placed his glass on the nearest coaster. "I cannot fathom why my own family continues to speculate on the intimate details of my relationship with Elizabeth. As I said to your father again this morning, Elizabeth and I are not lovers."

Geoff could only laugh at the sudden change in his cousin, and Darcy clearly was not pleased to be the object of his mirth. "Laugh all you want, but just remember this moment when you are stuck in London on Thanksgiving."

"Well then, put the speculation to rest and date again," Geoff suggested. "How long's it been?"

Darcy slouched down in his chair and took another swallow of brandy. "August since the last date; May since I got laid."

"May! You must be ready to explode by now!"

"Let's just say I've joined a very exclusive group who are dedicated to elevating masturbation to its own art form."

"Let me guess who else is in that group. The only person I can imagine whose love life is as pitiable as yours must be Elizabeth. With all the publicity your 'friendship' has been generating, every man on the planet must think she's engaged to you." Geoff got up to refill his glass. "Why don't you back off and at least let Elizabeth date?"

The flash of anger in Darcy's eyes was unmistakable. "Elizabeth is free to see whomever she pleases."

"Fine, then you won't mind if I ask her to dinner when we get to New York." Geoff turned from the bar just in time to witness the anger in Darcy's eyes turn to abject misery.

"Oh no!" Geoff moaned. "You've got it bad! How long have you been in love with her?"

Darcy turned his face away. "I said nothing of the sort."

"Damn it, Darce, you don't have to! Have you looked in the mirror lately? You practically light up when you talk about Elizabeth, and just the thought of someone else seeing her... well, let's just say I've never seen you look more miserable, and you're normally a pretty miserable bastard."

Darcy's continued silence gave further proof to his feelings. "So, what's the problem?" Geoff asked. "Just tell her how you feel."

"It's not that easy. First, I don't know how Elizabeth feels, and second, I don't want to know."

"You don't want to know? Darce what's wrong with you? This isn't about Rebecca is it? Good God, Darcy. That happened seven years ago!"

Darcy turned his face toward the fire, knowing he couldn't explain his reasoning to his cousin. Geoff didn't know how it felt to be the fool and have everyone you loved and respected looking upon you with disappointment. Darcy could still see his father's grim expression, his mother's tears and his Aunt Catherine's unrestrained pleasure over the incident with Rebecca Wickham.

"Look Darce, this makes no sense. Everyone already thinks you're together, so what difference does it make that it's not the truth? I'd bet any amount of money that Aunt Catherine is already spouting off the usual threats. You've handled the foundation too well for her to take it from you, so why deny yourself some modicum of happiness?" Seeing Darcy was unmoved, Geoff spat out in disgust, "So you're going to live your life as some martyr to the name 'Darcy?' Elizabeth is nothing like Rebecca. What the hell are you afraid of?"

Darcy turned back to Geoff, determination etched on his grim face. "I do not ask you to understand my decision, only to respect it. This discussion is now closed."

Geoff was incensed. "*This discussion is now closed?* Just because you're Fitzwilliam 'Fucking' Darcy does not mean you can dismiss me! This is not Pemberley, and I am not one of your damn servants!"

Darcy stood, his composure completely gone as he shouted, "You weren't there! While you were gallivanting across Europe, my life was a living hell!" He stormed to the door. Then, before leaving, he took a deep breath to calm himself and, without turning back, said, "Forgive my outburst. If you can accept that I will not discuss this subject any further, then be at the hangar by ten tomorrow morning."

THANKSGIVING DAY WAS CLEAR AND cold in Manhattan. Elizabeth met Darcy, Georgiana and Geoff at the subway station near Longbourn for the short ride to Times Square to watch the *Macy's Thanksgiving Day Parade*. As the streets would be blocked off, they could not take a car; however, bundled up in heavy coats, hats and scarves, no one recognized them as they made their way through the crowds to find where several of Elizabeth's students had stayed up all night to reserve a prime viewing spot. Georgiana greeted her friends warmly as they settled into folding chairs to await the start of the parade.

Soon the street was filled with marching bands, elaborate floats and gigantic helium-filled balloons in the shapes of America's most beloved cartoon characters. The parade first marched down Broadway in 1924, and ever since it was first televised in 1945, Americans across the country began their Thanksgiving Day watching it on television. When the final float carrying Santa Claus passed through Times Square, it was considered to be the official start of the Christmas Season. As the years passed, the parade became more commercial, but watching it was still considered one of America's best-loved traditions.

Thanksgiving dinner was originally to take place at Elizabeth's co-op, but as Elizabeth had spent too many Thanksgivings alone as a student, she wanted to invite all of her students who could not go home for the holiday to share in the feast. As most of these students were also Georgiana's friends, both women appealed to Darcy to host the meal at Lansing instead. Faced with the two women he cared most about in the world, Darcy could not help but acquiesce.

Elizabeth insisted that Darcy's staff be given the day off, for she wanted Thanksgiving dinner to be prepared, consumed and cleaned up by all in attendance, thereby making it more of a community effort. Jane and Bingley had offered to miss the parade to a keep watch over the roasting turkeys; however, once the gang followed Elizabeth and Darcy back to Lansing, the immense kitchen buzzed in a flurry of activity. The guests who could either brought dishes they had prepared at home or the ingredients to prepare once they had arrived.

Given the diversity of Longbourn's students, the meal represented a combination of cultures. When Darcy questioned the apparent lack of a common theme, Elizabeth reminded him that the first American Thanksgiving was also a melding of cultures; therefore, it was more than appropriate to find fried rice and baked plantains alongside the sweet potatoes and chestnut dressing.

Geoff felt as if he had been dropped into an episode of *The Twilight Zone*.[20] He kept expecting Darcy to frown at the noise or balk at some menial chore that was asked of him, but it never occurred. It was inconceivable that Elizabeth had somehow managed to convince his controlling cousin to allow such chaos into his home. Geoff nearly dropped the case of wine he was carrying up from the cellar when he entered the kitchen to see Darcy roll up his sleeves and plunge his arms into a sink full of dishwater to locate a colander for one of the numerous people digging through his cupboards and raiding his pantries. Geoff was sure no Darcys' hands had ever touched dishwater before, and he swore he could hear five hundred years worth of ancestors turning over in their graves.

Occasionally, Darcy would stand back, appearing a little overwhelmed by all the activity. Geoff noticed that at those moments, Elizabeth would immediately come to his side, touch his arm and speak softly to him. It only took a few words before Darcy was smiling and ready to rejoin the fray.

Somehow, Elizabeth and Jane had managed to coordinate everything so that it was all ready to eat at the same time. By two o'clock in the afternoon, all twenty-eight guests were seated around the dining room table.

After dinner, the younger guests volunteered to do all the clean up out of gratitude for the effort necessary to put together such a huge meal. Exhausted, neither Jane nor Elizabeth offered any resistance to the scheme, and Georgiana and Jake led their friends back to the kitchen to tackle the monumental task. The remainder of the group moved to the large couches in the game room to

---

20 A science-fiction television series originally running from 1959 to 1964, created by Rod Serling

watch football or participate in another Thanksgiving tradition: the post-dinner nap. Once the younger group rejoined them for coffee and dessert, the room took on a festive atmosphere.

Geoff kept a close watch on Darcy and Elizabeth. Several times, he caught them locking eyes across the room and smiling. When they passed one another, Darcy would reach out and touch the small of her back as they spoke briefly; then, they would smile into each other's eyes before separating. The situation was obviously far worse than Geoff suspected. They looked…happily married!

Geoff suddenly had a moment of clarity. Without a doubt, his cousin's body had been taken over by beings from outer space. At any minute *Alien Darcy* would pull out his ray gun and blow them all to smithereens!

While Geoff was meditating on what all of this implied, a soft feminine voice blew past his ear. "They're cute, aren't they?"

"Excuse me?" He turned to find one of Elizabeth's friends standing next to him.

"Charlotte," she introduced herself.

Geoff took in her appearance. She was tall and slim, her straight dark hair falling below her waist. Charlotte's face was not what most people would call beautiful, but she gave off an aura of class that Geoff found enticing. Her voice was deep and sensuous. "Geoff," he finally responded. "Who's cute?"

"Darcy and Lizzy. I've noticed you watching them."

"So what do you think of this 'friendship' thing?" Geoff's tone sounded far too critical for Charlotte's taste.

"I think it's great. Did you notice how frequently they finish each other's sentences? It's just so sweet. Why he's not banging her boots is beyond me."

Geoff let out a sarcastic laugh. "That's what makes the whole thing so twisted, don't you think?"

Charlotte took offense. "You sound a little jealous if you ask me. Look, Buster, if you're looking for dirt on Lizzy and Darcy, you've come to the wrong party!" With that she turned to walk away, but Geoff took hold of her arm and gently pulled her back.

"No, I just am a little confused, that's all. I've never seen Darcy like this before. I have to admit, it's a little unsettling, but believe me, I think he should be 'banging her boots' too."

Charlotte smiled. "You must be the cousin."

Geoff knew in an instant it was a smile he wanted to see again. "Yes. How do you know Elizabeth?"

"Lizzy and I were roommates her first year at Longbourn. I left after the second year, deciding I'd rather design clothing than play the cello, but we've remained friends."

"Ah, so you're the famous Charlotte Lucas. Are you related to William Lucas?"

"Yes, he's my father. I rather disappointed the old man with my change in career."

"I suspect I disappointed my father, too. I come from a long line of soldiers but decided to become an attorney. So you and Elizabeth are very close?"

"About as close as one can get to Lizzy. She's warm, friendly and would give you her last dollar if you needed it, but she's guarded about letting people get too close."

They both looked at the subject of their conversation to find her beaming at Darcy again. "Except Darcy," Geoff added. "They're a lot alike."

Charlotte could only smile in agreement before tilting her head to the side and narrowing her eyes. "Are you sure you're not jealous?"

"Any hope I may have entertained about Elizabeth would seem pretty foolish after seeing her and Darcy today." Geoff could not stop his eyes from raking down the front of Charlotte's body.

Charlotte noticed his glance and returned one of her own. She liked what she saw. He looked to be about six feet even and obviously took very good care of his body. He was easy on the eyes, and the British accent didn't hurt. This man was a studmuffin if ever there was one. Hell, Lizzy and Jane each had their own Brit. Why shouldn't she grab one, too? "Then why don't we focus on something else?"

A space large enough for two opened up on the couch behind them and Charlotte moved to sit down, tugging playfully on Geoff's tie indicating he should join her. When he settled in beside her, Charlotte let her large green eyes slowly travel from his face, down his neck to his chest. Geoff felt every hair stand on edge in response.

"What's with the tie?" she asked.

Geoff glanced down at the tie he had purchased two days before. "It's my 'lucky tie.'"

"Get rid of it," Charlotte said bluntly as she moved to remove the tie and toss it to the table behind the couch. "You look better without it." She then proceeded to unbutton the top two buttons of his shirt. "There, that's nice," she purred. "Now, tell me all about you."

Geoff's examination of Darcy and Elizabeth was over. His cousin would just have to sort out his own love life. Geoff's examination of Charlotte Lucas, however, was another thing entirely.

By 7:00 p.m. all the guests had left Lansing. Georgiana had gone to Jake's dorm room, and Geoff was over an hour late from taking Charlotte home. Darcy was lying on the couch in the music room while Elizabeth played Chopin's Nocturne No. 17 on the piano he had bought Georgiana for her birthday. He had specifically requested she play that piece, and Elizabeth was happy to oblige.

"It was worth it," he announced when she had finished.

"What was worth it?" Elizabeth asked as she left the piano.

"All those people invading my house." Darcy moved his feet so Elizabeth could sit down on the couch; he then placed his feet in her lap. "I've only experienced small family gatherings during holidays, so I had no idea what I was missing. Having all those people here today in such an informal setting…" Darcy couldn't find the words to express his contentment. The day had been rewarding. Even now, sitting with Elizabeth left him with a sense of peace he could never recall feeling before. Once again, she had pulled him out of his comfort zone, and he felt his life was richer for it.

Elizabeth placed a pillow on the coffee table before her and rested her feet upon it. She understood exactly what Darcy meant, so she did not try to force him to vocalize his feelings. She was happy he had made the effort to enjoy the day, and because of him, it had been the best holiday of her life.

It was nearly an hour later that he offered her a glass of port. When he handed her a cut crystal stem filled with Graham's 30 Year, Darcy settled in beside her, tucking his arm behind Elizabeth's shoulders. "Comfortable?"

Elizabeth leaned her head back into his shoulder and closed her eyes. She most certainly was not comfortable. The fire of desire coursing through her body was far greater than the heat she felt as the port glided down her throat. This picture of domesticity, instead of making her feel relaxed in contentment, only reminded her of how badly she wanted Darcy to carry her upstairs and *do* her. Getting up, going home and ending this torture would be the smart thing to do, and Elizabeth knew she was smart; but she also knew she was addicted to his warmth, his voice and that constant scent of soap and starch that always emanated from his body. She would never get enough.

"Elizabeth." She opened her eyes at the sound of his voice. "Am I holding you back?" She wrinkled her eyes in confusion, so Darcy clarified his question. "Am I keeping you from dating?"

"God, no!" she replied emphatically. "Where did you get such a ridiculous notion as that?"

"Geoff told me I should let you date."

"Like it would be *your* decision," Elizabeth said indignantly. "I hope you set him straight." There were a few more moments of silence before she asked, "Am I holding *you* back?'

"No! I have no desire to date right now. I'm quite happy to leave things as they are for the time being." He hesitated before blurting out, "Geoff wants to ask you out to dinner."

Elizabeth's heart sank. "You want me to go out with him?"

Darcy hesitated again before replying, "Only if that's what you want."

"No, I don't want to date Geoff. Besides, he looked pretty cozy with Charlotte this afternoon."

Darcy let out a breath of relief. "Yes, he did. Perhaps she'll keep his attention away from my love life."

"That didn't work for Jane. She and Charles are practically living together, and she's still managing to butt into mine."

"Why can't people just leave us alone?" Darcy asked incredulously. "Why do they all act as if our friendship is some kind of violation of the laws of nature?"

"I don't know. We just can't allow them to ruin this for us. Right?"

Darcy pressed a kiss on her temple, causing a rush of heat to run down Elizabeth's already burning body. "Right."

Elizabeth could bear no more. If she didn't go home now, she was going to start tearing Darcy's clothes off. "I'm going to walk back." She rose abruptly and started for the hallway.

"Hey! Wait! Where's the fire?" Darcy asked as he followed her.

All over! "I've really got to go."

"Stay and play for me again," Darcy asked. "You promised six songs of my choice if I hosted dinner today. You've only played one."

"No more tonight." Elizabeth was a little more abrupt than she wanted to be.

"Did I do something wrong?"

"No, of course not! If you had, you know I would say something."

"Then why are you going?" Darcy took her shoulders and turned them so that she faced him. "Tell me."

Elizabeth knew she could not lie and was furious that he was forcing her to admit her predicament. "I want you, damn it! Do you think you're the only one of us who gets horny when we're together?"

Darcy's hurt expression melted into a heart-stopping smile. "You want me?"

Elizabeth blushed furiously as she reached into the closet for her coat.

"You want me!" Darcy stated in wonder as he held up her coat while she slipped her arms into the sleeves.

"Enough!" Elizabeth cried. "It's not like you didn't know."

"Yes," he admitted, "but this is the first time you've said it. It makes it more real somehow."

"Like your ego needed more stroking!" Elizabeth rolled her eyes as she pulled her hat over her hair.

"You want me!" Darcy waggled his eyebrows at her as she passed out onto the front steps.

Knowing that when they left the sanctuary of the house his public persona would prevent his retaliation, Elizabeth reached behind him and squeezed his butt. "You, Fitzwilliam Darcy, are a horrible tease!" The sudden widening of his eyes was the only indication that she had successfully exacted her revenge. She smiled as she made her way back to her co-op, pleased at the certainty that she was not the only one who would soon be taking a very cold shower.

CHAPTER 15

AN UNWELCOME VISITOR

The day after Thanksgiving in the United States is known as "Black Friday." It is the day most stores open ridiculously early for overly zealous Christmas shoppers. Elizabeth, Jane and Charlotte chose to avoid the 4 a.m. crush but couldn't resist the sales entirely. By twelve noon they each had an armload of shopping bags.

They stopped for a late lunch at *Bubba Gump's* in Times Square, and as they waited for the popcorn shrimp appetizer to arrive, they gazed across Broadway at their next planned destination, *Toys Я Us*.

"Remember, Aunt Maddie said 'only *quiet* toys,'" Jane warned Elizabeth sternly.

"She'll never forgive me for the toy instruments I sent last year," Elizabeth laughed as she explained her aunt's warning to Charlotte. "Little Clare took to banging the drum, while blowing on the trumpet for hours on end. I was hoping to send a small keyboard to her this year, one with an attached microphone."

"Don't you dare!" Jane warned. "I have been given strict instructions to monitor your purchases."

"Are you and Darcy exchanging gifts?" Charlotte asked Elizabeth.

"We haven't talked about it, but I'm planning to give him something. Unfortunately, I don't have a clue what to buy. He epitomizes the phrase: 'the man who has everything.'" Elizabeth turned to Jane. "What are you getting Charles?"

"I'm not buying a gift for Charles." Jane averted her eyes from the other women. "He's leaving town before Christmas, and in all honesty, I don't know if I'll ever see him again."

"What?!" Elizabeth and Charlotte cried out in unison.

"Last night he told me that he's flying off to Russia to begin shooting a photo essay on the effects of global warming on the Siberian plain. He will be gone indefinitely." Jane finally looked back to Elizabeth and Charlotte. Noticing their expressions of shock she continued, "A photojournalist travels on the spur of the moment from one exotic location to the next. Charles was bound to leave sooner or later."

"Charles is running off to *Siberia*?" Elizabeth asked incredulously.

"We've only been seeing each other for a few months. It would be rather unrealistic to expect him to turn down this opportunity for me. So, I'm determined to be supportive. It's just that things were going so well for us, and I allowed my expectations to rise. I should have been more guarded."

"Did you tell him you'd like him to stay?" Charlotte asked. When Jane shook her head, Charlotte threw her hands in the air. "What is the problem you Bennet girls have with telling a man you love him?"

Ignoring Charlotte's frustration, Elizabeth reached across the table and squeezed Jane's hand. "I'm sorry, sweetie." Jane looked out the window, her eyes filled with unshed tears.

Jane then quickly glanced about the restaurant while dabbing at her eyes with the back of her hand. "Can we talk about something else? I don't want to cry in front of everyone."

At her friend's request, Charlotte began a discussion on where they should have dessert. Elizabeth wanted to go to *Maxie's Delicatessen* for brownies, while Charlotte preferred the cheesecake at *Roxy's*. The subject of food soon led to a detailed recounting of Thanksgiving Day. "So, Charlotte, why did it take four hours for Geoff to see you home?" Lizzy raised her brows suggestively.

"We stopped for a drink on the way, started talking and the hours passed by. While I was sure he was feeling the sparks between us as much as I was… *nothing* happened." Charlotte's disappointment was obvious. "Geoff is just so yummy! I'd have skipped all this," she motioned to her shopping, "to spend the day in bed with him. Somehow, I just couldn't get him there. He brushed off my every subtle suggestion."

"Subtle suggestion?" Elizabeth raised an eyebrow in disbelief. "Charlotte, your suggestions are about as subtle as a freight train! Perhaps you scared him off."

Charlotte shrugged her shoulders. "He asked me to call him this afternoon. The man is a mystery — a beautiful, god-like mystery."

Elizabeth excused herself to the ladies' room. She was not gone but five minutes when she returned to eat her shrimp salad. "You're suddenly very quiet, Lizzy," Charlotte teased. "You're not pouting because we're not going to *Maxie's*, are you?"

"No, of course not," Elizabeth responded; however, several times during their meal Charlotte and Jane exchanged concerned looks about Elizabeth's sudden loss of vivacity.

At *Toys Я Us*, Elizabeth purchased several quiet toys for the Gardiner children before claiming a splitting headache. She left her companions, but not before paying for a small harmonica without Jane's notice. Expertly hailing a cab, Elizabeth was soon ringing the bell at the gate outside Lansing.

Darcy was concerned by the expression in Elizabeth's eyes as he escorted her into his study. "Are you all right?"

"Of course I'm all right," Elizabeth insisted. "Get me a brandy, please." A moment later Darcy handed her a snifter, and she downed the generous portion he had poured in one gulp. "I think I just met her," she revealed as Elizabeth began digging frantically through her purse. "Rebecca Wickham."

Darcy froze at the name.

"A woman approached me in the ladies room at *Bubba Gump's*. She must have been following me all morning."

Darcy squeezed his eyes shut trying to make sense of what he was hearing. "How can you be sure?"

Elizabeth finally extracted a snapshot photo from her purse and handed it to him. It was a picture of a younger Darcy, his arm about a raven-haired beauty. "She gave this to me. Is that her?"

Darcy forced down the bile that suddenly rose in his throat. "What did she say?" He did not wait for an answer, but rose to pour a larger brandy for himself, downing it even faster than Elizabeth had.

"She wants me to meet her tonight."

Darcy continued to stare at the photo in his hand. He had hoped never to see Rebecca again, and now she had appeared out of nowhere.

Elizabeth watched as Darcy began pacing back and forth. "Did she say anything else?"

"She said she had some advice for me and that she would be in the Atrium Lounge of the Marriot Marquis at ten."

Darcy finally stopped pacing. "I can't imagine she was remotely pleasant."

"She wasn't, but I refused to give her the satisfaction of seeing me dash immediately from the restaurant." A mischievous smile came to her lips. "By the way, according to Miss Wickham, you are exceedingly well-endowed, and I need to learn to suppress my gag reflex."

Darcy closed his eyes again. "This is not the time for your teasing, Elizabeth."

"You don't have to go." Elizabeth knew before the words escaped her lips that he would not take the suggestion, but she pressed on anyway. "I say let's not give a rat's ass about Rebecca Wickham. We'll convince her of her insignificance by ignoring her."

Darcy reached for his phone. "I'll handle this."

Elizabeth stayed his hand. "Don't shut me out. You're not the only person in this room with the IQ of a quantum physicist."

"You don't know her!" Darcy's voice rose in intensity.

"That's because you haven't told me about her!" Elizabeth stood to face him. If he wanted an argument, she was happy to give it to him.

"I don't have to tell you anything. Must I remind you of the rules?"

"Fuck the rules! This woman is following me around, and I have a right to know why!"

"This is not your concern!"

"She's made it my concern. Look, it's obvious she's played some really sick mind games with you sometime in the past and she's trying to do it again. Don't give her that power over you!"

"I know how to handle Rebecca!" he insisted, the volume of his voice increasing to match hers.

"Humph!" Elizabeth could only roll her eyes. "If you did, she wouldn't freak you out so much. Look at you!" She pointed to their reflection in a mirror that hung over the fireplace. "The blood still hasn't returned to your face."

Darcy reached for his phone again, and Elizabeth let out a stifled scream of frustration, picked up her coat and purse and headed out of the room shouting, "Why is it perfectly acceptable for you to help me face my demons, but you have to deal with yours alone?"

"This is different!" Darcy put down his phone and followed her into the hall. "If you only had a bloody bodyguard —"

"I don't want your bloody bodyguard —"

"What's with all the shouting?" Geoff called out as he walked down the stairway.

Darcy ignored Geoff as he followed Elizabeth into the front entryway. "You are the most obstinate, headstrong..."

Elizabeth shouted back, "...arrogant, insufferable, controlling..."

"...argumentative, illogical..."

"...egotistical, adorable..."

"...frustrating," Darcy suddenly paused. "Wait a second — adorable?"

Elizabeth hissed through her teeth. "You're adorable when you're angry, and those damned dimples should be registered with the police as lethal weapons! You, Fitzwilliam Darcy, do not fight fair!"

Geoff suddenly appeared at Elizabeth's side to hold her coat as she slipped her arms into the sleeves. "First fight?" he asked cheekily with a large smile on his face.

"Go away, Geoff!" Darcy grabbed Elizabeth's hat from his cousin's hands.

Geoff was calmly insistent. "I think you two need a referee. The rate you're going, someone's bound to get hurt."

Elizabeth snatched her hat back from Darcy. "You want to shut me out? That's your prerogative." Forcefully she pulled her hat over her head. "I've got papers to grade. Let me know how it all works out."

"Elizabeth," Geoff interrupted again, "don't storm off. Let's sit down like—"

Elizabeth reached down to retrieve her shopping bags as she shouted, "Go away, Geoff!"

Darcy was furious. "I know how much you hate the idea of a bodyguard, but surely you see that Rebecca being able to approach you demonstrates how vulnerable you are!"

"Enough with the bodyguard!" Elizabeth reached for the handle of the door.

"Rebecca?" Geoff asked in alarm. "As in 'Rebecca Wickham?'"

Darcy and Elizabeth turned to him and said together, "Go away, Geoff!"

Darcy turned toward the coat closet. "I'll get my coat and walk you home."

"I am perfectly capable of walking the four blocks to my co-op."

"The reporters —"

"The reporters shout questions for the first block and then just snap pictures until I get in the front door. I *refuse* to let *them* change my life."

"Do you at least have your mace?"

Elizabeth pulled the small canister from her coat pocket to show that she had it. "See?" she said with sarcasm. "The permit is in my purse."

"Be careful!" he directed angrily.

"You too!" Elizabeth demanded loudly before masking her face in an exact replica of Darcy's expression of cold indifference. Opening the door, she left in a flurry of camera clicks.

As soon as the door closed, Darcy leaned back against it, closed his eyes and exhaled loudly. "She's going to be the death of me!" he muttered.

He opened his eyes when he heard his cousin's low chuckle. "I don't know if I agree about you being adorable, but Elizabeth is downright breathtaking when she's angry." Geoff added knowingly, "You really want to shag her right now! Don't you?"

"Go away, Geoff!"

REBECCA WICKHAM LOOKED CAREFULLY AT the small lines beginning to reappear around her eyes. She reached into the black leather bag on the counter and pulled out a disposable syringe and a bottle of Botox. Her face was her greatest asset, and she needed to keep it in top condition — no lines, no bags, no dark circles. Time was her enemy, and she was determined to stay one step ahead of it.

Moving to the closet of her suite at the Waldorf-Astoria, Rebecca looked through the vast array of clothing hanging before her as she thought about what would be the best thing to wear for her meeting with Elizabeth Bennet. *Poor girl! She is definitely playing outside of her league!* Rebecca chose leather pants and a black silk blouse. Both would accentuate her height and model-like proportions. Black stiletto boots would complete the outfit.

Before leaving the closet, she grabbed a red scarf. *He might just show up instead. That would be very interesting!*

Rebecca did her research on Elizabeth and knew the type well: perpetual victim, abused child star, sheltered academic. Elizabeth could not handle the pressure of the real world. There was no doubt that she would be painfully insecure. Rebecca was actually disappointed in Darcy. He was still playing the hero, rescuing helpless maidens. As she was about to get dressed, the ringing of her mobile phone interrupted her.

After checking the caller ID she flipped open the phone and hissed, "What do you want?"

"Hello, my lovely! Where are you?"

"What makes you think I would be stupid enough to tell you? What do you want?"

The man laughed uncomfortably, *"I'm a little strapped for cash. I was hoping you could give me a few thousand to hold me over until —*

"I don't want to hear your sad story, and you know I wouldn't believe a word of it."

There was another pause before the man asked, *"Well, can you?"*

Rebecca huffed with annoyance. "I'll transfer some funds into your account within the next twelve hours."

"Thanks, beautiful! You know I think the world —" Rebecca hung up. Just because George was her one weak spot didn't mean she had to listen to his empty flattery.

She turned once again to dress when there was a knock at the door.

"Contessa Alberghini," the young concierge addressed her with adoration, "I have your messages as well as the tickets to tomorrow night's performance of *Wicked*. Front row, center, just as you requested." He triumphantly waved the envelope before her.

"Grazie, Mr. Thorpe!" Her Italian accent was sexy. It should be, she had practiced it for weeks. Thank God that Thorpe spoke Spanish and not Italian, for Rebecca's command of the language was rudimentary at best. "However, I should have asked you to only obtain one ticket. I'm afraid the Conte will not be joining me after all."

"You really should not be about the city unescorted, Contessa."

Rebecca smiled. *Another knight in shining armor. How predictable!* "How very gallant of you!"

Rebecca figured the man could be no more than twenty-two, fresh out of college and eager to begin his career in hotel management. A quick glance to his crotch confirmed that the clingy silk robe she wore was having the desired effect. She looked him up and down suggestively before licking her lips. Not an original gesture, but one she knew he would understand. Thorpe did not need a second invitation; he stepped inside the door and pulled her into his arms, crushing Rebecca against his chest and plunging his tongue deep into her mouth. *Yes, eager indeed!*

As they tumbled into the bedroom, Rebecca knew John Thorpe was not going to be the greatest lay of her life, but she needed the release and like the old cliché: What the boy lacked in expertise, he made up for in enthusiasm.

Her only concern during their interlude was that she had to concentrate. To suddenly scream out, "Fuck me harder!" in a British accent would be a major *faux pas*. She thought that stealing the identity of an Italian aristocrat would be a bit of fun. Now, as she was unable to surrender completely to the moment, she was glad she would soon be ending her tenure as Contessa Maria Alberghini.

Half an hour later, Thorpe lay dozing as Rebecca looked at the theatre tickets. The hotel invoice showed a charge of five thousand dollars for the pair. Fortunately, the real Contessa had very deep pockets and Rebecca was doing her best to empty them before she left New York.

"You must go, my sweet!" she purred. "Wake up!" Rebecca approached the bed and gently shook Thorpe's shoulder. "My friends are coming to take me to dinner. They cannot find you here!"

Standing, Thorpe tried to shake the cobwebs from his head as he quickly pulled on his clothes. "May I see you later, Maria?"

Rebecca's first instinct was to refuse; however, as she watched Thorpe pull his shirt over his broad shoulders, she changed her mind. "You may return at midnight if you bring someone with you? Someone whom you would not mind…sharing." Rebecca pressed her body against Thorpe as she ran her tongue across his throat. "Surely a man of your talents knows…someone?"

There was a long pause before Thorpe asked, "Male or female?"

Rebecca smiled wickedly against his chest. Yes, people had become so very predictable. It would all be so incredibly boring if not for… "You choose," she responded.

An hour later, she was standing fully dressed before her mirror, applying a little more concealer to cover the remaining redness from the Botox injections. She took the moment to focus on exactly why she was in New York City.

For years, Rebecca had studied the tabloids, devouring every article about Fitzwilliam Darcy's love life. Rebecca thrilled at the evidence that she had ruined Darcy for all women, for all time. She saw his reputation as a playboy as a big bronze statue erected in her honor.

Things began to change in her contented universe when this woman, this Elizabeth Bennet, began to show up in the press. She was different from the others in every way, and that was troubling. As the weeks went by and it became obvious that Elizabeth was not just another in a long line of meaningless romps, Rebecca became angry — furious that somehow, someone had managed to break through the impenetrable wall Rebecca had erected around what little was left of Darcy's heart.

Now that they were engaged, Rebecca had to do something. It was risky, but it was time to rattle Fitzwilliam Darcy once again. Her ego demanded it!

TJEAN'S WAS AS CROWDED AS usual. The music was loud, the drinks were cold and the karaoke singers were in great voice. Elizabeth and her friends sat at their usual table, surrounded by their usual admirers, but Elizabeth's cosmopolitan sat untouched before her as she sat back and let her winning streak at karaoke come to an end. She kept looking at her watch and then her mobile phone. By 10 o'clock she was ready to admit that she was too worried to enjoy herself. She would go home and hope Darcy would call.

She was pulling out a twenty to cover her part of the check when a familiar voice caught her attention. "You're not singing tonight?"

AT NINE O'CLOCK, REBECCA SAT quietly at a table near the closed sushi restaurant, *Katen*, well away from the busy front bar area with its windows overlooking Times Square, but close enough to the Atrium Lounge for a waiter to bring her a drink. She was early just in case she misjudged Elizabeth and Darcy arrived in her place. Darcy was always early.

She had a perfect view of the glass elevators so that she would have significant warning of anyone's arrival. The photographer was in place. A few pictures of Elizabeth and her sent to Darcy, or a few pictures of Darcy and her sent to Elizabeth would certainly stir up trouble. The trap was set. All she needed was for someone to step into it. Still certain it would be Elizabeth, Rebecca passed the time replaying all the wicked things she would say to undermine Elizabeth's obviously weak self-confidence.

Time passed slowly. Each time an elevator would rise or fall before her, Rebecca would search for Elizabeth, but no one appeared. Finally, after eleven she realized that no one was coming. Obviously, she had underestimated her adversaries.

Frustrated and more than a little angry, she signaled for the photographer to leave, settled the drink tab and headed for an elevator. Suddenly her instincts rose in alarm at the sight of the two men who entered the confined space with her. For the first time in her life, Rebecca Wickham panicked.

ELIZABETH TURNED IN HER SEAT to see the cool blue eyes of Fitzwilliam Darcy. It was 10 p.m. and he was there with her, but she stated the obvious anyway. "You didn't go!"

"Oh, I was going to, but then I decided that I didn't give a rat's arse." Ignoring her shocked expression, he pulled out the list of karaoke songs available. "I'd really like to hear you sing this one…"

"It's 'rat's ass'…not arse." Elizabeth ignored the list. She was happy that he had taken her suggestion, but she was unsure as to what she could or could not ask about how he arrived at his decision. Rebecca somehow remained the only topic on which they could not have an honest discussion. "I was on my way home."

"Come now," he teased, "you'll never find the 'lucky bastard' that way. Surely there must be someone in this establishment that strikes your fancy."

Elizabeth was not in the mood to be teased and his smug attitude only served to irk her. Well, she could be smug too. "There's a guy over there who's been watching me all night. Do you think I should ask him to dance?"

Darcy looked over her shoulder and smiled, "Come now Elizabeth, the man's twice your size. He'd crush you in a second."

Elizabeth contradicted, "You're twice my size. He's like three times." She took a long drink from her warm cosmo and then waited until Darcy had a mouth full of martini before delivering her next line. "Of course, he can't dance with me and do his job at the same time."

Darcy suddenly coughed and felt the cold sting of gin being forced through his nose. "Job?" he sputtered out with the gin.

"Yes, his job as my bodyguard." Now it was Elizabeth's turn to smirk while Darcy frantically looked for a napkin to wipe up the mess.

Once he was somewhat dry, Darcy could only ask, "How did you know?"

"The man is far from inconspicuous. I noticed him following me the moment I left the co-op to come here. What is he, ex-Marine?"

"Navy SEAL, I believe, and he's not supposed to be inconspicuous. The knowledge that you're protected serves as a deterrent." Darcy had a long and logical explanation prepared which he had fully expected to give to Elizabeth after he had taken her home. Seeing her expectant expression, he realized that once again his carefully thought out plans had been for naught. "Elizabeth, I can explain…"

"Explain outside. I want to get out of here." Elizabeth grabbed her coat and, without waiting for Darcy, stood and walked toward the exit. Both Darcy and the large man followed her.

In the cold night air, they walked silently for some time before Elizabeth stopped, turned to the man walking twenty feet behind them and motioned for him to approach. "What is your name, sir?"

The man looked to Darcy first and then answered, "Benwick."

"And are you the only person who will be watching me?"

Benwick looked to Darcy again, and at his employer's nod, he responded. "There are a number of us, but a Mr. Harville and I have been assigned as your primary security."

"Thank you." Elizabeth's tone was dismissive, so as she and Darcy walked on, Benwick fell back to resume his duties. Elizabeth could not help but notice the effect of the bodyguard on the photographers. They stayed at least another twenty feet behind Benwick.

Elizabeth remained silent, and her lack of response was killing Darcy. "If it's any consolation," he added, hoping to appease the anger he was sure she was suppressing, "Georgiana and I now have bodyguards, too. I cannot tell you how angry *she* was." He looked to Elizabeth nervously. "However, I'm sure you know exactly how she feels."

Approaching the door to her co-op, Elizabeth again waited to address Benwick. "Will you be with me 24/7? Do you need a room here?"

"No," Benwick responded. "Mr. Wentworth and Mr. Darcy agree that the security procedures Mr. Anthony has established here are more than adequate. Therefore, once you're home for the night, we'll be released until the following morning."

"I suppose you already know my schedule for tomorrow."

"Harville and I will be here at 8:00 a.m. for a meeting with you and Mr. Anthony to discuss security procedures. We should be finished in plenty of time for your first music lesson at the Community Center. If you decide you need to go out before then, call this number." Benwick pulled a card from his pocket and handed it to Elizabeth.

"Good night, Mr. Benwick." Elizabeth swiped her key card as Darcy nodded to the bodyguard. Once Elizabeth and Darcy were securely inside the building, Benwick walked away.

In the elevator, Elizabeth addressed Darcy. "If Benwick's leaving, who's following you home?"

"I have Sparks on-call tonight. He and a Mr. Price will see me safely to Lansing."

Her question answered, Elizabeth was silent again. Once they were inside her co-op, Darcy could take it no longer. "Elizabeth, shout at me, flip me over and slam me on the floor, but please — I beg of you — talk to me! I realize that you're angry —"

"I'm not angry," she interrupted as she emerged from the kitchen with two bottles of water. She handed one to Darcy before taking a seat on the sectional. She waited for him to sit down before she continued. "At least I'm trying not to be. I've done a lot of thinking since our argument this afternoon."

She explained her reasoning. "You are a rich and powerful man. The rich and powerful cannot help but attract enemies. Now that you're even more in the public eye, the danger has increased. The least I can do is cooperate. This is yet another price we both have to pay to be friends."

This was not what Darcy had expected, but he was grateful for it. "I must admit I'll sleep easier knowing you are protected from any insane person who might want to hurt you."

She knew it was shaky ground, but Elizabeth asked anyway, "Is Rebecca Wickham insane?"

"No, at least I don't believe she is. Everything with Rebecca boils down to money." *Sex and money.* "I trust she's been arrested tonight."

"Arrested?" Elizabeth's eyes rose in surprise.

"I had Fred Wentworth run a check on her through Interpol. It turns out that the police departments of several European states have been looking for her for some time. We simply informed the FBI where she would be tonight. It was very careless of her to come here and use her real identity, even if it was only to you."

Elizabeth looked warily at Darcy. "The woman who screwed up your life comes out of nowhere and is simply arrested and carried away. It all just seems too simple, too easy."

"Sometimes, it is easy. Not everything in life has to be one long, drawn out drama."

"So does this mean we can talk about her now?"

Darcy sighed heavily. "I don't think I'll ever be able to talk about what happened…before. Please accept that."

Elizabeth took Darcy's hands. "You haven't seen her for years, she's now on her way to jail, and yet you're still allowing Rebecca Wickham to control your life."

Withdrawing his hands, Darcy turned away with a cold expression. "The way I see it, I've taken complete control of my life."

Elizabeth understood. "It all comes down to control for both of us. That's why I didn't want you to hire a bodyguard for me. I need to be in control of my own protection. What if you decided our friendship was no longer worth all this trouble? What if you walked out of my life tomorrow? If I depended on you to keep me safe, then where would I be?"

A flash of alarm crossed Darcy's face as he quickly took Elizabeth by the arms and locked his eyes with hers. "Never! That will never happen. You will be my friend — my very best friend — forever!"

He stared intently at her for a few moments before she suddenly burst into giggles. "That makes me your BFF."[21]

Darcy felt the tension melt with her laughter and allowed his fierce hold to relax. "Precisely."

She looked into his eyes, liquid silver in the soft light of her living room, and caught her breath. God, he was beautiful! Elizabeth gently pushed on his arms in a silent plea to release her. "Sometimes, it's just so tempting to screw this up with sex."

"Or sex this up with screwing," he teased gently. Also feeling the heat from their close proximity, Darcy let his hands drop and stood up. "All right, my BFF Elizabeth! You still owe me several more songs on the piano, so get to it."

Elizabeth made her way toward the instrument. "You are so right, my BFF Darcy! My fingers await your orders."

He glanced at the sheet music she had scattered about, when a title caught his eye. "I'd like you to play this one."

Elizabeth smiled as she noted his selection. "*Puff the Magic Dragon*? Interesting choice."

Darcy shrugged his shoulders. "I'm feeling nostalgic this evening."

Chuckling in response, Elizabeth prepared to strike the first key, but paused instead. "What's this I hear about Charles running off to Siberia?"

---

21 Text speak meaning 'Best Friend Forever,' the use of which is usually associated with teenage girls.

CHAPTER 16
THE BRICK WALL

December 7th, New York Post
Photo caption: Fitzwilliam Darcy and Dr. Elizabeth Bennet attend the
Riverside Community Center Holiday Concert.
Story: The annual Holiday Concert at the Riverside Community Center was
made even more festive last night as William Lucas, President of Longbourn
School of the Performing Arts, announced a joint project...

December 7th, Celebrity Watcher (U.S.)
Photo caption: Is Elizabeth Bennet hiding a baby bump? This loose fitting dress
by Charlotte Lucas seems to suggest so.
Story: Rumors are flying that Elizabeth Bennet and Fitzwilliam Darcy are
expecting a child to arrive this spring...

"So, let me see if I have this correct?" Geoff asked as he and Darcy were walking through Riverside Park toward the fencing club. "Charles believes that Jane doesn't love him because she *hasn't* begged him *not* to go to Siberia; and Jane thinks Charles *doesn't* love her because he took the job in Siberia in the first place?" Darcy nodded his head. "Good Lord! Can this be any more screwed up? We are talking about two grown adults here, are we not?"

"One of whom is a bloody psychiatrist!" Darcy huffed in exasperation.

"So why don't you and Elizabeth just sit them down and get it all out in the open?"

"We can't very well shout at everyone for trying to interfere in our relationship and then turn around and interfere in someone else's. They're going to have to work this out on their own."

"He's leaving in four days!"

"I know! I know! Elizabeth and I are having dinner with them tonight. Perhaps you and Charlotte would care to join us. It's promising to be a rather morbid evening otherwise."

Geoff hesitated before continuing. "Charlotte and I are not 'together.'"

Darcy looked confused. "I was under the impression you two had hit it off."

"I like her a great deal, but we've only seen each other a few times. Plus, we live on different sides of an ocean. That is not very conducive to a long-term relationship."

Now Darcy looked even more confused. "Since when did you start looking for a long-term relationship?"

"I've been watching you and Elizabeth, and I've decided that I want what you have."

Darcy laughed mirthlessly. "You're joking."

"I am perfectly serious. I'm going to find the perfect woman. We're going to become the best of friends and then, unlike you," here Geoff glanced mischievously at Darcy, "I intend to shag her rotten for the rest of my days."

"I didn't realize Elizabeth and I had begun a trend. So you've determined that you and Charlotte cannot be friends?"

"Perhaps we can; however, all I've determined so far is that Charlotte wants to get into my pants!" They shared a laugh at his jest before Geoff ventured further, "Elizabeth has changed you. I couldn't help but notice that you haven't been early for an appointment in weeks."

Darcy only smiled again in response.

"Quite frankly, I am still in shock that you didn't burst a blood vessel when you found that Carter boy sneaking out of Georgie's bedroom last night."

Darcy's smile disappeared. "I had a long talk with her this morning, and it appears we all owe you twenty pounds." Darcy frowned but appeared resigned to the situation. "Apparently they've been *together* for some time."

"What did you think they were doing when she would go back to his dorm after dinner?"

"Studying?"

Geoff laughed out loud. "You sound like a clueless parent. So why is Jake

Carter not wearing a foil through his chest?"

"I realized I have no right to demand a higher moral standard of Georgiana then I demand of myself. They're taking precautions. I can ask no more than that."

Geoff was sorely tempted to tease his cousin even more over this new realization about his little sister's sex life but decided not to push his luck. "A very reasonable response. I'm impressed."

"Don't give me too much credit. I was seeing bloody murder at first, but then I called Elizabeth, and she helped me place it all in perspective. Georgiana is happy. There were times last year I thought never to see her so again. I should be grateful."

At Geoff's look of skepticism, Darcy added, "I said I *should* be grateful. I'm still working on it."

Their discussion was effectively ended as they arrived at the door to the fencing club. Darcy and Geoff entered the club, followed closely by Mr. Price. They found the lobby deserted; even the receptionist had abandoned her post.

"That's strange," Darcy observed. "Usually this place is packed on a Saturday morning." He approached the front desk and peered around looking for someone to check them in.

"Elizabeth's here," Geoff indicated toward Mr. Harville who was seated in the lobby with a clear view of the door. "I thought she taught music lessons on Saturdays."

"The Concert was the last event at the Center until the new year." Darcy approached Elizabeth's bodyguard. "Good morning, Harville. Where is everyone?"

"Good morning, Mr. Darcy." Harville nodded to Price who took a seat on the opposite side of the waiting area with a clear view of the hallway to the fencing rooms. "A short time ago, Dr. Bennet was rather dramatically challenged to a match by a very unpleasant woman named Caroline. It created quite a stir, and everyone ran off to watch."

Darcy and Geoff looked to one another in alarm. "This way!" Darcy called out as he dashed down the hall with Geoff hot on his heels.

"That is strange," Harville said coolly to his fellow bodyguard.

Price smiled slightly in response. "Apparently you have yet to be briefed on Miss Caroline Bingley."

It was not difficult for Darcy and Geoff to find the room where the match was taking place. However, once inside they needed to push through the crowd to find an open space of floor from which to watch. Dalton himself was refereeing the match and the score was two points to one. Caroline was in the lead.

As the action passed back and forth across the piste, each giving and then receiving the right of way, Elizabeth could feel Caroline's advantage over her. Caroline had been fencing for nearly ten years, and her experience and talent were evident in her every move. Elizabeth steeled her nerves and waited for Caroline to make a mistake she could exploit. In spite of her efforts, the buzzer sounded as Caroline scored another point.

At the opposite side of the piste, Caroline was pleased with how the match was progressing. Just two more touches and Elizabeth Bennet would be properly put in her place. Taking a moment to glance across the crowd, Caroline spotted Darcy and his annoying cousin. This was exactly what she had hoped for. Darcy would witness his little friend's fall from the pedestal everyone had placed her on; surely, he would see Caroline then for the superior woman she was.

Caroline removed her mask in a show of adjusting her long white ponytail. She looked to Darcy with her most stunning smile and witnessed the look of absolute adoration that fell across his face…directed at Elizabeth. Inwardly, Caroline seethed in anger. The smile disappeared from her face as she narrowed her eyes at her opponent. *Elizabeth Bennet, you are going down!*

Dalton called out, "En garde," as the two women resumed their starting positions. When the word "fence" echoed through the room, Caroline attacked. Furiously she thrust at Elizabeth, refusing to back away. "Halt!" Dalton's voice stopped the match. "Foul to Bingley." Caroline looked up to find Dalton looking at her with distaste. "You failed to give the right of way when Bennet initiated her last attack!" Caroline scowled. Who cared about "right of way?" She had a point to prove!

When they began fencing again, Caroline resumed her aggressive assault. "Halt! Foul to Bingley," called out Dalton again. Caroline pulled off her mask and looked at him in fury. "Caroline, you must parry before launching a counterattack! You know the rules of fencing as well as anyone here! Point to Bennet! The score is three to two."

Caroline approached the centerline, her anger in open display. Calmly, Elizabeth removed her mask and met her. "When I win this match," Caroline announced loudly enough for all to hear, "you will walk out the door of this club and never come back again."

Elizabeth's raised eyebrow was her only reaction.

"Caroline," now Dalton was seething as his former student was severely testing his patience, "only I can ban a member from this club!"

Never before had Caroline felt so furious. She was now filled with indignation on Darcy's behalf, for Dalton was unfairly protecting his lover right before Darcy's eyes. Caroline glanced into the crowd expecting to see Darcy's disgusted reaction. The glare of disapproval was there, but it was directed squarely at her.

Caroline was aghast! How could they all be so ignorant of how this little nobody was playing them for fools? Turning back to Elizabeth she demanded, "When I win this match, your little 'friendship' with Darcy is over. You will stay away from him!"

Elizabeth's eyes flashed briefly before she calmly responded, "I would never agree to such a wager." Turning on her heel, Elizabeth resumed her place on the piste and replaced her mask.

Dalton pulled Caroline aside. "Get a hold of yourself! Don't you see how ridiculous you look?" Instead of calming her down as intended, Dalton's remarks only served to incense Caroline further. When the fencing resumed, she launched across the piste, and with both hands firmly clasped on the handle of her foil, she thrust the blunt blade into the flesh of Elizabeth's right thigh.

Elizabeth crumpled to the floor in pain. Dalton cried out "Halt," but Caroline was too angry to care. She stood triumphantly over her fallen rival.

In a flash, Darcy was crouching down beside Elizabeth, checking her injured thigh while Dalton approached Caroline, took her foil and, in a fit of anger, proceeded to snap the blade in half over his knee. "Match Bennet!" he called out into the room.

"What?!" Caroline shouted in disbelief. Certainly it was a foul, but she should not lose the match over a foul!

Dalton grabbed Caroline by the arm and led her away from Elizabeth. "You deliberately injured another fencer! Not only have you lost the match, but your membership as well. Get out!"

Caroline turned back to Darcy for support. "Darcy, you must come and talk some sense into Dalton. Can you imagine all this fuss over a little foul?" Instead, she watched in alarm as the object of her affections walked past her, carrying Elizabeth Bennet in his arms.

"Get out, Caroline," Darcy's steely voice cut her to the quick, "before I run you through myself!"

ONCE THEY WERE AWAY FROM the crowd, Elizabeth asked Darcy to put her down so she could walk off her injury. "I don't think that's a good idea," Darcy said. "Let's ice it down and see how you feel in a little while."

"I'm all right," Elizabeth insisted. "It just hurts like hell." Reluctantly, Darcy put her down but refused to release his grip on her arm while Elizabeth took a few tentative steps. "Damn! That's going to leave an ugly bruise." Forcing herself to keep walking, Elizabeth sucked up the pain, determined to recover quickly.

Geoff approached and, once assured that Elizabeth was all right, went off to change into his fencing gear. Then Dalton appeared to inform them that Caroline was cleaning out her locker and would be removed from the premises, forcefully if necessary. "I've got some ibuprofen in my office. Darcy, you may go. I'll take care of Elizabeth."

"I would prefer to stay with her." Darcy's expression darkened.

"Then make yourself useful and go get an ice pack and a bottle of water from the front desk," Dalton spoke dismissively as he unlocked the door to his office and waited for Elizabeth to enter.

Darcy bristled under Dalton's condescending tone; however, he was rational enough to realize that both the water and ice pack were a good idea. Glaring at Dalton, he turned toward the front desk, reminding himself that Elizabeth could handle any unwanted advances Dalton would undoubtedly make.

Once inside the office, Elizabeth heard the click of the lock as Dalton closed the door. "Take off you breeches," Dalton demanded. "I want to see how serious your injury is."

"The skin is not broken; my thigh is simply bruised."

"Come on, Elizabeth. Let me have those breeches."

"I am not removing my breeches," Elizabeth insisted. "I will, however, accept the ibuprofen."

Dalton placed his hands on her shoulders. "You are so stubborn!" He softened his voice as he added, "Why can't you accept that I know what is best for you?"

Elizabeth realized he was no longer talking about her injury. "Why can't *you* accept that I'm not interested in sleeping with you?"

"Is it because of your friend out there?" Dalton glanced toward the door.

"It's because of many things. Would you please just give me the ibuprofen?"

Dalton became insistent. "I could give you so much, Elizabeth. You are an amazing talent. I have no doubt that soon you could be nationally ranked. If you would just submit to my guidance, trust in my experience, you could someday make the Olympic team."

Elizabeth replied with mild sarcasm. "I wasn't aware they gave gold medals for the horizontal tango. Please, just give me the ibuprofen," Darcy's insistent knock rattled the door, "and unlock that door."

Reluctantly, Dalton complied. "How are you feeling?" Darcy asked upon entering the room. He gave Dalton another angry glare before handing Elizabeth the bottled water. "I have an ice pack. Here, let's have a look at that leg."

"She won't remove her breeches…" Dalton interjected, but realized that Elizabeth was leaning against Darcy for support as he helped her ease her breeches over her hips. Elizabeth sat down on a chair while they both examined the red bruise forming on her thigh.

"It's not as bad as I expected," Darcy observed as he gently pressed the ice pack over the bruise. "Is that too cold?"

"No." Elizabeth smiled warmly. "Thank you."

Dalton groaned as he watched Darcy tenderly fuss over Elizabeth. Realizing where he was not wanted, Dalton pulled a bottle of Ibuprofen from his desk, placed it near Elizabeth and left his office.

As soon as Darcy realized Dalton had left, he excused himself from Elizabeth for a moment and caught up with the fencing master not far from the door. His voice was cold and stern. "The receptionist was surprised you sent me to her as you have a refrigerator stocked with both ice packs and bottled water inside your office."

Dalton smiled mischievously. "All's fair in love and war, my friend."

Darcy stepped closer, towering over the shorter man. "Look Dalton, I'm warning you off Elizabeth."

An amused smile touched Dalton's lips. "Has something changed? My understanding was that in spite of the press reports, the two of you were nothing more than friends."

"The state of our relationship has nothing to do with it."

Dalton refused to back down to the taller man. "It has everything to do with it. As long as Elizabeth is unattached, she is fair game. Now, don't threaten me in my club. I'm perfectly capable of revoking more than one membership today!" Dalton smiled and gave Darcy an indulgent pat on the shoulder. "You're too tense, my friend. I suggest you work off all that animosity before you say something else you might regret."

As Darcy watched Dalton's retreating back, he forced his anger to the back of his mind. Reprimanding himself for behaving like a jealous lover, he focused on returning to assist Elizabeth.

"So, did you and Dalton finish your pissing match?" Elizabeth teased as Darcy returned to the office. "I've told you I can take care of myself."

"I imagine he hit on you again," Darcy grumbled as he once again kneeled beside Elizabeth to check the bruise.

"He's harmless," Elizabeth assured him.

"Harmless as a snake."

"A little green garden snake," Elizabeth added sweetly as she tried to get Darcy to abandon his foul mood. Darcy could not help but smile at the picture she presented. Her breeches were gathered below her knees revealing a pair of shapely thighs and pretty pink knickers. Distracted from his pique with Dalton, they talked about the plans each had for traveling over the upcoming holidays as the ice soothed Elizabeth's thigh.

Half an hour later, Elizabeth declared her leg to be fine, so fine she wanted Darcy to go through warm-ups with her and then join her in a match. "How am I to learn to parry your superior thrusts if you never use them against me? I think it would be an excellent learning experience."

Darcy was not comfortable with the idea, but somehow half an hour later he found himself standing at the opposite end of a piste from Elizabeth.

"Loser buys coffee?" she playfully called over her shoulder as an assistant helped to hook up the wireless scoring system to her lamé.[22]

"Winner buys coffee with the loser's money!" he amended the wager.

"Agreed! Don't hold back on me, or you may find you're out twenty bucks."

"You're so charming when you talk trash!" he teased.

"Are you ready?" The referee interrupted their tête-à-tête to remind them it was time to begin. "En garde!"

In no time at all, Elizabeth had managed to score three points on Darcy. She removed her mask and approached the centerline of the piste. "What are you doing?" Although her words were spoken calmly, the familiar flash of her eyes told Darcy she was not pleased.

"Fencing," he replied, irked that he was forced to state the obvious, while curious at what he had done to bring about her bad mood.

"No, you're toying with me," she insisted. "I should not be able to score one point on you, let alone three."

"I don't know why you're taking this so seriously."

---

22 Name give the metal mesh vest worn by fencers, which triggers the automatic scoring system when touched by a foil.

"You're letting me score! I know it, you know it, and," here she motioned to the crowd who had gathered to watch as news that Elizabeth was fencing again so soon after her injury flew through the club, "they know it. What's it going to take to make you put forth an effort? A bigger wager? Tell me Darcy, what do you want?"

Knowing he could not possibly ask for what he really wanted, Darcy smiled indulgently, "I'm concerned about your leg. We should take things easy."

"Don't you do it, Darcy! Don't you dare underestimate me!" Elizabeth's irritation was now clearly visible to everyone in the room. "If you do, you will find yourself on your knees before me like every other overconfident jerk I've fenced in the last six months."

His indifferent expression indicated to Elizabeth that her arguments were having no effect. Furious at what she perceived as his patronizing behavior, she searched her mind for some way to make him angry. Her eyes glanced to the crowd and she saw Dalton watching their argument, a self-satisfied smirk on his face. Turning her attention back to Darcy she said, "You were right. Dalton hit on me when he sent you off like some errand boy to get water. First he tried to get me out of my breeches, and then he tried to convince me that he could make me an Olympic fencer if I just submitted to him."

Darcy glanced over at Dalton and saw the smirk. Jealousy flared in his breast, feeding an unreasonable anger and clouding his judgment. Facing Elizabeth again, he allowed his heart's desire to spill forth angrily from his lips. "When I win this match, I want a kiss, at least twenty seconds in duration…" he took a step closer to Elizabeth so that she had to crane her neck to keep eye contact, "slow and *exceedingly* wet!"

Elizabeth realized with satisfaction that she had hit her intended mark. "Agreed! And if you should let your guard down, I will take this match and you will have to bow down before me and kiss my hand."

"In your dreams!" he whispered before turning to the assistant. "Agreed!"

The wagers were noted, masks were replaced and positions taken. As soon as the fencing resumed, Darcy used every ounce of skill he possessed. Fueled on by the overwhelming need to wipe the smirk from Dalton's face, he quickly and expertly scored five points on Elizabeth.

"Match Darcy," the referee declared.

The assistant called out, "Performance wager, Bennet to Darcy. To be performed immediately."

At his end of the piste, Darcy stood holding his mask in one hand, his foil in the other. His face was expressionless as he awaited his due.

Elizabeth handed her mask and foil to a bystander and, scanning the room, found a pile of fencing manuals that she carried over to stack on the floor immediately in front of Darcy's feet. When she stepped up on the books, she was face to face with her opponent.

"Twenty seconds," she called out to the timekeeper, "beginning...now."

Elizabeth immediately clasped the back of Darcy's head and pushed her open lips to his. It was Darcy's intention merely to open his mouth for her kiss while remaining firmly in control by keeping perfectly still. He was going to enjoy this. What he didn't count on was the incredible pleasure of her soft lips moving against his mouth and her tongue deftly caressing his. He tasted the sweetness of her mouth and felt the fire of her passion.

After only ten seconds, the room echoed with the sound of Darcy's mask and foil hitting the floor as his arms suddenly encircled Elizabeth's body. He pulled her tightly against his chest as he abruptly changed from passive recipient to aggressive participant in what had fast become an exceedingly passionate kiss.

"Twenty seconds," the assistant noted, but Darcy and Elizabeth were no longer aware of anything except the need to devour one other. The room was still and quiet as all were stunned by what they were witnessing. The ice queen had melted, and in spite of the tabloid reports, most were surprised it was not to the infamous Dalton.

In that moment, if Darcy had been capable of caring about Dalton's reaction, he would have been quite pleased to see the deep scowl that had replaced the aforementioned smirk. Consciously done or not, the message was effectively delivered and received. Elizabeth was attached.

However, at that moment, Dalton was the last thing on Darcy's mind. "Forty seconds," the timekeeper whispered, hoping to bring the opponents back to reality. If nothing else, he was sure they would soon have to break for air.

Being very intelligent beings, both Darcy and Elizabeth knew it was quite possible to breathe through their noses while their mouths were more agreeably engaged. Therefore, they were perfectly capable of continuing their kiss until one or the other collapsed from exhaustion or lack of nourishment. The timekeeper's wishes were in vain.

"Sixty seconds," the assistant shouted loudly. This seemed finally to permeate Darcy and Elizabeth's consciousness. Slowly their lips parted, and reluctantly they released each other from their embrace.

When their eyes met, a heavy anxiety began to take root in each rapidly beating heart. Suddenly everything felt awkward and uncomfortable.

Darcy cursed himself for his weakness in proposing the kiss, while Elizabeth chastised herself for accepting the wager. As Elizabeth numbly replaced the manuals and Darcy gathered his equipment from the floor, neither cared that every eye in the room was on them. Instead, they were each deeply concerned over how their friendship would be affected by what had just transpired.

They had kissed before, but this time was different. They both instinctively knew they had thrown off the delicate balance that had allowed two strongly attracted individuals to remain nothing more than the closest of friends.

Darcy followed Elizabeth as they exited the fencing room. Outside the women's locker room, he finally found his voice. "Elizabeth, I'm sorry…"

"Forgive me," she pleaded softly. "I baited you. It was unfair."

"No, don't apologize. You were right. I should not have treated you with kid gloves."

They continued to stand, unwilling to leave each other and yet too uncomfortable to look one another in the eye. Finally, Elizabeth could bear the silence no longer and attempted some semblance of normalcy. "Dinner will be ready at eight, but you're welcome to come over earlier." She failed miserably.

"Yes," he agreed. "I'm sure you could use some help with Bingley and Jane." After another long and increasingly difficult pause, he asked, "How's your leg?"

"Fine, thank you. I'll see you later." Elizabeth forced a smile he didn't see and then finally stepped into the locker room.

Darcy was grateful that Geoff was silent during the walk back to Lansing. Over and over again he replayed his actions in his mind: his unreasonable jealously over Dalton, the kiss, and the loss of the ease he and Elizabeth felt with one another. *This is insanity.* He admitted that things had come to a head with Elizabeth, but none of the alternatives was acceptable. He could not be Elizabeth's lover and, God help him, he could not leave her.

SOMEHOW, DINNER WAS EVEN MORE awkward than either of them could have predicted. Jane and Charles kept glancing at each other in misery when each thought the other was not looking. Darcy and Elizabeth could not look at each other at all. As the evening passed with only forced conversation, Elizabeth could not help but feel that her stubborn pride had caused a mess from which she was not sure how they could recover. She felt as if she and Darcy had suddenly hit a brick wall with nowhere to turn.

Hearing her sister sigh again triggered the transference of Elizabeth's anger with herself toward Jane and Bingley. Here were two people, clearly in love with one another, who had none of the baggage she and Darcy had standing in the way of their being together, and yet they were about to let the best thing that ever happened to them slip through their fingers.

Suddenly Elizabeth could bear it no longer. She stood and shouted in exasperation, "Charles, Jane does not want you to go to Siberia. She has been absolutely miserable ever since you told her you were leaving!" Jane immediately turned to Elizabeth with a look of absolute horror on her face.

Apparently sharing in Elizabeth's frustration, Darcy had risen also. "Damn it, Bingley! Tell her! Tell Jane that you don't want to leave her." As if they had a will of their own, Darcy's eyes finally looked to Elizabeth's. "Stop being an idiot and tell her you love her, that you need her, that you..." No longer sure whether he was speaking to Bingley or himself, he abruptly turned away. "I have to go."

Without further explanation, he grabbed his coat and headed for the door. When he reached for the handle, he found Elizabeth's hand on top of his. Darcy kept his eyes averted as he whispered, "It seems I am always apologizing to you."

"Yes," she agreed, "and it's always unwarranted. I understand that you have to go."

Elizabeth released his hand and watched helplessly as Darcy stepped through the door. Suddenly he turned, grabbed her and placed a hard, rough kiss upon her cheek. "I'll call you tomorrow." Then just as suddenly, he was gone.

Leaning back upon the closed door for several minutes, Elizabeth tried to clear away the oppressive atmosphere that surrounded her before entering the living room to deal with Charles and Jane. She found them locked in a crushing embrace. Jane was crying as Charles was desperately trying to kiss her tears away while repeating over and over again how much he loved her.

Try as she might, Elizabeth could muster little joy over her sister's newfound happiness. She walked back to her bedroom and silently closed the door. She lay in the dark room, staring unseeing at the ceiling and surrendering to the feeling of hopelessness that overwhelmed her.

CHAPTER 17
FRIENDSHIP INTERRUPTED

The next morning Elizabeth awoke suddenly, completely disoriented, her heart beating rapidly in her chest. Reaching about blindly to determine how, where and when, her dazed mind finally concluded that the phone was ringing.

"What?" she said into the receiver in a startled voice. After Jane and Charles had left the previous evening, Elizabeth found sleep evasive, not drifting off until after 4 a.m. The phone had interrupted what must have been a very sound sleep. She glanced at her clock to see 5:30 a.m. shining in bright blue numbers.

"Dr. Bennet, this is Tony at the security desk. I'm sorry to wake you, but there are two agents demanding to see you immediately."

Her confused mind was trying to decipher what Tony was saying. *Agents, 5:30 a.m., immediately.* None of it made sense and as the blood continued to pump at a maddening pace through her ears, all she could croak out was another astonished, "What?"

"There's an Agent Robert Martin from the FBI and an Agent Harriet Smith from the British Secret Service standing at my window. They insist that it's important they speak to you right now. Shall I send them up?"

Somehow, this additional information only triggered more questions. The FBI wouldn't show up if someone had been in an accident and the British Secret Service... *Wait a minute... What has Frannie done now?* "Will they tell you what it's regarding?"

There was a moment before Tony's voice responded, "They will only say it is a matter of international security."

Finally, Elizabeth's heart had slowed down enough for her to think more clearly. "Give me ten minutes to get dressed, and then send them up."

Rapidly, Elizabeth pulled on a pair of jeans and a sweater, brushed her hair and swept it up into a messy bun, and then managed to wash her face and start a pot of coffee before there was a knock at the door.

Two agents entered the co-up, both holding identification badges. "Miss Bennet," the one called Martin addressed her tersely, "We would like to speak to Fitzwilliam Darcy."

"Then I suggest you look for him at his home," she replied.

"We thought he might be with you," the one named Smith suggested politely.

"The security guard downstairs could have confirmed for you that Mr. Darcy is not here. What's this about?"

Ignoring her last question, Martin asked earnestly, "Do you know where Mr. Darcy is at this moment?"

"I imagine he is at his home on Lansing Street, most likely fast —"

"We have just come from Mr. Darcy's home," Martin interrupted again. "He left it at approximately 3:00 a.m. this morning. He is not answering his mobile phone. Do you know where he's gone?"

"He may have gone to the Manhattan Fencing Club. Did you ask his cousin, Geoffrey Fitzwilliam?"

Smith gave her irritated associate a warning glance before calmly replying, "Mr. Fitzwilliam accompanied Mr. Darcy to wherever it is he has gone."

"Did you ask Mr. Darcy's bodyguards or his driver?"

Martin stood and approached Elizabeth in frustration. "You expect us to believe that your boyfriend left town and did not inform you?"

Elizabeth's eyes grew large in surprise. "He's left town?" Suddenly, alarm bells were sounding in her head. "Please, tell me what is going on!"

Martin began pacing before her. "This is pointless! Look Miss Bennet —"

"*Dr.* Bennet!" she corrected again more forcibly. All Elizabeth knew for sure was that Darcy and Geoff were in some kind of trouble and the FBI agent in front of her was beginning to piss her off.

Martin continued in anger, "We suspect your boyfriend is illegally attempting to interfere in an international incident. He is way over his head in this matter, and if we can't stop him, he will most likely end up dead! Now, if you don't mind? Just tell us where he is."

Elizabeth looked to both agents in horror as she insisted, "I honestly don't know. What kind of international incident?"

"I'm afraid that's classified information." Smith stood, approached the increasingly belligerent Martin and motioned for him to take a seat before she calmly asked Elizabeth, "Is it possible he's left you a voice mail or an e-mail?"

Elizabeth went to her bedroom to retrieve her mobile phone. After confirming there were no messages, she then pulled her laptop from her briefcase. It took a few minutes to fire it up and open her e-mail. "Damn him!" she said out loud after reading the message she received at 2:55 a.m. Sighing heavily, she turned the laptop around so both agents could read the monitor.

Geoff and I have just been informed of a matter that requires us to leave New York immediately. While gone, it will be difficult, if not impossible, to contact you. Hopefully this matter will be resolved quickly and I'll return very soon.

I will not explain further so that if and when the authorities come to question you, you may be completely honest with them.

I know I can count on you to take care of Georgiana. Jacob Carter is with her now, but I know she will need you at Lansing after you wake.

I am certain you are now furious with me, and therefore, I can only wish I were there to see you. It has recently been brought to my attention that you are breathtaking when angry.

Your BFF,
Darcy

"BFF?" Martin asked sarcastically. "Tell me that doesn't mean 'Best Friend Forever.' Surely two people of your intelligence could come up with something better than that!"

In no mood for insulting comments, Elizabeth replied with equal sarcasm, "That's secret, evil-genius code instructing me to activate the giant laser we've built on the moon and to send my demand to the U.N. for one hundred billion dollars." If looks could kill, Elizabeth would have lain dead on the floor.

"Cute," Smith interjected in a poor attempt to diffuse the tension between Elizabeth and Martin. "Dr. Bennet, do you mind if we have a look around?"

"Whatever for?"

A loud ring cut off her query. "Smith here," the agent spoke crisply into her mobile phone. "Right." She returned her phone to the holder on her belt and turned toward Martin. "The plane took off at 0345 hours."

"Damn!" was the man's response.

Smith spoke in a more insistent tone to Elizabeth. "We're looking for anything Mr. Darcy may have left behind that would indicate his destination or who he was meeting."

"There's nothing like that here," Elizabeth answered honestly.

Apparently her answer touched off another nerve for Martin, who walked back to confront Elizabeth. "If you continue to refuse to cooperate, we'll come back with a search warrant. After our people have finished taking this place apart, you will be lucky to have it all cleaned up within a week!"

"Excuse me!" Elizabeth was too angry to put up with Martin's bullying. "You come into my home, accuse me of lying to you and now you threaten to rip apart my co-op?"

Martin stood directly in front of Elizabeth, staring menacingly into her eyes. "Perhaps we should take you to the nearest police station to continue this conversation!"

Furious, Elizabeth held out her wrists in front of her. "Do you want to put the cuffs on before or after I put on my coat?"

"Wait!" Smith stepped between them. "I'm sure it will not be necessary to take you anywhere, Dr. Bennet."

Snorting in disgust, Martin stepped back as Smith continued politely, "We are looking for a laptop, notepad, briefcase, a business card…"

"Darcy would never leave anything like that here," Elizabeth responded.

"What about personal items? Clothing, coats, toiletries?"

Elizabeth made a mental inventory of her apartment. "There are four bottles of Guinness in the refrigerator and a tin of Earl Grey Tea in one of the kitchen cupboards. Other than that, I have nothing here that belongs to Darcy."

Martin snorted again in disbelief, stalking off to the other side of the living room while Smith discreetly lowered her voice. "You must forgive my partner's rude behavior, but we know *exactly* how often Mr. Darcy is here."

Elizabeth did not miss the implication of Smith's words. Obviously, the paparazzi were not the only people keeping an eye on her and Darcy. "Then you should know he does not sleep here. We are not lovers," she insisted.

"And we are not idiots!" Martin responded loudly from across the room.

Smith smiled at Elizabeth as if the two of them were in on some joke at Martin's expense. "He hasn't had any sleep. Just ignore him."

Elizabeth fought the urge to roll her eyes. *Did they practice this good cop/bad cop routine before they got here, or are they just making it up as they go along?* Realizing the inevitability of the situation, Elizabeth commented to the good cop, "You're not going to be satisfied until you go through my co-op, are you?"

"I'm afraid not," Smith answered sympathetically.

"Very well," Elizabeth acquiesced.

As the two officers walked down the hall to her bedroom, she poured herself a cup of coffee and noisily tried to make a toasted bagel so that she could not hear her privacy being violated by the opening and closing of drawers and closets. Frustrated at her lack of success, she sat on the sofa sipping her coffee and searching her brain for some clue as to why Darcy left town. She steadfastly tried to ignore the words of Agent Martin: *He will most likely end up dead!*

Struggling to control her anger, she put down her cup and imagined all the embarrassing things the two agents might find in her home: her finger-tip vibrator, the rhinestone-studded demi-bra Lydia sent her for her birthday last year, and that picture Charlotte gave her of Albert Einstein's head Photoshopped onto the body of a well-endowed *Playgirl* centerfold with the caption, "Lizzy's Dream Date!" printed across the top.

This would not do! Elizabeth focused instead on fulfilling Darcy's wishes and resolved to go to Lansing and Georgiana as soon as the agents left her co-op. If these two were as charming to Darcy's sister as they were to her, Georgiana had to be terrified.

Methodically the two agents made a preliminary search of the co-op, finding nothing they had hoped for. Once the search was completed, they approached Elizabeth, and Smith handed her a card. "This is a number where we can be reached. If Mr. Darcy contacts you, tell him to call me. I hope you will impress upon him how important —"

"If you are done," Elizabeth interrupted, "I would like you to please leave."

Smith nodded her head, and after issuing her parting thanks for Elizabeth's cooperation, she and Martin headed for the door.

On the way down in the elevator, Smith's pleasant expression turned sour. "Shite! We're both going to have our bloody arses in a sling over this. The whole reason we were assigned here was to prevent Darcy from running off! First he gets his plane off the ground hours before we discover he's left his house, and then his sister and that Bennet woman were no help at all!"

"You need to relax, Harriet. We can't change what's happened. However," Martin took a deep cleansing breath, allowing his tense features to dissolve away into an almost boyish mien, "it wasn't completely unpleasant." At his partner's look of confusion, Martin broke out into a huge grin. "*Dr. Bennet* is breathtaking when she's angry."

"Forget it," Smith deadpanned. "You don't look anything like Albert Einstein!"

"Come along, my BFF, let's grab some breakfast before we face our superiors. It's going to be a very long day."

THE SCENE THAT MET ELIZABETH and Mr. Benwick when they entered Lansing at 7 a.m. was as close to a Darcy nightmare as she could imagine. Police officers were leaving, each carrying white file boxes marked "Evidence" into a van parked outside. Photographers and news crews were greedily snapping pictures and taking video of every move the officers made.

Once inside, Elizabeth found that each room had been thoroughly searched. Drawers were upturned, the contents of cabinets scattered and closets completely ransacked. She made her way through the disheveled rooms with the understanding that her own co-op would have looked just as disastrous if she had not agreed to the preliminary search, and the frustration of knowing that the private and fastidious Darcy would be appalled at what had occurred in his home.

Looking through the rooms on the first floor, she finally found Georgiana and Jake in the kitchen. On the table in front of Georgiana was a document with the words "Search Warrant" clearly printed across the top.

Elizabeth was greeted with a fierce hug during which Georgiana proceeded to break down into uncontrollable tears. She haltingly explained that she had woken up a little after 2:00 a.m. to the sound of Darcy and Geoff shouting at one another. The argument revealed that Darcy had to go somewhere in his private jet and Geoff was insistent that not only was he going along but he was going to fly the plane.

By the time Georgiana had pulled on a robe and approached her brother,

Geoff had apparently convinced Darcy to acquiesce to his plan and had gone off to pack a bag. Darcy led Georgiana into his bedroom and told her that he and Geoff had to leave, that their reason was extremely important, but that he could not explain it to her. He then asked her if she could call Jake and ask him to come over so that Georgiana would not be alone until Elizabeth arrived later in the morning. As Jake lived on campus, it took less than twenty minutes for him to arrive.

"Why didn't he just call me then?" Elizabeth asked. "I would have come over right away."

"He knew you would try to talk him out of going — not that I didn't try myself. He was just so insistent that there was no choice, and Geoff agreed with him."

After another flood of fresh tears, Georgiana continued, "The most terrifying thing was that when they left, both Wills and Geoff hugged me so hard, like they would never get to hug me again. Then Wills gave me a list of emergency contact numbers and this." Tears flooded Georgiana's eyes once again as she handed Elizabeth a series of documents relating to the Darcy Foundation. The documents stated that in the event of the death or incapacitation of Fitzwilliam Darcy, Georgiana Darcy would become the foundation's new president.

Elizabeth felt an overwhelming grief grip her heart. "A Darcy will always be at the head of the foundation," she whispered, remembering Darcy repeating to her his father's words. It was clear; before he left, Darcy understood the danger that he may not return.

Elizabeth suddenly felt her feet give way beneath her as she unsteadily collapsed into a chair. Grabbing her hand in support, Georgiana said, "He explained it was only a precaution, Elizabeth. You know how he has to think everything out, plan for every contingency." However, Elizabeth found no comfort in Georgiana's words as she continued her story. "To avoid the photographers, they went out the back through the little garden and into the alley."

"A little after 5:00 a.m. the FBI came to the gate with this," Georgiana indicated the search warrant sitting in front of her. "They asked so many questions and they have left such a mess! I have no idea how I'm going to clean it all up."

Realizing that Darcy was counting on her to help his sister, Elizabeth quickly pulled herself together. Putting all her emotions in the back of her mind, she quickly assessed what needed to be done. She gently took Georgiana's hands and smiled reassuringly. "I'll call Charles and Jane. They'll come and help us clean up. In the meantime, we have to trust that your brother knows what he's doing." If only she could believe her own words.

They were interrupted by Mr. Price. "Miss Darcy, there is a Mr. Bertram here." He handed Georgiana a business card. "He said he was sent by a Mr. Christopher Brandon."

At Elizabeth's raised brow, Georgiana explained, "Chris Brandon is a friend of Wills from London. He was on the emergency list as an attorney to contact in case there was any trouble with the authorities. I e-mailed him a copy of the search warrant this morning." Elizabeth took the business card from Georgiana.

Edmund T. Bertram, Esq.
Practice Specializing in Criminal Defense

Jake offered to start putting the front sitting room back in some kind of usable condition while Georgiana and Elizabeth met Mr. Bertram in the only room in decent condition on the main floors — the dining room. To their surprise, he had a team of men carrying electronic equipment behind him.

"Miss Darcy, Dr. Bennet, before we speak," here he motioned to the men behind him, "These gentlemen are here to conduct an electronic sweep of the house. The agents who searched this house may have left behind electronic listening devices."

"Is that legal?" Georgiana asked in horror.

"If they have obtained a warrant to wiretap, it is; however, that doesn't mean that if you discover the devices, you have to leave them in place." Confused, Georgiana looked to Elizabeth.

"I think it's a good idea," Elizabeth advised. They sat in silence as the men swept their equipment through the dining room. Sure enough, it was not long before one of them removed a small tube containing wires from the candelabra above the table.

Elizabeth's anxiety grew. Due to all the bad press received by the current Administration over illegal wire-tapping, many articles had been written about the reluctance of judges to sign warrants to wiretap. A court order meant the authorities had probable cause to believe that something illegal was going on. *Darcy, what have you gotten yourself mixed up in?*

Edmund addressed the sweep team leader. "That was fast. I take it your equipment must be quite advanced."

"We have the most up-to-date detectors, but even they couldn't locate this baby. I found it simply by looking in the most logical places to plant a bug. I believe this room is now clean."

Edmund gave his thanks as the team moved into the hallway. He then turned to Elizabeth and Georgiana. "Now, before you begin with your questions, let me tell you I have no idea where Mr. Darcy and Mr. Fitzwilliam are or what they're doing there. Chris Brandon contacted me to do what I can to protect your rights until Mr. Darcy returns." At the look of dismay on the faces of the two women before him, Edmund added, "I'm sorry. This must be very difficult for you."

As Georgiana expressed her gratitude for Edmund's assistance, Elizabeth fought to suppress the cutting retort on her lips. It was one of her greatest faults; every time she felt afraid, it was a gut reaction to erupt in anger. It wasn't Edmund's fault that he had no information to give her, but she was terrified...for Darcy.

SOMEWHERE OVER PANAMA, GEOFFREY FITZWILLIAM was once again running over his fuel calculations as the Cessna Citation X flew on automatic pilot. Flying at the plane's top speed they had made excellent time. "Anything?"

"Yes, be quiet!" Darcy was listening on the radio as their contact provided coordinates and landing instructions. Frantically, Darcy wrote down the co-ordinates and the time frame they had in which to land. "We've got two hours to land here," he said handing Geoff the paper. "If we're late...it's too late."

Geoff nodded his understanding and plugged the co-ordinates into the GPS system. "As we suspected, it's in a very remote area. It will be tricky. Let's hope the runway is big enough and we have enough fuel to make it."

AFTER EDMUND LEFT, ELIZABETH SENT Jake and Georgiana upstairs to rest while she gathered the troops. Lansing's staff, all the bodyguards and the newly arrived Jane and Bingley were drafted in the task of putting the house back to rights. Elizabeth methodically moved from room to room, replacing the contents of drawers and closets. Eventually she found herself on the third floor of the townhouse, picking up the clothing that had been tossed on the floor of Darcy's closet during the search.

She noted the designer names inside the articles of clothing. He had a penchant for Armani suits, Versace ties and Gucci shoes while his casual attire tended toward American designers Ralph Lauren and Calvin Klein. Methodically, she placed his ties on the tie rack, sorting them by color. As she replaced each colorful strip of silk, she recalled when she had seen Darcy wear it, what they had talked about or where they had gone. When hanging his suit jackets and sport coats, she found herself caressing the sleeves, remembering how it felt when Darcy embraced her while wearing them.

Eventually the closet was in order, so Elizabeth made her way into Darcy's bedroom. There she replaced books on shelves and gathered items from the floor to place back inside drawers. She laughed briefly while picking up four small bottles of personal lubricant and placing them carefully in the drawer of his nightstand. Glancing about the room, she took note of the décor. Dark green wallpaper gave the room a masculine feel. The deep gold-striped bedding over white sheers matched the heavy draperies that hung from the windows.

A sitting area containing a wingback chair in a deep red and a small table with a Tiffany-style lamp were situated before a small fireplace. A deep-piled, Persian carpet in jeweled tones covered the rich wood floor. Elizabeth could only smile at the realization that there was not a decorative pillow in sight. This room was a perfect reflection of its owner, and Elizabeth sighed as she turned to make the bed, remembering that Saturday in September when Darcy stretched out on her own bed. It seemed like a lifetime ago.

Suddenly, Elizabeth felt her eyes drawn to the print of an old painting that hung over the headboard. In the upper left corner of the print was a great house, white and gleaming in the sun, surrounded by meticulously planted gardens. In the middle were fields through which a pair of riders jumped a fence on their steeds. Finally in the lower right was a forest into which a herd of deer was running. *Pemberley!* The more Elizabeth gazed at the print, the more the scene seemed to beckon to her. If the reality was half as inviting as the print, she could understand why Darcy loved this place above all others.

Lying down upon the freshly made bed, Elizabeth clutched Darcy's pillow to her chest, breathing in his scent as it escaped from its downy depths. Fighting the tears that threatened her composure, Elizabeth stared through the sheer curtains into the nothingness beyond the window.

Where is he? No matter how hard she tried, she could come up with no clues; nothing was said, and no hint was given. Whatever had taken Darcy away from her must have occurred suddenly and been of extreme importance for him to take Geoff, leave Georgiana, and face the possibility of death. *What could it be?* Facing the fact that no answers were forthcoming in the foreseeable future, she lay back and began methodically relaxing her muscles, beginning with her feet and moving slowly up her body.

As THEY APPROACHED THE RUNWAY, Geoff was sweating bullets. The fuel was about to run out and the runway was short and in poor condition. Geoff flew enough to fulfill the requirements to maintain his license, but never had he landed a jet under such conditions. White knuckled, he lowered the plane to the ground.

As soon as the wheels hit the tarmac, Geoff realized that things were not as they appeared from the air. The runway was smooth, and where he thought the tarmac ended in dirt, there was actually more runway which was painted to disguise its length.

As the jet powered down, Darcy looked around for their hosts. *Hosts? What other word would fit? Captors? Negotiators? Killers? Who knows? Elizabeth would know, she would have the perfect word to complete my sentence.*

Instinctively Darcy pulled out his PDA and noted he had five bars of reception. *In the middle of nowhere, I have perfect reception?* He thought of texting Elizabeth. Perhaps she would be able to text him back and tell him what was happening at Lansing. *No. The police could be with her, and I need to focus on the task at hand.*

Shoving his PDA back into his pocket, Darcy settled in to wait for what the fates had in store. He hoped they would be kind.

CHAPTER 18
FEAR AND HOPE

"You were told to come alone!" a harsh voice in a thick accent accused while the barrel of a rifle was shoved into Darcy's back.

"Necesitaba un piloto," Darcy responded. *I needed a pilot.*

A wide grin appeared on the man's weathered face, displaying a large gap where his two front teeth had once been. "Una respuesta lógica." *A logical answer.* Pointing his automatic rifle toward the closest jeep he said, "Entren." *Get in.*

As Darcy and Geoff approached the jeep, five men, each heavily armed, entered the plane. Two more searched them, confiscating their phones and the laptop Darcy was instructed to bring. The man with the missing teeth spoke, "Recuerde, mientras siga las intrucciones, permanecerá vivo." *Remember, as long as you follow instructions, you will remain alive.* After crawling into the jeep, both Darcy and Geoff were blindfolded.

"And so it begins," Geoff whispered as the jeep jerked forward and drove off.

"ELIZABETH," GEORGIANA'S SOFT VOICE GENTLY roused her from sleep. "I'm sorry to wake you, but we're serving a late lunch in the kitchen."

Elizabeth pushed herself up and brushed the hair from her eyes. "Excuse me. I know I shouldn't have stayed here."

Georgiana looked tired and anxious. "I'm sure Wills would want you here if it made you feel better."

209

Elizabeth reached over to squeeze Georgiana's hand gently. "It did."

That small gesture was enough to crumble the girl's façade of composure as she threw her arms around Elizabeth and began sobbing uncontrollably. "Do you think they really could die?"

Inside, Elizabeth cursed the agents. Surely, there had to be a better way to try to obtain information than scaring a teenage girl to death. Once Georgiana's tears again subsided, Elizabeth looked into her eyes and smiled. "When your brother comes back — and I have no doubt he will — *I'm* going to kill him for doing this to us."

Georgiana returned the smile through her tear-streaked face. "And *I'm* going to help you!"

Hand in hand, the two women walked down to the kitchen as Elizabeth ran a new mantra through her head repeatedly: *He will come back. He will come back. He will come back.*

THEY HAD BEEN RIDING IN the jeep for what felt like hours. Attempting to memorize their route by the number and direction of turns they made. Darcy soon realized it was hopeless. If they needed to escape, he would have no way to get them back to the airstrip without assistance. He chose to ignore the fact that, even if they had made their way to the airstrip, they had no keys to the jet, which was completely out of fuel.

The jeep curved suddenly to the right and stopped. The blindfolds were pulled from their heads and they were astounded to find themselves in the middle of a large, luxurious hacienda. Darcy and Geoff were lead to a small house near an Olympic-sized swimming pool and quickly hustled inside.

"This place is like a fortress," Geoff commented as he looked out the window toward the large house that stood in the center of the compound. "There are armed guards everywhere, even on the roof."

"I don't care if it's fucking Buckingham Palace. All I want is to get what we came for and get out of here — alive if at all possible."

Geoff turned and said guiltily, "I'm sorry. I should have come alone."

Darcy shook his head. "I'm the one they contacted. You know as well as I do that they would have shot you if you showed up alone, and that would have helped no one." Turning his attention to their accommodations, he said, "This reminds me of the pool house I stayed in when Charles lived in LA."

Although the house looked small from the outside, it was simply dwarfed by the larger house. Once inside, it was found to be spacious and comfortable. The first floor consisted of a large great room and a fully stocked kitchen. A staircase led to the second floor that Darcy had no interest in exploring. He hoped they wouldn't be there long enough to need to.

"Hey, our stuff is here!" Darcy turned to see the bag he swore he'd left on the plane now sitting on the couch. Panicking, he took a quick inventory, only relaxing when he found the book of essays on the movement for the global ban on land mines entitled *To Walk without Fear.*[23]

"What's so important about that book?" Geoff asked.

Darcy quickly flipped through the pages. "I didn't want to sit around waiting with nothing to fill the time."

"Are you kidding? I've never seen a plasma screen TV this big before, and there's not only a Play Station 3, but they've got a Wii[24] too!"

Darcy walked into the kitchen to check out the contents of the Sub Zero refrigerator, emerging with two bottles of water. Tossing one bottle to Geoff, he glanced about the great room, his eyes resting on a one-liter plastic container sitting in the middle of the coffee table. "Please, don't let this be what I think it is!"

Geoff came over to investigate the reason for Darcy's statement. His response was a long slow whistle followed by, "You've got to be kidding me!"

Taking off the lid, Darcy quickly ascertained that his suspicions were correct. In his hands was one liter of finely cut cocaine. Darcy laughed humorlessly. "Do you think it's some kind of welcome gift, like a fruit basket?"

"Perhaps, but if they can afford to leave this amount of product lying around, they don't need your money. What do they really want?"

"I've been contemplating that same question since we left New York. I don't know what they want, but I'm not about to let them think they're dealing with idiots!" As he opened the front door, Darcy was greeted by two automatic rifles to the face. Undeterred, he shoved the container to the guard on his right. "Llévese esto!" *Take this away!* Without waiting for a response, he drew himself back inside the house and closed the door.

IT IS A TRUTH UNIVERSALLY acknowledged that you don't really know a person until you've lived with them, and that day Elizabeth found she still had

---

23 *The Global Movement to Ban Land Mines*, by Maxwell A. Cameron (Editor), Brian W. Tomlin (Editor), Robert J. Lawson (Editor), Oxford University Press, Ontario, Canada 1998.
24 A video game system by Nintendo

a great deal to learn about Darcy. From the place in the closet that his wool overcoat was hung, to the placement of the silver tray on which he deposited his keys in his study, she discovered that Darcy was a man who had a place for everything and everything was in its place. At least until his sister got her hands on things.

"I like to let him know he's not the only person who makes the rules around here," Georgiana said playfully as she moved the silver tray to the opposite side of the table. With the activity of putting the house back in order to keep their thoughts away from their concerns, both Elizabeth and Georgiana found they could inject a little humor into the day.

"Now who's living dangerously?" Elizabeth teased.

Georgiana whispered conspiratorially, "Go ahead, Elizabeth! You give it a try."

All afternoon Elizabeth had listened to the maids twitter about how Mr. Darcy liked everything placed "just so!" Quite frankly, she was ready to ruffle the master's feathers a little.

Giving a sly smile, she moved one of the four, perfectly sharpened pencils from the pencil cup on the desk and placed it inside the front drawer. She then removed a beautiful Mont Blanc pen from the drawer and placed it inside the pencil cup. "There! Have I caused enough chaos, do you think?"

"Bold move! Bravo!" Georgiana applauded.

"Perhaps just a bit more mischief…" Elizabeth then took the coaster from the top of Darcy's desk and opening the lowest drawer, unceremoniously dropped it inside before firmly shutting it with her foot.

Georgiana's eyes grew wide in mock horror. "I think you may have upset the delicate balance of the universe with that one!"

"So be it!" Satisfied that the rest of the room was in order, the two young women moved on to the game room. "Tell me, does your brother have a specific place to keep the remote controls?"

GEOFF TOOK A BREAK FROM the video game *Trauma Center*[25] after successfully performing a kidney transplant. "It's starting to get dark."

Darcy made no response, but continued to stare into the open book he held in his hand. Although a favorite, he had no desire to read the book again. It simply was the first one he found that was large enough to secret away inside a

25 *Trauma Center: Under the Knife*, Video game Atlas Publisher, for the Nintendo Game Systems, 2008.

photo of Elizabeth taken at the Longbourn Gala. As he studied her beautiful face, he repeated his new mantra over and over: *I will return. I will return…*

The sudden opening of the front door commanded both gentlemen's attention. Three men entered; one held his gun on Geoff while the other two grabbed Darcy by the arms and dragged him to the kitchen table, forcing him to sit.

"Señor Darcy." The toothless man entered carrying Darcy's laptop, which he set on the table before him along with a yellow piece of paper on which a series of numbers was written. "Tiene diez minutos; diez minutos para transferir cinco millones de dólares a esta cuenta." *You have ten minutes to transfer five million dollars to this account.*

As midnight approached, Elizabeth pulled herself from the guest room bed. Sleep would not come, and so, in an effort to burn off her nervous energy, she dressed, grabbed her iPod and headed for the basement where Darcy told her he kept a treadmill. Upon finding the room, Elizabeth could not help but laugh. Inside was a state-of-the-art treadmill, a full set of free weights, a Bowflex machine and a sauna.

It took several minutes for Elizabeth to figure out how to turn on the treadmill. In trying to program a simple hour-long run, she came across a record of Darcy's use of the machine. Nearly every morning at 7:30 a.m. he logged onto the treadmill and ran six kilometers. Not 7:25 a.m. or 7:40 a.m., but precisely at 7:30 a.m. A precise routine fit perfectly with Darcy's personality, and her overwhelming desire to tease him about it only made her miss him even more.

Turning her attention to the problem of how to play her iPod once it was inserted into the keypad of the treadmill, Elizabeth began her own six-kilometer run.

Darcy was on edge. Before the money transfer, he was somewhat confident that everything would work out as planned, but now that his host had his five million, there was nothing to stop the man from reneging on the deal, killing both him and Geoff and dumping their bodies in the forest, never to be seen again.

Geoff also seemed to sense a change in the atmosphere. He simply sat on the couch staring unseeing at the television. They found the compound had perfect television reception and access to hundreds of channels, undoubtedly provided by the huge satellite dish positioned near the pool. "How much longer will we have to wait?" Geoff shouted aloud to no one.

The answer to Geoff's question was immediately provided when once again three armed men burst through the front door of the pool house. "Rápido," *Quickly*, they shouted, "Muévanse." *Move*. Without being given the opportunity to gather their belongings, Darcy and Geoff found themselves back in the jeep, this time without blindfolds, driving off into the blackness of the surrounding forest.

This journey was once more several hours in duration. When the jeep finally stopped, Darcy's heart sank when he realized they were being pushed to the front of the jeep to stand alone in the headlights. Hearing Geoff softly whisper, "And so it ends," only served to confirm his supposition. This was it. They were going to die.

In the blink of an eye, his life seemed to pass before him. His only regret about the life he led was not the incident with Rebecca Wickham, or that he may not have lived up to his parents' expectations, but that he had not spent the last four months of his life making love to Elizabeth Bennet. *I am a complete idiot!*

"Mr. Darcy!" A voice from behind called out jovially in perfect English. "You look as if you were expecting a firing squad." Stepping into the light was a man of about forty years of age with dark hair and dark eyes.

"Renee Estoban, I presume." Darcy's voice was steady, hiding the minute relief he felt within. If they were to be shot, it would not be at that moment.

The man smiled. "No, I am his brother, Pierre. My elder brother is less hospitable. I hope you have enjoyed your stay at my little cottage in the woods." At Darcy's silence, Estoban suggested, "Walk with me?"

The question was rhetorical as a new set of guards surrounded him and Geoff. Darcy was led to walk beside Estoban while Geoff was forced to follow several meters behind. Guards carrying high-powered flashlights and the ever-present rifles led the way.

In no mood for idle banter, Darcy cut to the chase. "Why am I here?"

A deep laugh filled the darkness as Estoban puffed on a Cuban cigar. "You are a clever man, Mr. Darcy — clever enough to realize your money is nothing to me. When I realized my brother held something you would value, I convinced him to allow me to use it to bring you here. The five million is but a token for his trouble; with a little luck I can convince him to return it. You are here because I wanted to meet you face to face."

Exceedingly puzzled, Darcy waited for Estoban to continue. After several moments of silence, the older man continued, "You see Mr. Darcy, we have something very important in common."

Darcy suppressed the urge to contradict that statement.

"I see you do not believe me, but let me assure you we do. We are both very important to one person in particular: Elizabeth Bennet."

Darcy's steps faltered as he asked suspiciously, "Elizabeth? How do you know Elizabeth?"

Resuming their pace, Estoban said, "Many years ago I had the privilege of seeing one of Miss Bennet's concerts in Sao Paulo."

"*Dr.* Bennet," Darcy interjected.

Estoban laughed again. "At the time she was a teenage girl, just beginning to show the promise of the ravishing woman she has become."

Fuming at Estoban's description of Elizabeth, Darcy fought to remain silent. An outburst of jealous temper would not help anyone.

"I approached her mother and asked her to arrange a private concert at my home in Rio de Janeiro. I wanted an intimate performance, just my mother and myself. Mother was a concert pianist with the Orchestra of Paris before my father brought her here. So you see, Miss Bennet's music would have been the perfect birthday gift."

"Confident that her daughter would agree, Mrs. Bennet permitted me to wait outside of Miss Bennet's dressing room for confirmation. Imagine my shock to hear that Mrs. Bennet interpreted my request as something else entirely. I can still hear Miss Bennet's shouts that she would never sell her body to any man and Mrs. Bennet's insistence that she would. Can you imagine such a mother, Mr. Darcy?"

Darcy responded, "I am aware of Frannie Bennet's unnatural proclivities."

"I will admit I was smitten with the girl, but I am no molester of children. To realize that this beautiful flower was at the mercy of that woman, with no protection... well, I could not stand idly by and do nothing. At that moment, I appointed myself Miss Elizabeth Bennet's protector... a kind of guardian angel."

Darcy could not prevent the note of disbelief in his voice. "And exactly what have you done for Elizabeth as her 'protector?'"

Estoban stepped over a fallen log, illuminated by a flashlight. "I am not a man to boast of my actions; however, given the purpose of this meeting, I shall tell you that it was I who saw to it the Child Protection Authorities in Vienna removed Miss Bennet from her mother's custody, and it was I who guaranteed that Billy Ray Collins was advised to plead guilty by his attorneys. The Collins family is very powerful in Kent County, but even the powerful have a price, and I did not want to see Miss Bennet testify in court. She had been through more than enough at the hands of that animal."

Darcy again held his tongue. It seemed ironic that a man whose family supplied most of the world with a never-ending flow of cocaine saw himself as some kind of hero. Colombia was a nation filled with warm, hard working people, trying desperately to free itself from the grip of men like Estoban who held their economy and stability hostage. So while grateful for Estobans actions toward Elizabeth, Darcy could not bring himself to thank him. "So exactly what is the purpose of this meeting?"

"So I may sketch your character! You are to marry Miss Bennet, and while I know you have the resources to protect her, I know nothing about what kind of man you are. Your Google results give conflicting opinions. On one hand you are a humanitarian and philanthropist; on the other, a ruthless business-man and womanizer."

A mirthless laugh escaped Darcy's throat. "So what have you decided?"

"You have come all this way, paid a great deal of money, risked the threat of death and faced certain arrest upon your return. That speaks well of you ... and of course, you refused my little gift upon your arrival. All I need to know is whether you love her enough to give up all other women for the rest of your life?"

"I will not discuss my relationship with Elizabeth with you." Darcy stopped walking and faced Estoban. "All I will say is that, for the most part, Elizabeth is strong enough to protect herself. In those areas where she needs assistance, *I* will protect her. She no longer needs *you* to be her 'guardian angel.'"

Estoban laughed again. "You are a reserved man, Fitzwilliam Darcy, but your eyes betray you. I am glad we had this little meeting." Motioning through the trees, Estoban directed their steps toward a flood of lights ahead. As they came closer, the runway and Darcy's jet could be seen. "I will pull back, keeping a lookout only from a distance and trust that you will keep your word. Soon I will send you my files on Mrs. Bennet and Billy Ray Collins. You will need all the information you can get once that dog is released from prison."

When they approached the jet, Estoban stopped Darcy and said, "Warm up the engines as soon as you are aboard. Stay inside the plane until the helicopter has cleared the runway. If you leave the plane before then, *everyone* on the runway will be shot. These are not simply instructions; they are a warning! My brother is not only less hospitable than I, he has no patience whatsoever for disobedience."

Darcy waited for Geoff at the bottom of the stairs into the jet. As he began to climb the stairs, Estoban called out in a cold, authoritarian voice, "If you prove my trust is misplaced, I will not hesitate to step in again." A curt nod of the head was Darcy's only response as he and Geoff made their way into the jet.

Once inside the cabin, Darcy was not surprised to find all his belongings lying on the floor. Placing his PDA back into his pocket, he made his way to the cockpit where Geoff was firing up the engines. "Can you believe this?" Geoff asked incredulously. "The fuel tanks are full!"

"At this point I wouldn't be surprised to find a bloody *McDonald's* in the trees."

The thumping sound of helicopter blades prevented Geoff from offering any further comments on the resourcefulness of their host. Anxiously, the two men watched the runway in front of the jet as an Agusta A109 Power-Elite helicopter alighted. The door of the craft slid open and a man who Darcy knew must be Colonel Forster of the U.S. Army Special Forces began to climb out onto the runway. Apparently the man was not moving fast enough for those within, for a foot abruptly kicked out, causing him to fall to the ground. Then Darcy and Geoff could only watch in horror as a body wrapped in a green tarpaulin was tossed from the helicopter onto the runway.

"Let me go!" Geoff cried in anguish as Darcy tackled him to the floor of the cabin. Geoff lashed out against his cousin, catching Darcy with a right to the jaw that sent him flying back into a leather-covered, cabin chair. Darcy recovered in time to lunge at Geoff's feet, pulling him down before he could open the hatch.

For several minutes, they struggled with one another until Darcy finally called out, "They're gone! They're gone!"

Geoff was the first down the stairs, running across the runway, bypassing Colonel Forster and falling to his knees beside the tarp. Desperately pulling at the plastic, he froze once he finally saw the bloody, battered face of the man inside.

Darcy collapsed beside Geoff and, upon seeing the condition of his cousin, cried out in anguish, "Oh God, no!"

The swollen, purple eyelids of Colonel Richard Fitzwilliam fluttered briefly before his dry and raspy voice whispered, "Darcy, it's about bloody time you got here."

ONCE RICHARD WAS SECURED IN the stateroom of the jet and Colonel Forster was strapped into one of the reclining seats of the cabin, Geoff prepared for takeoff. Darcy stared unseeing into space. For the briefest of moments this night, he felt that he and Geoff were a heartbeat away from death. A few moments ago, he was certain his cousin, Richard, was dead, too. He was astounded that by some miracle, all three of them were alive and on their way back home.

Home? No, not home. Darcy knew he was not returning to some building, and as much as he loved them, he was not returning to Georgiana or his Aunt and Uncle Fitzwilliam. Darcy was returning to Elizabeth. He was done suppressing his feelings for her and denying how much he needed her.

"Wait!" Darcy called out as he grabbed his PDA.

Geoff looked at him angrily. "We're getting the fuck out of here now!"

"No!" Darcy shouted as he fumbled for the stylus, briefly cursing his fingers for being too large to use a model with buttons effectively. "Give me a just moment!" Rapidly, before they took off and all reception was lost, he sent what he felt was the most important text message of his life.

I TRIED TO SLEEP IN my room, Elizabeth reasoned as she found herself again lying in Darcy's bed. *I will only stay for a few minutes until I start to drift off. Then I'll go back to my room.*

It was 3:00 a.m. on the longest night of her life. No mind-relaxing technique, no attempt at meditation would allow her a respite from the pain and fear that had overwhelmed her once the house was quite and everyone else had gone to bed.

She loved Darcy. Even though she had never been in love before, there was no doubt in her mind that what she felt was real, honest and could never be duplicated with anyone else. All her life she had hid behind her need for self-preservation, never allowing anyone to get too close. Even Jane was kept at arm's length. And then, without even making an effort, Darcy had managed to pass through the thick walls of her defenses like a ghost in a gothic novel. Now, when all her well-rehearsed reasons for avoiding intimacy were revealed to be nothing more than smoke and mirrors, Darcy was gone, perhaps forever.

The vibration of her mobile phone interrupted her painful thoughts. Her heart leapt into her throat when she saw who it was from, and her fingers trembled as she tried to pull up the message:

My BFF, I have broken the most important rule.

CHAPTER 19
TO BE OF USE

December 15th, New York Times
*Photo caption: The Federal Bureau of Investigation removes Evidence from
Fitzwilliam Darcy's New York Townhome.*
*Story: "Billion Dollar Blunder!... Authorities have yet to issue a comment
explaining why Federal authorities searched the home of..."*

December 16th, The Daily Insight(U.S.)
*Photo caption: Elizabeth Bennet is left to face the music as boyfriend
Fitzwilliam Darcy escapes Federal authorities.*
*Story: "Darcy on the Lam! Sources say that Fitzwilliam Darcy and his cousin,
Darcy Company attorney, Geoffrey Fitzwilliam, have embezzled billions from
Company coffers and have disappeared to some unknown hideaway to spend
their ill-gotten gain."*

*T*he mist was so stereotypical it was irritating. "Enough with the stupid
mist!" Elizabeth called out into her dream. "Bring him to me!" However,
the dream was not cooperating. The mist thickened to where she could feel
it form a clammy sheen on her skin. She began to run, hoping that somehow the
mist would part and Darcy would appear before her, but no matter how far or
how fast she ran, it was always the same: only mist.

Frustrated anger rose in her chest and she began to scream, "Where is he?"

She repeatedly screamed her question into the void of mist. In response, the mist turned into rain, covering her face in a deluge of water as she was left alone and unanswered in the dark.

The phone was ringing and Elizabeth quickly forced herself from sleep to grab it. The caller ID was the first thing checked, and she nearly sobbed in frustration upon realizing it was not Darcy. She took a brief moment to calm herself before answering the phone. "Hey, Gran."

The soothing voice of Isabella Bennet filtered through the earpiece. *"Oh, Lizzy dear, you sound terrible. Do you want me to fly up? I can be there by dinner time."*

Elizabeth realized her voice sounded stressed, and she touched her cheeks to confirm they were hot and awash with tears. She cleared her throat, annoyed at her own weakness. "I'm all right, Gran. There's a lot of press here, so we're trapped in the house. You know I love you, but you tend to go a little crazy if you can't get outside to stretch your legs every day."

"If I remember correctly, I'm not the only one. All right sugar, just call me if you need me, no matter what time, no matter how late... and don't let your father bother you! The man's got a one-track mind where your friend is concerned."

The call lasted a few more minutes. Isabella was supportive and did not press Elizabeth for any details of what was happening with Darcy. Elizabeth was grateful, for she had no details to give. The call was ended with another promise from Isabella to be available to Elizabeth at any time.

Elizabeth did not have time to put the phone back on the nightstand before it rang again.

"Hey, Daddy."

"Lizzy, what has that man got you mixed up in?" Thomas Bennet was more than concerned, he was angry. *"Has he been arrested? Were you implicated? Do you need a lawyer? I think you need to come home, now!"*

Elizabeth thought to herself that Hunsford had never been her home and nothing could induce her to go back there... ever. "I have final exams this week, and besides, I want to stay here."

"Whatever that friend of yours has done, Lizzy, you owe him nothing. You need to get away now."

"I'm staying put! Now, I have to go, Daddy. Bye!" Elizabeth hung up the phone and settled back into Darcy's pillows. The last thing she needed at that moment was a suddenly over-protective father. Her phone rang again and she looked to see that her father was calling once more. She pressed the button to send the call directly to voice mail. "I'm sorry, Daddy," she said to herself. She was not going to allow anyone to say anything disparaging to her about Darcy that day. Any negative comments would be reserved solely for herself…and perhaps Georgiana.

She walked over to the window and glanced through the sheers at the sea of photographers outside Lansing. "Vultures!" she hissed. At the reminder that she had no other means of exercise, she threw on her sweats and headed for the treadmill.

MEXICO CITY WAS BRIGHT AND brilliant in the blazing sun. How long Darcy had been in the city was anyone's guess. There was no clock in the room where he was sequestered, but judging by the height of the sun over the buildings next door, he guessed it was well past noon.

The memories of the previous night were a blur. As soon as they cleared the runway, Geoff headed to Panama City. Richard was obviously in serious condition, and both Darcy and Geoff felt it was imperative to fly him to the nearest major hospital; however, Panama refused them permission to land. The jet was listed by both U.S. and British officials as holding possible fugitives, making finding a country willing to allow them to land impossible. Frustration built as they continued to fly north and country after country refused them entry. Finally, Mexican authorities gave them permission to land at Benito Juárez International Airport.

Police officers took Darcy and Geoff into custody immediately upon disembarking, confiscating everything except the clothes on their backs and placing them in handcuffs. He expected them to be taken to a Mexican jail, so Darcy was surprised to find that they were instead taken along with Richard and Colonel Forster to the American British Cowdray Hospital. There Darcy had been placed in a secure room, and a doctor had come in to examine him.

The doctor was kind, and after a few minutes of conversation, he confided that as a child he had learned to play the guitar under a program funded by The Darcy Foundation. Although it was against policy, the doctor informed Darcy that Richard had suffered severe internal injuries, a concussion, a broken leg and several broken ribs. Richard was taken into surgery, but was expected to pull through. Colonel Forster's injuries were minor and he was already on his way back to the U.S. Geoff was being held in a room down the hall.

Because he was exhausted and sleep deprived, Darcy was then subjected to several hours of questioning by representatives of both the U.S. and British governments. He told the truth several times over and from every angle imaginable until everyone seemed to accept that he had either given all the information he had, or all he was willing to give.

Darcy felt he owed nothing to Pierre Estoban. If not for the man's unusual interest in Elizabeth, Richard and Colonel Forster would simply have been shot to death as neither the U.S. nor British governments negotiated with kidnappers for the return of their own. If the information Darcy provided helped the authorities to capture the man, however unlikely, so be it.

Darcy pondered over how useless that information truly was. Given the long drive from the runway to Estoban's hacienda, it could be located anywhere within a three hundred meter radius of the airstrip, and the Bank in the Cayman Islands would never turn over any information concerning the account into which Darcy transferred the five million dollars.

Regardless of his intentions to pay a ransom for his cousin, Darcy gave a large sum of money to a known drug lord. Both the U.S. and Great Britain had what amounted to a no-tolerance policy for this type of offence, which was covered under each government's anti-terrorism policies. This classification allowed them to question Darcy without an attorney and hold him wherever they wished for as long as they desired without formally charging him with any crime.[26]

Although a stay in the infamous prison at Guantanamo Bay was not probable, the possibility of some form of incarceration loomed large over his head. He could lose everything: the foundation, The Darcy Company and his freedom.

He sighed heavily as he thought of Elizabeth. Pierre's fascination with her was the one bit of information he refused to divulge to anyone. Both governments were desperate to get their hands on the Estobans, and Darcy would not put it past them to try to use Elizabeth to trap Pierre. That was something Darcy simply could not permit.

Even without the picture of Elizabeth in his bag, Darcy could still conjure her image in his mind. It seemed ironic that the event that cleared away his last mental barrier to an intimate relationship with her was also the reason they were

26 *MPs will buy 42-day Detention*, BBC News Online, April 14, 2008, http://news.bbc.co.uk/1/hi/uk_politics/7345932.stm

Emergency Powers and Terrorism by Professor Wayne McCormack, Military Law Review, Fall 2005, Volume 185, Page 69.

Detainees at Guantanamo Bay, NPR Online, May 5, 2008, http://www.npr.org/templates/story/story.php?storyId=4711397

to be kept apart. It was fortunate that he was a wealthy and connected man. There was no guarantee, but Darcy was determined to use every means at his disposal to return to Elizabeth as soon as possible…however long that might be.

His thoughts turned to Georgiana. He had no doubt that Elizabeth was with her, but he wondered how she was holding up under the stress of his and Geoff's disappearance. His sister's spunky disposition may cause others to forget how insecure and vulnerable she was inside; however, Darcy was keenly aware of how easily she could be wounded. If only there had been some way to rescue Richard without alarming Georgiana. Hopefully someone would soon inform her that all were alive and well.

Pushing his regrets aside, Darcy took comfort in the knowledge that he and Geoff could now return Richard alive to his parents, and that alone made any sacrifice on Darcy's part worthwhile. *Didn't it?* Unable to stand or think any longer, Darcy fell into the bed and slept like the dead.

OVER THE NEXT FEW DAYS, life at Lansing developed a routine. In the mornings, Mr. Sparks would drive Georgiana, Elizabeth and their security guards to Longbourn. Once there, Elizabeth would administer and Georgiana would take final examinations for the semester. As soon as possible, all would be returned safely to the house.

The media was a constant, almost menacing, presence. With no statement from the authorities as to why the police searched Lansing and Darcy's lack of public appearance on either side of the Atlantic, the insatiable appetites of those who needed to know all things celebrity became voracious. To feed those appetites, a host of reporters and photographers from the so-called legitimate news sources joined the paparazzi to make it nearly impossible for anyone to either come or go from the house. Eventually Elizabeth discouraged even Jane and Bingley from trying to visit. Only Jake was brave enough to take on the thundering horde to see Georgiana each day.

The other constant was the telephone. Whether mobile or land line, Elizabeth spent hours each day talking to Chris Brandon, Edmund Bertram, The Earl of Matlock and anyone else who she thought could place pressure on both the British and American authorities to give them any information they had on Darcy and Geoff's whereabouts.

Elizabeth was convinced that if the authorities did not know the men's location, they would have been a constant presence at Lansing, waiting for either Darcy or Geoff to contact them. She knew in her gut that someone, somewhere, was keeping their location a secret, and Elizabeth would not rest until she found out just where they were.

Agents Smith and Martin soon regretted giving Elizabeth their phone numbers. First, she hounded them for information and, when unsatisfied, hounded their superiors and then the superiors of their superiors until even Agency Heads and Cabinet Secretaries could not escape her. The woman was tenacious and, unfortunately for the authorities, extremely well connected.

Edmund Bertram turned out to be a surprising ally. The son of Congressman John Bertram of New York State, who also happened to be head of the Senate Intelligence Committee, Edmund convinced his father to take up Elizabeth's cause. Chris Brandon was using contacts established throughout years as a human rights attorney that were not available through standard channels. However, Elizabeth's greatest help came from Geoff's father. As a retired Colonel and a member of the House of Lords, The Earl kept Elizabeth updated on his progress as he called in favors from associates. With the lives of his son and nephew on the line, only Elizabeth could match his stubborn determination to find them.

In between phone calls, Elizabeth graded final exams as Georgiana studied. After dinner, the two women would curl up together in the game room and watch CNN and BBC America, hoping for any late-breaking story that might shed light on what happened to Darcy and Geoff. Usually Jake would join them, but he also had finals to prepare for and needed to spend a great deal of his time on campus.

During the long nights when sleep was impossible, Elizabeth and Georgiana would sit at the piano, playing duets and singing pop songs. They tended to gravitate toward light, funny and sometimes ridiculous tunes, allowing them to smile and occasionally laugh, but they could not lighten the gnawing anxiety embedded in their chests. They lived in limbo with no end in sight.

Six days after Darcy and Geoff's disappearance, Elizabeth hung up from her second call of the morning from the Earl. She looked through the vertical blinds that covered the kitchen windows out to the crowd of paparazzi preventing her from taking even a casual walk in Lansing's small garden. "Vultures!" she hissed again through her teeth.

Suddenly, a plan hatched and a smile turned up the corners of her mouth. She grabbed her phone and, after receiving the hearty approval of all her allies, called Frank Churchill.

That evening as she, Georgiana and Jake took their usual places on the couch in front of the television, BBC America reported the following:

What you are seeing on your screen is a scene occurring live outside Number 10 Downing Street where protestors began gathering at about six this evening. Even though it is now midnight, the crowd is continuing to grow to such alarming proportions that the military has been called in to assist the police in controlling the protestors.

All of this is in reaction to an announcement made by Frank Churchill, spokesman for the family of Darcy Company CEO and Philanthropist, Fitzwilliam Darcy. The family is accusing the governments of both the United States and Great Britain of withholding the location of Mr. Darcy and his cousin, Mr. Geoffrey Fitzwilliam, son of member of the House of Lords, James Fitzwilliam, the Earl of Matlock.

Darcy, who is to receive a Human Rights Recognition Award next month, is unpopular with authorities in both countries for what is considered his interference in matters involving human rights. Now the champion of human rights appears to be a victim of the very violations he has fought to eliminate, causing an outpouring of sympathy not only here in Britain, but also in the United States where protestors are also gathering in Washington D.C. and New York City...

Confused, Georgiana turned to Elizabeth. "What's happening?"

Elizabeth voiced her growing hope. "The vultures are finally going to be of use."

Georgiana was prevented from asking for clarification by the ringing of the phone. Looking at the caller ID, Elizabeth recognized Chris Brandon's number.

DARCY STARED OUT OF A small window into the darkness, imagining the soft green hills in the distance. Standing at the window had become his favorite pastime since he had arrived in England four days before. Well, it was his favorite activity next to imagining Elizabeth naked; however, he suspected he was being observed, and it would not do to masturbate before an audience, so he needed to find some other activity to occupy his mind.

He had seen Geoff on the plane when they left Mexico, but they were seated far from each other and not permitted to converse. Not seated at the window, it wasn't until he saw the peaks when they disembarked at a military base that he was sure he was in England.

The cell he was held in was small, containing only a bed, a chair, a table and a toilet. There were no bars, but the room locked from the outside and the sole window was too narrow to climb out of even if he had considered breaking the glass to attempt such a thing. He had no television, radio, or contact at all with the outside world. That in itself would have been of no consequence to Darcy if he had not also been denied access to anything else to occupy his mind.

After four days, he would have paid a fortune for a book, even a cheap paperback romance or, heaven forbid, a copy of Celebrity Tattler. But his jailors made it quite clear: this was not a vacation. Therefore, he spent his days staring out of the window, reviewing whatever he could recall in his photographic memory and desperately trying to keep his baser thoughts of Elizabeth at bay.

The jingling of the lock alerted him to a visitor. Light flooded the dark room, causing Darcy to squint his eyes, and when his vision cleared, he recognized his visitor instantly.

"Thornton, isn't it a little late for a social call?"

John Thornton, head of British Intelligence, glared back at him as he sat down in the chair. "Why, Darcy, do you remain the proverbial thorn in my side? There I was, lying in my bed...alone, because my lovely wife was sitting in front of the telly watching some protest about your supposed unlawful imprisonment..."

"Protest?"

"Yes! Thanks to you, Maggie blew her top at me after your bloody mouthpiece made his statement this evening. She was insistent that I knew where you were and furious that I hadn't done anything to help you! Of course, she was right, but that doesn't absolve you for getting involved in this whole mess in the first place. How many times have Richard and I told you that one day your superman routine would go too far? Well, like I said, she was watching the television and the phone rings. Suddenly the Prime Minister is demanding I do something about you immediately."

Darcy had too many questions and was not sure which to ask first, so he did what he knew Elizabeth would do. He simply raised and eyebrow and remained silent.

"We know you're hiding something about Pierre Estoban. Five million dollars is nothing to these people, so what *did* you give him for Fitzwilliam and Forster?"

Darcy repeated the same story he had told over the past five days. "Estoban is a powerful man with a celebrity obsession. When he realized I was Richard's cousin, he contacted me to broker a ransom so that I would fly down to Colombia and he could meet me. Given my history, he had every reason to expect me to come. Even without that history, I would have done anything to save Richard. Lord knows neither Her Majesty nor Uncle Sam were going to step in on his behalf."

"Richard understood that when he took the job."

"Richard did, but that doesn't mean I had to. How is Richard? I haven't had any news since shortly after we landed in Mexico City."

Thornton hesitated a moment before answering. "He was well enough to be flown back to London last night. His parents will be notified as soon as he's settled. However, your story still doesn't explain why the elaborate ruse just to meet you. As far as we know, Estoban's not gay. Why you?"

"Somehow that question didn't seem important to me at the time. There's been too much death in my family, and I was not going to sit back and let my cousin die."

Thornton stood angrily. "So what you did was step into the middle of a failed U.S./British operation to capture the Estobans. Damn it, Darcy! Your company holds the economies of half the developing nations of the world in its hands. Surely you realize the damage that could be done with your sudden death!"

Darcy was adamant. "No more damage than my sudden disappearance with no explanation will. Come on, John, charge me or let me go!"

Thornton sat down again. "You're being punished. The Americans want your head on a platter, and the higher-ups in the Defense Ministry have had enough of you making them look bad. You've pissed off the wrong people this time, Darcy, and they want you to feel it."

"I'm feeling it. So, how much longer am I to be punished?"

"We *were* planning to keep you until we figured out how to charge you without exposing our operation in Colombia or causing a world economic crisis."

Darcy's eyebrow arched again, "Were?"

"Your uncle and that girlfriend of yours have been putting pressure on all the right people for days now. Today's press conference was the last straw. You've become more trouble to keep than to let go." Thornton rose and knocked on the door. As he waited for the guard outside to come and release the lock, he turned back. "Are you coming, or has the charm of this place induced you to remain our guest of your own free will?"

Darcy rose, not quite convinced that the implications of Thornton's statement could be fact. "What about the five million? I've broken more laws than even I can count."

"Funny thing about that five million — it reappeared in your account three days ago. The bastard gave it back, just as you suspected he would." Thornton allowed his frustration to enter his voice. "None of this makes sense. What did Pierre Estoban get in return for Fitzwilliam and Forster?"

Darcy avoided Thornton's piercing gaze by watching the door as it unlocked, allowing him to pass through into freedom.

The two men walked down a long hallway. "So, I'll be seeing you and Maggie at the awards dinner in New York?" Darcy couldn't help the dig. Maggie Thornton was the current President of the International Human Rights Society who was presenting Darcy with the award. Thornton glared for a moment before shaking his head and smiling.

They stopped in front of the door to a conference room. Thornton opened the door; inside sat Geoff and Chris Brandon. "You're a sight for sore eyes!" Darcy said as he crossed the room to embrace his friend and then his cousin. "Let's get out of here!"

"No so fast." Thornton said, indicating the documents lying on the table next to Darcy and Geoff's bags from the plane. "First you need to sign these confidentiality agreements. The Securities and Exchange Commission in New York will release a press statement indicating that you were assisting in an investigation into insider trading on the Stock Market. That will explain the documents removed from your house and your disappearance."

"Wouldn't that make me look like a guilty man you couldn't find anything on?"

"Not the way we've worded it. You'll sound like a hero." Thornton brought Darcy's attention back to the documents before him. "We brought Brandon here as your attorney to read over the documents and answer any questions you have, but the terms are non-negotiable. You sign, you leave. Don't sign, and I'll take you back to your little home away from home immediately. I'll leave you alone for a few minutes to look everything over." Thornton turned to leave, and as he walked through the doorway, he called back. "You also need to check your bags and report anything that's missing."

"There goes my book deal!" Geoff grumbled as he scanned through the mountain of papers.

Darcy simply looked through for the places to sign his name and quickly executed the documents without reading a word.

"Do you think that's wise?" Brandon asked.

Darcy handed the documents to Brandon so that he could witness Darcy's signature. "I have no desire to reveal what happened to the public; I do, however, have a burning desire to get out of here."

Darcy pocketed his PDA and then began checking off the contents of his bag against an inventory sheet. When he reached the book, he quickly scanned through the pages. The picture was gone. Scanning the pages one last time, his eyes caught an unfamiliar handwriting. Written in pencil so light, he had trouble making out the words, Darcy read:

Surely you would not begrudge me this memento. –P

NEITHER ELIZABETH NOR GEORGIANA COULD sleep. After receiving Chris Brandon's telephone call saying he was going to meet with Darcy and Geoff, they sat together watching Elizabeth's cell phone on the coffee table, willing it to ring. At 9 p.m. Jake reluctantly left for his dorm room, but Elizabeth and Georgiana maintained their vigil. Finally, at 10:05 p.m. the phone rang. Elizabeth checked the caller ID; it was Darcy's cell phone.

Elizabeth, seeing the hopeful expression on Georgiana's face, handed her the phone. "It's him."

Georgiana grabbed the phone from Elizabeth with trembling hands, and was already in tears by the time she opened it up. She gasped out, "Wills?"

Elizabeth strained to hear his voice as he spoke to Georgiana, but it was impossible as the poor girl was crying so loudly.

"Yes, we're all right. ... Yes, Elizabeth is here with me. ... No, she's sitting right beside me. ... It was awful, and I'm so mad at you! Elizabeth and I are ready to kick your sorry arse for running off like that, and you know she could do it too! ... You're all right? ... Geoff too? ... Yes, finals finished today. ... I think I did well. ... Yes, I'll leave tomorrow as soon as I can get a flight. ... I love you too! ... Here she is." Georgiana happily handed the phone to Elizabeth.

Elizabeth put the phone to her ear. "Hey, Darcy," she said softly. Her heart seemed to stop beating as she waited to hear his response, to know she was truly hearing *him*.

When his voice drifted through the phone, it was as soft and affected as her own. "Hey, Elizabeth." There was a long pause where each bathed in the comfort of being connected to the other. A week's worth of pain and uncertainty was ended. Reluctantly Darcy broke the silence. "I'm on my way to Pemberley with Chris Brandon and Geoff. Chris told me everything that's happened since we left and everything you've done. That stunt with Churchill at the press conference was brilliant."

"Thanks. You're all right? You're not hurt? They're not going to arrest you?"

"No, I'm fine — just exhausted. I was taken into custody, but it's over now. It's all over." There was another long pause before Darcy asked hesitantly, "Did you get my text…last Sunday morning?"

Elizabeth's heart skipped. "Yes." There was so much she wanted to say but they each had an audience, and most of those things were best said face to face. "I'm afraid I've had quite a bit of trouble with that particular rule, too."

"Really? I thought it would be a bit much for me to hope for, but I wanted you to know…my position on the matter." His voice was hopeful, almost desperate in his desire for her to understand him.

Elizabeth felt frustrated that it was necessary for them to have such an important conversation in code. "Yes, Fitzwilliam. In fact there are a few more rules I think we need to renegotiate."

She could almost hear his smile through the phone. "It's going to be a few weeks before I can get my passport back. I know you planned to go to your grandmother's soon, but…is it possible for you to come here? I realize it's a great deal to ask, however —"

Elizabeth interrupted. "Yes…I'll come as soon as I can get a flight."

"Good. That's…good. I can have my people book a flight for both you and Georgiana as soon as possible. A helicopter will pick you up at Heathrow and fly you directly to Pemberley."

"Sounds…good."

"I should let you go then. From what Chris has told me, you've had even less sleep than I have."

"I'm just so happy you're safe."

"Until tomorrow then…and thank you, for taking care of Georgie."

"That's what friends are for… Are you sure it's over?"

"Yes. It's over. I'll explain everything when I see you. Everything."

"Good… I'll see you tomorrow… Stay safe."

"I will. Sweet dreams…Lizzy."

DARCY STOOD AT THE DOOR that led to the family apartments at Pemberley. He waved tiredly as Chris Brandon drove off with Geoff.

"Welcome home, Master Wills."

Darcy turned to see the hopeful eyes of his housekeeper, Mrs. Reynolds.

"Thank you, Mrs. R. It is good to be home."

Soon he was pulled into her embrace. "I was just catching the morning news. That was so brave of you to help the Americans in their investigation, but you have no idea what you've put us all through — especially Miss Georgie and that lovely Dr. Bennet. Such a darling girl."

Darcy returned the embrace of the woman who had been a constant in his life since before he was born. He could feel the tears she shed wetting his shirt. Mrs. Reynolds released him and said, "Well, enough of that. You're home now and that's all that matters. You look very tired and much too thin."

Having no desire to resist her pampering, Darcy soon found himself in bed with a breakfast tray. Too exhausted to sleep, he thought about Elizabeth. Soon she would be at Pemberley.

Carefully he planned his strategy. Step 1: He would tell her everything about Richard, Pierre and Rebecca Wickham. Step 2: He would tell her how he felt about her. Step 3: He would prove to her that he was ready for a committed relationship. Of course, she would have misgivings about giving herself to a man who had so adamantly declared his aversion to love; therefore, he would strive, everyday, to prove himself to her.

Darcy was determined that he would allow Elizabeth all the time she needed to feel confident in his changed convictions and, hopefully, come to love him in return. How long might all this take? Weeks? Months? Only then, if he were very fortunate — Step 4: He would make love to her.

Their encrypted telephone conversation had allowed him to hope that all this was possible. He turned to his side in an attempt to find sleep, noticed the empty pillow next to his own and imagined Elizabeth lying there, smiling back at him.

He realized that if he could earn her trust, *he* would be the first man to make love to Elizabeth. He would be the "lucky bastard." Suddenly, the weight of all that implied hit him full force. Her first time should be glorious! Elizabeth deserved nothing less, and yet, would he be able to live up to that expectation? How would it be different from what he had experienced in the past? *Good God, I could hurt her!*

Suddenly he sat up and grabbed his laptop. He rarely Googled, having always had staff to research whatever he needed; this, however, was a matter he could not possibly delegate.

CHAPTER 20
MUSIC AND MORE

December 17th, The London Times
Photo caption: The Director of the SEC gives a press conference concerning the recent activities of Fitzwilliam Darcy.
Story: Early this morning, Securities and Exchange Commission Director, Edward Rochester, gave a press conference to publicly thank Fitzwilliam Darcy and his cousin, Geoffrey Fitzwilliam, for assisting his organization in an ongoing investigation…

Georgiana thoughtfully pointed out the sights as the helicopter flew over the Peaks. The view was spectacular; however, Elizabeth found it difficult to attend to the young woman's commentary. Her mind was focused on the newspapers she had purchased at both JFK and Heathrow Airports. The story they reported was incredible: Darcy and Geoff had been assisting the U.S. Securities and Exchange Commission in an investigation into insider trading.

Elizabeth read the press statement over and over along with the accompanying stories. None of it made sense to her. Surely, this was something Darcy could have confided to either Georgiana or herself, and working with the SEC did not explain the involvement of both British and American intelligence agencies.

Georgiana became quiet and still. When Elizabeth looked up to check on why, she noticed the view, and her breath caught in her throat. The sun was setting, suffusing the cloudy sky in a wash of pinks, purples and oranges; before her was the house that had become so familiar to her over the last week: Pemberley. The print had not done it justice, for the reality was even more spellbinding. Its lines were perfection, its symmetry unblemished, and its white stone brilliant in the sunlight.

"I never tire of seeing it," Georgiana whispered. "Wills has considered donating it to the National Trust several times, but in the end... No matter where we travel or how long we are away, Pemberley will always be our home. "

As the helicopter prepared to land in the open space of the front lawn, the massive front doors opened and Georgiana's hand grasped Elizabeth's painfully as they watched a figure exit the house, his long legs quickly taking him down the expansive front steps and into the finely manicured grass. Suddenly how or why Darcy had disappeared was no longer important. All that mattered was that he was alive and well and standing before them.

The wait for the helicopter to power down and for the pilot to allow them to climb out seemed like an eternity. As they waited, Elizabeth and Darcy's eyes met. His expression was intense, and it took every effort not to risk having her head chopped off to dash out of the aircraft and hurl herself at him. Her heart was in her throat, and she felt that if she were not released soon, she would explode from the anticipation.

Her thoughts were interrupted by a stifled sob. Elizabeth turned back to see Georgiana's face covered in tears. The week had taken a terrible toll on her, fearing that she may have lost the only remaining member of her immediate family as well as a cousin who was more like a brother to her. Elizabeth made the same decision she had made with the phone the night before, she would defer to Georgiana. She was Darcy's sister while Elizabeth was... she did not know. Darcy's text and their brief conversation confirmed that things had changed, but how much and into what form was still a mystery.

At last the pilot opened the door and Elizabeth prepared to climb out and move aside to help Georgiana down; however, she immediately found herself wrapped tightly in a pair of strong arms, her face pressed into a familiar shoulder as the scent of soap and starch permeated her senses. For the first time in her life, Elizabeth knew what it felt like to come home.

THEY SAT TOGETHER IN THE family room. It was the place where the Darcy family had always gathered, and Anne Darcy found the name, although a little too American for George Darcy's tastes, far more fitting than "sitting room." It was warm and comfortable, and Darcy sat in the middle of a large leather couch with Elizabeth and Georgiana seated on either side. He kept an arm around each of their shoulders, unwilling to release either for more than a few moments.

He quietly told them of the late night call he received from Renee Estoban seven days before, informing him of Richard's capture, and then of his confrontation with Geoff. Darcy wanted him to remain behind to take care of Georgiana, but Geoff insisted on coming along to help his brother. They snuck out the back to avoid detection by the paparazzi, not knowing the house was also under surveillance by both British and American intelligence officers who had been watching since Richard first disappeared.

He then told them the same version of events in Colombia he had told the authorities and about his incarceration, release and finally about the confidentiality agreements. Being raised a Darcy, Georgiana had it ingrained in her psyche not to repeat family secrets, and Elizabeth had proved her discretion time and time again since Darcy first began confiding in her. He finished his tale, explaining that Geoff was now in London with Richard and his parents. In between sobs and exclamations of surprise and outrage, Georgiana asked many questions, and Darcy carefully and honestly answered them all.

Georgiana then told him of all that had happened in New York, the police search and wiretap of Lansing, the increased presence of the paparazzi and Elizabeth's efforts to locate him. Darcy expressed his remorse at all they had to suffer, but brother and sister agreed that it had all been worth it. They were safe, Richard was home and the ordeal was over.

Elizabeth's uncharacteristic silence concerned Darcy. The physical reminders of the toll the last week had taken on her were quite evident. She looked exhausted, but it was the pain in her eyes that struck him the most, and he wondered if his eyes reflected the same. He had come home a changed man; was it possible that she was changed too?

Mrs. Reynolds entered to announce that dinner was ready. Georgiana rose first and ran over to hug the older woman. Darcy then introduced her to Elizabeth. When Elizabeth stood to shake the woman's hand, Mrs. Reynolds scoffed, "We'll have none of that!" and she threw her arms around Elizabeth's shoulders and hugged her tightly. "I'm so happy to finally meet you, dear. Master Wills didn't say how long you would be staying with us. I hope it's at least through Christmas. There's nothing more lovely than Christmas at Pemberley!"

As Elizabeth pulled away from Mrs. Reynolds' embrace, she glanced briefly to Darcy. "We haven't discussed it yet."

"Well then, Miss Georgie, why don't you come into the dining room and tell me about that new boyfriend of yours while your brother and Dr. Bennet discuss it."

Georgiana and Darcy hugged again before his sister was released to Mrs. Reynolds. As she reached the door, Georgiana turned back and hugged Elizabeth. She smiled broadly and then followed Mrs. Reynolds, shutting the door firmly behind her.

Darcy and Elizabeth stood facing each other. "Mrs. Reynolds is wonderful. I called her frequently this past week. I told myself it was to raise her spirits, but I think it was my spirits that were raised instead."

"She is wonderful, although she tends to sometimes be a busybody."

They both allowed themselves a laugh; however, Elizabeth's abruptly turned to anger. It was as if in finally allowing herself to express any emotion, the most dominant one took over, and she suddenly lashed out, releasing all the fear she had struggled to suppress for the past week. "What would Georgiana have done if you and Geoff had been killed? You're all she has left!" She fought back the tears that threatened to fall.

Darcy closed the distance between them and took her hands. "If Richard had died, I don't know how I would have lived with myself, knowing I might have done something to prevent it."

Tears were now coursing unchecked down Elizabeth's cheeks as she grasped his arms and cried, "How would I have lived if you had died? I love you, you idiot! I broke that damn rule long before we made it. It took me a long time to admit it, but I believe I fell in love with you that day in my office when you said you would keep the change from my twenty and you flashed those damn dimples at me."

Elizabeth dabbed at her tears with the back of her hand. "Give me your handkerchief!"

This confession was the last thing Darcy expected. Flabbergasted, he silently pulled his handkerchief from his pocket and handed it to her. Elizabeth wiped her eyes and blew her nose as Darcy wrapped his arms around her and rubbed her back comfortingly. She leaned her head against his chest. "Look at me, I'm a complete mess! You're the only person who can make me cry."

Darcy kissed the top of her head and finally spoke. "You tend to scold me when I apologize. Will you let me tell you now how sorry I am that I hurt you?"

"No! I know you wouldn't hurt me intentionally." Elizabeth slowly regained control of her emotions and embraced his waist. "I understand now why you needed to go. I'm afraid I've become very selfish where you're concerned."

Placing his fingers beneath her chin, Darcy gently lifted Elizabeth's face so he could look into her beautiful violet-blue eyes. "Then will you allow me to tell you how very much I love you? I love you, Elizabeth."

He could see his feelings reflected in her eyes, as they seemed to pull him in. Again, he was falling into their deep blue depths, just as he had that day outside the community center when he had desperately tried to fight the sensation. Today there would be no resistance.

Breathlessly she responded, "Don't tell me. Show me!"

He lowered his lips to hers, and they both waited until the last possible moment to close their eyes. They were falling together into unknown territory, and as her mouth opened beneath his, a swirl of emotions and sensations overtook their minds and bodies. This was what it felt like to love and be loved in return. It could not be described. It could only be experienced.

The kiss was unhurried. Each pass of their tongues was accompanied by a new depth of understanding, a new thrill of discovery. They were embarking on a new journey, and together they would find the courage to proceed. When their lips finally parted, they found they were both grinning like idiots.

"We still have a great deal to talk about," Darcy said, as the remnants of his carefully laid plan still floated in his mind. He needed to regroup and re-plan; however, at this point one thing was clear. He needed to keep his libido in check until the remaining requirements of Steps 1 through 3 were completed, no matter how long it took.

Elizabeth gently nodded her head. "Yes, but I suppose it will have to wait until after dinner. I don't believe either Georgie or Mrs. Reynolds would appreciate us skipping out on them."

"No, they would not." Darcy reluctantly released her from his embrace but took her hand to lead her to the dining room. When they reached the door to the family room, he asked, "Stay through Christmas?"

"Of course. I hear there's nothing more lovely than Christmas at Pemberley!" This cheeky response caused Darcy to retaliate with another kiss.

As Elizabeth felt his warm, hard body press against hers, a plan of her own began to form. Now that they had finally acknowledged their love for one another, Elizabeth was impatient to take the next step. Tonight, she would seduce Fitzwilliam Darcy.

They finally pulled apart when they heard a soft rap on the door. Mrs. Reynolds had returned to remind them that dinner was waiting. The housekeeper was quietly pleased to hear that Elizabeth had agreed to stay for Christmas.

AS THEY ENJOYED A QUIET dinner, Darcy asked Georgiana for the details of her final examinations. "So what did you finally decide to sing for your voice class?"

"I won't say, but I will sing them for you after we've finished eating. That is, if Elizabeth will play for me? She helped me rehearse."

Elizabeth had just placed a bite of filet mignon into her mouth, so she simply nodded her head in the affirmative.

"You won't even give me a clue?" Darcy teased.

"I will only tell you that I had to sing two songs. One was to be either a classical piece or a show tune. The second could be anything of my choosing as long as Professor Elton agreed that it challenged my individual vocal range."

"That's no clue at all!" Darcy protested, so after everyone had finished eating, Darcy hustled Elizabeth and Georgiana into the music room, bringing Mrs. Reynolds along for good measure.

The music room was large, as all the rooms in Pemberley's family apartments appeared to be. The walls were yellow, and the furnishings were covered in soft prints of yellow, green and white. Against these light colors, the rich, dark wood of the concert grand piano stood out. Next to the piano were guitars, violins and a cello displayed in glass-covered cases. All the instruments were highly polished and perfectly tuned, just waiting to be played.

Turning one of the large chairs so that he would have a better view of the performers, Darcy settled in and waited as Elizabeth sat behind the piano and Georgiana stood in the curve of the instrument. With a nod from her accompanist signaling she was ready, Georgiana belted out "I Can Hear the Bells" from the Broadway show *Hairspray*.

Darcy was surprised at just how well Georgiana could sing, and he laughed along with her exaggerated facial expressions as she sung the humorous words to the song:

Round One. He'll ask me on a date, and then,
Round Two. I'll primp but won't be late, because,

Round Three's when we'll kiss inside his car,
Won't go all the way, but I'll go pretty far...[27]

When she sang the last note, Darcy stood and applauded. Then he playfully suggested, "I believe you've already gone all the way, young lady!"

Georgiana's response was to lunge at him, causing Darcy to fall back into his chair with his sister on top of him. A tickle-fest then commenced that left both brother and sister breathless.

Stunned at this new side of Darcy, Elizabeth turned to Mrs. Reynolds. "Does that happen often?"

"Oh, yes!" Mrs. Reynolds responded with a soft chuckle. "You'd think they would have grown out of it by now."

"Never!" cried Georgiana with one last dig of her fingers into her brother's ribs. She quickly stood up and moved out of his reach when Darcy attempted to once again strike back. "Although Wills has become far better at provoking me since he started hanging out with Elizabeth."

"That's because Elizabeth is the master when it comes to teasing, and I have discovered many new things to tease about." He raised an eyebrow letting her know exactly which things he was referring to.

Georgiana threatened playfully, "Do you want to hear the next song or not?"

Darcy sat up straight in his chair and resumed a posture of mock seriousness. "Of course, My Lady!"

Elizabeth took that as her cue to remove herself from behind the piano. She picked out one of the guitars, sat down on a wooden chair, and at Georgiana's nod, she began plucking a lovely ballad that immediately changed the atmosphere of the room.

And I love you so,
The people ask me how,
How I lived till now,
I tell them, I don't know.
I guess they understand,
How lonely life can be,
But life began again,

---

27 "I Can Hear the Bells", Music by Mark Shaiman, Lyrics by Mark Shaiman and Scott Witman, written for the Broadway Musical Hairspray, 2000

The day you touched my hand,
And yes, I know how lonely life can be... [28]

Georgiana's beautiful voice told the story of a lonely, loveless life, finally given meaning by love. As the simple lyrics washed over them, Darcy looked at Elizabeth to find her eyes shining back at him. The song was about Darcy, it was about Elizabeth, and it was about the change they had each brought to the other's lonely, loveless lives.

When the last chord of the guitar sounded, both Georgiana and Mrs. Reynolds realized that something was happening between the other two occupants of the room. Darcy stood and gently embraced Georgiana. He whispered his compliments, "That was lovely, Sweetling! You should be very proud."

Georgiana beamed under her brother's praises. Then she looked at Elizabeth and back to Darcy and said, "Thank you. It's nearly ten so I think I'm going to take something to try and sleep now. Perhaps I can avoid jet lag tomorrow."

"I think that's wise," Darcy agreed.

Georgiana kissed his cheek good night and then moved to do the same to Elizabeth who had placed the guitar back in the cabinet. "Thank you, Elizabeth... for everything!"

Elizabeth returned the gesture. "Good night, Georgie."

Mrs. Reynolds piped up, "I think I'll call it a night too, Master Wills, unless there's something else you need?"

Darcy assured her there was nothing, and with another round of "good nights," Georgiana and Mrs. Reynolds left the music room. Once outside the closed door, Georgiana turned to the other woman. "I think they're both goners!"

Mrs. Reynolds would never gossip about the master of the house but could not resist an enthusiastic nod of the head. "Now, Miss Georgie, you're not really going to go to sleep now, are you?"

Georgiana hesitated for only a moment. "*Super Mario Brawl.*[29] My room. Fifteen minutes!"

"Make that *Guitar Hero,* and you're on!"[30]

"Which one?"

"*Legends of Rock?*" At Mrs. Reynolds' assent, the two women hurried off in

---

28 "And I Love You So," Music and Lyrics by Don McLean, 1972
29 Super Smash Brothers Brawl, by Sora for Nintendo, 2008
30 Guitar Hero, Legends of Rock, Video Game, Activison Publishing 2008

different directions.

Back in the music room Darcy and Elizabeth again stood looking at one another. "So…" Elizabeth said to break the silence, "here we are."

"Are you tired?" Darcy asked, hoping her answer was in the negative.

Elizabeth looked at her watch. "I believe it's still only 4 p.m. in my brain. I've got hours until my internal clock will kick in the need for sleep." She closed the distance between them. Darcy's concern was sweet, but his gentlemanly behavior confused her. Weren't men supposed to have only one thing on their minds?

With each step Elizabeth took closer to Darcy, his alarm grew. He wanted her desperately, but he was certain that she would want to take things slowly, and if she came much closer, he couldn't guarantee he'd be able to control himself.

Elizabeth reached out to touch his arm. "Perhaps now would be a good time to renegotiate the rules. Now that we've both violated the most important rule, I think it's safe to simply throw that one away."

"Yes. I agree." Darcy's voice sounded as weak as his willpower. This would not do! He took a step back away from her. "What about the others? If I remember correctly, there was something about hand holding and dancing and…" His voice trailed off as Elizabeth took his hand.

"I think we should keep those. What about names? I was not allowed to call you 'Fitzwilliam' and you never called me 'Lizzy.' I hope we can toss those out too."

He closed his eyes in an attempt to control his galloping desires. The effect of his name spilling from her lips had lost none of its seductive power over the past months, and watching as she said it only made it all the more difficult not to immediately take her on top the piano. His mind grasped a possible diversion. "You said something that night about singing to me." He pulled her toward the piano bench. "Sing to me, Lizzy."

"Lizzy?" She smiled impishly. "That does *things* to me."

Darcy swallowed hard. This was not going at all as he planned. *"Things?"*

"Yes, *things*!" Elizabeth pulled him to sit beside her on the piano bench. "If I remember correctly, there was one particular song mentioned." Then placing her hands on the keys, she played the song, not fast like the recorded version, but slow, turning the song into a ballad of sweet seduction.

The night we met I knew I needed you so,
And if I had the chance I'd never let you go.

240

So won't you say you love me, I'll make you so proud of me,
We'll make 'em turn their heads, every place we go.
So won't you please,
Be my little baby,
Say you'll be my darlin',
Be my baby now.

Darcy came to the inevitable conclusion that having her sing as a distraction was not his brightest idea. He had dreamed of her singing this song to him more times than he could count, and each time it was during a very erotic scene. His body was heedlessly betraying his resolve as she continued.

I'll make you happy, baby, just wait and see,
For every kiss you give me, I'll give you three,
Oh, since the day I saw you, I have been waiting for you,
You know I will adore you, 'til eternity.[31]

She never was able to sing the second chorus as Darcy suddenly pulled her into his arms and kissed her. Elizabeth was elated. Her seduction was progressing nicely. As the song promised, Elizabeth returned his kiss, once, twice, three times. "Now, Fitzwilliam," she whispered against his lips, "the release of the ban on kissing is obvious, but what do you say to a little sex?" She then attacked his neck with warm, wet kisses.

A groan escaped from Darcy's throat as he pushed her gently away from him, "Lizzy, I need to tell you about Rebecca."

"Rebecca who?" she teased as she reached to pull him closer.

Darcy grasped her hands, keeping their small distance intact. "I should tell you everything that happened in Colombia, and I need to assure you that I'm ready for this."

"I know you; I trust you. We have forever to talk about all the things that kept us apart." Elizabeth's body was on fire for him, and Darcy's resistance was driving her crazy.

Reaching through his mind for all the reasons he was sure she would want to wait to make love, Darcy pulled out his last theory. "But, aren't you the least bit apprehensive? This will be your first time, Lizzy. There will be pain!"

31 "Be My Baby", by Jeff Barry, Ellie Greenwich and Phil Spector, 1963

Elizabeth laughed seductively. "Don't worry, I promise to be gentle with you."

"Not for me," he said with alarm, "for you!"

Taking his hands and placing them on her waist, Elizabeth ran her fingers up the warm front of his sweater before beginning to unbutton the top button of the shirt beneath it. "My girlfriends talk. Some say it hurt a little, some say not at all. Regardless, any pain will pass away eventually with practice."

"I've done quite a lot of research on the subject." Darcy pleaded with her to reason. "The degree of pain depends on the narrowness of the vaginal walls and the size of the penis. I don't mean to brag, Elizabeth, but... I'm going to hurt you."

"Then delaying the first experience will not lessen the pain." Her frustration was beginning to show in her voice. "What is this? Must the wanton virgin seduce the reluctant playboy?"

He could not help but laugh at her assessment of the situation before he became serious again. "I don't want you to wake up tomorrow with regrets. I couldn't bear that."

"If I've learned anything in the last week, it's that life can be taken away in a whisper. I love you. I've waited all my life for you, Fitzwilliam, and I don't want to wait one minute more." Wrapping her arms around Darcy's neck Elizabeth pulled herself as close to him as possible. "Baby, I *ache* for you!"

Her kiss reached into his soul and nullified every logical thought. With his last shred of resistance blasted into oblivion, Darcy stood and pulled Elizabeth from the bench and led her out of the music room toward the back elevator. Once the doors to the lift closed behind them, Darcy pulled her into his arms, kissing her deeply. By the time the doors opened on the second floor, Elizabeth had wrapped her legs around his waist, and he had shifted her weight from the wall of the lift to his arms around her butt and waist so he could carry her down the hallway.

"I'm taking you to my bedroom," he said between kisses. "Condoms," was his one word explanation.

Elizabeth barely nodded her acquiescence before they resumed kissing. Her heart was fluttering rapidly in her chest as Darcy continued to demonstrate his kissing expertise. Granted, her ride was a little unsteady as he was far too interested in continuing their present occupation above the waist than to watch where his legs were going; however, Elizabeth did not mind the occasional bump into the wall or an errant doorway. This was it. All her life she had imagined that she would love the man she eventually gave herself to, but what she felt for Darcy was far beyond her fantasies. All the clichés were true. She was head over heels; he was her other half; he completed her, and she wanted him more than Ralphie wanted a BB gun for Christmas.[32]

Darcy pressed Elizabeth against the wall, removed his hand from beneath her buttocks and reached out blindly to find the handle to his bedroom door. As he refused to turn his attention from Elizabeth's lips, he was utterly unsuccessful. As he fruitlessly grasped once more at the evasive hardware, he heard a small, "Allow me," and the soft clicks of the handle turning and the inside latch disengaging.

In alarm, both Darcy and Elizabeth turned their heads toward the voice to find Mrs. Reynolds holding the door open for them, her face beaming. For the first time in his life, Darcy flushed with embarrassment. There he was, standing in the hallway, erection prevalent, arms full of Elizabeth, caught by the woman who changed his nappies. There was nothing to say except, "Thank you, Mrs. R."

"You're welcome. Good night, Master Wills, Dr. Bennet."

---

32 *A Christmas Story*, 1983. In this classic American Christmas film, a young boy named Ralphie is consumed with a feverish desire to receive a BB gun for Christmas.

CHAPTER 21
GOOD REASONS

In his dreams, Darcy had gazed down at Elizabeth lying in his bed many times; however, this was not as he had imagined it. Elizabeth was laughing so hard that tears were running down her temples as she kept her eyes averted to the ceiling. Each time she allowed those impish blue pools to glance his way, a new burst of hysterics would wrack her body. He frowned in a manner that normally would have reduced most men to silence. In Elizabeth, the frown only served to inspire another wave of laughter.

Lying back, Darcy waited for Elizabeth's moment of levity to pass. "Come on." Elizabeth poked him gently in his ribs, and Darcy turned to see her smiling sweetly at him. "You must admit it is funny. She opened the door, she reached in to flick on the light switch and then she closed the door behind us. Mrs. Reynolds was just so...helpful!"

The embarrassment he had felt at his housekeeper's actions had worn off, but indignation over Elizabeth's laughter at his expense struggled mightily to keep a firm foothold on his emotions. Finally, the small grin he had fought against won out. He never could resist Elizabeth's teasing.

In response, Elizabeth pulled herself over his chest. "You are so incredibly handsome when you smile." With a throaty laugh, she playfully kissed the corners of his mouth, then pulled back to allow her eyes to caress every curve and angle of his face. Her teasing smile gave way as her eyes ignited in passion.

Slowly she lowered her lips to his, and the fiery kisses Mrs. Reynolds had inter-rupted were immediately resumed.

The faint scent of orange blossom and ginger teased Darcy's senses as the softness of her lips and wetness of her tongue reminded him exactly why they were there. Abruptly Elizabeth pulled away and stood. "Where's your closet?"

Confused at her question, Darcy asked, "I realize you're inexperienced, but surely you don't expect this to happen in the closet?" Propped up on his elbows, it was his turn to laugh at her glare of impatience. Darcy indicated a door to the left of his bed and Elizabeth disappeared inside. A moment later she emerged, a box of condoms in her hand. He was more than surprised. "How did you know where to find them?"

"You, my BFF, are a man who likes to have his belongings in their proper place." Elizabeth placed the condoms on a bedside table, slipped off her shoes and socks and then climbed back up on the bed. "I simply looked in the same location where you kept them at Lansing: uppermost right-hand drawer, next to your sunglasses." Elizabeth straddled his hips and leaned forward, pushing Darcy back against the mattress. "Why is that? Is your penis so godlike that one is required to wear shades to view it?"

"I don't know how I feel about you knowing all my secrets."

"Oh, I don't know them all," she teased seductively. "However, I believe I am on the verge of a major discovery!" The sweet pressure of her body over his was intensely arousing while the teasing words falling from her lips and her seductive smile were extremely provoking. The quiet, emotionally drained woman who arrived in the helicopter just a few hours before was gone, and the sassy, impertinent temptress who never failed to arouse him was back— with a vengeance. Darcy pulled Elizabeth against his chest and kissed her, hard. Soon their desires were once again boiling over.

With a forceful heave, their positions were reversed; her body was effectively pinned beneath his. Darcy kissed her cheek, her jaw and then laved his tongue beneath her earlobe. The delicate flavor of her skin seemed to cause a subtle tingling in his tongue that increased in intensity as it traveled down his throat and through his gut until it settled pleasurably in his rapidly expanding erection.

"This is your last chance to change your mind, Lizzy. If you try to stop me after this, I swear I'll die of disappointment."

"Oh, Baby, if you don't make love to me right now, I think I'm going to spontaneously combust!" Her words and the deep, breathy voice that spoke them set his entire being on fire. Never before had he experienced this level of sensual anticipation, and he began to fear losing control. As Elizabeth aggressively attacked his neck with her mouth and his buttocks with her hands, he knew one of them had to call a time-out.

Pulling his lips from her delicate throat, Darcy took hold of her hands and held them against the mattress on either side of her shoulders. "We must slow down, or this will be over far too quickly."

Nodding her head in agreement, Elizabeth stopped resisting, and they remained still to allow their ragged breathing to slow and the inferno between them to reduce to a simmer. It was difficult to wait as he could feel her breasts heaving against his chest, but eventually Darcy felt he could proceed.

He began again by cradling her head between his hands and kissing her slowly before saying, "I know how difficult it is for you to give up control, but if you touch me too much…it's going to be impossible for me to be gentle and I…must…be…gentle." He reached to still her hands, which had snaked their way under his jumper. Kissing her eyes and then her cheeks, Darcy's mind warred with his body, which wanted desperately to simply rip off her clothes and have at it.

"But I want so much to touch you," she pleaded as she tried to free her hands. "I've dreamed of it for so long." Her hands slipped from his and found their way under his shirt to the sensitive skin on the sides of his waist before blazing a trail up to his shoulders. Elizabeth stroked his back, her fingers splayed wide to explore every muscle. "Ummm," she moaned softly into his ear, "you feel so strong."

Darcy groaned as her soft hands caressed his hard flesh. Little did she know that he was feeling far from strong against her gentle assault. With his resistance rapidly deteriorating, he faced the fact that, if this night was not going to end up a disaster, he needed her to stop. "Please, Lizzy, just for this first time, lie back and let me make love to you."

At first, he thought she intended to ignore his plea as her hands continued their delightful torture, but then he felt them slowly retreat. "May I undress you at least?" Elizabeth asked with feeling. "God, how I want to undress you!"

Darcy contemplated the wisdom of acquiescing to her request. "In a moment," he answered. They stayed still for a few minutes more until Darcy felt he was once more sufficiently under control to start again. Then he released her from beneath him and stood by the bed. Holding out his hand, he assisted

Elizabeth so that she could stand beside him.

He waited patiently as Elizabeth pulled his sweater over his head. She became frustrated when a sleeve became stuck on his watch and tugged hard. "Hey!" He chuckled deeply at her impatience. "Be careful with my jumper."

Elizabeth's glare turned teasing as she carefully removed his watch, placing it on the table behind her. Then she gently removed his arms from the sweater before slowly turning it right side out and meticulously folding it. Now finding himself impatient, Darcy quickly snatched the sweater from her hands before tossing it over his shoulder. "I believe it's my turn," he declared.

Elizabeth laughed warmly as Darcy carefully unbuttoned the front of her shirt. When the last button was released, he slid his palms beneath the shoulders of the cotton jersey and gently pushed it down over her arms, revealing an unadorned navy bra. Her skin glowed in the soft lighting of the room and the simple undergarment seemed only to enhance the view of her white breasts swelling above the soft blue satin. He looked into her eyes, and with a voice clearly affected, he whispered, "Lizzy, perhaps I should be the one wearing sunglasses."

She smiled again as she reached out to unbutton his shirt. First, she took each wrist, and as the buttons were released on the cuffs, she slowly spread the fabric apart before placing a long, warm kiss on the newly exposed skin. By the time she reached up to unbutton the front, Darcy was once again fighting to keep himself in check. When her task was finished, Elizabeth splayed her hands on his stomach, running them up his chest and over his shoulders before easing the shirt down his arms to slip silently to the carpet below.

Needing to feel her skin next to his, Darcy pulled her to him. He glided his fingers over her arms and across her back. "You are so very soft," he whispered in adoration before kissing his way down her neck to her newly exposed shoulders. He was unsure if her skin was truly so much softer than any other woman's he'd ever known, or if his love for her intensified every sensation he was experiencing, making her feel superior in every way.

His fingers felt for the clasp at the back of her bra. He began to tug impatiently at the strap when he could not locate the mechanism which stood between him and the objects of many a midnight fantasy. "It's in the front," Elizabeth whispered.

When he pulled back to look he noticed her averted eyes and slight blush. Her modesty served to increase his considerable desire for her; however, he didn't want anything to make Elizabeth uncomfortable. "Would you like the lights off or on?" he offered.

Elizabeth's eyes moved to his face then traveled down his chest to rest on the prominent bulge of his erection. "On," she decided, "definitely on."

Her eyes then returned to his and out of respect for her feelings, Darcy held her gaze as he reached between her breasts to unclasp her bra. It was only after the bra was lying on the floor that he briefly allowed his eyes to drink in the sight of her beautiful breasts. He kissed her as his fingers brushed up her flat stomach, and then he flattened his palm up and over her left breast. He was rewarded with her sharp intake of breath, followed by a barely perceptible moan.

To feel the firm swell covered by soft skin was everything Darcy had dreamed it to be; but when her nipple hardened in his hand, he felt a sudden rush of inexplicable jealously. She had admitted to kissing other men, but the thought of another man's hands on her breast was driving him mad. He knew it was unreasonable, but the question passed his lips before he realized it. "Lizzy, has anyone else…?"

"No," she breathed against his lips, "only you…in London."

Briefly the memory of those hasty, passion-filled moments in his office flashed through his mind. At that time, he had been willing to take her body without caring to know the value of the gift she had offered him. Now he was grateful for Lady Catherine's interference, for it had afforded him this night — this experience — with Elizabeth.

As he gently caressed her breast, heard her sighs of pleasure and felt her body move against his in response, the knowledge that he was the only man to have experienced this with her was not only awesome to contemplate, but intensely arousing. What little blood remained in the rest of his body rushed to his already capacity-filled groin. "Oh, God, Lizzy, I love you!"

Forgetting the importance of taking turns, Darcy quickly opened the top of her jeans and slid them down her smooth legs, hefting them unthinkingly across the room. He then sat her on the bed to remove her matching navy blue knickers when he decided instead to remove his trousers, which had become unbearably restrictive.

He reached down quickly and pulled off his shoes without untying them, tossing them across the floor. As he slipped his socks from his feet he felt Elizabeth unbuckling his belt. Forcing himself to remain still he took a long appreciative look at her breasts as Elizabeth focused on pulling down the zipper of his trousers. She sat on the bed and hooked her fingers inside his briefs to pull both garments down at once. "Hey," he said with difficulty as his breathing was once again becoming erratic, "I thought we were taking turns."

"You cheated and took two turns in a row. I'm just catching up." She averted her eyes as she slipped his trousers and briefs down and off his feet. When she sat back up she was staring directly at his naked, straining erection. "Oh, my," she whispered, "I can't tell you how happy I am at this moment that we left the lights on!"

As Darcy's eyes devoured the sight of Elizabeth wearing nothing but knickers, he could not have agreed more.

Once more approaching his breaking point, Darcy turned to the table and removed a condom from the box. He pulled Elizabeth gently by the arms so she was positioned in the middle of the bed and then removed her knickers before surrounding her body with his own. He groaned involuntarily, not only from the pleasure of physical contact, but for the unexpected wave of passionate emotion that rose in his chest.

"No more foreplay," she said breathlessly as he bent his neck to kiss the hollow of her throat, "I'm beyond ready now."

Darcy shook his head as he slid the condom under a pillow. "Oh, there's going to be foreplay, Lizzy...even if it kills me!" He was determined that this time, her first time, was going to be something she would look back on in fifty years and remember...and smile.

He kissed her fiercely, trying to erase from her memory every man who ever kissed her before. His tongue thrust against her own, tasting, teasing and claiming her mouth. But this wasn't just any woman he was kissing. Elizabeth Bennet may have been inexperienced in the remaining acts of love, but she knew how to kiss...very well. Soon her fingers were grasping his hair and she was giving as much pleasure as she received. Darcy quickly became lost in the exquisite taste of her mouth, the way her tongue swirled and how the tip would flick beneath his own.

Abruptly, he pulled away. No, her mouth was a dangerous place to linger, and there were far more delights to be explored. Kissing a trail down her throat, his hand returned to her breast. Feeling her back arch in response to his touch only urged him to take her straining nipple into his mouth. She cried out in pleasure, and Darcy felt his own arousal pulse in reply. The texture of her nipple as it grew within his mouth was more than sensual; it was spiritual. As his fingers moved down to slip within the drenched folds of her vagina, his entire being, both physically and mentally, responded. In pleasing Elizabeth, he had found a new level of pleasure. Nothing before had ever been so sensual or so erotic.

Elizabeth cried out again as he found her clitoris. "Please, Baby, don't make me wait anymore!"

Lifting his lips from her breast, he raised his head briefly to kiss her lips. "You may not be able to come later if it's too uncomfortable. I want you to come now."

"No," she protested between heavy pants, "I need to feel you inside me. This is what I've wanted; this is what I've dreamed of."

All his plans about this moment centered on what he expected, what he wanted and what he thought she would want, and Darcy realized he was behaving selfishly. It was far more important that this time be the fulfillment of Elizabeth's dreams, not his own. Reaching under the pillow, Darcy retrieved the condom.

Soon he was settled between her thighs; however, before they went any further, there was something he simply had to tell her. Holding her eyes with his own, he confessed, "You once said you wanted to mean something to the man you gave yourself to. Know this, Lizzy... you mean everything to me!"

"I know," she whispered softly before she kissed him. It was one of those soul-searing kisses that would leave him spellbound for the rest of his life.

"I love you, Lizzy." As he again fell into the depths of Elizabeth's beautiful eyes, Darcy slowly pushed into her. The tightening of her body below him and the short catches of her breath, followed by the rapid opening and shutting of her eyes, effectively communicated the pain he was causing her. The understanding was sobering, slightly cooling his arousal to where he could withstand the warm tightness of her vaginal walls surrounding him without immediately exploding into orgasm. When he breached the resistance of her hymen, he caught her small gasp with his lips and then remained still until she encouraged him to continue.

The effort it took not to surrender to his desire to move rapidly and forcefully was evident in the light sheen of sweat that had broken out over his body; however, there was so much more happening within the man who was Fitzwilliam Darcy than the simple stimulation of his pleasure center. This may have been Elizabeth's first sexual experience, but Darcy was "making love" in the full sense of those words for the first time, and the experience was profound.

He moved slowly at first, in and out, watching her carefully for any signs that she wanted him to stop. As he felt her body relax beneath him, Darcy allowed himself to move a little faster, but even at that restrained pace his mental endurance was rapidly depleting as the sweet pressure of pleasure increased in intensity. Faster than he would have hoped he whispered, "I'm too close."

Her response was to reach down, grasp his buttocks and squeeze. Darcy reacted instantly to her touch, crying out in harsh, deep, feral rasps of voice and breath that filled the room as orgasm wracked his body.

When he at last opened his eyes, he looked down to see a beautiful smile and sparkling eyes brimming with unquestionable love and adoration. In that moment, the emotional pressure in his chest became excruciating. Six months before, the idea of feeling this intensely for anyone would have terrified him; Darcy now welcomed the sweet pain wholeheartedly.

Although his body screamed out for sleep, Darcy forced himself to roll to her side. He took Elizabeth's fingers and wrapping them over his own, guided them back down to her clitoris. "Teach me," he whispered as he kissed her, "show me how you want to be touched."

As Elizabeth moved his fingers in a complex dance across her clitoris, Darcy memorized the steps. Soon she released his hand and lay back to surrender to the pleasure he was giving her. Darcy watched the changes in her body: the flare of her eyes, the rapidly increasing respiration and the flush of arousal that colored her face, neck and chest. Fascinated, he could not tear his eyes away from her as she gave up the last vestiges of her precious control and exploded in release. To him, it was an amazingly beautiful sight to behold. Never before had he felt more sated and yet more alive.

This was the *more* he had been searching for.

Between soft kisses, he poured out his heart in the best way he could. "I'm not good with words of love as I never had use for them before. I never understood what it meant to truly love someone, and it took staring down the barrel of a gun for me to realize just how much you mean to me. I have wasted so much time!"

"Don't you see?" she replied. "It had to be this way. We never would have made it through each other's defenses otherwise." Of course, she was right. If he had attempted to date her from the beginning, she would have been frightened off; and if she had come onto him, he would have dismissed her out of hand. It was only through their friendship that they were able to find their way to this perfect moment.

Darcy nestled his head between her breasts, just as he had dreamed of doing practically every night since they first met. He sighed in utter contentment. "I love you, my Lizzy."

"I love you, too, Baby."

They were both exhausted. With the release of five months of frustrated desires and a week's worth of intense anxiety, both felt fatigue claim their bodies. They lay in silence, listening to the wind howl outside the windows, warm and safe in their newly found cocoon of intimacy. Darcy was beginning to doze when Elizabeth's soft voice brought him back to consciousness. "Do you know which room is mine?"

"You're not leaving," he growled as he tightened his arm about her waist.

"I'll come back," she whispered as he felt her lips brush the top of his head. "I just can't sleep until I've brushed my teeth and I'd like to shower."

"I'll go and get your bags," he offered. "Now that I have you in my bed, I don't want to let you leave it."

With great effort, Darcy pulled himself from Elizabeth's warm embrace and slipped on his trousers. Reluctantly he made his way to the door to walk down the cold hallway to Elizabeth's guest room.

He was too tired to be anything but grateful for Mrs. Reynolds' assumptions when he opened his bedroom door to find Elizabeth's bags waiting right outside. *I have to give that woman a raise.*

ELIZABETH AWOKE WHEN SHE FELT the warm weight, which had been resting between her breasts, rise and move away, and then a pair of strong arms pulled her over against a hard body. As she lay against Darcy's chest, Elizabeth nuzzled his neck briefly before reaching up to gently brush her fingers from his temple into his thick hair. Over and over she caressed him in this manner, finding simple pleasure in the feel of his skin and soft hair and the reassurance that he was there, he was safe and he was hers.

Through the heavy drapes, she could see the faint light of sunrise, and she was a little surprised at having slept longer than she could ever remember. She was also surprised to find that she felt different in a way beyond the slight ache between her thighs. It was not some sudden great transformation that comes from finally having performed the physical act of sex but the quiet peace in her soul that came from being both mentally and physically connected to Darcy. In giving up a small portion of control over herself, she had found something far more liberating then independence. She had found contentment.

Darcy had been gentle and tender when he made love to her. Of course, there was more discomfort then she had anticipated, but then again, there was *more* to him than she had anticipated. However, any pain was surpassed by the memory of pleasure. His touch, his kiss, his voice, his very breath thrilled her beyond her considerable expectations. Watching him achieve release was like watching the sun burst through the clouds after a storm and she basked in the warmth of his light.

He had been right; even with his gentle thrusting, there was too much discomfort for her to come, but then… Elizabeth smiled against his chest as she remembered how it felt to let go, to give him complete control of her body. It was heady, exquisite, and she found herself wanting more than anything to grant him that control again and again.

She was brought back to the present by the gentle stroking of his fingertips on her arm. Then his other hand captured hers from his hair and pulled it to his lips. He kissed her palm before placing her fingers back to his temple, encouraging her to continue her caresses. "Lizzy?"

"I'm sorry," she whispered, "I shouldn't have woken you."

"I've been awake for a while. I'd like to talk now, if you have no objections?"

She kissed his lips gently before propping her head on her elbow, waiting patiently for him to begin. "You told me once about a South American businessman your mother tried to…" here he hesitated to find the right word.

"…pimp me out to? What about him?"

"He's Pierre Estoban."

Elizabeth listened in stunned amazement as Darcy carefully recounted every word of his conversation with Pierre. Elizabeth found the story incredible, but it had to be true. What else could explain Billy Ray Collins' guilty plea? "He's been watching me? All this time?" Elizabeth felt a shiver run down her spine. "That is just too creepy and yet, how can I be anything but grateful?"

"I feel the same way, but I cannot help but hope he'll keep his word and leave you alone now that he believes we're engaged."

The word "engaged" hung in the air between them as if it were a neon sign blinking bright blue and white. It was a great joke when they were merely friends, but now it was something else entirely. As confounded as Elizabeth was over Pierre Estoban, it was nothing compared to the absolute bewilderment she felt over her sudden, overwhelming disappointment that she and

Darcy were not really engaged. She was only twenty-four years old, beginning her career and was just now experiencing love for the first time. He had only just allowed himself to fall in love, too. Certainly, it was ridiculous for her to even contemplate marriage!

Darcy broke the silence. "I don't want to think about Estoban anymore this morning, and there is one more story you need to be told."

He fixed his eyes toward the ceiling and she could feel a small shudder pass through his chest. Once again she began stoking his temple, offering him comfort for what she knew was going to be a difficult revelation about…

"Rebecca Wickham," he whispered her name. "I had met her many times growing up when her family would visit George's. She was five years older than I and everything a young boy idolizes: beautiful, aloof, unattainable. I had a crush on her beginning when I was about ten years old."

Darcy was silent for a few moments before he continued with a surprising question. "Would you care to guess how old I was when I had my first sexual experience?"

Baffled by the purpose of the question, Elizabeth answered hesitantly, "Sixteen?"

"No, guess again."

"Fourteen?" she asked with a small squeak, shocked that he could have been so young.

His laugh was mirthless. "Try twenty." She hoped her look of shock did not register in the dark. "My parents were very concerned about my education. Not even the most prestigious schools had programs for children like me…like us," he corrected as he looked pointedly to Elizabeth, "…that would allow me to be with children my own age. Being placed in classes with students two to four years older than me was very difficult. I was ostracized, alone and very unhappy. After a time my parents decided to bring me back to Pemberley where they hired tutors to complete my education. I loved being here, but I was isolated from the normal social experiences of a boy my age."

"At sixteen I went to Cambridge with Geoff and Richard. I was socially backward and very shy. Like you, I compensated by burying myself in my studies. It took several years until I was able to make friends; even then, I was still very guarded. I could never work up the nerve to even speak to a girl I found attractive. I always thought that I would be either rejected because I was too young or accepted purely because of my wealth and family reputation. So you

254

see I was not the suave lady-killer I have been portrayed to be."

Elizabeth kissed his forehead. Yes, they were very much alike. They had both experienced the pain and loneliness of being different as well as being isolated from their peers. It was no wonder they had so quickly developed such a deep connection to one another.

Darcy's eyes moved back toward the ceiling. "All that changed when Rebecca came to a party Geoff had thrown at our flat. I was still captivated by her, and within half an hour of her arriving at the party, she had completely seduced me. I won't pretend I wasn't willing."

"Rebecca was insistent that we use condoms, so I felt sure she wasn't looking to force me into marriage, and naive as I was, I believed she truly loved me. After a time, I convinced myself that I loved her too. She also convinced me that, due to our age difference, my parents would not approve of our relationship. As she traveled a great deal — supposedly a necessity for her position of employment — it was not difficult to hide it from them. Of course, Geoff and Richard would never betray my trust. My parents did not find out until…but I'm jumping ahead." Darcy took another few moments to reorganize his thoughts.

"Rebecca liked to point out to me all the little signs that indicated a woman or even another man was interested in me sexually. Although I was completely in the dark as to her reasons for this, after awhile I began to understand the power that the combination of physical attractiveness and money held over most people. I knew I never wanted consciously to use that power, and looking back, my refusal to do so became a source of friction between Rebecca and me.

"However, that was only one reason why I began to feel uncomfortable with our relationship. Rebecca needed constant excitement. Once the newness wore off for her, she suggested more public places for us to have sex. She got off on the possibility of discovery; however, I wouldn't tolerate it."

"Everything blew up in my face when I returned from a visit home to find that Rebecca was throwing a party…no, not a party…an orgy, in my flat. I was outraged and threw everyone out under threat of calling the police. Rebecca was not only unapologetic, but in her realization that I would not continue our relationship, she proceeded to inform me that I was boring, a prude and many more words that were far more ugly and hateful. After she left, I spent the weekend in a drunken stupor. When my parents finally showed up, I discovered that Rebecca had spent her weekend in a far more productive and vindictive manner."

"A few months earlier, I had convinced my father to allow me to set up a project for the foundation as a tribute to my mother. I organized fundraising for repairs to the stage lighting in the auditorium at the Derbyshire College of Music in Lambton. My mother had taught at the college throughout her lifetime. I also hoped that enough money would be raised to restore an antique grand piano at the college in hopes that my mother could be encouraged to perform there. She was so ill. I just wanted to do something to make her happy."

"The people of Lambton were very generous and donated not only their own money but also their time and energies to raise additional funds. Having known Rebecca from her visits to Pemberley, my father was happy she had volunteered to help with the project." Darcy's voice became very quiet as he continued. "Even though she never had access to the funds collected, somehow, Rebecca had managed to hack into the bank account online and empty it. It was not a great deal of money, but I was responsible for it's safekeeping. With the same amount of effort, she could have taken hundreds of thousands from my personal account, but no, she chose to steal from all those people who had worked so hard and to attack my mother's legacy. Out of all the things she could have done, that was the absolute worst!"

"I was mortified at my duplicity, but unfortunately that was not to be the end of this tragedy. I replaced the money easily enough from my own funds, but somehow my Aunt Catherine found out about the theft and attempted to use the knowledge to have me removed from the advisory board of the foundation. When my father refused her demands, she took the matter before the entire board. I was belittled and humiliated before everyone I loved and respected. There are not words to describe how I felt."

"A few months later I sat in the renovated auditorium watching my mother play the restored piano before the happy people of Lambton. While they all beamed with pride in their accomplishment, I sat miserable, knowing that it was my money, not theirs, that had paid for it all. I had let them down, betrayed their trust...and my mother knew..."

Elizabeth felt her heart breaking for Darcy. Knowing his tendency to blame himself when people he cared for were hurt and his fierce pride, she could not begin to comprehend how devastating this experience must have been for him. Wrapping her arms around him in comfort, Elizabeth laid her head against his chest.

"Just when I began to put it all behind me my parents died. It was only a few days after the memorial service that my Aunt Catherine unearthed the whole debacle again before the board as proof as to why I was not capable of taking over the foundation. Many of the board members agreed with Aunt Catherine, and I can't say that I blamed them. The absolute worst moment was when she suggested the board take the whole matter before the courts to have me declared incompetent to run the foundation."

"That's when my Uncle James suggested that he would be willing to serve as co-president of the foundation with me until such time as the board felt I was prepared to take over on my own. Aunt Catherine adamantly opposed the idea, but the remaining members of the board accepted it wholeheartedly. It was less than two years later that my Uncle resigned, with the endorsement of the entire board...except for Aunt Catherine."

Elizabeth raised her head to look into his eyes. "And that's why you never wanted to fall in love again?"

"In the weeks after the money disappeared, I realized that I was far more mortified that Rebecca had played me for a fool. I cared about her, but if I had truly loved her, I would have felt the loss of her more. No, I just didn't want anyone to be close enough to humiliate me like that again."

"It was six months after my parents died that I started using The Service. I foolishly thought that, since I was experiencing the physical release, I wouldn't need the emotional connection. I thought I had it all figured out...until you. Try as I might, I just couldn't stop myself from falling under your spell. I think I was a lost man the moment I first looked into your eyes."

Darcy turned his eyes from the ceiling and Elizabeth could feel their intensity as they bore into her own. "I can barely recall the first time I had sex. I could tell you where it occurred, but I couldn't tell you what had happened or how it felt. It was over quickly and was utterly forgettable. I wanted your first time to be so much more than just sex."

"It was so much more," she assured him with small kisses pressed across his cheeks. Elizabeth luxuriated in the feel of his stubbled cheek brushing her lips, his bare chest beneath her hands, her pelvis pressed against his hip and her leg wrapped across his strong thighs. "I believe that, as per our earlier agreement, I may now touch you all I wish."

Elizabeth did not want to pepper Darcy with questions, and knowing how difficult his confessions had been to make, she was willing to accept the story as he told it. At that moment she was more than willing to allow the memory of both Pierre Estoban and Rebecca Wickham to fade away, and given Darcy's response to her kisses, he was feeling the same way.

Half an hour later, Elizabeth was climaxing blissfully around Darcy's gently penetrating erection. Soon thereafter, they both fell back onto the pillows, chests heaving and covered in sweat.

"So that's what the big fuss is all about?" she said dryly to the ceiling.

Darcy, who was just marveling over how fantastic it felt, looked to her and answered defensively, "Yes! It most certainly is!"

Still trying to catch her breath Elizabeth turned to him and smiled teasingly. "Good reason!"

AFTER BREAKFAST, DARCY AND GEORGIANA took Elizabeth on a tour of Pemberley. The public rooms of the great house were bustling with activity as decorators worked frantically to complete the trimmings for the upcoming Christmas holiday.

Before lunch, they received a jubilant phone call from Lord and Lady Matlock informing them that Richard would soon be released from the hospital and shortly thereafter, the entire Fitzwilliam family would descend upon Pemberley in time for Christmas.

CHAPTER 22
THE CHRISTMAS ANGEL

December 20th, The Celebrity Tattler(U.K.)
*Photo caption: Fitzwilliam Darcy, sister Georgiana (left) and girlfriend
Elizabeth Bennet Christmas shopping in Lambton, Derbyshire, England.
Story: The quaint shoppes of Lambton were the setting for Fitzwilliam Darcy's
first public appearance since last month's media frenzy over his assistance
with an investigation... Lambton's citizens have always been closed mouthed
concerning the Darcys, and as the press converged on the quiet town, the locals
closed ranks against the horde in support of their native son. The few tourists
who did speak to our reporter did so anonymously. "He (Darcy) held Dr.
Bennet's hand and they were always smiling at one another. The sister seemed
very happy too..."*

December 24th, The London Times
*Photo caption: The great house at Pemberley is decorated in preparation for the
annual Anne Darcy Memorial Christmas Concert by the Derbyshire Choral
Society. Tickets for tonight's event are sold out.*

Darcy entered the family room to find it dark except for the flames in
the fireplace and the warm glow of the Christmas tree. Elizabeth was
flat on her back in the middle of the floor and he would have been
concerned if not for the look of total contentment on her face as she watched

the twinkling lights of the tree. "Hey," he called out softly.

Slowly her eyes moved from the tree to him, a beautiful smile spread across her face and the light in her eyes outshone the lights of the tree. "Hey. Do you want to join me?"

He sat down beside her on the rug. "Exactly what are we doing?"

"It's my own little tradition. Every year on Christmas Eve, I would sneak downstairs after everyone else had gone to bed and lie just like this, watching the tree."

"Waiting up for Father Christmas, no doubt." Darcy stretched out on his side next to her, propping up his head with his hand. "Did you ever see him?"

"Of course not!" she laughed lightly. "He's far too clever. However, for the longest time I firmly believed that it was he who carried me back to my bed after I fell asleep."

"You must have been devastated when you learned that..."

"Don't you say it!" Elizabeth silenced him with a finger to his lips. "Santa Claus is alive and well, thank you very much, and I refuse to hear any opinion to the contrary!"

A deep chuckle reverberated in his chest as he kissed her forehead. "Very well."

"I am perfectly serious!" She could not resist stretching her neck to brush a soft kiss upon his lips. "He lives inside each one of us, and we feel him with each gift we give at Christmas."

He returned her kiss with one of his own, "That's a lovely thought. I hope Father Christmas brings you everything your heart desires."

"I believe he already has." To demonstrate her point, Elizabeth pressed her mouth to his. When she gently pushed her tongue against his lips, he happily allowed her entrance. He loved the way she kissed; her tongue teased him with a combination of sweetness and fire that could not fail to stir every fiber of his being and immediately send all blood rushing to his groin.

His overwhelming desire for her, always carefully restrained just below the surface, demanded to be let loose. As his arms pulled her tightly against his body, he took control of the kiss, thrusting his tongue forward to ravish every taste bud, salivary gland and tooth in her mouth.

Quickly he made a mental inventory of the occupants of the house: Georgiana, Geoff and Richard were watching a movie in the theatre room, his Aunt and Uncle had retired for the night and Mrs. Reynolds had left immediately after the concert to spend the holiday with her daughter in Kympton. After a rather embarrassing debacle in the kitchen a few days before involving anatomically correct gingerbread men, frosting and a half nude dash above stairs, Darcy had taken to carrying a condom in his back pocket at all times. Now it appeared that his penchant for planning for every contingency was about to pay off. His mind was settled; he was going to take her right there in front of the Christmas tree, and she would never hear the song *O Tannebaum* again without blushing.

He pulled back to look at her. Elizabeth's hair fanned out beneath her head: a rich brown halo glowing in the firelight. Her eyes held him spellbound as her lips moved to speak, "So, Fitzwilliam, what do you want Father Christmas to give you this year?"

He rose to lock the door, and the moment he returned to her side, he slid his hand down her cashmere-covered stomach, over the zipper of her jeans and suddenly he grasped her crotch. "This!" he whispered hoarsely against her lips. "I want this!"

Elizabeth gasped, "Oh, God!" when he grabbed her. The passion in his voice and his brazen words sent a rush of arousal through her body so fast she was breathless.

He continued to kiss her as his fingers pressed through the heavy material to find that spot...the one that drove her crazy. "Do you want to know why this is the perfect gift?"

She opened her eyes to find him staring intently, demanding she answer. Elizabeth somehow managed to croak out weakly, "Yes!"

His fingers deftly unbuttoned the top of her jeans and quickly pulled down the zipper. In a flash, his hand was inside her panties, stroking the moist folds therein and then finding her clitoris, pressing firmly while swirling his fingers over the tiny bundle of nerves. Elizabeth could not stifle the cry of pleasure that erupted from her throat.

"Because, *this* completely arouses all five of the senses. *This* is warm, soft, wet," he slipped two fingers inside of her, "and oh so very tight! My fingers know it, they want it, and they need to touch it, to feel your desire grow, to feel the promise of the ecstasy to come."

Elizabeth felt his words wash over her like molten waves, each phrase leaving her burning and desperate for the next. He was weaving an erotic spell — transporting them to another time and place where the only things that mattered were the sensations he was awakening in her body and his rich, seductive voice.

Finding her jeans too constricting, she pushed both them and her panties down her legs and off her feet. Darcy sat up to allow her room to maneuver; however, he never lost contact, continuing to tease her clitoris. She flung her jeans and panties away, not caring where they landed. When Elizabeth lay back upon the rug, Darcy remained seated and used his free hand to further part her thighs and drink in the view.

"I love to see you, every part of you. You are so beautiful, Lizzy, especially here where you are the most feminine. When you are aroused, *this* becomes red and swollen, and I can see how wet you are. I know this reaction is to me … for me. It is the most arousing picture my eyes have ever beheld, and I cannot see enough."

Never in her most explicit fantasies had Elizabeth imagined something so erotic would ever happen to her. She kept her eyes on his, watching them become darker as they remained focused between her thighs. Trapped between the need to find the release his teasing fingers promised and the need to hear more, she remained silent. The ragged breath panting from her chest was the only sound in the room beyond the crackling of the fire, his beautiful, sensual baritone, and something else … something she could not name but most certainly could feel.

"Do you hear that, the sound of my fingers moving in and out of you? There's no other music like it … moisture and flesh separating and coming together. It is the most sensual music, and Apollo himself could not have crafted a more beautiful instrument."

She should come. God knows she wanted to come, but Darcy stubbornly now avoided all direct contact with her clitoris. His eyes raised and locked with hers and she knew he understood exactly what he was doing to her, exactly how badly she wanted release, but he silently told her there were two more senses to go, and there would be no relief for her until he had finished. His eyes returned to the current object of his adoration before he lowered his head and inhaled deeply.

"When I recognize this scent, I know you are beyond the point of no return. It enters my nostrils, fills my sinuses and permeates my brain, setting every nerve in my body on fire. It reminds me that, no matter how much I strive to possess you, it is you who truly possesses me, for one whiff and I am lost."

He continued to inhale deeply while trailing small kisses slowly down the inside of her thigh. His breathing was now as ragged as hers, and she could feel a slight trembling in his fingers as he continued to tease her. As he wrestled with his self-control, Elizabeth silently prayed he would not stop, for if he did, she would surely explode, and she had no wish to die before his lips had finally reached their destination. Her entire body shook as his tongue reached out to caress her quivering flesh.

"This tastes like fresh pears, ripened on the tree and drizzled with spring honey. This is your essence: ambrosia from the gods, water to a dying man. I was dying…inside…slowly allowing myself to become nothing more than a hollow shell until you possessed me, filled me and made me whole. I am yours, Elizabeth, utterly and completely, and all I ask in return is this…"

Elizabeth braced herself, for she knew the moment he said that word, the word that he had referred to repeatedly but not voiced, she would become undone. She would surrender more than just a part of her body, but all of her. She now understood that was his object all along. He wanted it all: every inch of her body, every corner of her mind and the depths of her very soul. Everything he had offered to her, he now wanted promised to him in return.

"…this…*cunt*." As the word escaped his lips, he pushed them between her folds and sucked in her clitoris. Elizabeth's reaction was instantaneous. She arched her back as pulses of ecstasy flooded her body. Over and over the pulses came, as he continued to suckle, holding tightly to her hips as her body writhed violently beneath him. Her cries of rapture echoed from the walls until she finally collapsed. Only then did he release her.

While her body still shook with aftershocks of pleasure, she felt him kiss her lips as the weight of his body settled over her hips and he thrust deep inside her. His sweater was gone, but trousers still encased his legs as if he had been in too much of a hurry to remove his shoes to pull them off.

Elizabeth knew that, since their first night, he had been holding back during intercourse, constantly aware that he could again cause her pain. But this time, he did not hold back. He thrust roughly into her repeatedly, losing himself completely in the pleasures of her body.

Her legs wrapped around his trouser-covered thighs as he made love to her with complete abandon. His rhythm became more rapid, and sweat covered his body above hers.

"This is yours," she whispered in his ear as she kissed him there. "I'm yours! I always have been. I was yours before we met. Baby, I was born yours."

Her words seemed to send him over the edge. His body jerked, stiffened and she could feel him pulse within her. The moan that came from his chest was almost wild.

At last his body relaxed. Darcy rested his head against her shoulder as he continued to support his upper body with his forearms. He panted heavily as he trailed short kisses up her collarbone to her neck and then finally to her lips where he kissed her long and sweetly. "My Lizzy!"

"My Baby," she whispered between kisses. He rolled onto his back and gathered her into his arms. Exhausted, they both watched the blinking lights of the tree.

They began to doze, each too spent to move to dress or try to climb onto one of the couches. It was only by the small kiss Elizabeth placed on his chest that Darcy was aware she was not asleep.

"Marry me?" he whispered.

He could feel the muscles move in her face as she smiled against his chest. "Yes."

THEY STIRRED WHEN THE CLOCK struck eleven. Realizing the fire was dying and the movie the others were watching would be nearing its end, they reluctantly rose to dress.

Darcy wrapped the condom and its wrapper in a sheet of paper and tucked it back into his pocket to dispose of in his room. The last thing he wanted was anyone else in the family discovering it in the wastebasket near the desk. He reckoned the smell of the fire along with the scent of the Christmas tree would cover any remaining scent of sex. He smiled confidently, knowing no one would be the wiser about the activities that had taken place in that room.

"Damn, I can't find my underwear!" Elizabeth frantically searched the floor, under the couches and between the cushions.

Darcy tried to help her. "What color are they?" He was pulling up the cushions on the chairs to look underneath.

"Red, with little reindeer on them!" She became frantic. The last thing she wanted was for someone else to find them.

Darcy noticed her pale derrière as she continued her search. "I think you'd better put on your jeans before everyone else arrives to say good night." As Elizabeth slipped on her jeans, Darcy came up behind her and embraced her around her waist. "I'll be sure to write Father Christmas a thank you note for my gift!"

Elizabeth, however, refused to be distracted from her search. "You smell like sex, Baby. You'd better clean up before Georgie kisses you good night!"

He quickly did as he was instructed and returned to continue to look for the missing panties as Elizabeth took her turn in the nearby cloakroom.[33]

They were still searching when there was a soft knock on the family room door. It opened immediately and Georgiana slipped inside. Geoff and Richard soon followed.

"I'm going to bed," Georgiana announced as she walked over to kiss Darcy on the cheek. "Happy Christmas, Wills!"

"Happy Christmas, Sweetling!" Darcy returned the gesture.

Georgiana then crossed the room to repeat the process with Elizabeth. "Wish Jake a Merry Christmas for me!" Elizabeth called to Georgiana as she exited the family room.

"I'd like a brandy," Geoff announced as he strode over to the table holding a number of ornate cut crystal decanters. "Anyone want to join me?"

Richard settled into one of the couches, turning so he could rest his broken leg on the cushions as he set his crutches against the nearby table. "That sounds like an excellent idea. Darcy, would you mind throwing another log on the fire."

Darcy looked to Elizabeth and shrugged. The panty hunt would have to be postponed as the Fitzwilliam brothers settled in.

Accepting a glass of port, Elizabeth sat in a chair next to Richard as they discussed the movie shown in the theatre room. "…Then the teacher asks, 'Where's Flick?' and the other children just look about the room as if they had no idea the poor bloke was standing right outside the window in the middle of a snow storm with his tongue stuck to the flag pole!"

A Christmas Story[34] was one of Elizabeth's all time favorite movies, so she couldn't resist getting involved in the discussion. An hour later, everyone retired, the panty problem completely forgotten until Elizabeth undressed for a quick shower.

"I'll search for them before my run tomorrow," Darcy offered when he finished brushing his teeth. "No one else will be up before then, and it will be daylight so they should be easier to find."

They shared the shower and soon snuggled together in the warm bed, drifting off into a peaceful slumber.

---

33 British expression for a small bathroom containing only a toilet and sink. Named so because when older homes were renovated with indoor plumbing, the small rooms where the servants would place cloaks and coats (the 'cloak room') were turned into half bathrooms.

34 *A Christmas Story*, 1983. In this classic American Christmas film, a young boy named Ralphie is consumed with a feverish desire to receive a B.B.Gun for Christmas.

DARCY ENTERED THE FAMILY ROOM to find it dark except for the flames in the fireplace and the warm glow of the Christmas tree. Elizabeth was flat on her back in the middle of the floor and he would have been concerned if not for the look of total contentment on her sleeping face as it was illuminated by the twinkling lights of the tree.

The beautiful form of his love changed into that of a small child. She looked to be about three or four years of age. Her long, dark curls were spread around her little head like a halo, and she was dressed in a warm, red flannel nightgown printed with little reindeer.

He carefully picked her up in his arms, and as he adjusted her small weight against his chest, the girl wrapped her arms around his neck and pressed her little face against his throat. He carried the warm bundle to the nursery. It was decorated just as it had been when Georgiana was a child, all pink and white with ponies and butterflies. As he laid the child in her small bed, she roused and blinked. Large, dark blue eyes focused briefly on his face, and as he tucked the blankets around her, she sleepily whispered, "Good night, Papa."

Her skin was warm and soft beneath his lips as he gently kissed her forehead. "Good night, Sweetling. Did you see Father Christmas?"

"No," the child yawned before sighing and pulling the soft pink blanket under her chin, "he is much too clever." She yawned again and closed her eyes.

Darcy knew the child was not real, but that didn't stop his heart from breaking when he realized that soon the dream would shift or he would awaken and she would be no more.

ON CHRISTMAS MORNING, DARCY AWOKE as Elizabeth sang softly while gently teasing his brow with a sprig of mistletoe.

Santa Baby,
Slip a sable under the tree, for me.
I've been an awfully good girl.
Santa Baby,
Hurry down the chimney tonight…
Think of all the fun I've missed,
Think of all the fellas that I haven't kissed…[35]

---

35 Santa Baby, Words & Music by Joan Javits, Phil Springer & Tony Springer recorded by Eartha Kitt, 1953

"And you won't be kissing any more fellas next year either," Darcy raised his head from between her breasts and covered her face with kisses, "except me." Her soft laughter was silenced as the kisses became more passionate. "You did agree to marry me last night!"

"Yes." She tugged his T-shirt over his head. "You have a lover and a fiancée. Both things a month ago you swore you'd never acquire. Now it only makes sense you'd want a wife, too!"

He returned the favor, and as his hand closed around her breast, words tumbled unheeded from his lips. "I want children, Lizzy."

His statement made her stop kissing his neck to make sure she heard him correctly. Elizabeth narrowed her eyes suspiciously as she cocked her head to the side. "I specifically recall you telling me that you didn't like children."

"Yes, I did, and even though you adore children, you agreed to marry me anyway. God, you're wonderful! I love you so much!" Darcy tried to kiss her again, but Elizabeth moved her face to the side so she could think. Therefore, he began to amuse himself by nibbling her earlobe.

"Are you only saying that you want children to make me happy? I don't believe I want to be the sole parent who loves our child."

He stopped kissing her ear and held her face in his hands so he could look into her eyes as he spoke. "I didn't believe having children was a possibility since I was determined I'd never marry. I think I was trying to convince myself I didn't like children to lessen the disappointment that I would never be a father. I want a little girl just like you," he kissed her briefly, "and at least four or five more just like her!"

"Five daughters?!!" Elizabeth was astounded. "I was thinking more along the lines of only one child of any sex, to do our part for population control."

Darcy frowned. "I've felt alone for so long, Lizzy. I want a large family so if something happens to either or both of us, they'll have each other. How about four of any sex?"

"I'll compromise at two of any sex," Elizabeth stated firmly.

"How about I agree to two but hold open the option for a third if neither of the first two is a girl, that is if we 'get busy' working on number one immediately."

"Immediately! Hold on cowboy! We're not engaged twelve hours yet."

Darcy laughed. "You *are* so very breathtaking when you're angry."

"You have become a horrid tease," she pouted prettily.

He kissed her nose. "As much as I would love to marry you tomorrow, bring you here to Pemberley and fill you with babies, I understand that is too much to ask. Everything has happened so quickly the past few weeks. Would you believe I had a plan to wait six more months to ask you to marry me?"

"Really?" she laughed. "So what happened?"

"It went the way of every carefully thought out plan I've made since the day we met — to hell!" They laughed together at that. "When I was lying on the floor with you last night, it just felt right. So, I asked. I was a little surprised but exceedingly pleased that you accepted."

Elizabeth reached up to run her fingers gently across his brow. "I accepted, Fitzwilliam, because I couldn't bear the thought of living my life without you."

As she spoke his first name, long, low and sultry, he felt his blood stir again, and his morning erection began to reassert itself against Elizabeth's thigh. "I do believe," Elizabeth said seductively as she reached down to the front of his pajama bottoms, "it's time to try and guess the first of my Christmas presents. This one feels big and hard and..."

Elizabeth was very good at guessing gifts, and Darcy missed his morning run.

As Elizabeth tried to wrestle her curls into some semblance of order, Darcy made his way down to the kitchen to pull out the large basket of muffins Mrs. Reynolds had left for the family breakfast and start two pots of coffee.

This was another Darcy family tradition. Christmas breakfast required that no member of the staff would need to give up spending Christmas morning with their own family to wait on the Darcys. When Darcy was a child, his mother would cook eggs, toast and bacon, and the Darcy, Fitzwilliam and Bingley families would sit around the large kitchen table to eat their breakfast. Darcy chuckled when he recalled how his Uncle James would purposely take his time eating to provoke the children who had to wait until everyone had completed their meal and the dishes were cleared before they were permitted to go upstairs to the family room.

Darcy was pulled from his memories by the sound of a throat clearing. He looked up to find Richard, supported by his crutches, standing in the doorway. "Happy Christmas, Darcy!"

"Happy Christmas, Richard! Can I pour you some coffee?" Richard sat down at the table as Darcy brought him a cup along with the pitcher of cream.

Richard took a long sip, watching his cousin bustle about, pulling out juice glasses and setting them on a tray. "I was just up in the family room admiring the tree."

"Ah, you know that's not permitted until everyone has finished breakfast. If your mother knew she'd box your ears."

Richard laughed, "That she would. I happened to notice there were some new ornaments this year."

"Elizabeth's grandmother sent her a box so she wouldn't feel too homesick: glass icicles and a few hand-blown Santas. So anything unfamiliar on the tree must have come from her." Darcy continued to load the tray with jars of jam and honey.

"Well then, I must say I'd like to meet Elizabeth's grandmother." Darcy stopped in his tracks when he saw the flash of red in Richard's hand. "She must be a *very interesting* woman!" Darcy glanced up and, sure enough, held up between Richard's fingers was a pair of racy, red, reindeer panties. "I mean, how many grandmothers would actually wear knickers this sexy, let alone hang them on the Christmas tree. Christmas in North Carolina sounds like my kind of holiday!"

Now it was time for Darcy to clear his throat. "They were on the tree?"

"Actually, they were draped across the angel on the top. I had one hell of a time getting them down, especially in my condition. This was one instance where having crutches was an advantage."

"How much?" Darcy asked as he narrowed his eyes at his cousin who was obviously enjoying this way too much.

"Let's see, first there's the twenty I lost to The Squirt when you and Elizabeth failed to wait until next week to shag. Then there was this little wager I made with her and Geoff last night while we were watching the film..."

Darcy signed heavily. This was definitely not going to be cheap! "What wager was that?"

"You see, I commented to Geoff that you most likely had left us to return to the family room to bonk the very alluring Dr. Bennet. Both my brother and your sister insisted that you would never consider doing such a thing anyplace but behind the closed door of a bedroom. So a wager was made and I, as the lone assenting party, had to prove that said bonking did occur or pay up. Hence my early morning foray into the family room. I was just beginning to despair over the lack of evidence and was briefly considering where I might locate a black light to scan for bodily fluids when, like the herald of an angel on the first Christmas, your treetop angel brought me glad tidings of great joy!"

"How much!" Darcy growled.

"If I turn this sexy little thing over to Geoff and Georgie, I'll clear a cool forty pounds."

"I'll make it fifty."

"But then, it's hard to put a figure on the entertainment value of watching everyone in the family tease you mercilessly for days on end and again every Christmas from now until eternity! No, I'll never look at that angel the same way again!"

"You wouldn't do this to Elizabeth! I thought you liked her."

"In the last two days I've come to adore Elizabeth, but you know better than to think any one of us would ever say anything in front of her. No, this humiliation would be reserved for you alone."

Darcy was losing his patience. Never before had he wanted to throttle a man on crutches; however, Richard was about to be the first. "One hundred! That's my final offer!"

Richard whistled long and low. "That makes this one very expensive pair of knickers!" Richard peeked at the tag inside. *"Lady Racy Stacy's.* Isn't that the store on Bond Street, between Twirling Way and Tasselton Street?"

Darcy growled in frustration.

"Here," Richard handed the panties to Darcy, "Just watching that little vein throb in your neck for the last five minutes was payment enough. Consider this my little Christmas gift to you."

"Wanker!" Darcy hissed as he stuffed the panties into the pocket of his jeans.

"You should be grateful! Because I've spent the last few weeks laid up, you'll be the only person to get a gift from me this Christmas!"

Not trusting himself to remain civil, Darcy silently returned to putting out the breakfast. A few minutes later, Elizabeth walked into the kitchen. "Merry Christmas, Richard."

"Happy Christmas, Elizabeth!"

Elizabeth wore a deep green V-neck sweater, black skirt and black boots. Her hair was pulled up into a twist. She approached Darcy who could not help but shed his black mood to admire her. When she came close to Darcy, she whispered into his ear, "I'm going to slip up to the family room to look for my panties."

"I have them." At her questioning look he said, "Richard found them." Elizabeth's eyes flew open in horror. "Don't worry," Darcy reassured her, "he won't say a word to anyone else."

270

Elizabeth looked to Richard and realized he must know the topic of their whispered conversation. He smiled sympathetically and she immediately relaxed.

"Thank you, Richard." Elizabeth crossed the room to where he sat. "I would have died of embarrassment if anyone else had found them. You're my knight in shining armor."

"Just call me Sir Richard," he said as Elizabeth placed a kiss of gratitude on his cheek.

Richard looked over to his cousin and smirked.

Darcy glared!

Soon the remaining family members entered the kitchen, and after breakfast they moved as a group to the family room. Gifts were exchanged over the course of the morning between glasses of champagne mixed with fruit juice and the occasional story of holidays past.

The value of the gifts given was not measured in monetary figures, but by the thought and effort put into each by the giver. While everyone else was marveling over the silver earrings Elinor had custom made for Georgiana, Elizabeth slipped over to Darcy to give him his gift from her.

"Excuse me, madame," Darcy teased in a whisper, "but I believe you gave me my gift last night."

Elizabeth could not help the blush that spread up her throat to her cheeks. "Stop it, please. It's bad enough I think of last night every time someone mentions Father Christmas!" Darcy didn't dare tell her he had the same response every time someone mentioned the new ornaments on the Christmas Tree.

Darcy opened the box to find a pair of hand-tooled leather gloves. At first, he struggled to hide his disappointment at such an impersonal gift. Sensing his trouble, Elizabeth asked him to try one on. "Ohhh!" he said in realization of the rabbit fur lining which provided warmth with very little bulk. The feel of the incredibly soft fur was more than warm; it was sensual, almost erotic as it snugly surrounded his hand and fingers, reminding him very much of the gift he received the evening before. "These are excellent and they fit perfectly."

"Mr. Smithson at the leather shop in Lambton guaranteed they would fit."

"I should have recognized the quality of the craftsmanship. He's been making my gloves since I was a child."

"And, look here," Elizabeth said indicating the design discreetly embossed in the palm of each glove.

It was so small, Darcy had to hold it up to the light to see. "There are initials. B.F.F.!"

"That is to remind you each time you wear these that even though our relationship has changed, you will always be my very best friend, forever."

He was deeply touched by her gift and allowed himself to lean forward and place a chaste kiss on her cheek in thanks; but his lips apparently had a mind of their own and before he knew it he was kissing Elizabeth quite soundly before one and all.

It was the deafening silence in the room that brought them back to their senses. Darcy and Elizabeth turned their heads to find not the expressions of surprise they expected, but five sly smiles, as if everyone else was in on some private joke but them. "Oh, come on!" Darcy exclaimed in exasperation, "You didn't bet on when we'd kiss in front of you?"

Richard held out his hand to the remainder of his family, "Darcy, you have made me a very happy man!" One by one the remaining family members each put a twenty-pound note in his hand.

"Darcy," he turned to see Elizabeth's confused expression, "What's this all about?"

"I'm sorry, Elizabeth," Darcy said in a reprimanding tone directed at his relatives. "I'm afraid it's time to tell you the horrible truth about my family's gambling addiction!" His statement was greeted with peals of laughter from his unrepentant relatives. "Very well!" Darcy stood and pulled Elizabeth to her feet. "If you will excuse us?" he said to the rest of his family as he led Elizabeth out into the hallway.

"Did we really have to leave?" Elizabeth asked. "Surely we can withstand a little teasing."

"I didn't want them around when I gave you this." Darcy held out his hand to reveal a small box. "Happy Christmas, Elizabeth."

She smiled as she took the box and carefully removed the wrapping paper to reveal a black velvet jewelry box within. She lifted the lid to find a small gold heart, floating on a very fine chain. It was simple, made to be worn every day and it suited her tastes perfectly. "It's lovely!"

Darcy took the box from her hand and carefully removed the necklace. "Turn around, please." Elizabeth found she faced a mirror and watched as Darcy passed the heart over her head and before her face to rest just below her throat as he fixed the chain behind her back. He then looked over her shoulder and their eyes locked in the mirror as he slowly let the length of the chain drop. The heart glided over her skin, down inside her sweater until the cool heavy metal rested between her breasts.

No explanation was necessary. They continued to stare silently at each other in the mirror, until Darcy could bear it no more. He leaned down and kissed her neck as his hands moved from her waist to her breasts. Sighing in pleasure, Elizabeth leaned back into him. "We should go back in," she said with regret. "I'm sure they're expecting us to return."

Darcy reluctantly released her. "Oh, I'm sure they're betting on it."

CHAPTER 23

FRIENDLY REACTIONS

December 27th, The Daily Gossip (U.S.)
Photo caption: The main gate at Pemberley, the Darcy family estate in England,
where Elizabeth Bennet has been making some surprising changes.
Story: Family Feud! Rumors abound that Fitzwilliam Darcy's sister
Georgiana despises future sister-in-law, Elizabeth Bennet. Sources report the
teenager's complaints that Elizabeth has usurped the younger girl's role as
mistress of Pemberley, making sweeping changes in the staff and décor of the
great house…

"Richard," Elizabeth called out warmly upon discovering him alone in the library. "Your brother insisted last night that he has some contracts he wanted me to see today, and now I can't find him anywhere. You wouldn't happen to know where he's run off to?"

Richard studied her fine figure over the rim of his coffee cup as she settled into the chair next to his. "Darcy sent him and my father off to London in a helicopter first thing this morning, apparently on some urgent business about which I am happily not informed."

Elizabeth raised an eyebrow in disbelief. "You don't appear to me to be a man who likes to remain uninformed of anything."

"Typically you are correct; however, I am on holiday for the next several years I hope, during which time I want no stress, be it physical or mental." To demonstrate why, he tapped the removable cast on his right leg.

Elizabeth nodded her head in understanding. "How are you feeling this afternoon?"

The word "fine" was on his lips until he noticed the sincere expression on her face. No, she was not simply making conversation. Elizabeth was genuinely concerned, and he found himself speaking the truth. "The pain killers manage to take the edge off, but I refuse to take them all the time. I'm a man who likes to keep my wits about me. A brandy or *three* in the evenings ensures I fall asleep."

"I won't attempt to lecture you on the dangers of mixing alcohol and prescription drugs. I shall assume you know what you are about."

He smiled and nodded his head. "Thank you. I wish my mother held the same opinion."

"If I were your mother, *then* I would lecture you."

"If you were my mother, I'd be beating my friends off with my crutches." He liked her laugh and, not for the first time, briefly cursed Darcy's luck for meeting her first.

"You're not already? Elinor is lovely."

He appreciated her diplomatic dodge. "I do have a very beautiful mother, but surely you are aware of the effect *you* have on men."

"I think you are exaggerating, but I appreciate the flattery nonetheless."

"Now don't start confusing me with my brother. I never exaggerate, but if the truth is flattery, so be it. My suddenly lovesick cousin is the prime example of your considerable power over the opposite sex."

Elizabeth felt uncomfortable with the turn of the conversation. "I was under the impression that Darcy was the irresistible sex god in our relationship."

As they shared another laugh, she eyed Richard carefully. Except for a small scar over his left eye and a more severe haircut, he and Geoff were identical in appearance — like a set of beautifully matched bookends — but where Geoff was jovial, Richard was deeper. Even when joking with the rest of his family, there was always a darker edge to his character. One could tell that the wheels were always turning inside his head and his eyes were always watching, completely aware of everything and everyone in his surroundings. Elizabeth leveled her eyes at his. "What is it you really want to know?"

"You never cease to amaze — always so quick and clever and yet with an open sweetness that has captured the heart of every member of my family. You're lovely, smart, tactful, funny, kind, and generous and yet it is all tempered with just enough reserve to make it all so genuine."

"Enough with the flattery, Richard," Elizabeth's voice was calm, but determined. "Your words are flirtatious, but your tone tells me there's no seduction intended. I think you're fishing for something, and I don't like to be toyed with. Out with it!"

Richard laughed in astonishment. "And you are brutally to the point! Very well, I'll be brutal, too. I'm suspicious by nature; and you, Dr. Elizabeth Isabella Bennet, appear too good to be true. I've only known you for a few days, and I find I like you immensely — an occurrence that has never happened before and only serves to raise the hackles on the back of my neck. I'm looking for your faults, Elizabeth, something to make you more human than the picture of perfection I see before me. A hint of vanity? A whisper of excessive pride? A slight glimpse of calculated materialism?"

Now *this* made sense to Elizabeth. Perhaps she should have been offended, but everyone had welcomed her without question. It was actually a relief that someone was on their guard.

"I thought you were on vacation," she teased to let him know she understood his motives.

"I am, which is why I am determined to satisfy my suspicions. They're cramping my style."

"I'll do what I can to help." Elizabeth thought for a moment to gather her thoughts. "To answer your question, I am aware that men find me attractive, but I have a sister who makes me look like chopped liver. Whenever I become too vain, I am checked by all the comparisons to her in which I come up short. I must admit, I am a little jealous."

"We're all a little jealous of someone," Richard interjected, "and if your sister was so superior, Darcy would be with *her,* and I think you're more than smart enough to realize that. No, you're going to need to do better than that."

"All right, I'm a control freak. I hate to clean and cook and do both only out of necessity. I have a tendency to jump to conclusions about people, and I know, without a doubt that I am the best damn concert pianist of the last 100 years!"

"Bravo!" Richard briefly clapped his hands. "Controlling, non-domestic, judgmental and vain! I take it my cousin is aware of all these faults?" Elizabeth nodded her head in the affirmative. "Although I can't imagine they would bother Darcy too much as he shares nearly all of them with you."

Elizabeth smiled. "Well, that last one I've never admitted to anyone before.

Oh..." she added, "I also have a few very nasty skeletons in my closet. Darcy is aware of those, too. So you see we are sharing our closets as well as our faults."

"So you know about Rebecca?"

"I do."

"I must admit I never expected that." Richard picked up a cup and reached out for the coffee service on a table nearby. Noticing his wince of pain, Elizabeth stood and took his cup to refill it. "Thank you. Of course I'm dying to know about those skeletons of yours, but if you are as much like Darcy as I suspect, you won't be volunteering that information."

"You are correct."

"You have humanized yourself quite well, and I feel infinitely better. I didn't think it was possible, but your faults only make me like you more." Richard took the cup with his right hand, and to Elizabeth's surprise, he took her hand with his left and briefly kissed it. "Welcome to the family."

"You know!" Elizabeth was disappointed. Although she had left it up to Darcy as to how and when his family would be informed of their engagement, she assumed they would be together when he did.

Richards' eyes flew open wide as he put the pieces together quickly. "I was speaking figuratively, but apparently that is no longer the case!"

"Shit!" Elizabeth fell back into her chair dejectedly. "I would have made a terrible spy."

Richard chuckled loudly. "The worst! So, when did this happen?"

"Why?" she groaned. "Have you all placed bets on it?"

"I don't think it's occurred to any of us that things would progress so quickly. We're all still getting used to the fact that Darcy is hopelessly in love." Richard suddenly laughed out loud. "Aunt Catherine will be furious! I would love to be a fly on the wall when she finds out. Her shouts of anger will be so loud the foundation of every major building in London will tremble."

"Darcy has told me a little about her, but each time the subject comes up he visibly cringes." Elizabeth bit her bottom lip in concern. "Do you honestly think she will be *that* disappointed?"

"*Disappointed* will not begin to describe it. My aunt's position in society as 'Lady Catherine de Bourgh' was not her first choice. It is well known within the family that what she really wanted was to marry George Darcy."

Elizabeth was trying to make sense of the story. "So your aunt was heartbroken when Mr. Darcy married her sister?"

"Her heart, if she has one, had nothing to do with it. The power, wealth and prestige attached to being a Darcy extend beyond the boundaries of the U.K. It's global. That is what my aunt wanted. Uncle George, however, wasn't interested in Aunt Catherine."

"Anne Fitzwilliam Darcy," Elizabeth reasoned aloud, "thwarted her sister's plans."

"I'm certain Aunt Anne didn't intend to usurp her sister's imagined place as Mrs. Darcy. She simply fell in love with my uncle, and he loved her fiercely in return. I'm told that once their engagement was announced, Aunt Catherine didn't speak to either of them for more than fifteen years. That's when she married Louis de Bourgh who, on top of a rather convenient terminal illness, had wealth, a title and a daughter who reignited my aunt's delusions of gaining some control of the Darcy legacy through her stepdaughter's eventual marriage . . . to Uncle George's son."

"And now her plans will once again be thwarted," Elizabeth said, "this time by me."

"Her plans never had a chance at succeeding. Darcy started out being gentle but direct about his intentions never to marry, let alone marry Anne. When Aunt Catherine refused to take him seriously, Darcy became blunt, but she is still determined."

"And while she waits for Darcy to marry Anne," Elizabeth reasoned, "she tries everything possible to undermine his authority with the foundation."

"Precisely. As a member of the advisory board, it's the only aspect of his wealth in which she has any say. If she is going to retaliate because of your engagement, that will be where she strikes."

"And Anne — how will she feel? She seemed so fragile when I met her last summer."

"Anne needs to stand on her own two feet. You and Darcy can't be held responsible because she would rather play the willing victim to her stepmother's plots."

At that moment, Elinor, Georgiana and Mrs. Reynolds entered the library. "I don't know what all the excitement is about, but Darcy told us to come here and wait for him."

"Where is he?" Elizabeth asked.

Georgiana answered, "I believe he's looking for you."

The steadily increasing sounds of a helicopter approaching caught their attention. "That would be Geoff and Dad. Perhaps now we will find out what this is all about."

At that moment, the door to the library opened and Darcy entered. "Elizabeth! I'm going to have to get you a new phone so I can beep you when I can't find you."

"No thanks!" she responded with an irritated wrinkle of her nose. "I have no intention of ever using one of those things."

Darcy frowned but let it pass. "I have a surprise for you." When Elizabeth pushed on her hands to stand Darcy stopped her. "Just stay where you are. The surprise is coming to you."

With a look of childlike anticipation, Darcy sat on the arm of her chair and turned his attention to the door of the library in time to see it open as Geoff, the Earl and two gentlemen Elizabeth didn't know stepped inside. She watched in wonder as one of the two strangers approached her to place a large, metal briefcase flat on the coffee table before her.

Darcy performed the introductions. "This is Frederick Wentworth, my head of security, and this is Mr. Henry Tilney. Henry's company, Tilney & Sons, has been the Darcy family jeweler for ten generations. Fred, Henry, this is Dr. Elizabeth Bennet —" Elizabeth rose to offer her hand when with a huge grin Darcy added, "— my fiancée."

Outside of the engaged couple, only Richard and Henry did not freeze with looks of happy shock upon their faces. Georgiana was the first to break the silence with an enthusiastic, "Shut up!" as she threw her arms around her brother's neck. Elinor quickly hugged Elizabeth and soon the entire room was awash in heartfelt congratulations.

Suddenly the Earl sobered and looked to the case on the table. "When you sent us to the bank to collect Tilney and that case from your vault, I assumed you were giving Georgie some of your mother's jewels; but given your news this must be . . ." he looked to the case in awe.

"The Darcy diamonds!" Lady Matlock whispered as she sat near the case, looking at it with unabashed wonder.

"There really are Darcy diamonds?" Geoff sat beside his mother. "I thought that was just some myth."

"Oh, they're very real," said Tilney as he extracted a small key from a chain tucked inside his shirt. "Do you want to tell Dr. Bennet the story, Darcy, or shall I?"

Darcy sat Elizabeth back in her chair and, taking her hand, explained, "In

1790, my ancestor, George Albert Edward Darcy, went to India on a diamond expedition and returned with a number of uncut diamonds. Since then, it has become a tradition that when a Darcy heir marries, he selects one of the stones for his bride's wedding band. The tradition evolved over time, and since the early 1900's, the stones were set into engagement rings."

"And what of the Darcy females?" Richard asked with a wink to Georgiana. "That hardly seems fair."

"Only with my grandfather, Alexander, were the Darcy women included in this legacy. When she turns twenty-one, Georgiana may choose a stone to have made into whatever she wishes." Darcy looked at his Aunt. "Mum told me of her promise to you...that you would be present the next time this case was opened, so I decided to make this a family unveiling." He then turned to Elizabeth. "Do you mind?"

"No," Elizabeth whispered as she stared at the case, suddenly filled with anxiety over what she had gotten herself into. She knew Darcy was wealthy, but the realization of just how wealthy was more than a little unsettling. Still, she was dying to see exactly what was inside that case.

"There's only one restriction," Henry said as he unlocked the case and raised the lid, "You are not permitted to take more than twenty carats worth."

Looking to Darcy with wide eyes, Elizabeth repeated before swallowing hard, "A twenty carat diamond?"

Henry turned the open case toward Elizabeth and as all eyes were glued to the black velvet within, he carefully removed the protective covering, revealing numerous black oblong shaped rocks, several of which had pieces removed from them. After putting on a pair of white cotton gloves, Henry removed a small piece that was black on one side and cut in many facets on the other and held it out to Elizabeth.

With a trembling hand, she took the piece, which was the size of a robin's egg, and held it up to the light. "It's blue!" she said as she passed the stone carefully to Lady Matlock.

"They're blue diamonds," Henry explained, "perfect in clarity and deep blue in color. They are extremely rare and therefore, priceless!" After the stone was passed around the room, Tilney returned it to the case and pulled a sketchbook out from his briefcase. "So, shall we get down to business? Do you have any idea of the size you would like for the stone?"

With the unveiling of the stones, the show was over, so the rest of the family left the library, leaving Darcy and Elizabeth to design their engagement and wedding rings.

AFTER A CELEBRATORY DINNER, ELIZABETH and Darcy settled into a couch in the drawing room. Although more formal than the family room, it was quieter and more private when the house was full of guests. Darcy amused himself by reading the latest Martin Amis book that Geoff had thoughtfully given him for Christmas as Elizabeth read through the contracts Geoff had finally produced for her.

"Baby, I keep thinking about the ring. How am I supposed to wear it every day, knowing how much it's worth? I'm terrified that I'll lose it or it will be stolen."

Without looking up from his book, Darcy responded, "It will be insured, and you chose to have only a four-carat ring. That should make it less conspicuous."

"*Only* four carats?!!! It's huge!"

Putting down his book, Darcy tightened his arm about her shoulder and said, "This ring is supposed to make you happy, not give you a fit of nerves."

"I am happy, and it will be a very beautiful ring, but…"

"…but?"

"How rich are you?"

It was a fair question, Darcy thought, especially now that they were getting married. "Actually or figuratively?"

"Figuratively, please! I suspect the actual amount in pounds may give me a heart attack."

He smiled slyly and whispered in her ear. "I'm filthy rich!"

"That's perhaps a little too vague. Are you richer than the Queen?"

"Yes."

"Do you have more money than Bill Gates?"

"Bill and I have an agreement," Darcy teased. "We *tell* everyone he has more money than I do. It looks good for his business and keeps my fortune out of the limelight."

Elizabeth began to feel nauseous. "Oh, God! That's *very* wealthy."

Sensing her distress, Darcy took her hand. "Look at me, Lizzy. I'm just a man, a man who loves you very much. Over the next few months we'll make a lot of decisions about where and how we'll live. If it makes you more comfortable, I'd be happy for us to move into a small row house in Meryton, New Jersey."

Seeing the sincerity in his eyes, Elizabeth smiled and embraced him tightly.

At that moment, she decided she was not going to be missish about Darcy's wealth. "I don't think that will be necessary. If possible, I'd like us to eventually live here at Pemberley."

"Really?" Darcy's excitement was overflowing. "I thought you might prefer Manhattan."

"Really! I love it here. It's quiet, spacious, and even with the steady stream of tourists going through the public rooms, I feel safe here."

After several kisses, she couldn't resist asking, "You really would have moved into a row house in Meryton for me?"

"Of course!" Then Darcy added in a low voice, "It would have been surrounded by bodyguards and a twenty-foot-high, electric fence, but..." They were still laughing over the logistics of their imaginary row house when Elizabeth's cell phone rang. Seeing it was from her grandmother, she took the call.

Elizabeth and Isabella Bennet began by discussing the beauty of Pemberley and the quaint charm of the Outer Banks in winter. Then, as they confirmed Elizabeth's travel plans, Darcy tightened his arm around her shoulder and frowned. The idea of separating from each other was difficult to accept, but Elizabeth simply had to go to North Carolina for New Years. She was trying to sound happy about the trip when her grandmother surprised her. She rested the phone momentarily on her chest. "Darcy, Gran would like to speak to you. Do you mind?"

Darcy wrinkled his brow as he took the phone. "Hello, Mrs. Bennet?... Right, Isabella, then I am just Darcy. ... Are you sure? ... Frankly, Elizabeth has told me about Professor Bennet's opinion of me, and I have no desire to be the cause of any problem during your holiday. ... Thank you for your invitation. I'd be very happy to accept if Elizabeth has no objections." Darcy looked to Elizabeth who nodded her head vigorously. "She has agreed; therefore, we'll see you in two days. ... I will. Thank you again. Goodbye." Darcy handed the phone back to an astonished Elizabeth. "She's rung off, due to some race of some sort on the beach; but I'm to tell you she loves you and to give you this..." Darcy gently kissed her cheek.

"There's always a race on the beach," Elizabeth laughed softly as Darcy's lips brushed from her neck to her throat, "but I can't believe she told you to kiss me like this."

"I must admit I made that bit up." He took her earlobe in his mouth and sucked lightly. "I just assumed she'd want to kiss your cheek goodbye, and the rest I'm just improvising for my own benefit."

"Ummm," Elizabeth moaned softly as he continued his improvisation. "I'm so happy you're coming to North Carolina with me. I was dreading spending the week apart."

"I'm surprised at Isabella's invitation, but I'm not about to question it. I couldn't bear the thought of letting you go," he confessed between the kisses he trailed down her breastbone as his fingers nimbly unfastened the buttons on her blouse. "I find that I still cannot get enough of you: your voice, your teasing and this spot right here..." Darcy removed the gold heart before kissing between Elizabeth's breasts. "I believe I never will."

Enjoying his attentions very much, Elizabeth suggested, "Bed?"

"Bed!" Darcy stood and, taking Elizabeth's waist, lifted her over his shoulder like a sack. As she laughed at the absurdity of her position, Darcy smacked her once playfully on her bottom and carried her off to bed.

CHAPTER 24
READY...SET...GO!

December 29th, The Daily Gossip (U.K.)
Story: Prisoner at Pemberley! It has been several days since Fitzwilliam Darcy has been seen outside the gates of Pemberley. Sources tell us that Elizabeth Bennet has refused to allow him to leave the premises out of an irrational fear that Darcy will again disappear as he did earlier this month while assisting the Americans in....

Elizabeth felt a small thrill at how the rented Jaguar handled the turns of the narrow, brick streets of Netherfield, North Carolina. The town looked lovely as the quaint restaurants and tiny shops were tastefully decorated with small white lights, pine garlands and red and gold bows. Here the usual, hectic frenzy of the outside world seemed to melt away, replaced by the enchantment of the sleepy, charming atmosphere of North Carolina's Outer Banks in winter.

Elizabeth loved Netherfield, and the pleasure at once again viewing the place that held her few moments of childhood bliss was increased by the knowledge that she was released, at least for the next week, from chauffeurs and bodyguards. Yes, her movements would be restricted, but there would be no shadow following her wherever she went, and she could drive! If she tried very hard, she could imagine that she had returned to the life she had known before all the craziness of the past few months; however, there was one very notable and most welcome exception.

"Is it much further?" Darcy relaxed back into the passenger's seat after closing up the laptop full of reports he had been reading since they had landed at Raleigh-Durham Airport. He hadn't protested when Elizabeth offered to drive from the airport to her Grandmother's house. It was another example of how two control freaks were learning to compromise.

Of course, all was not roses. At seven o'clock that morning, Elizabeth was frustrated with Darcy's apparent lack of concern over his passport, which was still in the hands of the British government. As the time arrived for them to leave Pemberley, with no word from Geoff, she became distressed over the idea that she would have to leave Darcy behind, which in Elizabeth Bennet was expressed in anger. That she would question his judgment was, in Darcy's opinion, outrageous, and he found himself becoming angry in return. When they exited the helicopter at Heathrow with still no contact from Geoff, Elizabeth felt her tirade over Darcy making promises he could not fulfill was more than justified… until they arrived at the hangar to find Charles Hayter waiting with Darcy's passport in his hand.

Predictably, the knowledge that everything had worked out did little to immediately cool either of their considerable pique. For Darcy, she *was* quite breathtaking when angry; while for Elizabeth, his steel blue eyes, the hard set of his jaw and the barely repressed anger were a stirring sight to behold. Therefore, immediately after takeoff, they took their argument to the stateroom of the private jet and redirected their energies in a rather tumultuous introduction for them both to *The Mile High Club*.[36]

Elizabeth downshifted into third as she took another turn. Damn, if she didn't love a standard transmission! "The house is only about ten minutes away, and the view from the shore road is amazing."

As if on cue, the town fell away, and before them was the beautiful expanse of Netherfield Town Beach. Crowded and choked with traffic during the summer, it was practically deserted except for a few hardy souls who enjoyed walking the beach in a brisk December wind. The waves were high, crashing white foam that lapped hungrily at the soft sand.

Leaving the Jaguar standing starkly in the empty parking lot, they made

---

36 A term collectively applied to individuals who have engaged in sexual activity while on board an aircraft in flight at least 1 mile (5,280 ft/1,609 m AGL) above the Earth. There is no known formally constituted club so named.

their way toward the beach. Hand in hand, they silently strolled the weathered boardwalk path over the dunes to the water's edge, the only sounds being the crashing of the waves and the cries of the gulls. The few people they passed on their walk nodded their heads in friendly greeting, and a group of half a dozen hearty surfers in full wet suits braved the cold air to attempt to ride the large waves.

After awhile, they sat on the dry sand near the dunes, warmed by the winter sun and protected from the wind. Elizabeth, sheltered between Darcy's bent legs and leaning back into his chest, sighed as his arms enveloped her. Together they watched the tide slowly advance. It was idyllic.

"What do you think your father's reaction will be?" Darcy's question brought Elizabeth back to the realities of the day.

Their time together at Pemberley had been perfect. The short days were spent exploring the estate, riding the beautiful horses of Pemberley's stables and enjoying the company of Georgiana and the Fitzwilliams. Their nights were spent in a passionate discovery of everything a loving, intimate relationship could be. They were happier than they had ever been before, and when they had revealed to the rest of Darcy's family that they intended to marry, they were able to share that happiness with people who were overjoyed at the news.

Unfortunately, that would not be the case here in North Carolina. "I suppose we can put it off no longer." Elizabeth stood and reached out her hand to help Darcy up. "Let's go find out."

THOMAS BENNET STARED OUT THE front door of his mother's home, waiting for Elizabeth to arrive. "Daddy," Jane said as she approached from the dining room, "if you're that worried, call her cell phone."

"I already have," he replied grumpily. "Lizzy said she would be here twenty minutes ago. I should have asked her if *that man* was driving. He's probably driving on the wrong side of the road as we speak."

"Tom, if you can't be pleasant, you can return to Hunsford." Isabella Bennet's voice drifted from the living room. "I'm sure they'll be here soon."

Jane patted her father's shoulder supportively, and he turned to give her a quick hug. "Darcy's a nice man, Daddy." Jane smiled in an attempt to have her father give her a smile in return. She failed miserably.

Thomas Bennet was determined to hate Fitzwilliam Darcy, for *that man* brought with him all the things Elizabeth never wanted: wealth, fame and the attention of the press. *That man* was all wrong for her, and his only comfort was the knowledge that Darcy and Elizabeth were not lovers; but the fact that she had spent Christmas with his family and was now bringing him to her grandmother's house was worrying. "Why did *he* have to come?"

"Because I invited him," Isabella answered as she walked into the foyer. "He's Lizzy's friend, and we should all take the time to get to know him before we condemn him outright. I think it's wonderful that he was willing to come and meet all of her family."

"I already know him," Tom grumbled. "He's British!" Since his divorce from Frannie, Tom had developed an acute dislike of all things originating in the United Kingdom.

"So is Charles, Daddy," Jane admonished gently, "and the two of you have been getting along like two peas in a pod since he got here."

As if on cue, Charles Bingley entered from the dining room, carrying a plate on which sat the remains of his third piece of red velvet cake. Yes, Charles was the exception. Tom liked him because Charles was uncomplicated and obviously adored his Janie. The young man enjoyed life and everyone in it, and he repeatedly assured Tom Bennet of the one thing he wanted to hear more than anything else: *that man* and his favorite daughter were no more than good friends.

Without even meeting him, Tom just knew *that man* would be a whole other animal. He pictured him dark, overbearing and arrogant. If he was anything less, Tom would be extremely disappointed.

His eyes flew toward the door as a Jaguar pulled up in front of the house.

"Take a deep breath," Elizabeth teased Darcy as she gently patted his knee. "They'll only be strangers for the first few minutes, and then they'll be family." As she removed the key from the ignition, she could see he was uncomfortable. They had yet to leave the car, and already he was wearing his cold mask of indifference.

Darcy had every reason to fiercely dislike Thomas Bennet. It simply was impossible to respect a parent who had turned a blind eye to the sufferings of someone who was supposed to be his favorite child. Darcy pictured him constantly smiling, carefree and willing to find amusement at anyone's expense. If he were anything less, Darcy would be extremely disappointed.

"I'm not uncomfortable," he lied.

"Bullshit!" Elizabeth gently admonished. She knew he would make an effort for her sake, and she was confident that Darcy would get along well with everyone, except her father...and perhaps Lydia.

She was barely out of the car before Lydia came bounding up from the beach path. "Lizzy! Lizzy!" Elizabeth turned and could not help but smile at the sight of her youngest sister running toward her; soon the two were hugging tightly.

"Let me look at you." Elizabeth pulled back to look into her sister's exuberant face. "You're wearing far too much eye liner! Other than that, you're simply gorgeous!"

"Yeah, yeah, yeah," Lydia groaned playfully, "and you're still acting like a mother hen. But, I've missed you too. Now that you're here, we'll have so much fun. Gran's had the piano tuned, and Jane's boyfriend has the cutest accent! Kit and Mary have gone into town for... *Whoa!* What have we here?"

Elizabeth watched in dread as her sister moved toward Darcy who was standing on the other side of the car. Lydia's demeanor changed instantly from innocent teenager to shameless flirt. It was not just a change in facial expression. It was as if her whole body suddenly exuded sex. "No one told me *you* were coming. You are even more babe-alicous in person!"

"Lydia!" Elizabeth hissed her warning into her sister's ear. As Darcy was still wearing his sunglasses, Elizabeth couldn't read his expression, but she was sure he was shocked.

Elizabeth made the introductions. "Lydia, this is Darcy...only Darcy...not Handsome, Honey, Sugar, Hot Stuff, Studly or any other cute little nickname you may dream up. Got it?"

"Got it!" Lydia at least had the sense to look apologetically toward her sister. She knew she should not be flirting with Lizzy's friend, but flirting was Lydia's forte. She had been born to attract the attention of men, and this one was handsome, rich, famous and unattached. She simply could not help herself, but for Lizzy, she would at least try.

Darcy *was* shocked by Lydia. She was rude, loud and wore more eyeliner than Amy Winehouse; however, she showed a great deal of affection for Elizabeth, and so Darcy was determined to be civil. He simply needed to remember that somewhere, under the over-sexed attitude and heavy makeup, was an eighteen-year-old girl. He politely removed his sunglasses before speaking. "I'm pleased to finally meet you, Lydia. Your sister's told me a great deal about you."

"Good Lordy!" Lydia squealed. "Your eyes are gorgeous!"

"Lydia!" Elizabeth reprimanded, more loudly this time.

"Sorry!" Lydia whispered too loudly to her sister. "But are you sure you're not crazy, because you must be if you're not jumping this man's bones?"

With an apologetic look toward Darcy, Elizabeth steered them all towards the house in hopes that having her more sane relatives about would help curb Lydia's behavior. On the front porch, she found her grandmother, father, Jane and Charles waiting for them.

The house was a large, gray, two-story structure with white trim and deep wraparound porches on both levels. Situated atop a complex web of stilts, it had a spectacular view over the dunes to the beach beyond. The inside was a combination of comfortable elegance and warm southern charm, reflecting the personality of its owner.

Jackson and Isabella Bennet built the house in the early 1970s, and although considerably larger than most houses on the Outer Banks at the time, they dreamed of eventually retiring there. After Thomas married Frannie, Jackson sold his successful law practice in Raleigh, and he and Isabella realized their dream of becoming year-round residents of Netherfield. It had been five years since Jackson passed away from a sudden heart attack, but Isabella refused to consider living anywhere else.

Charles walked down the front steps to help Darcy with their bags, giving Elizabeth a chance to greet her relatives first. Isabella was generous with her affections, hugging Elizabeth tightly as she kissed her cheek, and Jane was equally happy to see her sister; however, Tom held back until Darcy had reached the porch before embracing his favorite child. "I've missed you, Lizzybear!" His eyes then locked with Darcy's as he enthusiastically hugged her more tightly.

Darcy's eyes narrowed. Elizabeth had warned him about Tom Bennet's fierce dislike of him, and the message on the older man's face was clear. Elizabeth was *his* daughter, and *he* was the most important man in her life. Darcy felt no sympathy that the man was in for a rude awakening.

Sensing her father's hostility toward their guest, Jane stepped forward to kiss Darcy's cheek, hoping to make him feel more welcome. Then Isabella warmly shook his hand and thanked him for coming. When Tom and Darcy shook hands, it was cold, precise and anything but welcoming.

"It's getting cold out here, darlin'," Tom cooed smoothly to Elizabeth as he took her hand. "Let's get you inside."

Elizabeth gently pulled her hand from her father's and then, smiling sweetly, reached out to Darcy. Darcy would not openly compete with Elizabeth's father for her affections; there was no need. However, he could not resist looking directly into Tom's eyes as he took Elizabeth's hand, allowing a small yet triumphant smile to curve his lips.

"Elizabeth will be in here with Jane," Isabella said with a smile as she showed Darcy and Elizabeth to their rooms. "And Darcy, you will be sleeping over there with Charles. I hope you don't mind doubling up, but with the whole family in residence for New Years, space is becoming pretty short and —" Isabella suddenly stopped speaking.

"Gran?" Elizabeth asked with concern.

"Lizzy, dear, is there something you need to tell me?" Elizabeth then noted the direction of Isabella's gaze. "I don't mean to pry, honey, but I've never seen two friends before who couldn't let go of each other's hands."

Darcy and Elizabeth looked at each other and smiled. Holding hands had become something they did without thinking. "Things have changed," Elizabeth responded as she waited for her grandmother's reaction.

A huge smile broke out upon the elder woman's face. "That's just great, Sugar!" She hugged Elizabeth tightly. "But you better tell the others soon, especially your father. This is something you don't want him to figure out on his own, and the way you two are beamin' at each other, that will take about two minutes flat!"

"I will, just as soon as we get our bags unpacked."

"Well then, I think I'll let you four work out the sleeping arrangements between the two rooms. When it comes to this sort of thing, I take Mr. Clinton's approach: 'Don't ask. Don't tell!'"[37]

After Isabella left them in the hallway, Darcy looked into both bedrooms. "There is no way we're sleeping in a room with two single beds." Grabbing their suitcases, he headed to Jane and Elizabeth's room before placing their suitcases in the middle of the king-sized bed.

"Baby, I don't think Charles and Jane are going to give this room up without a fight, and look," Elizabeth indicated a nearby table that held objects obviously belonging to both Jane and Charles. "Possession is nine-tenths of the law!"[38]

Darcy looked at the big bed and narrowed his eyes in determination, "We'll just see about that! Now, let's go face the music."

---

37 Former President Bill Clinton's famous and unpopular policy toward gays in the U.S. Military.
38 Is considered to have come from Old-English Common Law. It is means that once someone already has possession of something, it is nearly impossible to take it away from him or her.

"You're what?!" as Tom Bennet's angry voice was swallowed up by the wind, Elizabeth was grateful she had insisted on telling her father about the engagement alone, outside and away from the others. "Are you out of your mind?"

In no mood for his condemnation of her newfound happiness, Elizabeth fixed him with a determined stare. "We're together, Daddy, and we're engaged."

"Don't you remember why you quit performing? You wanted a normal life! How normal do you think your life will be with *that man*?!"

Elizabeth stepped closer to her father to insure he heard her clearly. "I will never have a normal life, because I'm not normal. I'm a fucking genius, and as wonderful as that sounds, you know as well as I that it's a lonely existence. I will no longer spend my life hiding away, waiting for a normal man who will worship me with glassy eyes while I talk circles around him, or one who could care less about my intellect because he's far too obsessed with my appearance. Darcy and I are equals in every way. He makes me happy, and I know I will never find that with another man, ever!"

"Lizzy, you can't even go into town with your sisters because you left your bodyguards in New York! The press is already hounding you, and once word of this gets out, you won't have a moment's peace. You will be miserable!"

"Then what do you suggest I do? Should I follow your example? Marry someone who's my intellectual inferior but looks good at University functions? Someone who won't disturb me while I pursue my academic passions? And eventually become so disconnected from my family that I am not aware of what is going on under my very nose? Your IQ is higher than mine, Daddy. You should have known better."

Tom Bennet riled at his daughter's accusations. "I loved your mother!"

"You never knew my mother! You dated her for how long — a week before she became pregnant with Jane? Yes, she was beautiful and knew just what to say to make you feel that everything was fine, but when people you knew and trusted tried to tell you it wasn't fine, you refused to listen because that would mean that you would have to come out of your library and deal with it! And then, when it all finally fell apart, did you deal with it? No! You stayed in your library and allowed Uncle Ed, Aunt Maddie and Gran to pick up the pieces."

Stunned, Tom could only stare at his daughter in silence. Was that truly how it happened? Had he been so wrapped up in establishing the University Library, so enthralled with his career that he refused to see the problems within his family? Was he so busy engaging in intellectual debate with his peers that he refused to see Frannie's obvious failings and Elizabeth's misery? No, it couldn't be!

"I'm sorry to be so blunt," her voice had noticeably softened, and Elizabeth gave him a brief hug, "but I've tried it your way for the last eight years, and it doesn't work for me any more. I'm going to marry Darcy, and I'm going to be deliriously happy."

As she turned to walk back into the house, Tom reached out and grabbed her hand, pulling Elizabeth into a tight embrace. "Lizzybear, please don't do this."

She looked sadly into his eyes. "Don't make me choose between the two of you." She quickly kissed his cheek and pulled away. "You'll lose."

THE SILENCE AT THE DINNER table was palpable as Darcy observed the reactions of the Bennet family to Elizabeth's announcement of their engagement. Elizabeth kept her eyes diverted from her father, but the remaining Bennet women all had their gazes fixed firmly upon him, waiting for his reaction. Darcy knew what to expect since Elizabeth had informed him of her discussion with her father that afternoon, so he passed the moment by assessing the five women who made up Elizabeth's family.

His first thought was that they were a very attractive family. Jane, of course, was angelic in appearance, and Mary and Kitty looked very much like her, each blonde and delicately featured. Their personalities, however, were very different.

Mary had spent a good hour with Darcy discussing her curriculum at the seminary in which she was enrolled. While Darcy did not agree with many of the beliefs she put forth, he had to respect her determination, commitment and unyielding faith. He could only imagine how difficult it would be for the men of her future church to keep their minds off her considerable attractions and on the content of her sermons.

Catherine, also known as Kitty or Kit, was a sweet girl but not living up to her potential. A junior at North Carolina State University, her focus was more on keeping her grades up so that she could remain a cheerleader than on any benefit she may be receiving from her education. She behaved like the stereotypical dumb blonde, but Darcy sensed that beneath the airy exterior was a girl of far more substance then she let on.

Lydia! There was a girl obviously in need of direction and discipline who was sorely lacking in both. Her flirtations were outrageous, and her naiveté only meant that someday she was going to end up in trouble that was way over her head. Darcy only hoped that when that day arrived, he and Elizabeth would not be called upon to pick up the pieces.

Isabella Bennet was everything Elizabeth had told him she was: intelligent, kind, and generous with an aura of pure class. In her late sixties, she was still a very attractive woman and, with her fair skin and violet eyes, the source of both Lydia and Elizabeth's sensual beauty. It was obvious that she was aware of the faults and foibles of her family and did her best to check them without overstepping her role as grandmother — a fine line that she somehow managed to walk upon with both grace and dignity. Darcy could not help but admire her.

Finally, his eyes rested upon Elizabeth, clearly the most beautiful of them all. She bravely awaited whatever would come next, and Darcy reached beneath the table to squeeze her hand gently in support.

"Engaged!" Charles was the first to break the stony silence. Bounding from his chair, Charles approached Darcy and vigorously pumped his hand. "That's fantastic!"

The remaining Bennets were still subdued, looking to Tom to judge his reaction. When the man refused to look up from his plate, Isabella stood, glared at her son's bowed head, turned to Elizabeth and Darcy and said enthusiastically, "Yes, it is fantastic! Congratulations, Lizzy dear. Darcy, I couldn't be more pleased!" With the matriarch's approval, the others quickly followed with their own congratulations and a flurry of hugging and hand shaking commenced.

Tom Bennet's exit from the room was noticed but not commented upon.

"I hoped you two would come to your senses," Jane said with a satisfied smile.

Lydia unceremoniously grasped Elizabeth's left hand. "Where's your ring? If you were really engaged, Mr. Money Bags... I mean Darcy, would have bought you a big rock!"

Elizabeth gave her youngest sister the mandatory glare before answering, "A ring is being crafted. I should have it in a few weeks."

"Crafted?" Lydia snorted. "That sounds like it's homemade. Why didn't you just go to Tiffany's?"

"Lydia!" This time it was Mary who censured her youngest sister before turning a serene smile to Elizabeth and Darcy. "May God grant you a lifetime of happiness!" She gave them each a kiss on the cheek that felt more like a clerical blessing then a show of affection. Elizabeth would have none of that. She hugged Mary tightly, and soon both had unshed tears shining in their eyes.

"When's the wedding?" Kit gushed, obviously thrilled with the news. "Will you marry in Hunsford?"

"No," Elizabeth said a little too sharply, "the wedding will probably be at Darcy's family estate in England. We've not looked at dates yet, but it will be sometime this summer."

Lydia stood next to Darcy, the index finger of her right hand running up and down his forearm suggestively. "Will Brad Pitt and Orlando Bloom be groomsmen? I've read they're your best friends."

"You shouldn't believe everything you read in the tabloids," Darcy said as he took Lydia's hand from his arm and dropped it. "I have met them both numerous times at charity functions but would not claim to know either well enough to call them friends."

"Darcy," Charles pulled him aside from the feminine swarm as Isabella did the same with Lydia to remind her softly but firmly to keep her hands to herself. "You look like you could use some rescuing."

Darcy glanced back toward Lydia. "Thanks. Does she behave like that with you?"

"Oh yes, only far worse!" Charles laughed. "She squeezed my arse twice last night!"

"I find it astounding that Tom Bennet presumes to tell Elizabeth who she should or should not marry when he doesn't bother to check the behavior of his youngest child."

"He's not so bad," Charles offered, "once you get to know him, and this place has a kind of magic about it. Everything is so laid back, unhurried. It's taken me a week to get used to it, but I must admit, I've never felt so relaxed. I can understand why Isabella retired here." Charles than lowered his voice and whispered, "Now that things with you and Elizabeth are more...intimate, I suspect you wouldn't mind sleeping in our room with her tonight."

"I've seen the size of the beds in that room. As I'm a good five inches taller than you are, it stands to reason you would allow Elizabeth and me to have the larger bed."

Charles frowned. "Jane and I have already unpacked in the larger room."

"Yes, but you were under the impression that you would be moving into the other room today and Jane would be sleeping with Elizabeth. Therefore, it was not as if you did not anticipate a change in your sleeping arrangements."

"You cannot expect me to simply give up the large bed." Charles' voice was becoming a little louder.

Darcy scoffed, "You cannot possibly expect me to fit in a single bed, let alone with Elizabeth."

"Then we are at an impasse."

Elizabeth, who had guessed the content of the gentlemen's hushed conversation, approached. "Then we'll race for it," she suggested. "It's a Bennet tradition. When we argue over something, we have to race for it. We always walk on the beach after dinner, so we'll settle it then."

"This is wholly unfair!" Charles protested. "Darcy's legs are longer than mine."

"But Darcy is suffering from jet lag, which should even up the odds. Look at him. He's already dead on his feet."

Seeing the truth of Elizabeth's words and believing his chances to be significantly better than his friend's, Charles agreed to the race.

After dinner everyone headed down to the beach. The full moon provided the perfect illumination as the group, bundled up in warm coats, hats and gloves, walked near the surf. The wind had died down, and the musical laughter of the Bennet women drifted through the quiet, cold stillness of the evening.

"I've lost her," Tom whispered to his mother as they walked at the back of the group.

Isabella looked up to where Darcy and Elizabeth had stopped walking. Darcy stood behind her, wrapping his arms around her as Elizabeth pointed out the distant lights that marked the Cape Hatteras Lighthouse. "She was never yours to lose, Thomas. Elizabeth has been her own woman since she was sixteen. However, if you want to remain a part of her life, I strongly suggest you find some way to reconcile yourself to her and Darcy."

"You knew about them," he surmised. "That would logically explain why you invited *that man* here to ruin my New Years."

"There's another even more logical explanation. I invited Darcy because it would make Lizzy happy...and I needed to give him the file."

"Why?" Tom's surprise melted as the answer occurred to him. "Of course. When were you planning to do it?"

Isabella sighed. "I'll speak to him privately tomorrow morning while Lizzy is helping Kitty put up the decorations for New Year's Eve."

"If we're lucky, he'll run from the house screaming like a girl, never to be seen again."

"I think we should thank our lucky stars that he loves her," Isabella countered. "I think Fitzwilliam Darcy may be the best man to protect her."

Darcy and Bingley shed their heavy coats, and as they lined up for their race, Elizabeth and Jane carefully watched the starting line while Mary was at the finish, waiting to pronounce the winner.

"What are they racing for?" Tom asked.

Isabella laughed. "I have no idea."

"Ready," Lydia called out as Darcy and Bingley approached the line Kit drew in the sand.

"Set." Both men crouched down, waiting for the signal.

"Go!" And they were off…

An hour later Darcy stretched out fully beneath the blankets. "This is more like it!"

Elizabeth sat beside him, slipping off her robe. "You are a genius."

"So are you." Tired as he was, the feel of Elizabeth in bed next to him was still too new to ignore. His hands moved beneath her T-shirt, sliding it up and over her breasts before he sat up to take a rosy nipple into his mouth.

"Wait!" she said. "I've yet to properly get into bed."

"By all means, get yourself situated." When she laid her head back on her pillow, he moved his mouth back to her breast.

"I didn't say you could *start* yet," she teased.

Frowning he sat up again and watched as she punched her pillows, smoothed out non-existent wrinkles in the blankets and moved about in a pretext of finding the best position.

"Dr. Bennet, you are a horrible tease!"

She raised her eyebrows. "Ready?"

When he moved to touch her Elizabeth chastised in a sing-song voice, "Ah, ah, ah! I didn't say 'go!'"

"Insufferable woman!" Darcy grumbled.

"Set?"

So Darcy waited as Elizabeth enjoyed prolonging the anticipation.

"Go!"

Faster than she could have imagined possible, they were spent, lying on their backs and panting heavily. "We do hold a distinct advantage over Jane and Charles tonight," Elizabeth commented as they heard the distinctive sound of creaking bedsprings between hushed oaths from Charles. Darcy could only smile in agreement as he scrambled up from where they laid the two small mattresses together on the floor.

Two nights later, the Bennet family, including a grudgingly civil Tom Bennet, sat around a huge bonfire drinking hot, mulled cider and coffee spiked with Kentucky bourbon from Tom's flask. At midnight, the Town of Netherfield put on a huge fireworks display from a barge on Pamlico Sound to welcome in the New Year.

A HUNDRED MILES AWAY IN Hunsford, Frannie Bennet sighed in satisfaction as her companion rolled off her and stumbled toward the bathroom. She felt no guilt in having found comfort in a lover or two (or twenty) while Billy Ray was locked up. Given that Billy Ray's appetites were similar to her own, Frannie was sure he wasn't keeping celibate in prison, although she didn't like to dwell upon exactly what that meant. This lover, however, had the distinction of not only being young, handsome and virile, but also British and in possession of a great deal of personal information on Bethy's fiancé.

CHAPTER 25
FALL OF THE TITANS

January 3rd, Celebrity Watcher (U.S.)
Story: Make $1,000,000 instantly! Goulding/Long Publishers have upped their offer to $1,000,000 to anyone who can provide them with clear, printable pictures of British billionaire Fitzwilliam Darcy kissing Elizabeth Bennet either in public or in private…

January 30th, The Daily Insight (U.S.)
Photo caption: Dr. Elizabeth Bennet lectures her students at the Longbourn School for the Performing Arts.
Story: As predicted several months ago by this paper, Elizabeth Bennet has moved into boyfriend Fitzwilliam Darcy's New York City town house…

Her life felt like it was in a complete whirlwind. Since returning from North Carolina a few days after New Year's, Elizabeth had moved into Lansing with Darcy, started teaching the spring semester at Longbourn and, in a stoke of supreme luck, managed to rent her co-op out to Charlotte and her sister Maria. Life should have been perfect, but there was one very large problem: the paparazzi.

The couple's re-emergence in New York after Darcy's disappearance in December sparked a frenzy the likes of which they had not seen since Frannie's radio escapade. They could go nowhere without a horde of photographers relentlessly following. Dinners out were impossible, trips to the theater required the planning of a small military campaign, and walks in the park were out of the question.

Now Elizabeth sat in the only mode of transportation open to her, the Darcy limo, as Mr. Sparks drove her around the city in a useless attempt to replace her usual walks. She wracked her brain for a solution to their dilemma as cameramen on motorcycles circled about.

She knew the source of the problem: a tabloid media tycoon named Albert Goulding of Goulding/Long Publishers and that damn offer to anyone who could produce an authentic picture of Darcy and her kissing. It was infuriating that, because of one man's greed, she and Darcy were now living like fugitives in hiding. After the freedom of Pemberley and the relaxed atmosphere of her Grandmother's house, New York felt like a noose tightening around her neck.

Elizabeth knew she was feeling the sharp blade of the double-edged sword she wielded to have Darcy released last December. She had used the press, and now they were both paying the price.

The strain was nowhere more evident than at Longbourn. Three times photographers had snuck into her classes and disturbed her lectures as if Darcy would waltz in at any second and kiss her passionately. The situation was affecting her ability to teach and her students' ability to learn. William Lucas lamented that the increased donations due to the publicity of having Elizabeth on staff would be eaten up by proposed measures for increased security. Something had to be done — but what?

As Mr. Sparks drove past the Roseland Ballroom, the idea struck her like lightning. To confirm the details of her plan, she opened her new PDA and, connecting to the Internet, reviewed Goulding/Long's offer. Yes, it could work. Now, the only problem was to convince Darcy to do something totally against his nature.

She found Darcy in his study, frantically pulling everything out of his top desk drawer. He stopped whatever it was he was doing when he noticed her enter the room, and Elizabeth walked directly to him to curl up in his lap. "We need to talk," she began as she carefully explained her plan.

"Tomorrow night?" he asked uncomfortably.

"Yes. The event has received a great deal of press, and the city is already erecting a police barrier outside the ballroom to control the expected crowd of fans. The official press will be corralled together inside." Elizabeth could tell that Darcy was thinking it all through logically, and the severe frown upon his face confirmed that he had drawn the same conclusions she had.

"All right. Let's pass this by Geoff and Frank." They sealed their agreement with a kiss, once, twice, three times, and soon the dark clouds that had hovered over Elizabeth all day were forgotten; who could possibly care one iota about the paparazzi when she could stay in the room with this man when he smelled this good, felt this good and tasted even better.

"Elizabeth," he whispered seductively against her lips, "you wouldn't happen to know the location of the coaster that was on my desk?"

THE ENTRANCE OF THE ROSELAND Ballroom was awash with light as a long line of limousines pulled up to deposit the politically aware of the rich and famous at its doors. Awaiting their turn, Darcy and Elizabeth tried to distract themselves from what was about to happen.

Darcy reached across her lap to take her left hand, removed her glove and touched the ring that now adorned her third finger. It was stunning. Two tapered, white diamond baguettes framed the four-carat, radiant-cut, blue diamond, all set in shining platinum.

"Were you able to get through to Lady Catherine today?" Elizabeth asked.

He frowned. "She still was not at home when I called this afternoon. I was able to speak to Anne though. When I told her about our engagement, she gave me her best wishes, but I could tell from the tone of her voice that she was surprised and very disappointed."

"I'm sorry," Elizabeth said. "How is she feeling?"

Darcy smiled at her inquiry, touched that she could show concern for the woman who had spent the last ten years of her life hoping to marry the man who was now Elizabeth's fiancé. Regardless of how non-existent the possibility, he was not sure he could be as magnanimous if the situation were reversed. "She says she is feeling stronger."

"Good." Elizabeth glanced out the window, and all her attempts at distraction were for naught at the realization of the number of fans who lined the street waiting to catch a glimpse of the celebrities who were attending the International Human Rights Society Awards Dinner where Darcy was to be honored as Man of the Year.

Elizabeth felt Darcy squeeze her hand as the limo stopped in front of the ballroom. He nodded to Mr. Harville who exited and stood by, waiting for them. "We can do this," Darcy reassured her as he climbed out of the car.

Once in the cold, clear air, he looked about as a thousand camera flashes went off. Steeling his resolve, he reached in to help Elizabeth out of the limo. She looked lovely as the tasteful diamond studs that adorned her ears glittered in the bright lights. Her curls were artfully arranged at the back of her head, and her long evening coat of deep purple velvet reminded Darcy of the sensual dress of the same color that Elizabeth wore beneath it. He reminded himself to send Charlotte flowers tomorrow to express his personal thanks.

To the surprise of the crowd, Darcy and Elizabeth did not simply turn and walk into the ballroom. Instead, with Mr. Harville following, they crossed the street to approach the waiting fans, eliciting a throng of cheers. As the bodyguard kept a close watch, Darcy reached across the police barriers to shake hands with as many people as he could within a two-minute period. Elizabeth kept back a few yards, allowing him to have the limelight he so desperately hated.

As the flashes kept going off in his face, Darcy muttered under his breath, "Hold on, the real show is yet to come." Then with a huge smile on his face and a wave to the crowd, he walked back to Elizabeth, wrapped one arm around her waist, the other hand around her neck and then, gracefully dipping her over his left knee, kissed her.

The combined camera flashes that went off at that moment would have lit up a small city.

Once they were inside the building, Darcy and Elizabeth were quickly led to the pressroom where they were relieved of their coats. "That dress ought to be illegal," Darcy whispered to her as they kept their eyes toward the cameramen while standing together for pictures. The only outward sign of affection displayed between them was the hand Darcy kept firmly on the small of Elizabeth's back, which was completely exposed.

"Oh, I believe that in several countries, it is. Jealous?" Elizabeth teased, "There's no reason, for you're looking very sexy in your tuxedo . . . and I happen to know you look even sexier out of it." Before he could think of a reply to her tease, Elizabeth stepped away so that Darcy could be photographed alone.

Soon they were seated at their table inside the ballroom, where Elizabeth was introduced to John and Maggie Thornton. The two women hit it off immediately, sitting side by side and chatting as if they were lifelong friends. Before the dinner had a chance to begin, the ladies had exchanged e-mail addresses and phone numbers with plans to have lunch the next time Elizabeth was in London.

Darcy assumed his usual posture at public events: He sat back with his arm draped over the back of Elizabeth's chair, his thumb absently stroking her bare shoulder. He frequently exercised his right to glare at any man whose gaze rested on his fiancée for too long, not that he hadn't done so when he and Elizabeth were no more than friends, but now he no longer felt the need to be covert about it.

His eyes caught Thornton's, and both men realized their postures were mirror images of each other. Darcy could not find fault with Thornton's need to stare down anyone who ogled his wife, for Maggie was a lovely woman. Both gentlemen tipped their drinks to one another in silent acknowledgement of their shared activity.

Soon Maggie took to the podium on the stage at the front of the ballroom and spoke about the mission of the International Human Rights Society; then she gave out several awards of large sums of money to organizations throughout the world whose work exemplified those goals. Finally, the subject of her speech turned to Darcy. She informed the gathered elite of his history of protecting the defenseless with his money, influence and, on rare occasions, his very presence.

Elizabeth listened in rapt adoration as most of the incidents Maggie spoke of occurred before she knew Darcy and drew no media attention. She did not believe it was possible to love him more, and yet the more she came to know him, the more her heart seemed physically to ache with the overwhelming emotions he inspired within her.

When Darcy took to the podium to accept the award of $1,000,000 to his favorite cause, Amnesty International, he spoke of each of the incidents Maggie mentioned, humbly downplaying his own role while praising the efforts of others involved. Elizabeth fought back the sting of tears in her eyes when, at the completion of his acceptance speech, Darcy received a standing ovation from the crowd.

The dinner was a blur of elegantly prepared courses followed by a stream of congratulations and new introductions. Elizabeth could tell Darcy wanted to escape, but his deeply bred manners forced him to remain and attempt to make small talk, even though his stiff manner discouraged some from approaching him at all.

Later, when the evening finally drew to a close and she and Darcy were once again alone in the limo, Elizabeth attempted to express her feelings. "Fitzwilliam, I am so proud of you. You are truly the very best of men."

His eyes spoke of how much her words meant to him, and Elizabeth felt her heart would break with the sweet pain of loving him so much. She sought solace in his embrace, and as Darcy lowered his lips to hers, his fingers felt for the unfamiliar button on the console above his head.

Mr. Sparks waited until the privacy glass was completely closed before allowing the smile to break out on his face.

ALBERT GOULDING AND HIS MISTRESS were awakened by the ringing of the phone. An hour later, he was sitting behind his desk at the London headquarters of Goulding/Long Publishing, owners of *Celebrity Tattler, Celebrity Watcher, The Daily Gossip* and at least a dozen other tabloid publications across the globe.

"How did this happen!" Goulding thundered at his partner.

"I would like to remind both of you," interrupted the company's attorney, Conrad Phillips, "that I warned you this could happen. I specifically said you needed to limit the million dollar offer to the first picture received."

"But it was you who insisted that Fitzwilliam Darcy would never kiss any woman in public," David Long said accusingly to his partner, "and if by some slim chance he did, it was nearly impossible that anyone with a camera would see it long enough to get a photo."

"It was a brilliant idea!" Goulding insisted. "The frenzy we created was a huge news story in itself, growing steadily larger and larger until it practically took on a life of its own. We've sold four times the advertising in the past month than any month in the history of Goulding/Long Publishing!"

"Yes," Phillips shouted in anger, "but you turned two people into hunted animals."

"That's the price of being a celebrity!" Goulding defended his actions further by adding, "and that's our business! Conrad, don't tell me you've suddenly developed a conscience."

Phillips stood up to emphasize his next words. "Well, now the tables are turned. The pictures are pouring in, and everyone is demanding payment. How many pictures have you received?"

"About two hundred and twenty-five as of thirty minutes ago," Long responded in frustration, "Based on the size of the crowd outside the HRS Awards Dinner, we will likely receive hundreds more by the time the office opens at nine o'clock."

"We can dispute the authenticity of the photos," Goulding suggested, "claim the people in them are not Darcy and Bennet or that the photo quality is too poor."

Long took several of the pictures and tossed them in front of Goulding, "it was a clear night, and the area was well lit. No judge or jury is going to dispute that these pictures meet the criteria we set in the offer. It is obvious that Darcy and his people planned this specifically to make us suffer. We underestimated him."

Phillips pinched the bridge of his nose, trying to hold back the pain flaring behind his eyes. "As far as I can see, we have two choices. We can be stuck in litigation with our assets frozen for years or we can declare bankruptcy now. Either way, this will be the end of Goulding/Long Publishing."

Goulding's face began to turn purple with rage. "Damn Darcy!"

"BUT, MOTHER," ANNE SAID IN exasperation, "that is exactly what Wills told me!"

Lady Catherine looked up from her poached egg. "You must have misunderstood. Call your doctor this morning and ask if hearing loss is a possible symptom of an MS relapse."

"He did not just mention his engagement in passing. We discussed it for nearly a quarter of an hour."

"Impossible! If Fitzwilliam was engaged, he would have called to tell me himself."

Anne decided it was pointless to mention that Darcy did call to tell his Aunt, but she was not at home. It was clear that her stepmother was determined not to believe a word Anne said.

As Lady Catherine poured herself another cup of coffee, her personal assistant, Alan Jenkinson, entered the breakfast room with a worried expression on his face. He had been working for Lady Catherine for seven months, the longest of any assistant of the last two decades. He would have quit months ago if not for the kindness shown him by Miss de Bough; however, he suspected that today might be his final day of employment. The Lady had a penchant for shooting the messenger.[39]

"What is it, Jenkinson?" Lady Catherine barked. "Don't just stand there in that stupid manner."

Inhaling deeply before stealing a glance at Miss de Bourgh, Jenkinson

---

39 Derived from the saying "kill the messenger" which originated in Shakespeare's Henry V and refers to times of war when soldiers from one camp would deliver messages to the enemy commander. If the contents of the message were considered bad, the messenger may be killed. Today the phrase means to retaliate against the innocent bearer of bad news.

handed the morning newspaper to Lady Catherine and braced himself for her reaction. It did not take long.

"I want the Earl of Matlock on the phone immediately! GO!" Lady Catherine then slapped the paper on the table in front of Anne. "Look at this! That woman has no sense of decency, kissing Fitzwilliam in the middle of the street. This is outrageous!" She then opened the paper and, finding the page on which the story was continued, again voiced her disapprobation. "Look at this dress. Why there is little more than a drape of fabric covering her bosom! Who in their right mind would wear something like that in the dead of winter? Has she no shame?!"

As Lady Catherine continued her ranting, Anne looked at the pictures, not with the outrage of her stepmother, but with the eye of a woman who had accepted the inevitable. Darcy looked happy, and his Elizabeth was the picture of health and beauty. They would marry that summer, and Darcy would not provide Anne with an easy means to escape Lady Catherine. Anne needed to find the courage to break away from her stepmother and start a life on her own, but she had no idea where or how to begin.

Suddenly, something in the picture she was examining caught Lady Catherine's eye, and she stopped in mid-sentence. She took the paper from Anne and brought it up to her eyes so that she could examine it more closely. "Jenkinson! Come here! I need you!"

Jenkinson nearly ran into the room, "I'm sorry Lady Catherine, but the House of Lords is in session, and therefore the Earl cannot be reached."

"Forget that! Go to the newsstand and bring back a copy of every paper and magazine that has pictures of my nephew and that woman in it. Quickly! GO!"

In less than half an hour, Lady Catherine had a host of tabloid magazines spread out over the now vacant breakfast table. Carefully she examined them with a magnifying glass, hoping to find one that would refute the evidence so clearly before her. Elizabeth Bennet was wearing a ring on her left hand, and although a casual observer may not have noticed its significance, Lady Catherine recognized the color of the stone as identical to the one her late sister wore throughout her married life.

By lunchtime, Alan Jenkinson was packing up the few personal items he was permitted to have at his desk and wondering how late the employment office would be opened. Fortunately — or perhaps unfortunately — Lady Catherine changed her mind before he walked out the door.

Two weeks later, Darcy and Elizabeth were once again walking though Riverside Park on their way to the fencing club. Mr. Price was a respectable twenty feet behind them, and a small group of photographers was another twenty feet behind him. Since Goulding/Long Publishing announced they were filing for bankruptcy and a starlet named Lindsay had been caught drinking only twenty-four hours after being released from rehab, life quickly returned to what it had been like before the incident in Colombia.

"I found out something very *interesting*," Darcy offered.

"Really? This wouldn't happen to be gossip, would it?"

"Me? Gossip? Never! I'm simply sharing information with my BFF. I don't want us to keep secrets from one another."

"A new rule!" Elizabeth teased. "I must admit I like that one. By all means, reveal your secret."

"Thank you; however, to put your mind at ease over the possibility of gossip, I shall not mention names."

"Brilliant! Do proceed."

Darcy cleared his throat twice. "A certain cousin of mine has been speaking on the telephone nearly every day to a certain friend of yours... sometimes for hours at a time, and that same cousin shall be arriving in New York next week to visit said friend of yours."

"And how did you come upon such *interesting* information?"

"This cousin has a brother who contacted me in an attempt to discover the identity of your friend."

"And was the brother of your cousin successful?" Elizabeth teasingly raised an eyebrow.

"Of course not. *That* would be gossiping!" The ringing of Darcy's PDA interrupted their laughter. Checking the caller ID, he commented to Elizabeth, "This is *said cousin* calling now!"

Immediately after answering the phone, Darcy's smiling face clouded over as he stopped walking. He ended the call abruptly and turned back toward Lansing. Through clenched teeth he whispered, "I have to leave for London immediately. Aunt Catherine has demanded an emergency meeting of the advisory board for tomorrow morning!"

Darcy sat at the head of the conference room table, his elbows resting on the arms of his chair, his fingers tented in front of his chest, his expression a study in cold fury. Recently released from both cast and crutches, Richard sat to Darcy's right while Geoff sat to his left, their expressions identical to that of their cousin. Georgiana was nearby, sitting between Lord and Lady Matlock. All three were obviously trying to control their emotions. Sitting near her stepmother, Anne visibly flinched with each pound of Lady Catherine's fist upon the podium as she delivered her accusations. The remaining five members of the advisory board, all distant cousins of Darcy's, gave the speaker their reluctant attention.

The content of Lady Catherine's angry speech was uncomfortable for everyone. While the behavior of the president of the foundation was a concern, the advisory board was just that — a board to advise. They had no legal authority over the decisions of the foundation and certainly could not force Darcy out of his position, but that did not stop Lady Catherine from trying.

"Disappeared! For an entire week! Vanished off the face of the earth without a word to anyone about where he was or when he would return. And the speculation by the press! There were rumors that he was arrested! His home was searched. He was suspected of committing some great evil while the rest of us were left in complete confusion. Regardless of the service we later learned he provided to the Americans, his first priorities should have been to his name, his family and to this foundation!"

Lady Catherine felt her speech was going well and, judging by the angry faces surrounding her, was having the desired effect. She knew that the board could not remove Darcy as president of the foundation, but if he was aware that he had lost the confidence of his nearest relations, she was certain he could be persuaded to step down.

"And I'm sure everyone in this room has seen the headlines. How professional can Fitzwilliam's relationship with Dr. Elizabeth Bennet be if they are romantically involved? We all remember the incident seven years ago with Rebecca Wickham. Apparently, he did not learn from that mistake! As Fitzwilliam obviously has more important priorities than this foundation, it is clearly time that he made way for someone who does not!"

"And who should that someone be?" Lady Catherine asked the board as she prepared to hammer the final nail into her nephew's coffin. "Obviously, it cannot be Geoffrey Fitzwilliam as he joined his cousin in that little escapade, and as for Richard, his position with the military prevents him from taking on a more serious role. Georgiana is only 18 years old, and as for The Earl of

Matlock... his current responsibilities will not allow him to give the position the necessary time commitment to do a proper job of it. Thereby, as Fitzwilliam and Georgiana's closest relation, I am the only logical person to serve as the new president of the foundation. I have had years of experience with this organization and both the time and desire necessary to do the job credit —"

"That is quite enough, Catherine." The Earl stood from his chair. Knowing the true reason for Darcy and Geoff's actions in December, he had completely run out of patience with his sister. "You have made your point. Wills, do you wish to address the charges your Aunt has laid at your door? If you do not, then by God, I will!"

Lady Catherine had not expected this. Her brother James, of all people, should have been as outraged at Darcy's behavior as she was. Well, that meant she could no longer count on James' vote, and Elinor would vote against her, too. Georgiana would no doubt side with her brother, but that left the remaining cousins and, of course, Anne and herself to set matters to rights.

Darcy did not move a muscle, and his eyes never left his Aunt's. Throughout her speech, memories of a similar meeting seven years earlier came to the front of his mind, but instead of reawakening feelings of dread and humiliation, his Aunt's words filled him with righteous indignation. It was a cleansing experience.

"Thank you, Uncle James, but I believe I can handle this." There was silence — dreadful, terrifying silence as Darcy continued to lock eyes with Lady Catherine. It was Elizabeth who had taught him that there were times when silence could be the most effective weapon, and as he watched his Aunt begin to squirm, Darcy fully understood her lesson.

Finally, when Lady Catherine could no longer look him in the eye, Darcy spoke. "Aunt Catherine, there was a time when your opinion may have carried some weight with my decisions, but I am no longer a boy, and it has been some time since you could frighten me. So let me remind you of what my father said to you over seven years ago: I am the head of the *Darcy* family and the *Darcy* Foundation. The decisions regarding the care of both are mine alone!"

Darcy then made eye contact with each member of the board before he continued. "I cannot, and I will not be removed as president of this foundation. If any member of this board ever again attempts to challenge that fact, I will use my authority as president of the Darcy Foundation for the Promotion of the Arts... to disband it!"

Darcy stood. "As Lady Catherine has followed protocol in presenting her recommendations, then protocol requires they be voted upon. I will be in my office to await your *advice*."

ELIZABETH WAS WAITING FOR DARCY in his office, sitting in a corner of the couch while attempting to read the morning *Times*. When he entered, anger still darkened his features. "That bad?" she asked while placing the paper on a nearby table.

"The woman is insufferable!" he shouted before throwing himself on the couch. He lay back, placing his head in Elizabeth's lap. "It was exactly what we expected, but it still infuriates me to the core."

Gently brushing her fingers from Darcy's temple into his hair, Elizabeth offered her silent sympathy and smiled in satisfaction as she watched his eyes close, the angry lines slowly fade from his face and his breathing deepen. Darcy was so relaxed when Geoff and Richard entered the office, that he did not bother to open his eyes, let alone chastise them for not knocking first.

"Elizabeth," Geoff was grinning broadly as he crossed the room, "Darcy didn't tell us you accompanied him and Georgie to London. I would have thought you'd have classes to teach."

"I took a week of emergency leave," Elizabeth said quietly. "I simply had to come."

Geoff looked down at Darcy as he leaned over him to kiss Elizabeth's cheek in greeting. "It's amazing that, with everything going on, he's managed to fall asleep?"

"I'm not sleeping," Darcy stated flatly as he reluctantly pulled himself up to a sitting position, "and stop kissing my fiancée."

"We Fitzwilliams are very affectionate by nature," Richard said as he, too, leaned in to kiss Elizabeth's cheek.

"I think Aunt Catherine has given more than enough 'Fitzwilliam affection' this morning to last me for quite some time, thank you very much! So what happened?"

Geoff was the first to respond. "The Old Bat had to realize that once you threatened to disband the board, the game was up; however, as soon you left the room she entered into a shouting match with my father, which was a huge mistake." Geoff's expression changed to one of great irritation. "As her tirade continued, the focus changed dramatically from your management of the foundation to her anger over your relationship with Elizabeth. I don't think there was a person in the room who doubted that was her true motivation."

Elizabeth asked, "Has there been a vote?"

"We left when Aunt Catherine finally agreed to end the discussion and begin the vote; fortunately, that was after Georgie interrupted to tell her she was a vindictive, horrid woman," Richard beamed with pride. "You should have seen the shock on Aunt Catherine's face. Now that was a beautiful thing to witness."

The details of the meeting and the possible repercussions of the vote were discussed in detail until a knock at the door was followed by the admittance of the Earl and Lady Matlock, Georgiana and, surprisingly, someone else.

"Anne?" Darcy asked with concern upon seeing his cousin's stricken face.

"She voted against Catherine," the Earl calmly informed them as Geoff fetched Anne a bottle of water. "Anne will be staying with us until things between the two of them cool off."

Anne sat in one of the large leather chairs and took the water with a trembling hand. "I don't know how long that may be, Uncle James. Father left the house to me. If she doesn't accept that I will no longer kowtow to her demands, she will have to move out."

"Thank you, Anne." Darcy said as he took Elizabeth's hand. "That you would defend me, and in turn Elizabeth, means a great deal."

Georgiana piped up, "Oh she did so much more than that. There were three votes."

The Earl elaborated, "After the 9-1 vote against Catherine's recommendation, your little sister put forth a recommendation of her own: The removal of Lady Catherine de Bourgh from the advisory board. After everyone voted against her, Catherine vented her considerable frustrations at Anne before storming from the room."

Richard's long, low whistle broke the silence that followed as Darcy stood to embrace his sister. "You've grown into a more confidant, and apparently *more vocal*, young lady. I suppose we will all have to stop calling you 'Squirt.'"

"Never!" called out Richard and Geoff simultaneously.

"What was the third vote?" Elizabeth couldn't hold back her curiosity a moment longer.

Lady Matlock took the seat Darcy had vacated next to her and delivered news that Elizabeth had never considered as a possibility. "Anne recommended that, if Wills removed Catherine, *you* as the future Mrs. Darcy be given her seat on the board. The vote in favor was unanimous."

CHAPTER 26
NO MORE MR. NICE GUY

February 18th, The London Star Gazette (U.K.)
Photo caption: Fitzwilliam Darcy and Elizabeth Bennet attend a performance of "Aida" in London's West End.
(No story)

It was another cold, gray day, but as Darcy stared absently outside the windows of his office, he felt nothing but warmth. A contented smile formed on his lips as he remembered how he had left Elizabeth that morning in their bed: hair disheveled, lips red and swollen, a sleepy look of satisfaction on her sweet face and her body still glowing with a sheen of perspiration. It took a Herculean effort not to immediately fall back into bed with her, but pull himself away he did, for he had Mr. Thayer waiting for him in the drive and a 9 a.m. meeting with Lady Felicity Russell.

It had been four days since the showdown with Lady Catherine. Their trip to London was unexpected, and rather than return in another week as he had planned, he successfully moved all his meetings forward. Elizabeth had passed her time visiting a few of London's colleges and universities with well established music programs, laying the foundation for when she would seek a new position after her contract with Longbourn expired. If only he could have prevented Elizabeth from bathing, so that every man she met that morning at the Royal Academy of Music would smell him all over her.

While he calculated the exact number of hours and minutes before he could return Elizabeth to her previously disreputable state, the phone on his desk buzzed, informing him that Lady Russell had checked in at the security desk in the lobby and was on her way to his office. Reluctantly, he pulled his thoughts from more pleasant things to Lady Russell.

Having recently married a member of the House of Lords who was nearly thirty years her senior, Lady Felicity Russell quickly established herself as the new darling of London's charity circles. Within the past few months, she had managed to connect her name to every cause from feeding refugees in the Sudan to funding new exhibits at the British Museum. It seemed only a matter of course for her eventually to end up at his door.

After a firm knock, the doors to his office opened, and Charles Hayter announced Lady Russell. As Hayter withdrew back into the hallway, a beautiful woman who appeared to be in her late thirties entered Darcy's office. She wore a deep green business suit that fitted her voluptuous body like a glove, and she walked with a wiggle far too suggestive for someone entitled "Lady." Even as the hair on the back of his neck stood up in alarm, Darcy could not help but notice that her face, framed by a blonde fringe, looked vaguely familiar.

"Mr. Darcy," she said, "I'm so pleased to finally meet you."

"Who are you?" Darcy asked in a steely voice. "And what are you doing here?"

Her blue eyes sparkled as a deep sensuous laugh flowed from her throat. "Sugar, you really must do something about your appallingly inadequate security. All I needed was an appointment and a fake passport to get in to see you."

There was something in the voice he knew he should recall. She was British but had a slight Southern drawl. Recognition flashed in his brain: "Frannie Bennet!"

"Oh, my, you are a bright one!" Frannie sat herself down in one of the chairs in front of Darcy's desk, her skirt hiking up her thighs a little too far during the process of crossing her legs. As Darcy glared at her, Frannie ran her eyes up and down his body. She immediately decided that Bethy had done very well. This man was one tall, cool drink of water with his own conveniently attached straw. Suddenly she felt *very* thirsty! "Surprised to see me?"

Darcy was successfully hiding the shock of being confronted by Elizabeth's mother. Torn between the curiosity to find out just why she was there and the desire to hit a woman for the first time in his life, he sat down and sized up his opponent.

Frannie Bennet was not a tall woman, but she had an exceedingly fit body for her age. He refused to allow himself to be impressed, even though her actual age was somewhere approaching fifty. The reason she seemed familiar hit Darcy full force. She had Jane's face and Elizabeth's body — a dangerous combination. Now he understood how she could capture and hold the attentions of men far younger than herself.

Deciding he had waited long enough to reply to her question, he said dryly, "I had hoped to postpone the introduction indefinitely. I will ask you only once more, Ms. Bennet. Why are you here?"

She wrinkled her nose in a way Darcy was sure a lesser man would find endearing. "I want to see Bethy."

"Why?" Darcy could not stop the words from escaping, "Do you have another boyfriend you wish to pimp her out to?"

He didn't expect the laughter he received in response. "Bethy told you about *that* did she? You must be one *very* persuasive man to have gotten that story out of her. But then again, I think any woman would do just about *anything* you asked her to." Frannie saw the flash of anger in Darcy's eyes, but chose to interpret it as something else and pressed on. "You must know how talented Bethy is. She's very stubborn, but if she is managed correctly, she can once again be the star she was before. Imagine the fame, the money, the status! I'm sure you'd want that for her... for you." She wet her lips and dipped her eyes suggestively down his body before adding, "For *us*! Just let me talk to her."

Fighting the bile that rose in his throat, Darcy reminded himself he should not be surprised that Elizabeth's mother was coming on to him. It was a part of her character she'd obviously passed on to her youngest child; however, that was no reason to put up with this nonsense any further. He had his answers as to why she was there, and now it was time to send Frannie on her way.

"I can assure you, Elizabeth does not want to see you, *ever*! Now, I believe that concludes your business with me. I will see to it that security keeps your photo on file. I guarantee, Ms. Bennet, you will not be able to enter this building again under any circumstance, no matter how underhanded, illegal and well planned." With those words, Darcy picked up his phone and buzzed Hayter. "Call security. I want the woman in my office escorted outside immediately."

He hung up the phone to find that Frannie was now standing beside him. She leaned over and released the one button on the front of her jacket to expose a black bra that did little to hide her breasts. "Come now, Mr. Darcy. There is no need to be unpleasant. Now why don't you just call back your security people and tell them you were mistaken, and then I'm sure that you and I can come to some kind of friendly understanding." She lowered her voice to a breathy, seductive whisper. "I can see you are a man of fire, far too much fire for my little Bethy to handle." With that, Frannie fell to her knees and reached out for the front of Darcy's trousers.

Darcy managed to catch her wrist before she made contact. "You disgust me!" Without letting go of her wrist, Darcy stood and forced Frannie to her feet.

Frannie's reaction was to squeal in delight. "If you want to play rough, let me assure you, I like to play rough!"

"Then this is your lucky day!" Darcy twisted her around, pinning her wrist up behind her shoulder blades as he pushed her toward the door.

"Wait a cotton-picking minute!" Frannie yelled once the realization of what was happening finally filtered through her brain. George told her Darcy was too much the prude to fall for her seduction, but in Frannie's eyes, there was only one reason a man would refuse her. "I was right about you all along! You must be gay!"

Darcy refused to respond. He had wasted enough breath on this worthless piece of baggage. He hustled her to the door and opened it just as the security officers were arriving.

By this time, Frannie had let loose a stream of obscenities that made even the security guards blush. Once she was firmly in their custody, Darcy shouted to Hayter, "Call Fred Wentworth and find out who's responsible for this woman getting in here. I want him in my office in ten minutes." With that, he turned on his heel, re-entered his office and slammed the door.

Geoff heard the commotion from his desk and quickly sprinted to the source in time to see a woman being forced into the lift, spitting curses at the two security officers she was trying to escape from. He made his way over to a stunned Charles Hayter. "Who was that?" Geoff asked.

Hayter couldn't take his eyes off the doors to the lift, even though they were closed and the passengers well on their way to ground level. "That was Lady Felicity Russell," he said in shocked disbelief. "Mr. Darcy just had Lady Felicity Russell thrown into the street!"

"There's a resemblance, but that woman was not Lady Russell," Geoff reassured Hayter. "Darcy and I met Lady Russell at a UNICEF function last summer."

"Well whoever she was, she has the big guy in a lather!" Hayter jerked his head toward Darcy's door. "I've been his assistant for four years, and I've never seen him lose his temper, ever! Someone's head is going to roll over this. I just hope it isn't mine!"

"Don't worry," Geoff said as he slapped Hayter on the shoulder. "I'll go talk to him." Hayter remembered after it was too late that he was supposed to remind Geoff to knock before entering Darcy's office.

As Geoff made his way over to grab a bottle of water from the bar, Darcy moved from the window and stormed over to his phone to buzz Hayter. "I want a lock on this door by the end of the day. Get to it!"

"Yes, sir!" Hayter's hesitant voice responded before Darcy turned off the intercom and walked back to his place at the window.

"Take it easy on Hayter, Darce," Geoff suggested before taking the seat Frannie had so recently vacated. "You're scaring the poor guy to death."

Darcy continued to stare out the window. After a minute of silence, he asked, "Did you see her?"

"Yes," Geoff laughed. "Who was she — another overzealous fan?"

"That woman," Darcy spat with emphasis, "is my future mother-in-law!"

"Elizabeth's mother?" Geoff whistled long and low. "So what did she want?"

"To see Elizabeth," Darcy began to clench and unclench his fists, "and to suck my cock."

"You're joking!" Darcy turned his dark stare from the window to his cousin. Geoff's eyes flew open wide. "Good God! You're not joking!"

Darcy walked back over to his desk and buzzed Hayter again. "Where's Wentworth?" he shouted angrily into the speaker.

Hayter responded, clearly disconcerted with Darcy's tone. "He's just arrived. I was about to show him in." Darcy turned off the intercom without another word. Upon seeing Geoff's raised brows, Darcy cursed to himself before buzzing Hayter one more time. "Hayter," he said in a calmer tone, "please forgive my temper. I'm not myself today, and I fear I'm taking it out on you because you're too bloody convenient."

Hayter's voice expressed his relief. "Sure, Darcy."

Fred Wentworth was a man in his late thirties who had been head of security for The Darcy Company for the last ten years. Nearly as tall as Darcy himself, he was a formidable presence. "What's this I hear of you terrorizing my staff, Darcy?"

Although Darcy respected the man and considered him a friend, he was not backing down. "Your staff let in a woman using a false passport today. I want to know who is responsible."

Geoff stood to leave, but Darcy put up his hand to stop him. "Stay. I want Wentworth to bring you up to speed on Frannie Bennet."

Wentworth calmly sat down in the seat next to Geoff. He took a CD from inside a file folder and dropped it onto the desk while reciting the report from memory. "Frances Lydia Gardiner Bennet, born April 9, 19—, Harperbury Hospital, St. Albans, Hertfordshire; attended King's College on a scholarship won when crowned Miss Great Britain, 19—, majored in humanities, dropped out of uni in 19— to marry one Thomas Jackson Bennet, American, now Dean of American History, Hunsford University, Hunsford, North Carolina, USA; mother of five daughters, divorced September, 20—. Sister to Edward Gardiner of Gardiner Heating & Air Conditioning who, as of last August, holds a maintenance contract with The Darcy Company for this building."

Here Wentworth looked to Darcy. At his employer's nod, he continued. "This is where it gets unpleasant. Eight years ago, Ms. Bennet was arrested and charged as an accomplice in an assault against her daughter, Elizabeth, by a William Raymond Collins, also known as Billy Ray Collins. To avoid prosecution, she agreed to be treated at the Kent County Psychiatric Hospital where she remained for nearly two years. After her release, her entire criminal record was expunged by a court order issued by a Judge Jefferson Robert Collins, uncle of said Billy Ray Collins. Since that time she has remained a regular visitor at the Hunsford State Penitentiary where Billy Ray Collins is serving his eighth year of a ten-year prison sentence for the aforementioned assault against the future Mrs. Darcy."

"Charming woman," Geoff commented sarcastically. "So what does she want with Elizabeth?"

Darcy answered, "She seems to think that if Elizabeth goes on tour again, she will recapture the fame and fortune she gave up when she was sixteen. I assume she also wants Elizabeth's assistance in securing an early release for Collins."

Geoff shook his head in confusion. "Doesn't she realize that an adult pianist, regardless of talent, cannot possibly garner the same level of celebrity as a child prodigy? I have no doubt that Elizabeth could regain a great degree of fame, but nothing compared to —"

Darcy was growing impatient. "Frannie seems to have an 'alternative' sense of reality. Elizabeth is not interested in touring again or in ever seeing her mother. I shudder to think what could have happened if Elizabeth had come to the office with me today."

"Ah, so this snit you're in has nothing to do with Frances Bennet gaining access to you but everything to do with the possibility of her gaining access to Elizabeth!"

Ignoring Geoff's comment, Darcy picked up the file and began paging through the documents inside. He addressed Wentworth. "If you knew all this, how was she able to get in here?"

"Look, Darcy, last October you asked me to check her out, not put her under constant surveillance or tag her in the company's security database. Today my Annie checked the passport identifying her as Lady Russell at the security desk, and I'd stake my career on my wife's expertise in spotting suspicious documents. Whoever made that passport for Ms. Bennet was a professional forger. I run a tight ship here, Darcy. Like everyone else, she had to pass through the metal detectors and security scanners. She had no weapons."

Except for her mouth! "All right, Wentworth." Darcy tossed the file back onto his desk. "I want to know where Frannie Bennet is staying in London and how long she plans to be here. I wouldn't bother Ed Gardiner. Elizabeth and I had dinner with his family last night, and I'm certain he would have told us if he knew Frannie was in town. I also want everything you can get me on Billy Ray Collins by eight o'clock tonight when we'll meet back here." Darcy looked to his friend and paused. "That is if Annie doesn't object?"

Wentworth smiled in return. "No, I don't think she will. She and my sister are putting up the nursery tonight. You'd think after two children, the third would require nothing at all."

Darcy walked Fred to the door and shook his hand before whispering apologetically to his friend. "Fred, I hope I didn't upset Annie too much. Please, tell her I know she's the best at what she does and —"

"It's all right, Darce." Fred stopped him with a smile. "Annie's tough, and I know she understands why you're angry. Hell, she's angry, too! No one's ever managed to get by her before."

"Annie's an understanding woman. You're a lucky man, Fred."

"That's not what you told me at my bachelor party!"

Darcy smiled in remembrance of that night and whispered, "Is she still calling you 'Pumpkin?'"

"Thankfully, yes." Wentworth lowered his voice even further. "Tell me, what does your Elizabeth call you?"

Darcy couldn't stop a silent snort at the question. "She calls me 'Fitzwilliam.'"

"Sure she does!" he said sarcastically. "I'm going to find out the truth, Darcy, before *your* bachelor party. I owe you!"

After Wentworth departed, Darcy turned his attention back to Geoff. "If you have anything planned for tonight, I'd appreciate your getting out of it. I want you at this meeting, too, and bring Richard if you can. I think he's retired long enough, and I need the mind of a spy."

Geoff smiled encouragingly. "You have a plan?"

"The beginnings of one. I'll need a few hours to put my thoughts together. By the time we meet tonight, I should have a general outline for us to work with."

After Geoff left, Darcy met with representatives from a Kosovo conglomerate applying for funding to start a machine parts industry within the newly independent nation. Then he met with representatives of the Serbian Ministry of the Interior who were attempting to block the efforts of the Kosovars. In the end, he decided to suspend the application for six months to see if the political situation stabilized.

After completing his morning meetings, he found himself staring at his PDA, trying to gather his thoughts before calling Elizabeth. How was he going to explain to her about her mother's visit?

Finally, he pressed the speed dial, and she picked up immediately, answering in a soft, husky voice, "Hey, Baby!"

The tone of his voice mirrored hers in response. "Hey, my Lizzy! How was your meeting?"

"Productive. There's no question they want to offer me a position, and they appear willing to wait until my contract with Longbourn has expired..."

Darcy noticed her hesitatio. "Somehow I sense there's a 'however' at the end of that sentence."

Her sigh was audible through the phone. "However... I suspect their enthusiasm has more to do with your billions than my qualifications."

"My advice is to wait. You do not have to commit to anything this far in advance. Once their offer becomes concrete, you can decide based on *their* merits. You're brilliant, Lizzy. Their students will be lucky to have you, regardless of the motives of the administration."

"You are a wise man, Fitzwilliam. I love you."

"Mmmm," he groaned lightly into the phone. It had been two months but he still couldn't hear those three little words enough. "I love you, too."

"What's wrong?"

He smiled into the phone. Once again, she seemed to be able to read his mind. "I need to talk to you, but I just realized I can't do it on the phone. Do you have plans for this afternoon?"

"Nothing I can't break. Do you want me to come to the office?"

"No!" he nearly shouted in alarm. Not only was there a small army of paparazzi outside his office building, but Frannie's disgusting presence, like her heavy perfume, still seemed to haunt his office. "I'll meet you at home."

Suddenly the weight of what had happed with Frannie seemed to crash down upon him. She was there — in London — and she was trying to get to Elizabeth. The anger at this threat seemed to burst forth from the tight knot inside where he had successfully imprisoned it since Fred Wentworth had left his office, suddenly threatening to drown him in a sea of hatred directly solely at one woman.

"Fitzwilliam?" Elizabeth's soothing voice of concern pulled him back from the abyss, showering the heat of his anger in the cooling waterfall of his name tumbling softly from her lips. He could almost feel her fingers gently stroking the fever from his face and her lips sweetly kissing away the pain behind his temples.

Darcy's anger transformed into a familiar, all-possessing need to tell Elizabeth exactly what she meant to him. *An impossible task.* In a voice fraught with emotion, he confessed, "Sometimes, my Lizzy, there are no words."

"Then don't tell me, Baby. Come home and show me."

HALF AN HOUR LATER, ELIZABETH paced the hallway in front of the door to Oakland. Her eyes were focused on the door, waiting for Darcy to enter. His phone call had left her uneasy, wondering what new threat to their peace had turned up to cause such a reaction in her usually calm fiancé. One by one, she went through the possible scenarios. Billy Ray Collins was still in prison as was Rebecca Wickham. Caroline Bingley was little more than a pest and, therefore, could not be responsible for this degree of distress. Elizabeth had checked the news and found no report of a terrorist attack or the sudden financial collapse of The Darcy Company. That left two possible candidates: his Aunt Catherine and her mother. *Please don't let it be Frannie!*

His muted form through the leaded glass of the door caught her attention, and she froze in place, awaiting the news. As Darcy entered the door, his eyes locked with hers for a moment before he all but threw his briefcase onto a silk covered bench, followed immediately by his coat. *Oh this is bad!* Elizabeth thought. *Really bad!*

Without a word, he wrapped her in his arms and kissed her passionately, breathlessly, desperately. Elizabeth knew this was not the moment for words. They would talk later when they were exhausted and all was quiet. This moment was for communication of another kind.

Sweeping her up into his arms, he carried her up the grand marble staircase of Oakland, down the finely appointed hall and into their bedroom. Reverently, he laid her down upon their bed before quickly divesting himself of his clothes. When Elizabeth attempted to remove her dress, he stopped her hands, asking her with his eyes to wait. Finally free of his impediments he slowly began to deliver his message.

Before Elizabeth, he had been a non-believer. Sex was offered to idols, mere images of beauty. It was empty, shallow, heathen. Then Elizabeth slowly showed him the light and offered him salvation.

Elizabeth had become his goddess, and her body was his temple. Every moan from her lips was a liturgy, each kiss a blessing, and each brush of her hands and tongue upon his skin an anointment. In return, he offered his every caress as a prayer; every taste of her body became a holy communion, every rough embrace a cry for redemption, every playful touch a hymn and every gasp for breath a hallelujah. The very act of love was a sacred ritual, and he was forever transformed in the rapture. Finally, in the calm that followed, tender words of love became their benediction.

He worshiped Elizabeth with the reverence of the converted, and no one is more fanatically devout than a convert.

Later, as she was protectively enfolded in his embrace, he told Elizabeth about his meeting with her mother. Darcy held back nothing and spared no detail for he respected her need to control her own destiny. She raged and despaired while he listened and comforted. When her emotions were finally spent, he did the one thing he would have never before thought possible: He discussed with her his plans and asked her to come back to his office to meet with Wentworth, Geoff and Richard.

Elizabeth listened to his ideas with careful attention and made her own suggestions for improvement; soon they both felt a measure of relief at having a plan of action to deal with the situation. She offered no opposition to his assistance — proof to herself that she trusted implicitly his love and commitment. They had come a long way together, and together they would battle all their demons, no matter how evil they may be.

At 8:00 p.m., the gas fireplace in Darcy's office was lit to ward off the chill. Sitting before it on each end of the couch were Geoff and Richard Fitzwilliam like a pair of identical bookends. Fred Wentworth sat in one large leather chair. In the other sat Elizabeth, with Darcy perched on one of the large overstuffed arms, his own arm stretched protectively behind her.

Fred began his report. Frannie was not staying at a hotel, but according to the taxi driver who picked her up from the Darcy Company that morning, she was let off in a rather seedy section of the city outside a boarding house owned by an R. W. Younge. An examination of the trash revealed a number of take-out food containers and used condoms, indicating that either a man was staying with her or she had made *friends* with someone in the building. No identity of the man was yet made. Frannie travelled by round trip ticket; she had arrived the week before, and her return flight was scheduled in six days, two days after Lady Felicity Russell was originally scheduled to see Darcy.

The report on Billy Ray Collins was even more disturbing. During his prison stay, Billy Ray passed the time by taking college courses. Over the course of his confinement, he had managed to earn a Doctorate of Divinity with a less than mainstream Christian sect. Once released, he expected to become an ordained minister.

Unfortunately, that event would take place sooner than expected. Due to overcrowding in the Kent County prison system, all prisoners within 24 months of the end of their prison terms would be systematically released over the next year. Billy Ray Collins was expected to be out of prison in less than seven months.

Darcy felt Elizabeth's hand tighten where it rested on his knee. She showed no other sign of distress. "No parole hearing? No victim impact statements?" Elizabeth's voice was calm.

"No," Wentworth replied, his eyes full of sympathy although the rest of his manner spoke pure professionalism. "He has behaved himself in prison, and the county is in a financial crisis. They see no reason to spend what scant resources they have to keep him."

"When were they planning to tell Elizabeth?" Darcy asked.

"Kent County only requires a thirty-day notice to crime victims when the perpetrators of that crime are being released from prison."

Silence fell over the room while everyone absorbed what had been said. Finally Darcy stood. "Good job, Fred. Thanks for your help."

Fred Wentworth knew he was dismissed but suspected that something else was going on, something he was being kept out of. Darcy would never say he was about to plan something some might consider high-handed, even illegal. As much as he appreciated Darcy keeping him out of the loop in such matters, Wentworth really wanted to lend his expertise to his friend.

As Darcy escorted him to the door, Wentworth whispered, "I can help, you know."

Darcy simply shook his head. "Go home to Annie and the kids." At Wentworth's look of protest, Darcy continued, "This job has suddenly grown too large for you alone. Your responsibilities are the security of The Darcy Company and Pemberley. No matter what else happens, I know you'll keep them safe. It's like you said earlier today: You run a tight ship, Captain. That's what I need you to do."

Wentworth merely nodded in acceptance and left.

As soon as he resumed his seat beside Elizabeth, Darcy addressed Richard. "So, are you ready to begin working again? If so, I have a position for you."

Richard looked up from Wentworth's files on Frannie and Collins. "Somehow, I don't think you're sending me to that beach chair in the Caribbean."

"No, I'm offering you the position as head of my personal security." Darcy looked down at Elizabeth and corrected himself. "*Our* personal security."

"Sounds a little light for me. Why not just have Wentworth take care of it?"

"Wentworth plays by the rules. The paparazzi, Collins, Frannie, Aunt Catherine — these people do not. I need someone willing to think outside the box. You can hire whoever you want to assist you, and I won't interfere with your operations; we only request you keep us totally informed."

Richard looked to Elizabeth and could see by her determined gaze that she understood exactly what Darcy was asking of him. Usually women would be wary of such things, but what little Richard understood of Elizabeth confirmed that she was not the usual woman. "Even if you hadn't saved my arse in Colombia, I'd still do it. I'm in!"

Darcy turned to Geoff with a questioning glance. "Hey, do you even have to ask?" Geoff looked slightly offended. "Of course I'm in!"

"I must admit, I expected no less of either of you, but I had to give you the chance to bow out." Wasting no time, Darcy began explaining the plans he and Elizabeth had discussed that afternoon. "We refuse to simply sit back and wait for someone to attack us again. Our basic strategy is that we are going to take a proactive instead of a reactive approach with those we know are a threat to us. That means Collins, Frannie Bennet, Rebecca and George Wickham and Aunt Catherine."

"No more Mr. Nice Guy! I like it. So, what about Caroline Bingley?" Geoff added.

"Caroline?" Richard turned to his brother in disbelief. "She's a little misguided, but I don't think she'd hurt anyone!"

Geoff couldn't suppress the smirk directed at his brother. "She hurt Elizabeth in New York!"

Richard turned to Elizabeth, the shock registering on his face. "It was just a bruise," Elizabeth answered. "For what it's worth, I think you're correct about Caroline. We have bigger fish to fry."

"Speaking of bigger fish," Darcy interjected, "We need someone inside Aunt Catherine's organization. I want to know in advance when she's coming after me again and how. I also want to find out where George Wickham is and what he's doing. Richard, I think that's your department." Richard nodded his head in response.

Darcy continued, "Geoff, I want to know what's happening with Rebecca Wickham. Has she been deported from the U.S.? if so, where is she? I want to know the complete status of her situation and I want weekly reports."

The brothers were surprised when Elizabeth spoke up next as Darcy went to unlock a safe that was well concealed under the bar. "Geoff, we need you to find a way to prevent Billie Collins from getting a legal passport in the U.S. and see if we can obtain restraining orders upon his release to prevent him from coming anywhere near us in New York, London and at Pemberley. It would be great if we could protect my sisters and grandmother too. We can get everything in order before he's released and then, once he's out of jail, simply put things in motion. It won't stop him from getting to us, but it won't make it easy, either.

"Richard." His eyes lifted to hers. "You wanted to know about the skeletons in my closet. What do you think?"

"I've seen worse. What can I do for you?"

"This is where things get very sticky." She looked to Darcy who nodded his encouragement. "I want my mother picked up at the boarding house, taken immediately to the airport and forced on a plane back to Hunsford. I don't want her physically hurt, but don't make it a pleasant experience. She needs to think twice before she pulls another stunt like she did today. See if you can make her spill about where she obtained the fake passport. If *she* can get one, you'd better believe Collins will be able to get one, too."

Richard wrinkled his brow. "I'm not convinced that Collins is the threat you seem to think he is. He's been in prison for eight years. Could be he's ready to just marry your mother and live a normal life — however normal that might be."

"I wish I could agree with you," Darcy said as he walked back toward the rest of the group, carrying a large green folder he retrieved from the safe. From inside the folder he withdrew two CDs, handing one each to Geoff and Richard. "This is information from a special source. It contains transcriptions of private conversations held with Billy Ray Collins and his fellow inmates. The man has every intention of finding Elizabeth and finishing what he started eight years ago. He also claims he will kill any man who's touched her since he was sent to prison. That would mean me."

Both Geoff and Richard let out slow whistles. "Who is this special source?" Richard asked.

Darcy leveled his gaze at Richard. "Pierre Estoban. It's easy to see that he would have contacts within the prison that could provide him with this information."

Geoff looked puzzled. "How did you get this?"

Darcy proceeded to explain everything that transpired with Estoban in Colombia, as well as his discussion with Isabella Bennet on the day she gave him the file. Darcy had been surprised to learn that Estoban had been in regular contact with Isabella since before Elizabeth retired from performing. After the incident with Billy Ray Collins, Tom Bennet joined in, and together they had worked to do everything possible to keep her safe.

Darcy emerged from that discussion with a grudging respect for Tom Bennet. However, against Tom's insistence, Darcy immediately returned to Isabella's study with Elizabeth in tow, demanding they both tell her the entire story. In spite of Tom's desire to shield Elizabeth from knowing the full extent of the danger in which she was living, Isabella was grateful for Darcy's determination to be open and honest with Elizabeth.

"I'll review these files carefully," Richard suggested as he put the incredulity of the situation with Estoban out of his mind for the present. "I think we need to find some way to warn as many of Elizabeth's past lovers as possible. Collins may go after them first, thinking there will be less resistance."

Elizabeth looked into the fire as Darcy cleared his throat before responding firmly, "There are no others."

The silence in the room was long and deafening. Finally, Elizabeth looked to both Geoff and Richard, the steel in her eyes challenging either of them to question Darcy's statement.

Darcy was the first to break the silence. "I think we have enough to work on for now. Let's meet again before we return to New York."

Elizabeth excused herself to the washroom as the twins prepared to leave. As Geoff walked through the door, he stepped back and whispered to Darcy, "No others? Are you sure?"

Darcy narrowed his eyes in warning. "Absolutely positive."

"You," Geoff smirked, "are a lucky bastard!"

Darcy replied in a serious, even tone, "Yes, I am." He then lowered his voice. "Has Richard seen *her* since he's back?"

"She's still in the States, which is surprising, given the circumstances. I've been expecting her to show up at any moment."

Darcy nodded his head, acknowledging Geoff's statement, and then slapped him on the back in farewell.

When Elizabeth re-entered Darcy's office, she found him sitting on the couch, staring at the fire. "I can just imagine your thoughts, Mr. Darcy."

He looked up at her playful tone. "I think not."

Elizabeth sat down next to him, wrapped her arms around his neck and whispered against his lips, "You, sir, were thinking about what happened on this couch last summer and how insupportable it would be to suffer such a disappointment again." He kissed her slowly and she returned that kiss, once, twice, three times.

Darcy reached down to the coffee table in front of the couch and picked up what looked like a television remote control. Pointing the devise at the door, he pressed a small red button and a resounding "thunk" was heard as the door locked. Another button lowered the lights in the room. "I believe you are perfectly right!"

As he lowered her back onto the cushions of the couch, the call to worship was issued and obeyed. Sometime after the majority of their clothing was removed, the door handle could be heard turning, followed by a loud banging.

"Darcy!" Geoff's voice called through the door. "I think my keys fell out of my pocket... Darcy?..." Geoff would have sworn he heard soft laughter through the thick door. "Come on, I know you're in there!... Elizabeth?... Darcy?... DARCY!"

Geoff had to call a cab home that night, and the next morning, Charles Hayter received a mini-holiday to Paris, courtesy of his grateful employer.

CHAPTER 27
LIKE SANDS THROUGH THE HOURGLASS...

March 10th, The Daily Insight (U.K.)
Photo caption: Elizabeth Bennet's engagement ring is rumored to be worth upwards of two million pounds.
Story: Word has spread that the wedding of Fitzwilliam Darcy and Elizabeth Bennet has been postponed, sparking rumors that the couple is calling it quits.

April 3rd, Celebrity Watcher (U.S.)
Photo caption: Fitzwilliam Darcy and Elizabeth Bennet attend a performance of the New York Symphony Orchestra.
(No Story.)

Darcy picked up his phone on the first ring. "Hey, Lizzy."

"Hey, Baby. Guess what?"

"Hmmm." Darcy hesitated, giving her question serious thought. "You've been picturing me naked in your mind, and you called to ask what I was wearing?"

Elizabeth let out a soft purr at the thought. "I knew there was something I forgot to do this morning. Umm... what *are* you wearing?"

"I'm fully dressed, but I could change that in a flash."

"That's what I love about you — always willing to do for others."

"A gentleman could do no less. So, what's up?"

"I was fired."

"Pardon?"

"Fired. F.I.R.E.D. Let go. Sacked. Shoved off. Sent packing. Pink slipped…" Elizabeth's voice was light, as if announcing something amusing that happened every day.

"You're joking?"

"Okay, it was not *technically* a termination of employment, but the message Longbourn's attorneys delivered to me a few minutes ago was clear. As of the end of the current semester, I will no longer be teaching at Longbourn."

"On what grounds?" Darcy was angry. "What about your contract?"

"They're fully aware of my contract, so financially they'll honor the remaining year, but they don't want me on campus. They suggested I could be a guest lecturer or perhaps give a special performance for the alumni each semester. There was an obvious preference for the performance, of course. I imagine they could raise quite a bit of money from that."

"What about the project for the community center?"

"They still want me to oversee the project via the Internet, which shouldn't be a problem as all the set-up work will be finished by then.

"Is this because we're getting married?" It seemed the longer Elizabeth remained calm, the angrier Darcy became. "Did you tell them you weren't planning to move to England until after your contract expires?"

"I never got the chance. This is all about the paparazzi. Longbourn cannot afford the security measures necessary to ensure my safety and the safety of their students. They've decided that I'm more trouble than I'm worth, and I must admit…they are right."

"They're not right! We can fight this," Darcy insisted, filled with righteous indignation on Elizabeth's behalf. "I'm sure Ed Bertram knows someone local who's well versed in employment law."

"I'm sure he does," she said with a sarcastic edge to her pleasant tone. "Then we can force Longbourn to pay for millions of dollars in legal fees in addition to a state-of-the-art security system. After you withdraw your contributions, we could bankrupt the school in no time." She took a deep breath. "No, I'm not going to fight this. Longbourn was established to encourage free thought and free expression. I'm not going to be responsible for turning this campus into a prison during lockdown the next time our names hit the tabloids."

"You're angry." He thought that at least she should be angry. Perhaps Elizabeth was simply too shocked to realize it. "We'll talk about this when you come home. In the meantime I'll make a few phone calls —"

"No!" Elizabeth was now undoubtedly *angry*. "I don't need you to save me! I've given up my co-op, I've got a damn bodyguard and I miss my couch, but let's get one thing straight: I'm not going to give up control of my career!" She stopped short and he could hear her take another deep breath before she sighed heavily. "I'm sorry I snapped at you. I know you're just trying to help."

"I'm glad you snapped at someone." His voice had lost its edge, too. "I was beginning to fear for your sanity. So what did Bill Lucas have to say about all this?"

"The little shit's out all day," she hissed in unconcealed anger.

He couldn't help but laugh. "Now that's my Lizzy!"

"My eleven o'clock is about to start. I'll see you around five, and then I think a trip to the fencing club is in order. I need to work off some steam."

"Save some of that steam for me."

"I will. I love you, Baby."

"I love you too, my Lizzy."

Elizabeth arrived at Lansing precisely at five o'clock to find a welcome surprise. The two leather couches in the game room had been removed, and her comfy red sectional sofa had been brought out of storage and put in their place. As Darcy and Elizabeth once again snuggled in its corner, they discussed Elizabeth's options for dealing with Longbourn. Although he did not agree with her decision, in the end Darcy accepted that she would not fight for her position there. Her life was changing, and it was time to move on.

The silver lining was they could move to the security of Pemberley that much sooner.

May 1st, Tête-à-Tête Magazine (formerly Celebrity Watcher) (U.S.)
Cover headline: The Sexiest Couple Alive!
Story: Your votes have decided that Fitzwilliam Darcy and Elizabeth Bennet are the sexiest . . .

THEIR HANDS WERE LINKED, FINGERS entwined, heart's beating faster than normal, but this was no romantic encounter. When Agent Martin called to ask Darcy to meet him at the police station, Darcy assumed it was on some matter related to the incident in Colombia. At first, Elizabeth was going to remain at Lansing, but something in her gut told her to go along. Darcy was never as glad for Elizabeth's instincts as he was at that moment.

"She wants to see *me*?" he asked Martin incredulously as his squeeze on Elizabeth's hand tightened. "Did she say why?"

Martin sat behind the metal and laminate desk, absently drumming his fingers. "No, she simply said that she would reveal to you—and you only—the name of the person who makes her forged documents."

Darcy stared at Elizabeth's hand that he had pulled into his lap. It was so small compared to his. Her nails were neatly trimmed and polished in a light pink that was hardly noticeable except for the pretty shine it gave to them. Her fingers were long and slim: the fingers of a pianist. Their every movement was graceful, precise and perfect.

"Mr. Darcy." Martin interrupted his thoughts to bring him back to the subject Darcy's mind most wanted to avoid. "We suspect these documents are coming from a source operating throughout the United States and Europe. Millions in money and property have been stolen with them. We need that name."

"Can we come back tomorrow?" Elizabeth suggested, sensing that Darcy needed to plan for this meeting, to think out and anticipate every contingency for why Rebecca Wickham wanted to see him and what she might say.

Agent Martin pursed his lips before replying. "Ms. Wickham has been fighting her extradition for months, and yesterday she lost her final appeal. The Italians will be taking her later tonight, so I'm afraid it's now or never."

"All right," Darcy said quietly as his eyes fixed on the blue diamond sparkling brilliantly in the harsh fluorescent lighting. "Let's get this over with."

Darcy rose, followed immediately by Martin who said with relief, "Good. Dr. Bennet can wait here."

"Give us a moment, please," Elizabeth requested of Martin.

The agent nodded his head. "I'll be right outside."

As soon as the door closed, Elizabeth slipped her hands inside Darcy's jacket, linking them behind his back as she rested her head on his shoulder. "Don't give her the power to mess with your head. You're not the same man you were seven years ago. You know exactly what she is this time; you're older and wiser."

"And I have you." He hugged her tightly, kissed her forehead and left.

WALKING DOWN THE STEPS TO the holding cells, Darcy tried to calm his nerves. He reminded himself that as CEO of The Darcy Company, he dealt with far more calculating creatures than Rebecca Wickham on a daily basis. However, he couldn't stop replaying his last conversation with her in his head.

He had walked into his flat; the music was loud, and the smell of pot smoke was heavy in the air. "Richard! What the hell?" he called out into the semi-darkness. He didn't have far to go before he found the first tangle of thrusting, undulating bodies and immediately knew that whatever was happening, neither of his cousins had anything to do with it. As his eyes adjusted to the darkness, he finally realized that he was standing in the middle of an orgy and there on the couch, in between two men and partially covered by another woman, was Rebecca.

His first reaction was fury. As he shouted at the top of his lungs and threatening to call the police, the bodies scattered, grabbed at the clothing littering the floor and scrambled out the door—all except Rebecca, who stood completely nude before him, hands on hips and tapping her foot like a mother waiting for her child's temper tantrum to pass.

"Shit, Rebecca, you know how I feel about having drugs in this flat. If the police had been called…" he shouted in alarm. Then he suddenly went pale, "All those people… When the press gets a hold of this…"

"I didn't tell any of those people whose flat this is," she said matter-of-factly, as if this was an everyday occurrence. "And it was just a little grass and a few lines of coke to heighten the senses and relax one's inhibitions. Besides, no one called the police, at least not until you started ranting like a lunatic. So, your precious family's reputation is safe."

Darcy stormed around the flat opening the windows and turning on the lights. "How did you get in here?" Darcy asked accusingly. Because he shared his flat with Richard and Geoff, he never even considered giving Rebecca a key.

Rebecca began searching for her clothing, and as she pulled her shirt over her head, she said, "I told Richard I was planning a little surprise for you, so he let me in before he took Geoff to Heathrow."

Darcy stopped picking up the cushions from where they had been tossed on the floor. Suddenly everything became clear: She knew he was returning to the flat early, wanted him to find the "party" and had expected him to participate. He turned to Rebecca in horror. "Get out!"

"Come on, Darcy. You can't tell me you weren't the least bit interested?" She slipped on her knickers and began searching for her jeans.

Darcy was literally shaking with anger. "Get out! Please, before I do something rash."

Rebecca spit sarcastically as she slipped into her shoes. "Oh, please do something rash! You haven't done anything spontaneous, ever. You're predictable, up-tight and incredibly boring…"

Bristling at her tirade of criticisms he asked, "Doesn't what we had mean anything to you? Christ! You said you loved me."

"What we had? As in the past?" Rebecca's voice was filled with incredulity, as if what had happened was nothing more than a minor offense, like leaving the cap off the toothpaste, and Darcy was overreacting. "You're going to stop seeing me because I tried to open up your mind — expand your horizons?

"You can't possibly think that I would stay in a relationship with you after…this!"

"Why?" Rebecca suddenly began laughing. "Can't handle the truth? Can't bear the idea that you're not the only man I've slept with in the past year, that you alone aren't enough for me?"

Darcy felt each of Rebecca's insults to his ego like a knife in the chest. "Get out!" Darcy seethed once again. Too angry to think except for the fact that he wanted to break something — preferably Rebecca's neck — he walked back to his bedroom and slammed the door.

Fortunately, not long after that, he heard the front door open and close, signaling Rebecca's exit from his flat and, he hoped, from his life. Of course, that was not to be.

Agent Martin stood outside a large metal door. "There will be several of us in the room next door. We will be able to see and hear everything that happens. Whatever you do," Agent Martin reminded him, "don't leave that room before we find out the name of the forger."

When the door opened, Darcy's first impression was that either he had been led to the wrong room or that someone had put the wrong woman inside. The figure sitting at the table in the drab, grey jail uniform was almost painfully thin.

"So you've come." Her voice brought his attention to her eyes, and there, in their dark brown depths, was the woman he used to know. Those eyes took in his face and then, unabashedly, his body. "You're more handsome than I remember, even more so then your pictures in the tabloids. It's not fair. Here they won't allow me to have makeup or a decent hair stylist, and the wait for a manicure…"

Her face was devoid of cosmetics, revealing bright red patches on her skin, and there were dark circles below her eyes. She had no visible wrinkles, but when she smiled at her little joke, only her lips moved while the rest of her face remained frozen, reminding Darcy of a talking doll Georgiana received for Christmas when she was a little girl. *Botox? She's not old enough to even consider Botox!*

Darcy suppressed his surprise and asked unemotionally, "Why am I here?"

"Ah, the voice! Like warm chocolate." Rebecca lowered her voice. "I've missed it. I've missed you."

A sardonic snort flared Darcy's nostrils. *Let the games begin.* Sitting down in the chair opposite hers, he crossed his arms over his chest and glared at Rebecca, refusing to contribute to the conversation. There would be no sarcastic banter, no useless recriminations of her character and no pleasant trips down memory lane.

Rebecca's confident expression turned harsh. "Your Elizabeth has a tolerable body in a 'common tart' sort of way. She's a little 'vertically challenged' if you know what I mean, although whoever did those tits is worth every penny you paid."

Darcy's reaction was to remain silent and still, thereby denying Rebecca the satisfaction of angering him.

"Really, Darcy! She's not at all what I expected; but, if she's nothing more than a brood mare for your heirs, I can see where she might suffice."

Behind his stoic expression, Darcy was wondering if Rebecca had always been so vicious.

"I read somewhere that she's a genius, so I suppose the two of you must spend hours participating in deep intellectual discussions. My," she laughed cruelly, "I can just imagine the stimulating pillow talk!"

Darcy's eyes were suddenly drawn to Rebecca's hands which where handcuffed to a bracket in the middle of the table. Her veins were clearly visible and each joint was noticeably protruding. He had noticed hands like this on many of the models he had dated, the lack of body fat making them appear far too large for their bodies. "Man Hands" they were called in the tabloids, though Darcy had not paid much attention to the condition until that moment.

His level of discomfort abated at having found such an unexpected weapon. "Elizabeth's the loveliest woman I've ever met," he responded wistfully with a smile, his eyes still fixed on Rebecca's hands. "Everything about her is so feminine, especially her hands. They are so very delicate... so beautiful."

There was a tugging on the handcuffs and Darcy knew he had hit his mark. He did not need to look up to know Rebecca was unhappy. She continued to pull on the handcuffs, but there was no way to withdraw and hide her hands.

Leaning slightly forward, Darcy cocked his head to the side, narrowed his eyes as he continued to stare at Rebecca's hands and then…grimaced. Rebecca's reaction was more than he could have hoped.

"Stop that!" she shouted while yanking hard on the cuffs, in turn fisting and folding her hands in an attempt to cover them up, but Darcy would not divert his eyes. As the seconds ticked by, he continued looking only at her hands as Rebecca became increasingly distressed. "Get out! Get out right now!"

"Give me the name," Darcy demanded coolly, his eyes never wavering.

Rebecca's voice was panicked. "You bastard! Get out!"

His outward calm disguised his amazement when Rebecca began to sob; however, he would not move his eyes from her hands. "Tell me."

Rebecca shrieked, "Go away! Leave me alone!" Rebecca tried to stand but her feet were shackled to the legs of her chair. "I want out!" she shouted in the direction of the two-way mirror behind which sat Martin and his fellow agents.

Darcy fought hard not to enjoy the newfound power he had over Rebecca, for to do so would sink him to her level. Instead, he focused on the necessity of obtaining the name of the forger. "Tell me, and I'll go."

"Henry Crawford!" Rebecca attempted to look defiantly in Darcy's eyes, but it was impossible as they remained fixed exasperatingly on her hands. "He uses a copy shop in Manchester as his front."

"I think you're lying, and I'm not leaving until you give me an answer I can believe."

Suddenly Rebecca's struggles stopped. Slumping defeatedly back into her chair, she spoke so softly she could barely be heard. "George. It's George."

"Let's have his full name for the gentlemen listening in."

Rebecca's eyes fared in anger as she shouted, "George Wickham!"

Finally, Darcy moved his gaze from her hands to Rebecca's tear-stained face. "Where is he?"

"I haven't heard from him since my arrest."

Darcy took one last hard look at Rebecca. For seven years, he had allowed her specter to haunt him, controlling how he lived and, more importantly, how he loved. Now here she sat before him, no more than a clever and exceedingly vain woman terrified of aging. Like a child who discovers the monster under his bed is no more than a pair of old shoes, Darcy felt the long-seated anxiety lift from his chest. He was forever free of Rebecca Wickham.

Having obtained what he came for, Darcy rose to leave. That was when Rebecca called out, "We could have been amazing together. Between the two of us, there wouldn't have been a man or woman alive we couldn't con."

He turned back to her. "I never needed money."

"It's not about money you simpleton! It's about power — the power to control someone's mind: to take, punish and torture their very soul. That's why I took the money from the good people of Lambton — to punish you and teach you a valuable lesson about power. If you would have only tasted it, you would have found it intoxicating."

"Obviously, you know little about who I really am."

A little of Rebecca's cockiness returned. "Obviously, I could say the same to you."

"That is a mistake that has since been rectified." Darcy turned and knocked on the door so that he could leave. "Goodbye, Ms. Wickham."

"That's Mrs. Younge!" she declared defiantly, ready to deliver her last remaining blow. "I was married when we were together."

Darcy stopped momentarily upon hearing her words but continued on his way without looking back. If Rebecca thought her revelation hurt him, Darcy did nothing to disabuse her of the notion. What the woman did not fathom was that she had unwittingly disclosed the link that tied Darcy and Elizabeth's enemies together.

July 6th, The Daily Insight (U.S.)
Photo caption: Fitzwilliam Darcy, his sister Georgiana, Elizabeth Bennet and her sister Mary Bennet lunch at an outdoor café in Netherfield, NC.

ELIZABETH WALKED INTO THE LAW firm of Bertram & Bertram LLP, Mr. Benwick close behind. Her mind was still filled with conflicting emotions as she was led into Thomas Bertram's office. Tom was Edmund Bertram's older brother and was hired to represent Elizabeth's interests for one purpose only. She sighed heavily as she sat in the burgundy leather chair in front of Bertram's desk.

The months were passing quickly. Their vacation to the Outer Banks over the Fourth of July was very relaxing, and Elizabeth was happy to see Darcy become better acquainted with all her family, specifically her grandmother and the Gardiners, whom Isabella invited as a surprise for Elizabeth.

Georgiana, who was also graciously included in Darcy and Elizabeth's invitation, had no trouble making friends with Kit and Lydia. Elizabeth's father, while not exactly thrilled over her upcoming marriage, seemingly accepted it and made small attempts to get to know his future son-in-law. But now the holiday was over, and soon Charlotte would purchase Elizabeth's co-op, and the majority of Elizabeth's belongings would be moved to Pemberley, half a world away.

Except for the occasional semester abroad, New York City had been Elizabeth's home for the last eight years. Although her home would now be in England, Darcy would retain his townhouse on Lansing Street, not only for Georgiana to reside in while attending Longbourn, but also as a home to stay in during their frequently planned visits to the city. Still it was bittersweet to realize that she would no longer be a New Yorker, no longer reside in the same city as Jane and no longer have regular contact with her network of friends.

The planning of their wedding required the strategy and execution of a two-front world war. Realizing all that would be required to co-ordinate the event and an unforeseen problem with the availability of Pemberley Church, Darcy and Elizabeth reluctantly pushed back the date.

Keeping the paparazzi off the scent was the most challenging task. No official word of their engagement was released, but as pictures of Elizabeth's ring began surfacing in the tabloids, speculation grew. When an article was released disclosing that the wedding was to be held at Pemberley instead of in Hunsford, it became clear that someone within their small circle of friends and family who knew that detail had leaked the information.

Elizabeth and Darcy realized they had been careless. It did not matter to them from whom or how the information became public; they could not change the past. However, from that moment on, all details of their wedding plans would be kept on a need-to-know basis.

Of course, there is more to marrying a billionaire than the actual ceremony, and after four months of their attorneys hashing out the details, Elizabeth hoped finally to put aside a major hurdle to her marriage to Darcy.

"Dr. Bennet," Tom's slick voice interrupted Elizabeth's thoughts as he entered the office, "How are you today?"

"Fine. Is everything ready?"

Tom pulled out two, three-inch thick stacks of documents and set them before her. "Here it is: your pre-nuptial agreement."

"HERE IT IS," GEOFF ANNOUNCED with a flourish as he set the two, three-inch thick stacks of documents before Darcy, "your pre-nuptial agreement."

Darcy looked at the thing as if it had warts and a leer. "How did it become so large?"

"You didn't read my e-mails, did you?" Geoff accused with a frustrated sigh. "I've been sending you the various drafts as Tom Bertram and I hammered out the details. You approved each and every one! Good Lord, Darce, it's your business to review contracts every day, and you catch mistakes that have somehow managed to get past me, but this...this is probably the most important contract of your life, and I can't get you to even glance at it."

Darcy knew Geoff was right, but reducing his decision to marry Elizabeth to a list of facts, figures, financial statements, conjectures and promises, all due to the impossible possibility that they would someday divorce, was more than Darcy could bear. He detested the whole process, no matter how necessary it was. "I did review the financial requirements for Elizabeth's support as well as for the support of our children. I found Bertram's suggestions to be less than adequate."

"That was four drafts ago and those figures were outrageous! It would behoove you to remember that Tom's representing Elizabeth's interests, not yours.'"

Darcy quickly looked at the figures that were marked with a hot pink post-it note. "I can afford to give Elizabeth so much more than this."

"You could afford ten ex-wives — fifty if they were all as self-sacrificing as Elizabeth — but that's not the point. You need to understand exactly what it is you're signing. The section regarding the division of property —"

"Geoff, I'm tired of hashing out the details of this fantasy divorce!"

"You feel that way now, but trust me. If the time comes, you won't be feeling so magnanimous."

Darcy stated with determination, "There will be no divorce."

"You're impossible!" Geoff sat down, looking very tired. "Look, do you want me to represent you or not?"

"Do I keep Pemberley?" As far as Darcy was concerned, it was his only requirement.

Geoff gritted his teeth in frustration at Darcy's lack of concern over his remaining assets. Fortunately for his cousin, the future Mrs. Darcy was concerned enough for all of them. "Of course you keep Pemberley. Elizabeth was insistent that everything you bring to your marriage always belongs to you, regardless of the circumstances."

"But I wanted her to have Lansing! That woman is going to be the death of me. Go back to Bertram and renegotiate."

"Argh!!!! Give Lansing to your kids!" Geoff practically screamed, his patience completely gone. "I don't know why you and Elizabeth aren't at each other's throats over this."

"After that blowup we had over the push-to-talk phones, we agreed not to discuss the pre-nup directly with one another. That's what we pay you and Bertram for."

"For a pair of geniuses, you both can behave stupidly at times. Honestly, Tom and I are fed up with the pair of you!"

"You weren't here for the phone argument. If you had been, you would understand completely."

"That bad?"

"Ohhhh yeah!" Darcy grimaced in remembrance.

"Who won?" Geoff was teasing for he was keenly aware that Elizabeth was not carrying the standard issue, Darcy Company, walkie-talkie phone.

Darcy changed the subject back to the document before him. "I know you wouldn't ask me to sign something you felt would be to my detriment. However, I don't have the same confidence in Bertram's scruples to do the same for Elizabeth. Just give me your honest opinion, not as my attorney, but as Elizabeth's friend. Is this agreement fair to her?"

"Darcy, it's unethical of me to even speculate on Elizabeth's behalf." Darcy wouldn't give up until finally Geoff relented. "Don't ever even suggest I said this; however, it's very fair to both of you."

"Then show me where to sign." Darcy grabbed the pen. "Apparently there is only one way to ensure Elizabeth receives her due."

"And what would that be?"

Darcy smiled. "Never to divorce her."

"Brilliant," Geoff said sarcastically. "That will certainly show her who wears the pants in your relationship!"

Darcy signed his name on each page marked by a yellow "sign here" flag. "How's it going with Charlotte?"

"We are friends. Other than that, I'll not discuss our relationship with you."

Darcy could only laugh. "I see you are faithfully following the outline of my relationship with Elizabeth."

"Confirming that would be discussing our relationship, which I just professed I would not do. However, if you insist on interfering, I will have to go into an unpleasant snit and threaten to leave you behind while I go off to New York in the Darcy jet."

"That's not exactly how it happened," Darcy said dryly as he began to write his initials next to Elizabeth's on each and every page of the agreement. "Besides, we're already in New York. So, you won't tell me if you've reached the BFF stage yet?"

Geoff raised his eyebrows playfully as he used the same words Darcy did the previous November. "This discussion is now closed!"

"This discussion is now closed?!" Darcy said in mock agitation, proving Geoff was not the only one to remember their heated argument. "Just because you're Geoffrey 'Fucking' Fitzwilliam does not mean you can order me about like a servant."

"That's Viscount Geoffrey 'Fucking' Fitzwilliam to you!"

Geoff burst out in loud guffaws while Darcy tried to keep his countenance long enough to finishing executing both counterparts of the document. When the Darcy/Bennet Pre-nuptial Agreement was fully executed, the two gentlemen celebrated their superior understanding of each other with a brandy… or two.

CHAPTER 28
PLAYING GAMES

August 30th, The Celebrity Insider (U.K.)
Photo caption: An aerial view of Pemberley where Fitzwilliam Darcy and Elizabeth Bennet will host a lavish engagement party this Saturday.

"Lizzy!" Lydia shouted as she ran from the helicopter ahead of the rest of her family. "This is where you live? I thought the private plane and the helicopter were sick — but this! This is just *twisted*!"

Pulling herself from Lydia's embrace, Elizabeth said dryly, "Hello, Lydia. It's nice to see you too."

"Hello, Lizzybear," Tom Bennet hugged her next. His eyes swept across the broad expanse of the house. "I'm afraid this little cottage is much smaller than it appears on the Internet. Do you think you'll be happy here?"

"Yes, very, very happy." Elizabeth hugged him tightly and whispered in his ear, "Wait until you see the library." Then she turned to greet Isabella, Mary and Kit.

Tea had been set up in the library for Elizabeth's family who, after many hours of travel, were tired and famished. "This place is just lovely!" Isabella praised as she looked out at the fountain surrounded by the beautifully manicured front lawn. "How extensive are the grounds?"

"There are a little over six square kilometers of property within the gates. Near the house are the formal gardens, but not far from here you will find plenty of open meadows and woods." Elizabeth watched her grandmother's eyes widen with delight, knowing how the woman loved long walks as much as she did. "It's not the beach, but I believe there are enough winding paths to please even you, Gran."

"And what's the weather forecast for tomorrow?"

Elizabeth's smile lit up her face. "Perfect."

"Good!" Isabella leaned forward and kissed her cheek.

Turning to her sisters, Elizabeth apologized for the timing of the party since it interfered with their school schedules, but Mary and Lydia assured Elizabeth that they would not have missed it for the world. Tom, however, simply harrumphed as he selected a book from the shelves.

"I'm so nervous about meeting Darcy's family." Kit, who had been silenced in awe since catching her first glimpse of the Darcy jet many hours earlier, finally found her voice. "I've been trying to keep the titles straight. His Aunt and Uncle are Lord and Lady Matlock while his cousin Geoff is Viscount Fitzwilliam and his twin is The Honorable Colonel Fitzwilliam." Elizabeth was about to correct her sister when Kit began to panic. "That's not right! He isn't a Colonel anymore! What if I get confused and say the wrong name?" Kit then began a fit of nervous coughing.

Mary grabbed a nearby glass of water for her sister before saying solemnly, "In God's eyes, we are all the same."

"Mary," Isabella remarked firmly, "that hardly helps."

Elizabeth reassured her sister, "Just remember Lord and Lady Matlock. I'm sure the rest will want you to use their first names. After all, soon we will be family."

"Ha!" Lydia rolled her eyes. "It's nearly September and you and Mr. Eye Candy have yet to set another wedding date. The same thing happened to Bennifer I[40] and they never got married."

"*Darcy*!" Elizabeth growled in frustration. "His name is *Darcy*!"

"And exactly where is Mr. Eye Candy?" Tom Bennet said with a smirk as Lydia laughed at her father's tease.

"*Darcy* sends his apologies for not being able to greet you right away. He, Charles and Jane took the entire Gardiner family fishing this afternoon. Apparently, Darcy and little Clare went for an unexpected swim. He was heading

---

40 Tabloid nickname given to celebrities Ben Affleck and Jennifer Lopez who became engaged in November of 2002, but never married. Ben Affleck later married actress Jennifer Garner and their relationship was briefly referred to as Benifer II.

to the shower just as we received word you were about to arrive."

Isabella patted Elizabeth's knee affectionately. "So, are the children still as attached to your young man as they were at Netherfield?"

"Charles is gaining in popularity with all three of the boys, but Clare still follows Darcy around like a little shadow."

"Well, there's no accounting for the taste of a four-year-old," Tom said dryly as he selected a second book from the shelves. Elizabeth narrowed her eyes in warning, but Tom just smiled as he made his way over to a climate controlled display case. "What's this?"

"That's the Darcy family bible," Elizabeth explained. "In it are recorded all the births, deaths and marriages of the Darcy family for the last three hundred years."

While Mary's interest was piqued, Lydia looked at it and grimaced, "How boring! That thing looks like it belongs in a museum."

"Pemberley is a museum," Elizabeth explained. "The family occupies only one-fourth of the house. Although closed for this weekend, nearly 300,000 people tour the public rooms and gardens every year. Georgiana has offered to take you on a tour after you've had a chance to rest. I'm afraid I still have a tendency to become lost outside the family apartments, and there's still so much I have to do for tomorrow."

"I believe I will remain here," Tom said absently while scanning yet another shelf of books. Rather than tender a response the man was unlikely to notice, Elizabeth escorted the rest of her relations to their rooms.

DINNER WAS A GRAND EVENT, taking place in the formal dining room. Darcy sat proudly at the head of the table with Elizabeth at his right. As the current mistress of Pemberley, Georgiana sat at the opposite end with Jacob Carter nearby. Between them were the remaining 40 guests, all of whom would be staying at Pemberley throughout the weekend. An additional 160 guests were expected to attend the actual engagement party the following day.

Elizabeth was pleased to see her father in an animated discussion with Senator John Bertram and Lord Matlock while her grandmother was charming both of the politicians' wives. She watched closely as Geoff and Charlotte spoke quietly, their heads close together. Nearby Richard and Charles Hayter were chatting up the "Zandras" and Maria Lucas. Mary was involved in what appeared to be a deep discussion with Edmund Bertram and Henry and Catherine Tilney. Kit was staring with undisguised adoration at the dashing Christopher Brandon, whose arm was wrapped possessively about the shoulders of his wife Marianne, while discussing the current political climate in Venezuela with Margaret and John Thornton. Predictably, Lydia was flirting shamelessly with Tom Bertram and Frank Churchill, who were obviously amused by her antics.

"Dr. Bennet?" Elizabeth's attention was brought back to the man who was sitting at her right.

"Please excuse me, Dr. Knightley." As Lydia was too far down the table for Elizabeth to check her discreetly, she caught the eye of Jane, who, upon understanding Elizabeth's concern, turned her gaze to Madeline Gardiner, who looked to Isabella, who turned an effective glare at Lydia. Lydia's eyes flew open wide in indignation before she looked all the way back up the table to Elizabeth who simply gave her a stern nod of the head. With a huff, Lydia stuck out her bottom lip in a pout.

"I think you would make an excellent snooker player," George Knightley teased. "That was an incredible bank shot!"

Elizabeth was about to respond to Darcy's friend when a commotion at the door captured everyone's attention, announcing an unexpected guest.

Richard was the first to react, standing quickly, followed immediately by Elizabeth. Even though he was an expert at hiding his emotions, Richard struggled mightily to contain his anger.

Richard was not the only one displeased with the source of interruption. "How did she get in here without an invitation?" Darcy hissed at Fred Wentworth.

Elizabeth gave Darcy an apologetic look. "She has an invitation."

As Darcy stared at Elizabeth in confusion, she moved away from the table to greet Caroline Bingley. "Forgive us, Caroline. I did not receive your response to our invitation so we assumed you would not be joining us."

"I never need to R.S.V.P. to Darcy's invitations." Caroline voice was laced with venom as she looked down her nose toward Elizabeth. "He knows I will accept them with the greatest of pleasure."

The two women stood face to face. Elizabeth wore a simple but stunning red dress with matching pumps, her hair flowing down her back and Isabella's pearls gracing her ears and throat. In contrast Caroline wore a flowing, floor length, baby pink gown, her large matching wrap covering the bodice while revealing an over abundance of sparkling diamonds dripping from her ears and about her neck.

Isabella, knowing a scene-stealing diva when she saw one, was determined that the woman who just entered the dining room would receive no more of her notice and quietly resumed her conversation with Lady Matlock. The remainder of the room soon followed.

Giving a quick nod to the butler who walked briskly off, Elizabeth spoke graciously to Caroline, "Please take my seat. Another place setting will be brought immediately."

Running her gaze across the table, Caroline smiled broadly upon noting the location of the sole empty seat. She walked elegantly past the other guests without a look in their direction. Although she was keenly aware of the intense glare from Richard, she only had eyes for the man at the head of the table.

The gentlemen in the immediate vicinity of the empty chair rose as Caroline and Elizabeth approached. George Knightley held Caroline's chair as she sat, but before she could grace all assembled with her triumphant smile, she noted that a butler had brought a chair for Elizabeth and at Darcy's direction, placed it immediately next to his. Before Elizabeth could sit, Darcy announced to the table, "Excuse us for a moment please," and taking Elizabeth's hand, he led her from the room.

Satisfied with the apparent unhappiness between the lovebirds, Caroline waved to a butler to fill her wine glass.

Once they reached the privacy of the hall, Darcy had only one word for Elizabeth, "Explain."

Elizabeth took a moment to select her words carefully. "I've been looking at your mother's photo albums for the last several months and in nearly every candid photo of the children at Pemberley, Caroline is smack in the middle. Like it or not, she is just as much a part of your family as Charles, Richard, Geoff or Georgiana. It's been nearly ten months since you've had any contact with her. So, when Richard asked that I invite her —"

"Richard! I should have guessed!" Darcy turned momentarily from Elizabeth as he ran his hand through his hair. "Why didn't you tell me?"

"If Caroline had responded to tell me she was attending, I would have told you immediately. When she didn't respond, I assumed she wasn't coming, and therefore, there was nothing to tell. I should have known she would do something like this. Forgive me. I will find some way to get rid of her as soon as dinner is over."

Seeing the anguish in Elizabeth's face, Darcy gently pulled her into his embrace. "Of course I forgive you. Even geniuses make mistakes, although you must admit that this is a rather large one. A large, pink, blonde one." Elizabeth could only nod her head against his shoulder in agreement. "What made you think she would be willing to behave...appropriately?"

"Jane told me that Charles has severely limited his contact with Caroline since he confirmed our engagement to her. She's practically cut off from all her family, and I thought that would be enough to make her wish to reconcile. I enclosed a personal note with her invitation in which I expressed my desire to heal the extended family you both knew as children. I would have met her privately first. If she was not cooperative, I would have sent her away without causing a scene; but I did hope —"

"Ah, Lizzy, Caroline is beyond hope," Darcy sighed as his hands moved slowly up and down the soft silk of her dress. "I think Jane must be rubbing off on you," he teased as a hand moved to her buttocks.

"Oh!" Elizabeth exclaimed as he pinched the firm flesh beneath his fingers before bestowing on her a mind-blowing kiss. "Oh, Baby, I've missed you. Georgiana and I had a blast in Paris, but I wish you could have gone with us."

"I had too much work to do, and you deserved a break from all the stress of planning this weekend." He kissed her again. "And I'm sure I missed you far more than you missed me."

Between kisses, their disagreement about who missed whom more continued until Richard's voice interrupted them. "Darcy, this is not what I expected."

Darcy refused to break away quickly from Elizabeth simply because of Richard's interruption. It felt like ages since he had held her, so he indulged himself for a second or two more. When he pulled back, he caught the fire in Elizabeth's eyes and cursed the interruption before responding, "What exactly did you expect?"

"A situation dire enough to require my informing you that Caroline being here is my doing."

"Then you can help me get rid of her. Please wait for me in the front sitting room."

As Darcy and Elizabeth re-entered the dining room, they could hear Caroline remarking to the Knightleys and Fred Wentworth, "I mean, really! Colored diamonds just scream 'new money.' Every starlet in Hollywood has one. Nothing says sophistication and taste like a brilliant white stone."

Darcy made a show of kissing Elizabeth's left hand before assisting her with her chair. He then stepped back to whisper something to a nearby servant before turning a brilliant smile to Caroline. "Might I have a word with you in private?"

Caroline eyed him suspiciously. While there was nothing she wanted more than to have a private word with Darcy, she could not have missed the tender show as he returned Elizabeth to the table, and his lips looked rather…glossy. However, perhaps her superior fashion sense as well as the reminder of Elizabeth's tasteless choice of engagement ring had brought Darcy to his senses. Just to make sure he and everyone else understood which woman was by far best suited to be mistress of Pemberley, Caroline rose from her seat and allowed her wrap to fall to display the latest and most expensive in *haute couture*.

A collective gasp went up from all seated as the top of Caroline's dress consisted of nothing more than a whisper of the sheerest of pink silk, allowing her breasts to be clearly seen through it. Charles Bingley practically choked on his water while a chorus of whispers arose from the Bennet women, "Bless her heart!"[41]

"Valentino strikes again!"[42] Charlotte said uncharitably to Geoff, who could not contain his smirk.

After Darcy and Caroline left the dining room, Elizabeth resumed her earlier discussion with those seated nearby. A butler discreetly removed Caroline's chair and place setting before carrying her pink wrap from the room. In less than a minute, Darcy returned alone, spoke again to the butler and rejoined his guests. Once more, the butler set to work, this time quietly removing Richard's place at the table.

Soon the incident with Caroline was forgotten by the guests and the many courses came and went without further incident. As the champagne was poured before dessert, Tom Bennet stood to make a toast. "To my Lizzy: a beautiful, intelligent, talented woman who has always made me very proud and has managed somehow to get me out of my library and onto English soil. Not an easy feat, I assure you." Tom nodded to acknowledge the polite laughter about him. "And to Darcy, a man…with an excellent library. Congratulations on your engagement!"

Not rising to the bait of Tom's thinly veiled slight, Darcy reminded himself

---

41 An expression used by women of the South Eastern United States. The expression has many meanings.
42 Valentino designed the infamous see-through dress worn by Uma Thurman at the Swarovski Fashion Rocks Event in September 2007.

the man was simply hoping for an amusing reaction. After several months of dealing with Tom's eccentric brand of teasing, Darcy had learned how to respond in kind. He stood and raised his glass. "To Thomas Bennet, without whom there would be no Elizabeth. But before I thank you, sir, I feel it is incumbent upon me to remind you that your Lizzy, is now *my* Lizzy."

RICHARD FITZWILLIAM WAVED TO THE security guards as he drove through the large iron gates of Pemberley toward the Inn at Lambton where he had reserved a suite for Caroline. "Smile for the photographers," he said with obvious sarcasm. "You wouldn't want to appear in the papers tomorrow with that scowl on your face."

Caroline's face immediately brightened as she smiled toward the flash of cameras lining the street. Once they were past the paparazzi, the smile disappeared. "I can't believe I've been thrown out of Pemberley!" she said angrily, "I have more right to be there then that…that…that…"

"Elizabeth!" Richard suddenly shouted, clearly past his tolerance level, "Her name is Elizabeth, and you lost any privileges you may have possessed at Pemberley when you chose to insult her tonight. Damn, Caroline, what were you thinking wearing that dress?"

Caroline pulled her wrap more tightly to her chest. "It's a designer original, made exclusively for me! I'd bet the dress that…that…" at Richard's warning glance she rephrased her statement, "…*Elizabeth* wore was designed by that hack, Charlotte Lucas."

"Elizabeth's dress was appropriate for the occasion. Your *designer original* may be considered all the rage at a red carpet event, but in Pemberley's dining room, it was nothing short of vulgar. Aunt Anne is probably rolling over in her grave!"

At the mention of Anne Darcy, Caroline's scathing retort died on her lips. She hadn't thought that far when planning her little disruption of Darcy's celebration, and the idea that her behavior would have appalled the one woman she idolized as a child was sobering.

They rode in silence for several minutes until Caroline whispered, "Why can't he love me?"

"Chasing Darcy back and forth across the Atlantic and creating ridiculous spectacles to gain his attention are not ways to convince him to love you."

Caroline started to sniffle. "Then what should I do?"

"Nothing! Darcy's madly in love with Elizabeth. If you cared about him as much as you claim to, you'd be happy for him."

As Richard finished his sentence, Caroline began to cry. "You don't understand! I have to marry Darcy!"

Avoiding the front entrance, Richard parked the car in the side lot of the Inn. "Why Darcy? Why not Geoff? He's a bloody viscount for Christ's sake."

"Princess Katrina," Caroline sniffled while taking Richard's offered handkerchief.

Richard rolled his eyes. "That explains nothing!"

"When I was at the academy in Switzerland, Katrina wouldn't acknowledge my existence because I came from new money. When she discovered my connection to Darcy, she was impressed and suddenly *I* was important. When pictures of Darcy with other women began appearing in the tabloids, my popularity was threatened. So, I told Katrina that Darcy and I had an agreement. He was welcome to sow his wild oats, but when he was ready to settle down, he would marry *me*."

Richard was unsympathetic. "Why would any of that matter now? You've been back for more than three years."

"Katrina calls me now and then. Once the rumors surrounding Darcy's engagement to that...that...*Elizabeth* began to surface, her taunting intensified."

"Princess Katrina is twenty-six and on her third husband," Richard growled in frustration. "Why would you care what she thinks? Look what you've done! You've alienated yourself from everyone you care about, including your brother!"

"You still care about me, don't you?" Caroline peeked out from his handkerchief as she dried her eyes. She then reached over to touch Richard's hand. "I still remember that you were my first kiss and later, my first..."

Richard's eyes flashed dangerously as he pushed her hand away. "Don't play games with me! You made it quite clear when you came home from Switzerland that I was nothing more than the second son. Suddenly, being born twelve minutes late and without a title put me beyond your notice."

He got out of the car and then opened the passenger door for Caroline. After checking her in at the lobby desk, Richard escorted her to the door of her suite.

"Your bags will be along any moment." His voice was ice cold as he reminded her, "I'll have someone watching you until you leave Lambton. You are no longer permitted anywhere within the boundaries of Pemberley, ever. This was your last chance to make nice, Caroline, and you blew it!"

She began to cry again, only this time Caroline threw her arms around Richard's neck as she sobbed violently against his chest. "You'll speak to Darcy for me? He always listens to you."

"Stupid girl!" Richard was fed up with her manipulations and pushed Caroline back against the door and kissed her hard, his tongue pushing through her surprised lips while his hand snaked under her wrap to caress one barely concealed breast. After the initial shock, Caroline reluctantly melted into his long remembered embrace and moaned.

After a few minutes of heated kisses, he whispered against her lips, "Do you miss me, Caroline?" When she did not answer, he pulled his lips just barely out of her reach before demanding, "Do you miss me?"

"Yes, damn it!" she spat before grabbing his face to kiss him again. Desperately her hands caressed his neck before burying into his hair. With the familiarity of their passionate past, Richard kissed the spot beneath her ear that drove Caroline crazy while his fingers continued to tease her breasts.

Richard pulled back again as he felt her body arch hungrily against his. "Do you want me?"

"Oh, God help me, yes!" Caroline cried as she reached one hand down to grasp his buttocks and pull his erection tightly against her.

"Good!" Richard pulled himself abruptly from their embrace, turned and was gone, leaving a confused and thoroughly aroused Caroline with a great deal to think about.

CHAPTER 29
THE ENGAGEMENT PARTY

Darcy slowly drifted from the depths of sleep, his head slightly pounding, reminding him of the too many brandies he indulged in the night before. After dinner, the men said good night to the ladies to begin a long evening of cards, billiards and cigars. It was all going along swimmingly when, at about midnight, he was deep into a game of poker.

"I'll raise you ten, Reverend," Darcy said to Edward Ferrars as he threw his chips into the center of the table.

"Sounds good to me. What about you, Doctor?" Ferrars asked of George Knightley as he added his chips to the kitty.

Knightley smiled, taking a deep draw on his cigar. "I'm in." He then looked to Christopher Brandon. "How about you, Counselor?"

"I'll see you and raise ten more," Brandon relaxed further back into his chair as the chips clinked in from all those before him, meeting the increased stakes. "It's your turn, Mr. Secretary."

John Thornton looked at his cards for a moment and then took twenty pounds worth of chips and tossed them into the kitty. He then looked to Fred Wentworth. "Captain?"

"I'm out!" Wentworth said in disappointment as he tossed his cards away.

At the time, Darcy thought it was amusing when he turned to Wentworth, pointed his cigar at him and said, "What's wrong, *Pumpkin*? Too rich for your blood?" In the cold, hard light of day, he would blame his actions squarely on the brandy.

"*Pumpkin*!" exclaimed Brandon as Darcy raised another ten. "How could I forget? Wentworth, your bachelor party will forever live in my memory as 'The Night of the Pumpkin!' Darcy, you were in rare form that night!"

Ferrars took a long drink from his snifter before saying to his brother-in-law, "You've little room to boast, *Teddy Bear*!"

"How do you know that?" sputtered Brandon.

"We married sisters. There are no secrets between sisters, or between Eleanor and me."

"Nor between me and Marianne, *Sweet Lips*!"

The table broke out in laughter causing piles of chips to topple. Thornton cleared his throat. "Shall we get back to the game?"

"Come on, Thornton!" Brandon said defensively as he threw another ten pounds into the kitty. "Everyone in the Home Office knows Maggie calls you *Peaches*!"

"*Peaches*!" Knightley chuckled enthusiastically as he threw in his cards. "That's even worse than *Pumpkin*."

Thornton narrowed his eyes at Knightley as he met Brandon's raise. "You should think twice before crossing the head of British Intelligence. I read lips, *Love Monkey*!"

After recovering from a bout of hard laughter, Darcy threw in his ten pounds, "I'll see you and call." Darcy laid down his cards, showing a straight of hearts, queen high. Okay, Reverend, what do you have?"

"You can't call yet," Ferrars protested.

Darcy shrugged his shoulders. "You gentlemen are welcome to continue to pour money into the kitty if you wish, but I'm sure none of you can beat my hand, and it's Bingley's and my turn to be trounced by Elizabeth's father and uncle at the pool table. So, *Sweet Lips*, if you don't mind..."

Ferrars gave Darcy a quick grimace before laying down his cards, "Two pair, ace high."

"Too bad. Now the *Love Monkey* is out, so how about you, *Teddy Bear*?"

Brandon visibly bristled as he lay down a full house.

"Oh, so sorry, mate; that's not good enough," Darcy said in mock sympathy. "Well, *Peaches*, since *Pumpkin* here threw in, you're the only person standing between me and that rather large kitty in the middle of the table."

Thornton just folded his cards without showing them and tossed them away. Darcy smiled triumphantly as he reached in to grab the chips.

"Congratulations, *Baby!*"

Darcy froze, his hands still surrounding his winnings on the table. He couldn't believe what Wentworth had just revealed as he knew that Elizabeth never called him *Baby* except when they were alone, and she would never confide that bit of information to anyone, not even Jane.

Slapping Darcy on the shoulder Wentworth explained, "I had almost given up; however, the public rooms in Pemberley have security cameras, and while there is no sound, *your* Lizzy has perfect enunciation." The laughter started deep within Wentworth's chest and soon poured loudly throughout the room. "Revenge is sweet, *Baby!*"

"BABY!" The name seemed to echo off the walls of the game room along with the raucous laughter of everyone within. Wentworth seemed most pleased with his discovery, and in the same manner Darcy had at his bachelor party, proceeded to use the name over and over when addressing Darcy throughout the remainder of the night.

After another brandy, Darcy was able to take the teasing good-naturedly. After all, what was *Baby* compared to *Love Monkey?*

Now the daylight was filtering through his eyelids, and the warm scent of orange blossom and ginger, as well as the silky skin of his favorite pillow, reminded him exactly why he enjoyed waking up in the morning, even with a headache.

Lizzy! His hand moved up her side before changing course to caress the breast in front of his face. As he kissed the tender skin beneath him, he felt her fingers glide into his hair.

"Wait a minute." Darcy lifted his head to look into the fine eyes he loved most of all. The gold heart of her necklace stuck to the side of his face. "You're not supposed to be here."

"I don't sleep well without you, and Mrs. Reynolds snores like a lumberjack," Elizabeth whined with a smile as she pulled the heart from his skin. "You smell like cigars. Did you have a good time last night?"

"I did." He winced as his head reminded him of exactly how good that time was.

Elizabeth laughed at his suffering. "Will you be all right by eleven?"

"A few ibuprofen and I'll be fine. I don't need to ask you about your night. Charles and I snuck up to see how your little pajama party was going. What is it about women and ABBA?"

Her warm laughter bubbled from her chest. "So what did you see?"

"You, my Lizzy, are … without a doubt … *The Dancing Queen*!"

"You're too kind," Elizabeth laughed again as she bent her neck to kiss his forehead. "Last night we received a lovely gift from Jane, Charlotte and Georgiana?"

"The invitations said 'no gifts,'" Darcy grumbled as he eyed her breasts with undisclosed longing.

"Actually the gift was for me, but I suspect you'll like it very much. It came from a little shop called *Lady Racy Stacy's*."

Darcy's eyebrows rose. "Is that the place on Bond Street between Twirling Way and Tasselton Lane?"

"The very one."

A low groan came from deep within Darcy's throat. "It is not wise to torture a man who hasn't had sex in a month."

"It's only been five days…" Elizabeth took a quick glance at the clock before saying wistfully, "…two hours and twenty-seven minutes."

"It feels like a year since you took your beautiful body off to Paris."

"If I recall correctly — and I do — the shopping excursion was your idea."

"A rare moment of utter stupidity on my part. Since you returned, I haven't had more than a moment alone with you, until now…" he sighed heavily, "when I find you naked in my bed."

"Baby, I'm not completely naked," Elizabeth defended with a naughty glint in her eye. "I'm still wearing black silk panties."

Darcy groaned again in frustration. "I believe the Geneva Convention contains several articles banning such inhumane treatment. Get out of my bed, woman! Now!"

Laughing, Elizabeth scurried out of bed, quickly donning her pajamas. "I'll see you at eleven. If you have any trouble recognizing me, I'll be the woman in the white dress."

THE PARTY'S NOT UNTIL ONE O'CLOCK!" Lydia whined as Jane helped her zip up the back of her floral print dress. "Why do we have to be ready so early?"

"Lizzy's having pictures of the family taken," Mary said as she carefully placed the matching hat on Lydia's head. "There! You look lovely, refined, and very sophisticated."

Lydia looked into the large, full-length mirror at the reflection of the four sisters. "Lord, how droll! We look like we're off to watch the races at Ascot! Can I have my eyeliner back?"

"NO!" Jane, Mary and Kit called out in unison.

"Can I at least have my cell phone?"

"NO!"

Across the hall, Elizabeth was looking at her own reflection. She marveled that the woman staring back at her looked exactly like the woman she was before she met Darcy. Inside she felt warmer, calmer, lighter than she ever felt possible, and it seemed strange that these profound changes did not manifest themselves physically.

Her thoughts were interrupted by a soft knock on the door. "Come in."

The door opened slowly, almost reluctantly. before Tom Bennet's face peered around the corner. "I was sent with two missions," he said quietly as he entered the room. "The second was to bring you downstairs, but the first was to give you this." In his hand was a large, flat jewelry box.

Elizabeth's eyebrow rose in question. "Oh, it's not from me," Tom qualified. "It's from your future husband. I suspect it's something outrageously expensive to mark the occasion."

"I'm sure it is," Elizabeth said without thought, for her heart suddenly began beating rapidly as she slowly pulled up the lid.

Inside was a diamond necklace, and set in its center was a large, radiant cut blue diamond. Written on the card inside was:

My BFF Lizzy,

Here is the remainder of your twenty carats.

Love,
Your BFF Fitzwilliam

"Damn!" Tom whispered in awe as the morning sunlight caught the stones. Carefully he pulled the necklace from the box as Elizabeth removed the gold heart from around her neck, quickly looping the chain over her hand repeatedly until it formed a bracelet. Then standing before the mirror, she watched her reflection as Tom stood behind her and carefully placed the sparkling diamonds around her neck.

They were both speechless until their eyes met in the mirror. "He deserves you, Lizzybear."

"He does, but not because of this." Elizabeth gently caressed the stones below her throat.

An overwhelming sadness came to Tom's eyes as he looked at his daughter and marveled at how different she appeared from a year ago. She looked warmer, calmer, and lighter than he had ever hoped to see her, and he had only one man to thank for that. "I know, sweetheart."

ED GARDINER AND HIS THREE boys looked on as the women were gathered outside the front entrance to the house. Elizabeth's small group of close friends, all her sisters, Isabella, Madeline and Clare Gardiner, Anne de Bourgh, Lady Matlock, Georgiana and Mrs. Reynolds were posed before the house as Emma Woodhouse, photographer to London's elite and wife of George Knightley, captured the moment on film. They were interrupted when the doors opened and Elizabeth emerged on her father's arm.

Charlotte had outdone herself. The creation in white silk was an off the shoulder gown, fitted to Elizabeth's curves with the look of 1940's Hollywood. A comb of white diamonds held her dark hair in a simple shining twist as the blue diamond necklace graced her throat. Emma snapped a few candid shots as Elizabeth appeared to float down the staircase.

The group was speechless as the implications of Elizabeth's dress became clear. "Oh, Elizabeth!" Lady Matlock cried out as tears of joy slipped down her cheeks. "I've won the bet!"

The Bennet sisters were fighting back tears of their own, but fortunately, Tom Bennet had thought to bring handkerchiefs for all. Madeline and Clare kissed Elizabeth's cheek before Georgiana took her hand and led her toward the driveway.

Reminding them of the need to escape quickly before the house full of guests with picture phones became aware of their activities, Mrs. Reynolds hurried them all toward a waiting caravan of Range Rovers.

"Where are we going?" Clare called from her booster seat as the vehicles left the main road to drive across the grounds.

"I'm not exactly sure." Madeline looked to the other women that shared the second Rover in the caravan as if they could answer her daughter's question.

Lydia rolled her eyes as she careened her neck to look out the windows, "Isn't it obvious!" Turning to Georgiana she snorted, "What a good joke! Did you know about this?"

"I did. I hope you aren't angry," Georgiana said to the other women in the Rover. "This was the only way to keep the press away. If they knew the wedding was today, photographers would be scaling the fences to get pictures, and Pemberley Church is outside the grounds. So nearly everyone was kept in the dark."

Soon the convoy of vehicles was once again driving on paved road and, within a few minutes, was exiting Pemberley through the gate used only by maintenance vehicles. From there it was only a few miles to Pemberley Church. They arrived precisely at eleven o'clock.

AT PRECISELY ONE O'CLOCK, 200 guests were milling about under a large tent that shielded them from the brilliant sun. The champagne flowed like water as a string quartet played Mozart softly in the background. Family, friends and business associates greeted each other and made small talk as they waited for their hosts to appear.

The Earl of Matlock walked to the center of a small stage situated at the front of the tent and, taking a microphone, cleared his throat. As the room quieted, he asked everyone kindly to take their seats. Waiters dressed in black and white removed sheets of cloth from the sidewalls of the tent, revealing large television monitors. "Ladies and gentleman, I ask you to kindly direct your attention to the monitors placed along the periphery of the tent." Immediately the monitors blinked on, showing the words:

Pemberley Church
Saturday, September 1st 20__
11:00 a.m.

Soft guitar music filtered though large speakers, soon followed by a clear, sweet voice.

And I love you so,
The people ask me how,
How I lived till now,
I tell them I don't know …

Georgiana appeared on the screen, Jacob Carter accompanying her on the guitar. As the camera pulled back, the interior of Pemberley Church came into view. The Reverend Edward Ferrars stood before the altar and standing to his left was Darcy, in a light grey Armani suit, crisp white shirt and dark blue tie. In his lapel he wore a boutonniere containing a pale yellow rose.[43] By his side stood both Geoff and Richard.

There was an audible gasp from the guests as they realized what they were witnessing. Most were pleasantly surprised while a few were annoyed that they were not invited to the actual ceremony; however, all were amazed by the novelty of the entire proceeding.

The camera now showed the aisle trimmed in garlands of yellow and red roses as well as the few guests sitting on either side of it. The doors to the church opened and Jane entered, walking gracefully toward the altar in a deep blue dress, carrying a bouquet of yellow and red roses tied with a blue ribbon. When she reached the altar, Jane gave a surprised Darcy a kiss on the cheek before taking her place to the right of the Reverend.

All eyes in the church turned toward the doors as they opened once more to reveal Elizabeth and her father. The crowd in the tent sighed "Ahhh" in unison at the vision she presented. Tom looked at his favorite child with a mixture of pride and sadness, but Elizabeth's eyes were fixed squarely on the man who stood waiting for her at the altar, and she beamed. She wore no veil but carried a large bouquet of pale yellow roses.

And yet, I know how loveless life can be,
The shadows follow me, and the night won't set me free.
But I won't let the evening get me down,
As long as you're around me...[44]

They walked slowly down the aisle of the chapel and when they at last reached the altar, Elizabeth pulled her hand from her father's arm, kissed his cheek, and then walked the last few steps alone to Darcy before giving him her hand.

Their eyes were locked as Darcy raised her hand to his lips and kissed it before reverently tucking it into his arm. They both turned to face Reverend Ferrars as the last strains of Georgiana's song echoed throughout the church.

---

43 Yellow roses signify friendship — red roses, love.
44 "And I Love You So," Music and Lyrics by Don by Don McLean, 1972.

The ceremony was brief. The Reverend gave a small sermon on the importance of friendship and conquering fear with love. The vows spoken were traditional, rings were exchanged, and when Darcy and Elizabeth were finally pronounced husband and wife, their first kiss was too long to be thought chaste and yet too brief to be considered vulgar. Everything was perfect. When they turned to face their friends and family and were pronounced Mr. and Mrs. Fitzwilliam Darcy, the guests beneath the tent erupted in cheers and loud applause.

As the applause died down, the Earl of Matlock once again stood on the dais. "Ladies and Gentlemen... Mr. and Mrs. Fitzwilliam Darcy."

All stood as Darcy and Elizabeth entered the tent, their faces glowing in happiness. Darcy apologized to their guests for the elaborate ruse but offered little by way of explanation. He and Elizabeth then circulated throughout the tent to receive the congratulations of their guests until the first course of an elaborate lunch was served.

The string quartet played throughout the meal, but once the cake was cut, the speeches began. Some were warm and sentimental (Jane and Isabella's), some were dryly humorous (Lord Matlock, Tom and Richard's) and one in particular was rather bawdy (Geoff's). When the final toast was drunk, the quartet retired, and a disc jockey took over.

The celebration lasted into the evening when a lighter dinner was served to the many guests who remained. By nine o'clock, the area beneath the tent resembled a minor disaster area, but the disc jockey played on as Darcy and Elizabeth's closest friends and family continued to celebrate on the dance floor.

Darcy had never danced so much nor enjoyed a party so much in his life, but when Geoff took off his tie and wore it on his head like a sweat band while he and Bingley were belting out "Paradise by the Dashboard Light",[45] Darcy knew it was time to get his new wife out of there. "Lizzy, let's sneak out, now!"

"But Richard's asked me to dance the next one," Elizabeth laughed, her hair adorably disheveled. He knew she wasn't inebriated — Elizabeth had drunk only water most of the day — but he had been to enough clubs with her to know that a dance floor was one of the few things with which his fine physique had trouble competing.

Richard approached at that moment to claim Elizabeth. "Sorry, cousin," he said with no remorse and a cheeky smile as the drum beat at the beginning of

---

45 "Paradise by the Dashboard Light" words and music by Jim Steinman, performed by Meat Loaf.

Love Shack[46] vibrated from the nearby speakers. Darcy glanced up in alarm at the device the disc jockey was plugging into his equipment. It was Elizabeth's iPod.

Darcy knew Elizabeth's "dance" playlist and remembered that after *Love Shack* would come Meredith Brooks' *Bitch*,[47] My Chemical Romance's *I'm Not OK*[48] followed immediately by every hit ABBA ever released. If he wanted to make love to his bride before 2 a.m., he needed to do something now. Fortunately, he had planned for just such a contingency.

"Mrs. R!" Darcy found his housekeeper dancing with both Tom Bertram and Frank Churchill. "Please, now!"

Darcy followed Mrs. Reynolds out of the tent and in less than ten minutes, he returned, looking surprisingly *fresh*. Stepping onto the dance floor, he grasped Elizabeth's arm and turning her towards him, wrapped his hands about her waist as they danced. She raised her eyebrows teasingly, giving him a come-hither flash of her eyes, but Darcy was finished with dance floor foreplay.

He pulled Elizabeth close and as soon as her hand rested on his shoulder, the effect was instantaneous. "You changed your shirt," she said as the teasing light in her voice became smoky. From there it took little effort to bring her closer so that she could nuzzle his neck. He could feel her chest rise as she inhaled deeply. "You took a shower too," she moaned softly into his ear.

"I was feeling a bit sweaty after dancing all day, and Mrs. Reynolds was kind enough to press a clean shirt," Darcy said innocently as he felt her inhale again. "Now I'm ready to dance all night."

"Oh, Baby, let's sneak out now!"

THE DOORS TO THE ELEVATOR opened, revealing a now common sight: Darcy and Elizabeth snogging madly. With her wedding dress hiked up to her hips and her legs wrapped firmly around Darcy's waist, he carried her down the hallway with well-practiced skill. The longer than usual journey did not register in Elizabeth's head, for she was too enthralled with the scent of soap and starch, and the feel of his freshly shaved skin against her face to notice. Neither batted an eye when they heard Mrs. Reynolds' soft, "Allow me," before she opened the bedroom door, and the elder woman took no offense at their failure to issue their heartfelt thanks.

---

46 "Love Shack", words and music by the B52's.
47 "Bitch", words and music by Meredith Brooks
48 "I'm Not OK" words and music by Gerard Way

It wasn't until Darcy stood Elizabeth before him to pull down the zipper of her dress that she became aware of their surroundings. "This isn't our room."

"Yes, it is," he said as her dress fell to the floor. "This is why I sent you off to —" His hands skimmed down over her bare back then suddenly froze. "Oh God, Lizzy, what are you wearing?"

"Shoes," she said simply as she continued to kiss his neck and dispatch the buttons of his shirt. "...and my necklace, of course."

Pulling back, he held her at arm's length for visual confirmation. Sure enough, his bride was completely naked except for the diamond necklace and a pair of strappy white heels. His thoughts were written on his face. The idea that she had gone all day without wearing knickers beneath her wedding dress was clearly playing havoc with his already slim self-control. Elizabeth did not suppress her deep throaty chuckle at his expression of surprise mingled with unbridled desire.

"At the church?" he somehow managed to choke out.

"Well, it did seem disrespectful to enter a house of God in full commando mode, but as soon as we returned to Pemberley I got rid of my panties at the first opportunity."

"Why didn't you tell me?" he groaned.

"You have no idea what a turn on it's been, anticipating this very moment when you would find out. Oh, Baby," her eyes boldly dropped to the prominent tent in the front of his trousers, "you never disappoint."

Elizabeth closed the distance between them, feeling his body shudder when her hands slid beneath the crisp cotton of his shirt. As soon as her lips brushed his chest, Darcy's control shattered.

Their mouths collided, hungry, famished — no, starving — for one another. With the last vestiges of conscious thought, Darcy guided her toward the large glass doors that looked out over the east garden.

Surrounded in an erotic cloud of soap and starch, Elizabeth devoured the flesh beneath Darcy's shirt, working her way slowly and methodically down every millimeter of his chest. So absorbed was she in her task, that she didn't notice the loud boom in the background.

"Lizzy," he spoke with great difficulty between heavy breaths as she gracefully fell to her knees before him, "fireworks."

"If you think you're seeing fireworks now," she purred as his trousers glided down his legs to the floor, "I promise that soon you'll see nothing but stars."

At that moment, Darcy gave up all pretense of caring about the £100,000 fireworks display currently going off over the pond, for Elizabeth was rubbing her face in a very feline-like manner against his cotton-covered erection. "Oh, Baby, you starched your shorts too!"

It was only a few days after they first became intimate that Darcy discovered the power the simple scents of soap and laundry starch held over his Elizabeth, but as his boxers slipped over his hips and Elizabeth's lovely, full lips touched his cock, he could not help but wonder who at that moment held power over whom.

In these months of blissful intimacy, Elizabeth boldly followed his example, exploring every pore of skin, searching for every place on the body where touch and taste would cause a pleasurable sensation. She mentally cataloged the location and intensity of each reaction until she could use her knowledge to create an ebb and flow of excitement within his body. However, this was not just the cold execution of scientific theory, for each hypothesis was demonstrated with a level of intense tenderness — an expression of indescribable passion that frequently threatened to choke Darcy with overwhelming emotion.

Slamming his palms against the cool glass of the door, Darcy hoped for enough purchase to allow him to continue standing, for Elizabeth was demonstrating that, after nine months of constant practice, she had become a true proficient. The warm moist sheath of her mouth and the silken caresses of her tongue combined with the perfect intensity of suction and motion to create a riot of limb-weakening sensation. *God Bless the scientific method!*

As the fireworks thundered outside the window, wave upon wave of intense pressure built within his groin. He would not last long, but somehow he understood that was Elizabeth's plan. Their need for one another was too great for long, slow, reverent expressions of love. There would be time enough for that later this night. Still, he wanted the exquisite pleasure to last a few more moments so he kept his eyes diverted to the ceiling. Nothing would send him over the edge faster than a glimpse of the scene below his waist, and with all her physical attractions, nothing was more erotic then Elizabeth's eyes when they were filled with unbridled lust.

As a cluster of exploding bursts of color lit the night sky, Darcy's breath hitched violently for Elizabeth's fingers played a strangely familiar tune upon his testicles. His head jerked down in response and once his eyes took in the vision before him, he was lost. His moans that had filled the room over the last several minutes, immediately ceased. His eyes squeezed shut, his mouth flew open wide and with little more than a hiss of air escaping his lungs, Darcy's entire body tensed as he burst into ecstasy. As he gasped for breath, his orgasm continued; Elizabeth held tight, refusing to cease this most intimate of kisses until her new husband collapsed, spent before her.

They lay together against the glass. "I love you," Elizabeth whispered as Darcy rested his head against her shoulder.

"Me too," was all he could mutter as his embrace tightened about her waist. He could feel the intense fire radiating from her fully aroused body. "I'll need a moment to recover," he panted, "then I intend to reciprocate fully."

"You mean I shall see stars?" she teased.

"Entire galaxies, my Lizzy."

They both turned toward the window as the finale of the fireworks display turned night into day in a dazzling array of noise, color and white fire. "Fireworks!" Elizabeth exclaimed in childlike wonder, noticing them for the first time. "How thoughtful."

"I'll let you in on a little secret," he whispered. At the raised brow he received in response, he continued, "It was Charles' idea. You see, right before the finale, he intended to propose to your sister."

The light of happiness in Elizabeth's smile outshone any fireworks display. "That's wonderful! I'll let you in on another secret. This morning as I was returning to my room, I caught Geoff slinking out of Charlotte's."

"It appears Geoff has moved on to the 'shagging her rotten for the rest of his life' stage." At Elizabeth's questioning look, he laughed. "Now I want you to tell me another secret."

"I don't have any other secrets," she wrinkled her nose in thought, trying to guess his meaning. "That's against the rules."

Darcy took his index finger and smoothed the worried skin at the bridge of her nose. "I want you to tell me where you learned about that thing you did to me." As the wrinkles returned to her nose, he took her hand, and to demonstrate the nature of his question, placed her fingers around, up and between his testicles in imitation of her earlier actions. "Or did you simply come up with that little maneuver in that magnificent brain of yours?"

"Oh, that? It's something I saw years ago. I can't believe I remembered it. It just popped into my head."

His breathing having returned to normal, Darcy gently pushed her back against the rug. "That doesn't answer my question," he persisted. "Where do virgins acquire such knowledge?" As he trailed kisses down her neck, Elizabeth tried to divert his attention away from the subject at hand by removing his shirt. She was utterly unsuccessful. Taking both her hands, he pinned them over her head. "You're evading the question. So, now you have me even more curious."

Elizabeth blushed. "My second year at Longbourn, one of my roommates was getting married. To celebrate, there was a party just for the girls she knew at school during which they played a little DVD called, *Lucy Licks Leeds*."

"Liverpool," Darcy corrected, "It was *Lucy Licks Liverpool*." At Elizabeth's wide-eyed response, he nearly blushed himself upon realizing what he had just disclosed.

"I don't know what you saw, but I saw *Lucy Licks Leeds*, which was followed immediately by *Lucy Licks London*. I will admit that by the second film I was bored and left. If you've seen Lucy perform one blow job, you've seen them all."

"Perhaps Lucy has a series of films where she licks every man in every town in England that begins with the letter *L*."

Elizabeth smirked. "Are you complaining about the lesson Lucy taught me."

"Oh, not at all. In fact, I may just have to send Lucy flowers to express my gratitude. I just find it amusing to imagine my little Lizzy watching a porno."

"There are many things you have yet to learn about me."

"Well then, let's go exploring." Soon Elizabeth not only saw stars, but as promised, galaxies.

It wasn't until the next morning that Elizabeth noticed the changes Darcy had made to the master suite, which until the week before had remained unoccupied and exactly as his parents had left it.

That afternoon, after bidding farewell to friends and family, Darcy and Elizabeth flew to his family's villa on the Costa del Sol for a month-long honeymoon. It was the first time he had been to the villa since his parents' deaths, and as he and Elizabeth stood on the terrace overlooking the Mediterranean, Darcy felt as if he had finally laid to rest every ghost that had haunted him for the last eight years.

Two days later in Lancaster, aging porn star, Miss Lucy Steele, received an anonymous bouquet of roses.

Later that day, half a world away, Billy Ray Collins passed through the outer gates of Hunsford State Penitentiary and into the waiting arms of Frannie Bennet.

CHAPTER 30
BABY BLUE

December 15th, The London Times
Photo caption: The great house at Pemberley is decorated in preparation for the annual Anne Darcy Memorial Christmas Concert by the Derbyshire Coral Society. Tickets for the Christmas Eve event are sold out.

Fitzwilliam Darcy prepared to exit the Augusta A109 helicopter that had landed effortless on Pemberley's west lawn. He methodically unbuckled the safety belt, and gathering his PDA and iPod, he placed them into the right pocket of his Valentino wool overcoat before slipping his laptop into his Gucci briefcase. He carried out this routine in the same precise order three days a week as he returned from his commute to London — except for today. Instead of walking directly into the house, he took a detour through the garage and approached a metallic blue Jaguar XJ Custom Hybrid sedan. He reached out his hand to feel its bonnet, and his usual expression of cold indifference turned into a definitive scowl.

It took him five seconds, instead of the usual two, to enter the security code for the house. His briefcase, along with his overcoat, was tossed on a bench inside the door instead of being carried directly to his study, and he by-passed the kitchen without stopping for his customary bottle of water. To the un-trained eye, these little glitches in Darcy's routine would mean little; however, Fitzwilliam Darcy was nothing if not a man of routine. These minute changes in fact did signal that something very serious was troubling him.

The cause of this loss of equilibrium was on the second floor of the stately manor. Elizabeth had been ill for nearly two weeks, her usual lively disposition suppressed by bouts of extreme fatigue and nausea. At first, it was suspected that she had the flu, but as the days turned into weeks, Darcy became concerned that it was something far more serious.

Originally, he blamed her illness on her penchant for working too hard. Immediately upon their return from Spain, Elizabeth was contacted by Jay Austen, lead singer and songwriter for the alternative rock group, Excessively Diverted. The group was producing their own rock opera, and Jay wanted Elizabeth to co-write the songs with him. Not able to accept a teaching position because she was still under contract to Longbourn, Elizabeth read the script and then quickly jumped at the chance to be a part of the project and have some occupation with which to fill up her time.

Between writing the opera, overseeing the Riverside Community Project at Longbourn and doing her best to make sure her husband of only three and a half months did not feel neglected, it was no wonder she had become ill. But after more than two weeks, there was no improvement, and Darcy began to suspect that Elizabeth's illness may have had little to do with simple exhaustion.

Elizabeth was stubborn, and it seemed the more he pushed her to call a doctor, the more she procrastinated in completing the task. That morning as he once again sat on the floor of the bathroom beside his wife's heaving form, concern manifested itself into terror that she was suffering from something serious, perhaps life threatening. His only consolation was that today she had finally agreed to call his friend, Dr. George Knightley, and Darcy was anxious to find out how long she would have to wait for an appointment.

That the hood of her car was still warm meant she had gone out when he had specifically instructed her to spend the afternoon resting. Chastisement would be pointless as Darcy imagined the amusement she would find at his attempt.

He methodically searched her usual haunts. The library, her study, and the music room were all empty. That left only one logical place to check — their bedroom suite.

He entered quietly, hoping to find her sleeping; however, the bed was empty and undisturbed since the maids had tidied up that morning. He walked into the attached sitting room and found the red sectional sofa, moved all the way from New York just before the wedding, was also vacant. As frustration began to color his demeanor, he heard the sound of the shower coming from her bathroom.

Usually, Darcy would immediately doff his clothing and join her; but with her recent illness, he didn't entertain the notion. Desperate to find out if she had called Knightley, he opened the door to the bathroom and was greeted by a cloud of steam.

He watched the muted shape of her form through the fogged, glass walls of the shower as his mind easily filled in the details: wet chestnut hair lying flat against the fair porcelain skin of her finely toned back, breasts ornamented in soapsuds, long legs shining with rivulets of water coursing to beautiful feet and immaculately pedicured toes. It amazed him how each day he could be struck again by how beautiful she was.

He was about to speak to her when something unusual caught his eye. A long, strip of blue on the white sink commanded his attention. He picked up the device, looked at it carefully and raised his eyebrows in puzzlement. "Elizabeth, why is there a pregnancy test on the sink?"

Her voice answered him from behind the shower door, "I know it's ridiculous, but George told me to buy one. I tried to explain to him that I could not possibly be pregnant, but he said my symptoms could be related to any number of things and it was simple enough to eliminate this one before my appointment tomorrow afternoon. I peed on the damn thing before I got in the shower. It should be finished by now, so don't get your hopes up that it's going to turn blue anytime soon."

Darcy looked at the test carefully. He picked up the instructions lying nearby and examined the test again. "Elizabeth, dear, it's already blue."

"Not the outside plastic, Baby. The white square window in the middle turns blue if it's positive."

"There is no white square anywhere, Lizzy." Darcy turned it around in front of the light to make sure.

"Look on the flat side, that's where it is."

Darcy walked over and quickly pulled open the shower door, startling her. Elizabeth quickly wiped the water from her eyes and beheld her usually carefully composed husband. He had a ridiculously dopey smile on his face and held the test in front of her. "There's only one window on this thing and it's blue. Blue, baby blue, baby blue, blue, BLUE!"

Elizabeth's mouth flew open. "It can't be."

366

"But it is!" He was ecstatic.

"It must be a mistake!" She clearly was not.

"Lizzy, how accurate are these tests supposed to be?" It was a rhetorical question. As his wife stood by in obvious shock, Darcy couldn't contain his excitement on realizing that not only was his wife not fatally ill, she was pregnant. Armani suit, Breitling Watch, Versace tie, Italian shoes and all; he stepped into the shower and wrapped his arms around her. "It's blue... It's blue! You're pregnant, Lizzy!" He showered the top of her wet head with kisses, overjoyed with the turn of the situation.

Elizabeth, however, was still stunned with disbelief. She had taken her birth control pills every single day without fail. She could not possibly be pregnant, and yet, there was the test, obviously positive. Surely, there was some error. Either the test was faulty or she had done something wrong. It was simple... pee on the test and wait five minutes. How can one screw that up?

Who knows how much time they would have spent in the shower — he in his wonder, she in her puzzlement — if Elizabeth had not suddenly felt the need to dash for the nearby toilet. Naked and shivering, Elizabeth knelt in front of the fixture while dry heaves wracked her body. Darcy pulled several towels out of the closet to keep her warm until the storm in her stomach passed. She looked up from her position inside the bowl to see his face, still covered with that ridiculous grin, looking at her with adoration as he sat in his wet clothes beside her on the bathroom floor.

"You did this on purpose!" she accused before another wave of nausea hit her.

"Lizzy, I believe you too had some part in it." Darcy thought she never looked more adorable than she did right then: soaking wet, head in a toilet, vomiting wretchedly and totally bitchy.

For Elizabeth, the smile on his face was really pissing her off. "You wanted this to happen! Now look at me!" She felt awful, she was cold, she was tired and she wanted the waves to stop. Why did he have to look so damn happy?

Darcy continued to grin as he reached out to gently push a stray curl from her cheek back behind her ear. "Need I remind you, love, that you were the one who insisted we no longer needed to use condoms." He helped her up from the floor. "Do you need to finish your shower, or can I help you to bed?"

"Just put me in bed as I am." She was exhausted and wanted nothing more than to curl up in bed and sleep. "I still don't think this is possible. I won't believe it until I see George Knightley tomorrow."

After changing out of his wet clothes, Darcy came back to sit on the bed to watch her rest. Elizabeth huffed, "Can't you go be happy somewhere else?"

"No." He was still grinning as he bent over to whisper in her ear, "Blue, baby, blue… it's blue!" Elizabeth groaned in response and pulled the blankets over her head.

A few minutes later, she could hear him typing on his laptop as he sat next to her. Not long after, he picked up the phone. "Mrs. R., would you kindly bring a bottle of water and some saltines for Mrs. Darcy?"

She pushed back the blankets. "What are you doing?"

"I've found three websites that all agree morning sickness is exacerbated by an empty stomach and recommend saltines."

"It's not morning sickness. I cannot be pregnant."

He smiled mischievously. "It's blue, baby, blue."

"Prat!" When his response was nothing more than to continue to grin, Elizabeth dove again beneath the blankets.

She could hear more typing and in a few minutes a knock on the door. "Come in!" Darcy called. Elizabeth could hear Mrs. Reynolds' soft footsteps as Darcy acknowledged her. "Thank you Mrs. R."

Mrs. Reynolds took in the scene: Mrs. Darcy, as the mistress was referred to by the household staff, curled up under the blankets and Master Wills sitting beside her, typing on his laptop and smiling broadly. Mrs. Reynolds knew that smile better than just about anyone, and when she added that up with the saltines, she strongly suspected the truth of the situation. Her eyes flew to Darcy in question and his wink confirmed her suspicions. Master Wills *never* winked!

Her first response was relief. The entire staff was subdued with worry over Mrs. Darcy's recent illness. Her second response was pure, unadulterated joy. Finally, the halls of Pemberley would once again ring out with the laughter of a child.

"How is the poor dear?" she asked warmly.

Once more Elizabeth's head emerged from the blankets only to see the smile on Mrs. Reynolds' face nearly matched the one on her husband. It looked like a Bingley convention in her bedroom, and that was more than her exhausted nerves could bear. "Would you both just leave me alone? I am not pregnant!"

The smiles continued unabated, so Elizabeth again burrowed beneath the blankets.

"Elizabeth," Darcy spoke soothingly, "if you eat two —" Mrs. Reynolds held up four fingers. "— four saltines, I'll leave you alone."

"No. It's just the flu. Wait a few days and I'll be fine."

"Mrs. Darcy," Mrs. Reynolds spoke with her usual calm, "it wouldn't hurt to try."

Elizabeth wanted to tell her what she could do with her saltines but knew she could never bring herself to speak to Mrs. Reynolds in that way. She tried to come up with some other comment but did not have time to respond as her stomach forced her from beneath the blankets to heave into the basin, which had become a permanent fixture beside her bed. Mrs. Reynolds walked back to the bath to tidy up. She soon returned with a bundle of wet clothing and the pregnancy test. "Your suit and shoes are ruined, Master Wills. Do you want to keep the test?"

"Oh, most definitely!" Darcy answered.

Elizabeth glared again. Why anyone would want to keep a stick soaked with urine was currently beyond her comprehension.

Mrs. Reynolds left but returned five minutes later, handing Darcy the test, now undoubtedly hermetically sealed in clear plastic. Seeing that Elizabeth's nausea had subsided, Mrs. Reynolds removed four saltines from the package and held them out. Elizabeth recognized the look on her face; it would brook no dissent.

When she finally rested back on her pillows, she had eaten the saltines and drunk a few sips of water. The saltines did feel good in her mouth, and when they hit her stomach, the relief was almost instantaneous. Instinctively, Mrs. Reynolds handed Elizabeth two more crackers, which the suffering woman immediately devoured. Wisely, the housekeeper left the sleeve of saltines on the table next to Elizabeth, and with a backwards smile to Darcy, silently left the room.

"Well?" Elizabeth hissed.

"Well, what?"

"I ate the saltines, so leave me alone." Elizabeth glared at him once more.

"I'll stay for a little while just in case the saltines don't stay down. Once you're resting comfortably, I'll go."

Elizabeth huffed again and, turning her back to Darcy, pulled the blankets again over her head. Not ten minutes later, her slow, even breathing signaled to him that she was nearly asleep. Darcy carefully lay beside her, wrapping one arm across her body, and finally let relief flood his mind and body.

Darcy had watched his mother's battle with breast cancer reduce her from a warm, vibrant force to be reckoned with into a small shadow of her former self. Seeing Elizabeth suffer the last two weeks had brought back vividly the months he spent with his mother while she endured long courses of chemotherapy. The vomiting, fatigue and sickly pallor of his wife were reflections of his mother during her darkest days. He knew it was irrational to jump to conclusions concerning her health, but he found that, when it came to Elizabeth, he could become far from rational. Now that they knew the cause of Elizabeth's distress, he could allow himself to relax. She was not sick. The elation once again took over his emotions. She was pregnant!

He gently pulled the blankets down around her neck and nuzzled her ear. "I love you, my Lizzy."

She reached back briefly to stroke his cheek and whispered sleepily, "I love you too, Baby."

Twenty hours later, in the London office of Dr. George Knightley, Elizabeth sat before an empty desk, a sleeve of saltines on her lap and a bottle of water in her hand. To her left sat her husband who bounced his knee and still wore the dopey grin from the day before.

Elizabeth placed her hand on the bouncing knee and snapped at him, "Stop that, please." He cast an indulgent smile that angered her even more. "And you didn't have to flirt with the nurse. I'm sure Julielynn was quite capable of obtaining the details of my illness directly from me!"

Darcy refused to rise to the bait of Elizabeth's absurd accusation, for he understood this was hard for her. Everything had happened so fast; the development of their relationship, the overwhelming attention of the paparazzi, her relocation to another country, and their marriage were more changes than most people could face in just a little over one year. Elizabeth had handled it all admirably. Becoming pregnant was just the straw that broke the camel's back.

In spite of his sympathy, Darcy refused to rein in his enthusiasm. He was just too happy. He leaned over and whispered to her, "It's blue, baby, blue!"

Elizabeth was prepared to bite his head off when Dr. Knightley entered. "Our test confirms that Elizabeth is indeed pregnant." Knightley waited for their reaction before choosing his next words. If the couple was happy, he would respond one way, if not, he would respond in a completely different manner. The Darcys, however, had him baffled. Darcy was obviously elated as his smile spread into a huge toothy grin while he reached over to take his wife's hand

and kiss it tenderly. Elizabeth, however, just closed her eyes and groaned.

"George," Elizabeth looked at him pleadingly, "I assure you that for the last ten months I have never missed a day of those pills!"

"Elizabeth," Knightley came around to the front of his desk, sat on the edge of it and faced her, "99% effective is not 100%. Although this is just my personal opinion, I believe that sometimes the body's desire to reproduce is far greater than the methods used to prevent it." The doctor eyed her carefully. Regardless of his friend's reaction, it was Elizabeth who was his patient, and he needed to focus on her feelings at this moment. "I take it this is not good news."

She looked over at her smiling husband and back to the physician. "It's not terrible news, it's just...unexpected. I wanted to wait to have children." She leaned forward to rest her head in her hands.

Knightley spoke sympathetically. "Do you want time to consider the alternatives?" Even though he wasn't looking directly at Darcy, Knightley could feel the man's smile for his wife turn into a frosty glare directed at the physician.

Elizabeth's eyes snapped up to the doctor's face. "Of course we're going to have this baby!" Her voice then took on a tone of acceptance. "I just need for all of this to sink in." Darcy's face again morphed back into a huge smile. He knew Elizabeth would never consider aborting their child simply because the timing was inconvenient.

Knightley returned to his seat behind the desk. The next ten minutes passed as the doctor provided basic information on diet, exercise and morning sickness, as well as possible complications due to the birth control pills. He also provided them with a list of obstetricians he highly recommended. In a complete reversal of their usual roles, Darcy had numerous questions while Elizabeth preferred to remain quiet.

Eventually, all three of them rose from their seats. Knightley extended his hand to his friend. "Darcy, may I be the first to congratulate you! I can see how happy you are; you're beginning to resemble Bingley."

Darcy was practically bursting with restrained joy. "Thank you, George. However, I believe my behavior is a little more controlled than yours when you first discovered Emma was expecting."

"Did he ruin an Armani suit?" Elizabeth piped in. She was still feeling subdued but could not resist a little humor at Darcy's expense.

"No," the doctor replied looking embarrassed, "I'm afraid I barged into a women's locker room at Cambridge. Unfortunately, Emma was not the only woman I found there."

The drive back was long as Elizabeth felt too ill to ride in the helicopter and had no desire to stay at Oakland. For the first time in her life, Elizabeth felt that she truly had a home — a place where she belonged — and the serenity of Pemberley was exactly what she needed to help put her overwhelmed mind back in order. She slept most of the way back in the car, and the much-needed rest helped her brain function better than it had in weeks, allowing her better spirits to return.

Darcy was content to spend a quiet evening reading in their bedroom as his wife rested. The constant munching of saltines had allowed her to go the entire day with only a few bouts of nausea. She had actually consumed all three meals that day and kept two of them down.

Eventually, as the day neared its end, Darcy climbed into bed and gathered Elizabeth into his arms. "Feeling better?"

"Yes." She wrapped her arms around his waist and snuggled into his chest. "I have to apologize for being so irrational these past two days. It's all just so overwhelming. Forgive me?"

Kissing her forehead gently, he replied, "Of course."

"It was as if we both suffered a personality change. I was angry and irrational and you were downright bubbly," she teased.

"Absolutely no suffering on my part; however, I would describe myself as happy. I was hardly 'bubbly.'" He sounded slightly defensive.

Elizabeth could not help but tease him a little more. "You always let your reserve down when we're alone; however, that smile you're wearing would outshine Charles Bingley's."

"Well then, you'll just have to get used to it. I refuse to pretend I'm not ecstatic."

Darcy stroked the soft skin of his wife's back with the tips of his fingers. It had been two weeks since she had felt well enough to make love and nearly a week since she could bear to be touched at all. "I missed this, holding you," he whispered into her ear.

"I hope you won't be offended that I was too miserable to notice." Elizabeth reached up to kiss his neck and was greeted with the soft scent of oatmeal soap. "You smell wonderful." She continued to place light kisses across his neck as her hand gently caressed the skin covering the lean muscles of his abdomen.

"Lizzy," his voice became husky as he suddenly became aware of what he had been missing for the past two weeks, "you realize that does *things* to me."

"*Things*, Fitzwilliam?" she purred innocently against his throat as her tongue turned her light kisses into wet caresses.

"Yes, *things*," he growled softly as he slowly ground the proof of his assertion of "things" against her thigh.

Elizabeth could feel his amazing body respond beneath her hand and she marveled that she could have gone two weeks without wanting him. She had missed him; his warmth, his touch, his body and the emergence of full-blown desire would not be ignored.

"Do you want me to stop?" She laughed seductively.

For Darcy, the past two weeks had felt endless, lying next to her beautiful body without being able to make love to her. While his overwhelming concern had cooled his passions, his suppressed desires were now free to run amok, and run they did! His palm now joined his fingertips in stroking her back, pulling her body even closer to his. He could feel that she had become thinner over the past weeks. *Well, that will change soon enough!*

"Do you want me to start?" With these words, he began the game they both knew well.

"Ready," she whispered against his skin. She could feel the immediate tension in his muscles against her body.

"Set," his breath quickened as his hands moved to secure her waist.

He waited for her signal as he had numerous times before, the anticipation increasing both their ardor. She hesitated for what he felt was an eternity. "Go!"

In a flash, Elizabeth was on her back, his body on top of hers, his mouth crushed over her own as his tongue hungrily reacquainted itself with hers. His hands glided down, lingering momentarily over her breasts before moving to her stomach and thighs, stroking, reclaiming, demanding surrender. The long abstinence and her passionate response to his touch demolished any attempt at self-control. Sensing that his urgency matched her own, Elizabeth wrapped her legs around his buttocks, and he thrust into her immediately.

Their rhythm increased rapidly. Darcy could feel her climax building and pulled back his head to watch her. Elizabeth's dark curls were spread across the white pillow, her skin was flushed, her lips were swollen and her eyes were dark with passion. These were the eyes he had fallen into a year ago, and he could hardly fathom why he had fought for so long to discover the sweet pleasure he had found within their depths. This was the most breathtaking sight he had ever, or would ever, behold.

Soon the cries that came from her throat filled the room and pushed him over the edge as his shuddering body joined hers in a long and ecstatic release.

He remained within her as their bodies cooled and their breathing returned to normal. Soft sweet kisses between whispered words of love continued as he carefully moved his lower body to her side so that his weight would not cause her discomfort.

Eventually, he rolled onto his back and pulled her to lie against him, when her head suddenly rose. Anticipating her need, Darcy quickly reached for the saltines on her night table. Elizabeth immediately shoved one into her mouth, followed quickly by two more.

"You realize," she said between crackers, "we're going to be sleeping in a bed full of crumbs."

"That's all right," he kissed her on her forehead as he teased, "today I bought stock in the company that makes them, so at the rate you're consuming saltines, we'll make a fortune in no time." When she once again felt well enough to lay her head back down upon his chest, he whispered to her in wonder, "Lizzy, we're going to have a baby." He reached down to stroke her flat stomach.

"Yes," she whispered back, softly chuckling, "you said you wanted to bring me to Pemberley and fill me with babies. It looks like you got your wish. But, be warned, this child is going to be such a handful."

He was pleased at the return of her playful manner. "What makes you say that?"

"Look at the trouble he or she has already caused, and we didn't know it existed! Just imagine the mischief once it's out and running about."

"This baby will be a Darcy," he spoke in what Elizabeth called his "haughty" voice, usually reserved for non-cooperative board members, "calm, collected, regulated and well behaved."

"Really? Just look at how stubborn this baby's parents are. We'll be in trouble no matter which of us the baby takes after, and if both our traits are combined, heaven help us!"

Darcy could not help but laugh at the mental picture this inspired: a small toddler with dark curly hair, deep blue eyes and a huge pout on its lips throwing food across the kitchen, each spoonful meticulously and methodically aimed to cause the maximum amount of trouble for the adults present. *Perfect!* Once again, he quickly pushed her back against the mattress, but this time he went straight to her belly, covering it with short noisy kisses which resulted in

Elizabeth's squeal of laughter.

It was then Darcy began his first conversation with his child, "Listen here, I believe the time has arrived to take a stern hand with you since you are likely to be most troublesome. It would be greatly appreciated if you would be a little kinder to your mother. She's the only home you'll have for the next several months, so I suggest you be nice or she'll eat something you won't find the least bit palatable, like broccoli." At the mention of broccoli, Elizabeth quickly sat up and grabbed the saltines again. Darcy followed her ascent to continue speaking with his errant child.

"Now, perhaps you might want to consider emulating one of your aunts such as Georgiana or Jane. Both of these fine young women have the sweetest of dispositions, and we would not mind in the least if you would take either or both of them as role models. Do not even consider following in the footsteps of your Aunt Lydia or your Great Aunt Catherine. If you do, I predict you will spend most of your adolescence confined to your room and your teenage years locked in the closet."

Elizabeth looked down at her husband's serious face as he caressed and kissed her abdomen between sentences. Reaching down, she gently stroked his hair back from his face. He glanced at her tender expression and moved up to kiss her lips gently. "Please go to sleep, my Lizzy. I'm just going to have a few more words with the heir of Pemberley before I call it a night."

"I'll wait, Baby. I wouldn't miss this for the world." He smiled at the amusement in her eyes, kissed her again more deeply, once, twice, three times, and then moved back to address her belly.

"Pardon me, but we shall have to continue this conversation at another time as I wish to make love to your beautiful mother again. I suggest you get used to being jostled about." He placed one last kiss upon her belly before quickly pulling her hips down beneath him. Elizabeth's laughter was silenced as his mouth claimed hers in a long and passionate kiss. Darcy then proceeded to make love to her with all the tenderness due the mother of his child.

As they were drifting off to sleep, their legs and arms entwined, Elizabeth sighed with contentment. Somehow, after everything they'd been through and all the trials sure to come, life was bliss. "Good night, Baby."

"Good night, my Lizzy." His head suddenly rose from her breast. "If I'm your baby, and we're going to have a baby, won't that become a bit confusing?"

"Do you want me to stop calling you 'Baby?'"

Darcy was silent. Never would he admit to the joy and fire he felt each time Elizabeth called him "Baby."

"Don't worry, Fitzwilliam." She lifted her hand to caress his brooding face. "You'll always be my Baby." Elizabeth gently stroked her fingers from his temple back into his hair and began to softly sing: *"Be my, be my baby. My one and only baby."*[49]

His smile was a mile wide. "I love you, my Lizzy."

"I love you too, Baby."

49 "Be My Baby", by Jeff Barry, Ellie Greenwich and Phil Spector, 1963

CHAPTER 31
CAREFULLY THOUGHT OUT PLANS

April 15th, The Celebrity Insider (U.K.)
Photo caption: Elizabeth Bennet is one of the many celebrities rumored to be sporting a baby bump this spring.

The small hotel room in the Bronx was dull and lifeless. The man sitting at the pressboard desk was muscular, his arms a tapestry of brightly colored tattoos; a crucifix dangled from his neck as he spoke with an intelligent southern drawl. "Looks good," Billy Ray Collins commented dryly as he examined the four passports. "Excellent craftsmanship. We should have no trouble getting out of the country with these."

George Wickham said nothing in return. Frannie did enough talking for all of them, so the men tended not to speak unnecessarily. Instead, he poured out two generous portions of vodka and handed one glass to Billy Ray. The two men toasted each other in unison. "To sweet revenge!"

Not able to allow more than a few moments of silence to pass, Frannie rose from the bed nearby. Sliding up to the chair where Billy Ray sat, she let her hands roam over his well-defined pectorals. "Can we go to the theater tonight, my love? It's been ages since I've seen a musical on Broadway."

"Not tonight." He kissed her to prevent the whine that would soon follow if she were left to her own thoughts. Already nude, she offered her breasts to his mouth, but Billy Ray suddenly set her aside. "No fun now." He turned his head to George. "First we need to think. We've made it to New York City without anyone being the wiser. Now comes the hard part. We've got a plan, but we need an opportunity to strike when Bethy and her husband are out of the public eye and Darcy's bodyguard can be easily distracted and overcome."

"It's already been a week," George complained. "How much longer will they be in town?"

Frannie grabbed the vodka bottle and added a splash to her orange juice. "Janie's engagement party is tomorrow night. I spoke to her on the phone this morning, and she wouldn't say a thing about Bethy — not that I'm surprised. She hasn't told me a thing about her sister for years. Even Lydia has become tightlipped. Can you imagine that?" Frannie stared out the window at the cold spring rain. "I can't believe Janie won't let her own mother attend her engagement party! Bethy must be behind this — she and that gay husband of hers! It would serve them all right if we barged into that party, guns blazing..."

"The party is too public," Billy Ray spoke to George, ignoring Frannie's effusions. "We need to make our move when it's least expected. Bethy is giving a lecture at Longbourn on Monday night, so they're here at least until Tuesday morning. Where's Alan?"

"He should be back at any minute." George poured another vodka as he paced back and forth in front of the hotel window, disturbing Frannie's view. "I don't trust him."

Billy Ray laughed. "Why? You brought him in, and he's proved to be quite resourceful."

"Darcy's aunt was happy to lend him to us, and I know the Old Bat hates Elizabeth with a passion. Still, he's too...pure."

"You're just unhappy because you couldn't seduce him," Frannie accused.

"You couldn't seduce him either," George shot back.

"That's because he's gay!" For Frannie, that could be the only explanation.

Billy Ray gave them both a warning look. "I've got no problem with a man who refuses to mix sex with business. Besides, he hates Darcy as much as any of us."

"Really!" Frannie said with wide eyes as she slipped on a robe. "I haven't heard this story."

George sat on a chair next to the bed and gave Billy Ray an expectant look.

Billy Ray held up his glass for a refill. As George obliged him, Billy Ray explained. "Alan has an obsessive thing for Lady Catherine's stepdaughter, Anne. You should hear him go on about her: *'She's so kind and has the prettiest eyes.'* The man is one sick puppy! Anyway, Darcy turned Anne against his aunt, and as a result, the two women no longer live in the same house. Now, Alan is reduced to stalking Anne from afar. And he does, relentlessly."

"Poor man!" Frannie sympathized. "To be separated from his one true love…"

George stood up, walking back to the window. "Anne's rich, but she's not much to look at. I guess there's no accounting for taste."

The buzz of the door lock was followed by the entrance of Alan Jenkinson, soaking wet, three boxes of pizza in his hands and a triumphant smile on his face. "I've got something!" he said as he placed the pizzas on the table before them.

"What?" all three asked at once.

Alan held up a flyer from The Manhattan Fencing Club. "Opportunity! At least the possibility of opportunity."

Billy Ray read the flyer and passed it to George. "How do we know they'll enter Sunday's tournament?"

"I went inside the club, pretending to be interested in membership. There's a large board in the lobby where the matches are mapped out. Darcy's name is there, so he's entered the competition. Since the paparazzi are aware that he and Dr. Bennet are in town, I think Darcy will avoid the front entrance. I checked out the back exit, and the alley is the perfect place to hit them. I stood watching for an hour; there was little traffic and few pedestrians. I imagine it will be deserted on a Saturday."

Frannie opened a box of pizza and wrinkled her nose in disgust at the anchovies she found inside. She reached for another box. "What about Bethy? We can't very well kidnap her if she's not there."

"If she's not competing, she may attend just to watch," George suggested. "She's a member of the club too, so I imagine she has friends there she hasn't seen in awhile."

Billy Ray closed his eyes for a moment to think. "Tonight we'll check out the back of the club. If I agree with Alan's assessment, then Sunday morning George will watch for their arrival. If Bethy shows up with her husband and they use the back door, then we'll hit them when the tournament's over. Now, once again, let's go over everyone's part in the plan. Frannie?"

"I attempt to approach Bethy. The bodyguard will recognize me and leave Bethy and her husband to subdue me." She laughed throatily at the thought. Frannie loved submission!

George continued. "I hit the driver over the head and get behind the wheel of the limo."

Alan answered without prompting. "I use my gun to force both Darcy and his wife into the limo."

"And then —" Billy Ray smiled menacingly. "— I come out of hiding, save Frannie from the bodyguard and the two of us will jump into the limo and enjoy the look of terror on Bethy's face when she recognizes us."

Not daring to speak his true plan aloud, he thought through what would really happen next.

I shoot Jenkinson right between the eyes and then shoot Darcy in the gut.

As Darcy slowly, painfully dies, the last thing he sees will be me raping his screaming wife.

Once we arrive back here, I will shoot Wickham who, thanks to the privacy glass and a silencer on my gun, will have no idea what happened in the back of the limo.

I will leave the bodies with the limo in the parking garage and then move Bethy to the rental car.

I will drive to a little motel I booked right outside of Allentown, and when I think Bethy has suffered enough, which won't be for a very long time, I will slowly strangle her to death.

Then I fly off to Venezuela where I'll sell Bethy's engagement ring and live like a king!

Billy Ray suddenly realized everyone was waiting for him to finish speaking what they thought was his part of the plan. "Then Alan and I force Darcy out of the limo while we drive off with his wife, bring her back here and issue the ransom demand."

"And once the fifty million lands in the Cayman Islands bank account George set up," Frannie said dreamily, "we fly off to Mexico!"

"That's it, honey!" Billy Ray reassured her while thinking that she'd never see Mexico. Frannie would still be in the hands of Darcy's bodyguard as the limo drives off, left behind to take the rap for four murders. "You just keep dreaming about Mexico."

"DARCY, ELIZABETH!" DALTON VIVASH CRIED out when he saw them enter the club. "It's been too long!" He shook Darcy's hand and briefly hugged Elizabeth. "Whoa!" he said as he stepped back. "What's this?" His hand shot out to touch the baby bump, which to Darcy and Elizabeth seemed to have sprouted almost overnight. "You two didn't waste any time. When are you due?"

"The end of August," Darcy answered quickly as he too reached out to touch the bump, subtly brushing Dalton's hand away in the process.

Elizabeth gently pushed both their hands away from her abdomen. "This is my belly, and only I say who can touch it." She looked at Dalton and said, "You, never," then turned to Darcy and said, "You, later!"

Elizabeth walked off to meet up with Richard and Geoff, who both decided to accompany Darcy and Elizabeth on this trip to New York and had arrived at the club earlier. "Bitchy, isn't she?" Dalton said with a mischievous grin.

Darcy's smile was far more genuine. "Elizabeth's having a rough time of it. Would it be all right if we moved a chair into each of the rooms so she can sit down to watch the tournament?"

"I take it that's why she's not competing?" Darcy nodded his head in answer. "There's a folding chair in my office. That way you can easily transport it from room to room as needed. You're expected to win today, Darcy. I hope you won't have to leave early and forfeit the competition because of a sick wife."

"I assure you, Elizabeth wouldn't allow it."

"As an added incentive, I'll reveal the prizes to you. I am giving both the men and women's champion a sixteenth-century rapier from my collection."

The only emotion Darcy showed was a rising of his eyebrows, but he was very impressed. Dalton's collection was legendary. "Then you can be assured I will stay until that rapier is firmly in my hands. Who do you anticipate will take the women's prize?"

Dalton suddenly looked uncomfortable. He leaned close to Darcy and whispered, "I'm afraid I may have an unpleasant surprise for you."

RICHARD WAS ONCE MORE REASSURING Elizabeth when she suddenly felt that all too familiar watering in her mouth. Giving Richard and Geoff a frantic hand signal they had both become well acquainted with over the past few months, she dashed back to the women's locker room. She entered the large handicapped stall and, tossing her purse and tote bag on the floor, promptly lost her breakfast in the toilet.

As she was heaving into the bowl, Elizabeth tried to hold back her hair until she felt a feminine hand take it, pulling both sides gently to the back of her head. Then she heard a voice she couldn't quite place say soothingly, "I've got it."

When her stomach finally calmed, Elizabeth sat back against the cool tile of the wall and opened her eyes to see Caroline Bingley cracking open a bottle of water. Elizabeth realized that her voice was different because it was missing its customary haughty sneer. "I asked Dalton to warn you and Wills that he allowed me back into the club, but from the expression in your eyes, I can see he did not."

"No," Elizabeth confirmed as she took the water to rinse out her mouth. When she finished, she watched in amazement as Caroline walked over to retrieve a towel from the shower area. Elizabeth asked suspiciously, "When did you start calling Darcy, *Wills?*"

Caroline gave Elizabeth the towel. "I always called him Wills when we were growing up."

Still stunned over the behavior of the woman before her, Elizabeth watched in wonder as Caroline knelt down beside her. "Are you going to be all right? I've got a match in a few minutes."

"Yes," Elizabeth answered quietly. "This happens all the time."

Elizabeth stared in wonder. Just the evening before, she and Darcy were little more than grateful that Caroline made no attempt to speak to either one of them at the engagement party, and now, without a subtle insult or blatant put down, Caroline stood, clearly prepared to leave after being nothing but...*kind*. Elizabeth pulled herself from her amazement to call after her, "Thank you."

DARCY WAS WAITING FOR ELIZABETH outside the women's locker room when his eyes met those of Caroline Bingley.

"Caroline," he said coldly, nodding his head slightly.

"Wills." She could see his brows rise at the use of his nickname, and she cringed at the look of suspicion in his eyes. Awkwardly, she pointed her finger to the door behind her. "Elizabeth says she's fine. I'm sure she'll be out shortly." She glanced to the floor, then to the ceiling, clearly uncomfortable. "A baby! Wow, I never would have guessed." Her eyes then hesitantly rested on his. "Congratulations."

He nodded again, clearly dismissing her. She turned to walk away and then suddenly took a step toward him instead. Her voice was brittle and barely above a whisper. "Charles and Jane have graciously chosen to give me another chance, therefore it is unavoidable that we will run into each other. I'm not going to claim to be some miraculously changed woman, but rest assured that I will not attempt to insinuate myself back into your life or try to make you or Elizabeth uncomfortable in any way. This is not easy for me, but I'm trying... I'm really trying to move on, and whether you believe it or not, I wish you well."

Without waiting for a response, she blindly turned and walked straight into

Richard's chest. In an instant, a storm of emotion passed wordlessly between them. Caroline then quickly stepped past him and walked away.

The day passed quickly, and as predicted, both Darcy and Caroline won the prized rapiers. As they prepared to leave the club, Darcy rested his rapier against the wall near the back exit and embraced Elizabeth tightly. "I love you, my Lizzy."

"I love you too, Baby," she responded before they briefly kissed.

"Are you ready?" She nodded, and taking his hand, they walked into the alley.

WHILE ONLY TAKING SECONDS, THE events in the alley behind the Manhattan Fencing Club seemed to happen in slow motion to those involved. As soon as Darcy and Elizabeth exited the club, Mr. Sparks approached to open the limo door while Mr. Harville surveyed the alley.

As scheduled, Frannie appeared, calling "Bethy" at the top of her lungs. Harville ran forward to stop her from approaching Elizabeth; Wickham and Jenkinson then stepped out of a nearby doorway.

From there, Billy Ray Collins' carefully thought out plan went horribly astray. Instead of hitting Mr. Sparks on the head with the butt of his gun, Wickham found himself pushed hard against the side of the limo with the blunt end of Jenkinson's gun in his back.

Fifty feet away, Frannie found not just Mr. Harville, but Mr. Price holding her firmly against the wall of the fencing club.

Standing in front of the door to the club, Billy Ray quickly comprehended that his plan had gone to hell. In a last act of retaliation, he aimed his gun squarely at Elizabeth's head.

Across the alley, Richard and two FBI agents had Billy Ray in their sights, but before any of them could fire a shot, the point of a sharp, thin blade erupted from the front of Billy Ray Collins' chest.

Billy Ray's eyes registered shock before they glassed over, the blade retreating through his heart as he fell face forward onto the black top of the alley. Standing behind him was the frozen form of Caroline Bingley, Darcy's prize rapier held firmly in her extended right hand.

Frannie's scream pierced the silence, followed quickly by the clattering of the rapier as it hit the pavement. Caroline's legs suddenly gave out, but Richard caught her before she fell into the large pool of blood draining from Billy Ray's lifeless body. As the agents stepped forward to take Frannie and Wickham into custody, a stream of police cars, sirens blaring, raced into the alley.

Darcy and Elizabeth stood wrapped in each other's arms. As the chaos of sirens, Frannie's angry curses, and the shouts of the army of law enforcement officers circled about them, they were focused purely on one another and the thought that, finally, the nightmare that began nine years before was over.

Neither would feel remorse for Billy Ray Collins' death. If he had survived, there would have always been the possibility that he could have escaped from prison or been released again due to some political agenda. As long as Collins lived, the day would come when it would be his life or theirs. Darcy and Elizabeth could only feel grateful that that day had come, and they had survived.

They owed that positive outcome to Richard who, after recruiting Alan Jenkinson to keep an eye on Lady Catherine, was lucky enough to have that man placed smack in the middle of Billy Ray Collins' conspirators. Fully aware of all their plans, it was Richard who chose the time and place for the attack, and provided Alan with the location for the hit. In the end, Richard's carefully thought out plan worked perfectly, except for Caroline Bingley.

Caroline had seen Darcy and Elizabeth leave the club and noticed that Darcy had left his rapier behind. Leaving her own belongings in the hall, she grabbed the rapier and followed in hopes of catching them before their limo drove off. When she exited and saw Billy Ray leveling his gun, she reacted with little thought, pulling the rapier from its scabbard and thrusting it into the back of a man who wished to harm someone who, deep down, would always be her family.

Richard held Caroline as she began to cry hysterically. Picking her up, he kicked the bottom of the door to the fencing club, which had automatically locked behind her.

When Geoff opened the door, Richard passed inside, silently communicating to his twin that everything was all right. Terrified of the outcome of the expected attack and frustrated that he had promised Darcy to remain inside the club, Geoff affectionately hugged both his brother and Caroline. Then passing through the door and leaping over the dead body of Billy Ray Collins, he made a mad dash to embrace Darcy and Elizabeth.

September 7th, Tête-à-Tête Magazine (U.K.)
Photo caption: Socialite Caroline Bingley and The Honorable Richard Fitzwilliam drive through the gates of Pemberley...

CAROLINE SAT IN HER LONDON townhouse and placed the DVD she received that day into her laptop. The screen flashed blue before a picture of Darcy and Elizabeth appeared, both wearing beaming smiles.

"Hello," Darcy said to the camera, "Elizabeth and I want to introduce you to the newest member of our family." The camera panned back to reveal that Darcy and Elizabeth were sitting on a red couch, both wearing white button-down shirts, and Darcy was holding a squirming blue bundle in the arm that was not wrapped around his wife. The camera then zoomed in on the bundle and the blue blanket was moved aside to display a soft pink face and two violet-blue eyes.

"This is Bennet Fitzwilliam George Darcy. Ben was born here at Pemberley on our wedding anniversary, September 1st, at the ungodly hour of 3:45 a.m."

"He's eight pounds even and 20½ inches long. That's 52½ centimeters for those outside the U.S.," Elizabeth playfully piped in.

The baby stared directly into the camera before yawning adorably. Even Caroline could not resist smiling and saying, "Ahhh," in response, though this was not the first time she had seen the heir of Pemberley yawn. She had the pleasure of meeting little Ben in person two days previously, thanks to the man who would be his godfather and who was, at that moment, fast asleep on her couch.

Caroline and Richard were not lovers. Neither trusted each other enough yet for that; however, Richard understood the emotional trauma she suffered upon taking the life of another human being, even if that man hardly deserved the title. She still awoke suddenly during the night, screaming about the blood that she dreamt covered her hands. Richard was always there and promised he always would be for as long as she needed him.

No, they were not lovers, but over the past five months, they had become the very best of friends.

GEORGE WICKHAM HAD NO INTENTION to commit murder in the alley behind the fencing club, but since a man died during the commission of the attempted kidnapping, he was charged with murder nonetheless. Upon his conviction, he was sent to prison for life. His cellmate was a rather large man called "Butcher," who thought George was the prettiest piece of ass he'd ever seen.

Frannie Bennet's insanity defense did her little good, and she too was sentenced to prison for the rest of her life. For a woman who lived solely to be desirable to young men, a prison full of women was the closest thing to hell she could imagine. Elizabeth received the news of her suicide with little emotion other than sadness for the woman Frannie never could be.

Lady Catherine de Bourgh was horror stricken the day she was arrested for conspiracy in the attempted kidnapping of Elizabeth Bennet and Fitzwilliam Darcy. The testimony of Alan Jenkinson helped to put her in prison for five years. While the police searched her computer for records relating to that crime, they found enough evidence to investigate her further for another.

The investigators were shocked to discover that Lady Catherine was the brain behind a worldwide, high-priced prostitution ring referred to as "The Service." While prostitution was not illegal in the U.K., failure to pay taxes on the income she received from it was. As the majority of her records were little more than a series of numbers, none of her "girls" or clients could be identified. However, paying back taxes and fines bankrupted the woman, and "The Service" was effectively put out of business forever. Upon her release from prison, Lady Catherine wrote a bestselling book about her experiences and became the "Lady" of the lecture circuit for years to come.

Charlotte Lucas became a world famous fashion designer who lived on in the halls of *haute couture* history as the woman who dressed Elizabeth Bennet. It was during the christening party for Ben Darcy that Charlotte became better acquainted with Anne de Bourgh and learned that Anne did have one major accomplishment: she loved to design shoes and handbags. Soon after, the fashion powerhouse of *Lucas & de Bourgh* was born.

Anne de Bourgh and Alan Jenkinson lived together for ten years before he was able to convince her that her illness mattered little to him, only augmenting his desire to care for her for the rest of her life. They finally married, adopted three Sudanese orphans and lived happily in the home Anne's father left her when he died.

Georgiana Darcy eventually graduated from Longbourn and became a world-famous, Broadway singer. She and Jacob Carter dated for two years before they broke up; however, they remained the closest of friends. Nearly ten years later, they reunited and married.

Jane and Charles eloped the day after Jane finished her residency. Their honeymoon was spent in Siberia, where Charles finally shot the photo essay of his dreams. Jane used her extensive education and life experiences to write a series of books on the dangers of excessive positive thinking. The Bingleys had no children but spent their lives going happily from one exotic location to the next at the spur of the moment.

Caroline and Richard eventually became lovers and married a little over a year after Ben Darcy's birth in a double ceremony with Geoff and Charlotte Lucas. As *Mr. Bond* and *Studmuffin* stood before Reverend Ferrars with their respective brides, Lord and Lady Matlock thought they could not be happier until the host of grandchildren began to arrive. No one showed any reaction when Geoff stumbled through his vows halfway through the ceremony, but there were many curious glances afterwards when every member of the Darcy-Fitzwilliam family handed Elizabeth a twenty-pound note.

Elizabeth did not return to full-time teaching. She and Jay Austen completed their alternative rock opera titled *A Fit of Nerves*, which opened on Broadway to rave reviews and sold-out performances nearly two years in advance. When the opera was nominated for a Tony Award, Elizabeth gave her first public performance in ten years, playing lead guitar with Excessively Diverted as they performed the ballad, *Obstinate Headstrong Girl*. She and Jay Austen won two awards that night. The following year the opera was made into a film, and Elizabeth was contracted to write the soundtrack. She donated all her earnings to The Darcy Foundation for the Promotion of the Arts to ensure that the dream that brought her and Darcy together would last for many generations to come.

Darcy continued to expand the work of The Darcy Foundation as the program he and Elizabeth developed at Longbourn was used to expand music education in inner-city neighborhoods throughout the world. When he took over for Maggie Thornton as president of the International Human Rights Association, Elizabeth was made temporary president of the foundation with the unanimous endorsement of its advisory board.

When Ben Darcy was three years old, a little brother joined him in the nursery. Richard Geoffrey Charles Darcy was a rambunctious child who had no trouble living up to his name. Two years later, Isabella Jane Georgiana Darcy had her father twisted around her little finger the moment she first opened her deep violet-blue eyes. The Darcy children and their Fitzwilliam cousins all shared the same adventurous spirit, filling the house and grounds at Pemberley with laughter enough to please even Mrs. Reynolds.

As for Pierre Estoban, neither the Darcys nor the Bennets ever received another communication from him, but they knew he was out there, somewhere, watching...

EPILOGUE

D arcy entered the family room to find it dark except for the flames in the fireplace and the warm glow of the Christmas tree. Elizabeth was flat on her back in the middle of the floor, their three children sleeping curled up next to her. He smiled at the look of total contentment on her face as she watched the twinkling lights of the tree. "Hey," he called out softly.

Slowly her eyes moved from the tree to him, a beautiful smile spread across her face and the light in her eyes outshone the lights of the tree. "Hey. Do you want to join us?"

He sat down beside her on the rug. "I see the old trick of waiting up for Father Christmas has worked like a charm. Your father had the three of them so wound up after the concert, I was beginning to think they'd never settle down to sleep." He reached over a sleeping Richard to kiss his wife. "Shall we take them upstairs?"

As Elizabeth walked the sleepy boys to their bedroom, Darcy carried Bella in his arms, echoing the memory of his dream of eleven years before. She wrapped her arms around his neck and pressed her little face against his throat. Her room was decorated not with ponies and butterflies, but with dinosaurs. Bella was too busy trying to keep up with her brothers to care for anything remotely girly, and she could give the scientific name for over fifty species of dinosaur along with their preferred habitat, what they ate and which period of time they existed in. Yes, it was clear that all three children shared their parents' intellect, but somehow Darcy and Elizabeth had managed to preserve for them all the wonders of a normal childhood.

As he laid her in her small bed, she roused and blinked. Large, violet-blue eyes focused briefly on his face, and as he tucked the blankets around her, she sleepily whispered, "Good night, Papa."

Her skin was warm and soft beneath his lips as he gently kissed her forehead. "Good night, Sweetling. Did you see Father Christmas?"

"No," she yawned before sighing and pulling a stuffed tyrannosaurus rex under her chin. "He is much too clever." She yawned again and closed her eyes.

Darcy was still sitting beside Bella's bed when Elizabeth came in to kiss her good night. "I love these pajamas," Elizabeth whispered as she touched the sleeve of Bella's nightgown. "I can't believe you convinced *Lady Racy Stacy's* to custom make them for all five of us."

He stood and wrapped his arms around Elizabeth's waist, slipping his thumbs beneath the waistband of her pajamas. "They made this year's family Christmas picture my absolute favorite. Besides, my Lizzy, I've always loved seeing you in red flannel, covered with little reindeer." Darcy nuzzled her neck inhaling the soft scent of orange blossom and ginger.

"And they smell great too!" Elizabeth inhaled deeply near the collar of Darcy's pajama shirt. "Baby, did you ask Mrs. Reynolds to starch yours or did they come out of the box that way?" He only chuckled deeply in response. Elizabeth suggested, "Why don't you go kiss the boys good night and meet me in the family room," and then kissed him, once, twice, three times.

Darcy pulled back, smiled and waggled his eyebrows suggestively, "Ah yes, I believe it's time for the "Eleventh Annual, Shag My B.F.F. Madly under the Christmas Tree Extravaganza'!"

"Ready…" she whispered.

"Set…"

"Go!"

THE END

Breinigsville, PA USA
07 September 2009
223643BV00003B/34/P